D1564889

SILVER CITY

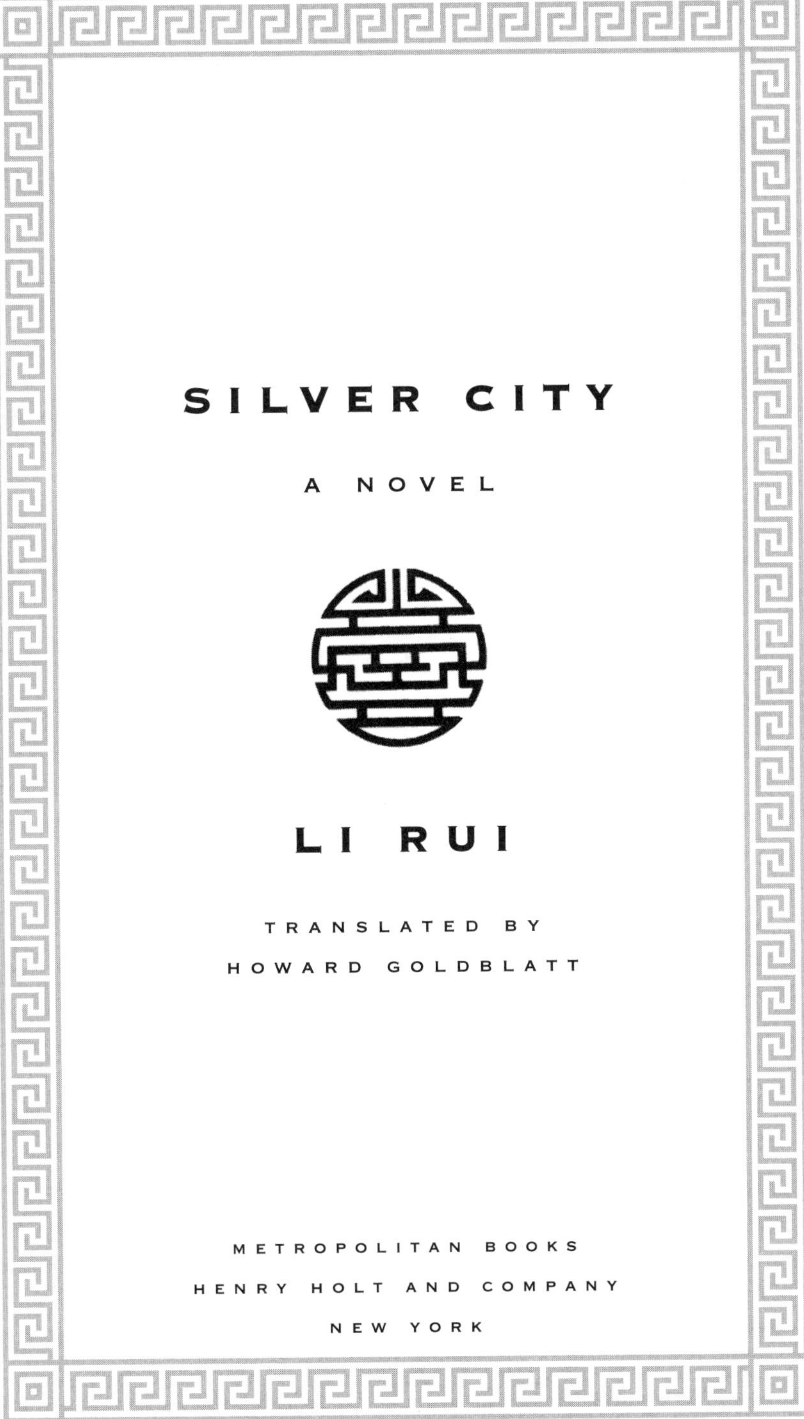

SILVER CITY

A NOVEL

LI RUI

TRANSLATED BY
HOWARD GOLDBLATT

METROPOLITAN BOOKS
HENRY HOLT AND COMPANY
NEW YORK

Metropolitan Books
Henry Holt and Company, Inc.
Publishers since 1866
115 West 18th Street
New York, New York 10011

Metropolitan Books™ is an imprint of
Henry Holt and Company, Inc.

Published in Canada by Fitzhenry & Whiteside Ltd.
195 Allstate Parkway, Markham, Ontario L3R 4T8
Originally published in China as
Chiu-chih by Shanghai Literature and Arts Publishing House in 1993

Library of Congress Cataloging-in-Publication Data
Li, Jui, 1950–
[Chiu chih. English]
Silver City : a novel / Li Rui ; translated by Howard Goldblatt.—
1st American ed.
p. cm.
"Metropolitan Books."
ISBN 0-8050-4895-2 (alk. paper)
I. Goldblatt, Howard, 1939– . II. Title.
PL2877.J826C45 1997
895.1'352—dc21 97-23508

Henry Holt books are available for special promotions and premiums.
For details contact: Director, Special Markets.

First American Edition 1997

Designed by Iris Weinstein

Printed in the United States of America
All first editions are printed on acid-free paper. ∞

1 3 5 7 9 10 8 6 4 2

SILVER CITY

SILVER CITY FAMILY TREE

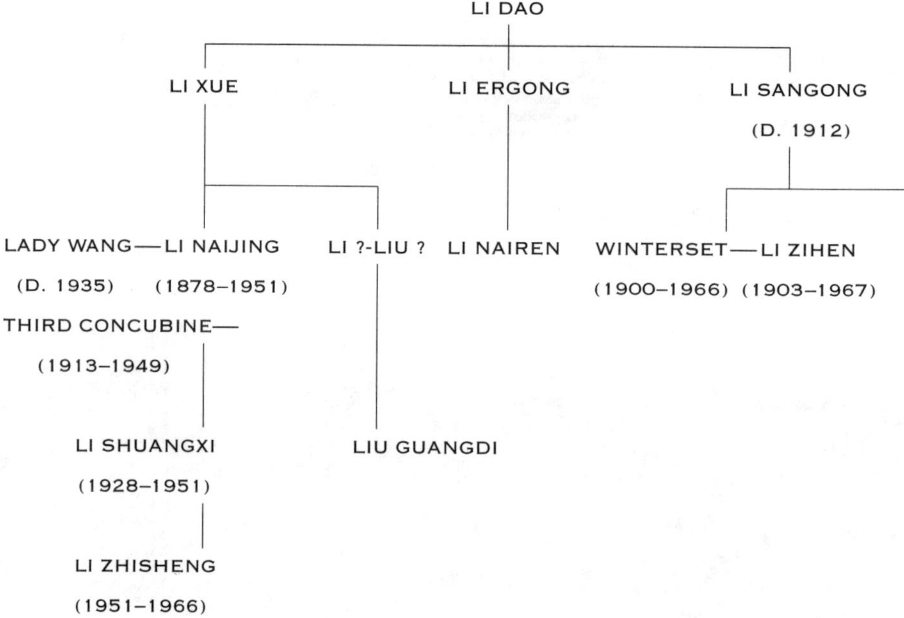

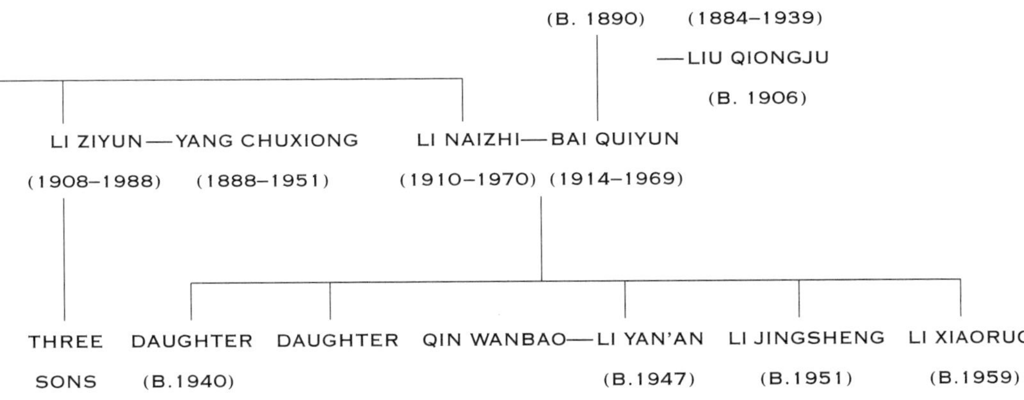
BAI RUIDE—LADY YANG
(B. 1890) (1884–1939)
—LIU QIONGJU
(B. 1906)
LI ZIYUN—YANG CHUXIONG
(1908–1988) (1888–1951)
LI NAIZHI—BAI QUIYUN
(1910–1970) (1914–1969)
THREE SONS
DAUGHTER (B.1940)
DAUGHTER
QIN WANBAO—LI YAN'AN (B.1947)
LI JINGSHENG (B.1951)
LI XIAORUO (B.1959)

CHAPTER ONE

1

Not until later did it occur to anyone that October 24, 1951 (the twenty-fourth day of the ninth month in the lunar calendar), happened to fall on Frost's Descent.

On that morning, Division Commander Three Ox Wang, valiant head of the Silver City Military Control Commission, displayed all the fervor and elation of a conquering hero as he raised his arm in a historic gesture, then swept it through the autumn drizzle, proclaiming in a thick Shandong accent:

"Drag the counterrevolutionaries to the execution ground and carry out the sentence!"

The hundred thousand citizens of the upper Yangtze city of Silver City were so stunned by the command—or else by the jarring strangeness of his dialect—that all two hundred thousand eyes turned to stare at Commander Three Ox Wang's fervent, elated face. The ensuing cold and gloomy silence was shattered only by the fateful commands of Liu Guangdi, the even more fervent leader of the execution detail. A hundred and eight counterrevolutionaries, white placards of the condemned around their necks, were shoved and dragged up to a whitewashed stone wall at the base of the mountain directly across from the cordoned-off parade ground by swaggering Liberation Army soldiers with bandoliers across their chests. Moss covered the wall, and the hundred and eight white placards lent the soft green growth a somber, even ghostly air.

Commander Three Ox Wang had personally chosen the number 108; the original list of counterrevolutionaries was far longer than that, but being from Shandong he'd always been partial to the famous hundred and eight heroes of Mount Liang and so settled on that figure at the assembly convened to suppress the counterrevolutionaries.

Liu Guangdi, who had checked the list of the condemned, knew that thirty-two of the hundred and eight were members of the Li clan, including virtually all the adult males from the three branches of Nine Ideals Hall. On the eve of the execution, he had submitted a request to the Military Control Commission to fire the first shot, so as to become the personal executioner of his own uncle, Li Naijing, the clan patriarch. Duty triumphed over family loyalty when a single crisp retort sent a bullet shrieking mercilessly out of the muzzle of Liu Guangdi's American-made carbine into the head of Li Naijing, whose shattered skull smashed into the mossy wall like so many shards of ceramic tile, spraying the area with bright red blood and the gray muck of brain. A hundred and seven times more, in rapid succession, identical splashes of red-gray muck stained the stone wall, until it had the mottled look of a forest in autumn under a settling frost. . . . To the right of the wall flowed Silver Creek, a swath of inky-green serenity that bisected the city before slipping beneath the mountain and twisting out of sight. Three enormous characters in the calligraphic style of the celebrated poet Su Dongpo proclaimed: Fish Listening Pond. The crack of rifle fire raised nervous white ripples on the placid, inky-green surface of Fish Listening Pond.

A shower later that night cleansed the wall of its sticky gray and red stains, washing away, too, the last blood-curdling shrieks of a hundred and eight bullets. Centuries of domination and expansion in Silver City by the Li clan had finally come to an end. Overnight, the many memorial arches to the civic virtues of the clan that dotted the lanes and byways were stripped of their splendor and majesty; now passersby saw only gouged-out stone mouths, terrified and ugly. Many years later a night-lit basketball court was erected on the execution ground. The thud of bouncing balls and the sight of writhing bodies scrambling for the ball inevitably reminded the remaining Li clan womenfolk of the crack of carbines and the hundred and eight sprawled corpses; they thought back to October 24, 1951, the twenty-fourth day of the ninth lunar month, which happened to fall on Frost's Descent.

The only adult male of the Li clan who did not face the firing squad that day was Li Naizhi, a fraternal cousin of the first man to die, Li Naijing. Years earlier, Naizhi had served as party secretary of Silver City's Communist underground and later rose to the position of provincial party secretary. At the time of the execution, he was sitting atop a Stalin 55 tractor, a Russian-style beaked cap perched above his intact forehead as he led the first graduating class of New China's tractor trainees in churning the rich soil of the Beijing suburb of Tandang. The engine roar was nearly deafening. Giant blades plowed the dormant soil, watched by rows of rapturous bronzed faces warmed by the autumn sun. Two news film crews and several journalists busily focused their cameras on this "swords to ploughshares" event, creating scenes that would become the defining images of New China's historic national project and find their way into documentaries of every description.

As the graduates were memorialized in these busy scenes of historic moment, Li Naizhi's first son, the sixty-ninth male descendant of the Li clan, was born on a wood-slat bed in the dilapidated clinic of the Tandang experimental farm. Li Jingsheng's birth transpired without a hitch, was so uneventful that the doctor and nurse in attendance might as well have been elsewhere. His mother, Bai Qiuyun, had already delivered three daughters. As a little girl playing on a swing in Silver City's renowned White Garden, with its jadelike purity, dressed in a virginal cotton dress like a Western girl, pushed by her father until she soared above the lush banana trees, she never dreamed she would someday marry a member of the party underground, never dreamed she would deliver such vital progeny, never dreamed that a womb could, under such circumstances, be so free of pain, could do its work so well, could overcome all obstacles, could complete its reproductive mission with the gentleness of flowing water. How different from the splattering of thirty-two brains and the grand historic gesture by Commander Three Ox Wang . . .

Even before the boy came into the world, his father had chosen a name, one that broke with the generational prescription for naming. Feudal legacies had been swept away by the victorious revolution and the establishment of the nation's capital in Beijing. Male or female, the child would proudly bear the name Jingsheng—Child of the Capital. And just as Li Jingsheng came naked and wailing into the world, two high-pitched public-address speakers mounted atop a water tower blared forth a stirring musical tribute to the first graduates of New China's tractor-driving course, heralding the spirit of the age and the ecstasy of victory. The lyrics celebrated the joy of peasants, who shared in the rewards of land reform as the wealth of landlords fell into their hands:

Three yellow oxen. Hooray! A single horse,
This old driver can't stop laughing,
Hurrah, ha ha, see me laugh.

In years past, this wagon here
Could never belong to a poor man like me,
But now, hurrah,
Big-wheel wagon, turn, turn,
Big-wheel wagon, turn, turn,
Turn, turn, turn, hooray!
That's the way,
Turn right into my yard!

A jubilant song that filled the void between heaven and earth.

Years later, Li Jingsheng came across some yellowed photographs of his father sitting atop a Stalin 55 tractor, a Russian-style beaked cap perched on his head, his face flushed with victory. Li Jingsheng was troubled by something he couldn't quite name. He sensed that his father was not grand enough, that he somehow failed to rise to the historic import of the moment; though he did not know it, Li Jingsheng was really yearning for the sort of historic gesture displayed by Division Commander Three Ox Wang as he raised his arm and then swept it through the autumn drizzle. When Li Jingsheng finally understood his feelings of disappointment, he realized that the gesture—a hand raised to the future—had already been claimed: it belonged to every statue of Chairman Mao, large or small, concrete or stone, in every public square, large or small, in every town and city in the nation. It had become the exclusive property of the Great Teacher, the Great Leader, the Supreme Commander, the Great Helmsman.

When Commander Three Ox Wang, filled with the heady elation of victory, raised his hand in that historic gesture in the dark, drizzly, cold autumn sky, when the brains of thirty-two adult male members of the Li clan stained a section of the stone wall, when Li Naizhi drove his Stalin 55 tractor into the fertile fields and Li Jingsheng came wailing into the world, a solitary, ashen-faced woman in one of the deserted homes of the Li clan sat shivering atop a stack of rush mats. At the moment when gunshots sounded near Fish Listening Pond and shattered skulls flew through the air, Li Naizhi's sister Li Zihen abruptly stopped shivering; her legs fell open inelegantly and she tumbled backward in a dead faint in the empty room. Her string of sandalwood prayer beads snapped as she fell, scattering her fears and despair on the floor.

Only one member of the Li clan put on white funeral garb and cried herself hoarse: it was Li Ziyun, Li Naizhi's other sister, but she was many miles away. Her grief was intended not for her clan but for her husband, General Yang Chuxiong, who had followed Chiang Kai-shek to Taiwan two years earlier, in 1949, only to die there still a young man. She cried for her piteous fate as widow, something no funeral, no matter how solemn, could alter, and for the harsh reality that she was destined to die as a guest in a foreign land, something no ceremony, no matter how dignified, could change.

2

In point of fact, the demise of the Li clan can be traced further back, to December 1927, when peasants in the five counties surrounding Silver City rose in rebellion.

In point of fact, that insurrection was doomed to fail before it began. Armed only with shouts of victory, five glorious red flags, and stirring revolutionary songs, the peasant forces were decimated by machine-gun fire.

In point of fact, the greatest significance of the failed insurrection was that it spurred Li Naizhi to turn his back on the magnificent arches of the Li clan and cast his lot with the revolution. Indeed, had it not been for Zhao Boru, Silver City's high school principal, who dressed in long Chinese gowns and wore pince-nez high on his nose, or for the peasant called Mongrel Chen and his hideous end, had it not been for all this, much of what has thus far been narrated would have turned out quite differently.

When the order from Communist Party Central to mount an insurrection reached Silver City, the party underground organization in all five counties could boast only fifty-seven members. Bereft of even the most basic experience, they had no idea how to mobilize the peasants and commit them body and soul to an insurrection. Yet those fifty-seven individuals went ahead and set up a command post. Their primary objective was to seize Silver City. Invoking the Communist-led insurrection months earlier in the mid-Yangtze cities of Wuhan, they took as their battle cry: "On to Wuhan, establish a Soviet!" First they fashioned five red battle flags, then they taught their peasant troops stirring revolutionary songs. Half a century later, when Li Jingsheng and his fellow students, who had organized themselves into a Red Guard unit during the Cultural Revolution, marched in Tiananmen Square, they sang one of those songs with such fervor that their voices grew hoarse and the blood ran hot in their youthful veins:

Workers, peasants, and soldiers—unite,
Stride forward, all hearts as one!
Workers, peasants, and soldiers—unite,
Stride forward, kill the enemy!
We are brave, we struggle, we are united, we forge ahead,
Storm the camp of imperialist reactionaries,
Final victory belongs to the workers, peasants, and soldiers!

But in the year 1927, victory was not theirs. Fifty-seven members of the underground, determined to follow the orders of Party Central and with the recent harvest uprisings as their models, made it a matter of honor to expose their youthful chests to a storm of bullets from enemy machine guns.

Under the command of Mongrel Chen, the Gao Mountain Farm red detachment of peasants led the insurrection, relieving the local forces of their weapons and lopping off the head of the wealthy landowner Gao Binghui. Then they slaughtered all the male members of Gao's family and parceled out his grain and his possessions. Finally they attached Gao's head to a bamboo pole with a hemp cord and paraded it around the area. Raucous crowds gathered everywhere they went: mountains swayed, the earth shook. Mongrel Chen stuck a captured Mauser into the waistband beneath his open shirt; he wore a red band around his head and wielded a gleaming sword with a red tassel. From the front of the column he shouted slogans: Down with local tyrants! Down with warlords! And as excitement mounted, he brandished his sword in the theatrical pose of the famous dark-faced Ming rebel:

I am Zhang Xianzhong returned!
I slaughter the greedy landlords!

True to his word, Mongrel Chen cut a wide swath with that sword, to which the heads hanging from hemp cords bore gory witness as they were paraded, like New Year's lanterns, up and down the streets and lanes of each hamlet he visited. Peasants who had known only hunger and cold for generations greeted the insurrection as if it were a holiday festival, thus shaming the fifty-seven Communists for underestimating the will of the masses. Some even called for a party meeting to criticize the capitulationist tendencies of certain individuals. But then an unexpected problem arose: the heroic Mongrel Chen took killing and pillaging to the next logical step. One day, after slaughtering the male members of a landlord family, he herded the females into the women's quarters, where he forced them to paint their eyebrows and lips, apply powder and fragrance, and strip naked. Grinning broadly, he "sampled" each fair-skinned hostage, virgin or not, after which he rewarded his troops by letting them share the fruits of conquest. News of this development rocked headquarters, where no one had anticipated that the resolute revolutionary Mongrel Chen could commit such a reactionary act. The leaders immediately censured him: Rogue activities fly in the face of the spirit of Bolshevism and Soviet principles, they said. Any reoccurrence will be dealt with severely. Mongrel Chen, who by then had grown arrogant, took this as a personal affront:

"What more do you want of me? Isn't killing people enough for you? Do I have to worry about Bolsheviks and Soviets too?"

One day, having sampled the wife and other womenfolk of a tyrannical old landlord, he continued on with the kitchen help and bondmaids, the kin of poor peasants and tenant farmers. This was the last straw. Unwilling to tolerate the lawless behavior of treating friends and foes alike, rebel headquarters sent an emissary with instructions to remove Mongrel Chen from command of the red detachment and, as a warning to others, place him under arrest. But before the emissary reached his destination, he was cut down by enemy machine-gun fire. The red detachment went on to fight harder, more courageously, and with greater determination than any other peasant force; only after the last man fell was Mongrel Chen, himself wounded, taken prisoner.

The rebels failed because they were vastly outnumbered and carelessly deployed. Silver City was protected only by the garrison of Commander Yang Chuxiong, who calmly watched rebellion sweep the countryside; not until panic-stricken salt merchants and rich gentry approached him with offers of pay and provisions did he offhandedly order five companies of soldiers to lay siege to the rebel counties. He gave a single command: "Set up machine guns and keep firing until you see the turtle scum turn tail and run!" It worked. Machine-gun fire had barely begun raking the fields when the peasants broke rank and fled. All that remained on the damp ground of the recently harvested fields were many corpses, many spears and sabers, many oversized baskets the peasants had brought to carry away the grain and other riches due them, and many gorgeous yet sorrowful white egrets circling overhead startled by the sound of gunfire.

The December 1927 Silver City insurrection took the lives of thirty-eight hundred peasants. None of the fifty-seven members of the Communist Party survived: their severed heads hung above the entrances to the five county towns for a full year, until the hair had fallen out, the flesh had rotted away, and they had become fifty-seven naked human skulls. In their quest for vengeance and, more important, in their desire to forever discourage future rebels, the victors brought two of their prisoners, the supreme rebel commander, Zhao Boru, and Mongrel Chen—whose exploits had become legendary—together with ten captured red detachment soldiers, back to Silver City, where they set up an execution platform at the base of the mountain directly across from the old parade ground. The city seemed to shake with excitement and apprehension, as the citizens clamored to see how the notorious Mongrel Chen would go to his death. Despised by his captors, he was first to face the executioner. He was tied naked to a rack, and the executioner was ordered to slice off his sizable genitals with a razor-sharp ceremonial knife. To members of the landed gentry from the five counties, that loathsome piece of anatomy, which had sampled the wives and womenfolk of so many of their peers, was the cause of far more hatred than any of the awkward, alien concepts such as "Soviet" or "Bolshevik." With a single sharp, cold stab, Mongrel Chen lost his manhood amid gushing blood, and when he saw the now-useless chunk of flesh tossed to the ground, he cursed wildly:

"I am the man! I was never happier than when I stuffed that up the wives and sisters of you turtle spawn! In twenty years I'll be back, stronger than ever, and ready to kill and fuck again . . . I am the Bolshevik, I am the Soviet! I am the rebel . . . Zhang Xianzhong will return and the slaughter will start anew . . ."

This final burst of invective was raspy and crackling, bearing little resemblance to human speech. The executioner turned back to Mongrel Chen and cut out his tongue, silencing him once and for all, though he squirmed and struggled on the rack, glowering through the wide circles of his eyes and savagely spitting out mouthfuls of hot, red blood. Everyone knew he was still cursing; the squirming and struggling and the garbled noises continued until suddenly the executioner produced a steaming human heart in his hand. The bystanders gasped in amazement. Those who had come to kill as well as those who had come to witness the killing were profoundly shaken by Mongrel Chen's earth-shattering rage.

Li Naizhi, a high school student in 1927, gaped first at the corpse of Mongrel Chen, his shouts and curses now stilled, then at Zhao Boru, the principal, next to emerge on the platform. Dressed as always in a long gown, pince-nez perched high on his nose, Zhao Boru moved in the calm, unhurried fashion that was his trademark, displaying his customary air of uncomplicated elegance. Yet when he raised his manacled hands to brush the hair from his eyes, he revealed the sallow face of a defeated man. Turning toward the mutilated figure of Mongrel Chen, stripped of heart, tongue, and genitals, he bowed deeply, then raised his hands and announced to the crowd that had come to see how he would meet his death: "They cannot kill off all the laboring masses, nor can they exterminate the Communists!" Clenching his fists and rattling the manacles, he shouted: "Mark my word, red flags will fly over the world of the future!"

Li Naizhi knew these words. As a member of Silver City's high school study club, he had often heard Zhao Boru echo this famous line by Li Dazhao, cofounder of the Communist Party, but never dreamed that one day the poetic ideal would step out of the textbook and classroom and into the terrifying, bloody scene now before him.

Three executioners mounted the platform. Two held the principal by his arms and forced his head down over a large, slimy wooden stump as the third man raised an ax high above him, then brought it down with a thud, severing the head that had been filled with so much knowledge and so many ideals, so many ideas and so much truth, so much poetry and so much passion. With the casual indifference of farmers slaughtering their sheep, they obliterated all that unhurried calmness, all that uncomplicated elegance, drowning Li Naizhi's ideals in a sea of blood. When his mentor's gore-covered head thudded to the ground, Li Naizhi fainted dead away.

After killing Mongrel Chen and Zhao Boru, the executioners dragged up the ten peasant soldiers of the red detachment and tied them to stakes buried in the ground. Fastened behind them with wire were buckets of kerosene, into which burning torches were tossed. Amid soul-shredding shrieks of agony, ten human beings were transformed into that many screeching bonfires. The crowd watched this hellish scene, absolutely terrified. Two days later, the ten charred corpses still twitched on their stakes.

As time passed, the insurrection would fade from memory, as would the name Mongrel Chen. In the quiet of evening, as oxen pulled plows through the wavy rice paddies, spectral egrets would greet the winds and accompany the rains, landing softly on this spot of land, which had once been blanketed with bodies of dead rebels but was now among the most fertile fields anywhere.

No one emerged more victorious from the December 1927 insurrection at Silver City than Yang Chuxiong. Soon after crushing the peasants' red detachments, he fell heir to the riches of a thousand salt mines in and around Silver City. Now in possession of immense wealth, he expanded his forces from a regiment to a division, and from there to a full army. Many years later, when Chiang Kai-shek controlled nearly all of China and had converted the troops of feudal lords into nationalist forces, Yang Chuxiong was a natural choice to become one of his senior generals.

3

In the second year in the reign of the Manchu Xuantong emperor, the year of the dog or 1910 by the unfamiliar Western reckoning, a bawling baby boy came into the world in the home of Li Sangong—"Elder Three Li"—on Silver City's Archway Street. His arrival drew a sigh of relief from everyone in the family. All the other members of the Nine Ideals Hall branch of the Li clan had plenty of sons and grandsons, all but Li Sangong, whose wife had presented him with three daughters in a row, the eldest of whom had died the year before. Now the lines that creased his brow were from the joy of having a son, an heir, the answer to his prayers. Clan forefathers had devised a couplet—Cao Shi Wei Ren Dao, Xue Nai Shen Zhi Bao, roughly translated as "Benevolence is a worldly measure, knowledge is a priceless treasure"—each word in succession to be used in the names of males for ten generations. Li Sangong named his son, a member of the seventh generation, *Nai*zhi. Among his fraternal cousins, Naizhi was ninth in the pecking order, so everyone called him Ninth Brother. After the eight elder male cousins of his generation had passed away, Brother Nine would become Elder Nine, patriarch of the Li clan, so long as the prescribed order was followed and all traditional conventions were observed. No one could have predicted that tradition would soon be swept away. Only one year after Li Naizhi's birth, a republican revolution would put an end to the monarchy that had existed uninterrupted since the emperor Qin Shi Huang first sat on the throne 2,131 years before.

As fate would have it, Li Sangong's wife died unexpectedly a month after the birth of her son. A scant year later, illness claimed Li Sangong as well. As he lay dying, having squandered his riches, he was comforted by the knowledge that he had produced an heir to carry on the line. Yet he left little of value to his son: three salt mines whose production had fallen off dramatically, ten acres of paddy land, and the family home. In his final moments, Li Sangong entrusted his soon-to-be-orphaned offspring to Li Naijing, who, as a member of the same clan and generation as Sangong's three children, would assume the role of father. That way, even after his departure for the Yellow Springs—the next world—his heart would live on, and he could gaze up to watch his son, Naizhi, grow to manhood. So Li Sangong passed on, leaving three grieving children to face life with neither father nor mother to care for them, and an uncertain nation, soon to be bereft of an emperor to lead it.

The three salt mines quickly dried up, the ten acres of paddy land were sold off piece by piece, and the family home was mortgaged. By the time Li Naizhi was a student at Silver City's high school, even though he walked down Archway Street on his way home every day, skirted the five-hundred-year-old locust tree, with its cloudlike canopy of branches, and passed beneath Silver City's two most imposing stone-carved arches before crossing the threshold of his home, he sensed that the triumphal expressions on the stone lions bracketing the doorway were beginning to fade.

In December 1927 the severed head of the Communist Zhao Boru hung from the city gate above Silver City citizens, who were busy, as in years past, with preparations for the Spring Festival, the celebration of the lunar New Year in late January. Overeager children tossed firecrackers into the sluggish final moments of the old year. Since the high school had been the heart and soul of the rebellion, its board of directors met after Zhao Boru was killed and decided to dismiss the teachers and shut the doors. Faced with that void and the terror that had created it, Li Naizhi lost heart. Lacking an outlet for his torment and indignation, he sat down at his desk and wrote a eulogy for his mentor—In memory of my teacher, the late Zhao Boru—placing the scroll with its dark lettering behind a pair of white candles mottled by wax drippings and a symbolic joss stick. Beneath that lay several books his teacher had given him: Lu Xun's *Cemetery* and *Outcry,* Liu Bannong's *Flourishing Whips,* Li Dazhao's *On the Victory of Bolshevism,* plus two treasured issues of Chen Duxiu's *New Youth* magazine that Zhao had saved from his college days at Beijing University. . . . The wholesale slaughter at Silver City in December 1927 gave rise to sorrow and fury in a young man who did not yet understand the dialectic of grief and strength and how to turn one into the other.

After the heads of Zhao Boru and Mongrel Chen had hung above the entrance to Silver City for a month, the citizenry displayed New Year's lanterns, as custom dictated: throughout the city, blood-red eyes peered through the cold night air. New Year's couplets above the stone lions at the Li home on Archway Street repeated the traditional message:

HONESTY AND TOLERANCE ARE A FAMILY'S LEGACY

ETIQUETTE AND PROTOCOL LAST FOR GENERATIONS.

On New Year's Eve, the patriarch, Li Naijing, led the entire clan to the ancestral hall, where every member, male and female, young and old, kowtowed before the ancestral tablets to pay respects to deceased elders. But the thoughts of Li Naizhi, as he knelt in the darkness, were on the most difficult decision of his life: once New Year's was past, would he accompany his sister, Li Ziyun, who was home for the holidays, to the provincial capital to attend school, thus relinquishing his family responsibilities as heir? If he went, how would he tell his older sister, Zihen? And after he left, how would she get by?

Li Zihen, the eldest daughter of Li Sangong, was twenty-four that New Year's season, an age well past the time when a girl should leave home and well beyond the limits of her cousin Li Naijing's tolerance. Having decided to look after her sister, Ziyun, and her brother, Naizhi, and to fight to keep the family together, she had rejected five marriage proposals, becoming the talk of Silver City, the little old maid who never strayed far from home. Years of standing in for her parents had turned her into a fierce creature who inserted herself between her brood and the prying eyes and cold looks of the outside world and protected it from the growing dissatisfaction of Li Naijing, now the clan patriarch. When she realized that her brother was seriously considering abandoning his education in order to stay home, as was expected of the eldest male, she did something that astonished the men of the Li clan and earned her the veneration of the women of Silver City.

On the sixth day of the new year, Li Naizhi was awakened by the sobs of his sisters. The minute he entered Zihen's room he saw the bean-sized burns all over her face. Two smoldering sticks of incense lay discarded on a nearby octagonal table, and the sickening odor of scorched flesh hung in the air. A white ceramic Guanyin bodhisattva holding a jade washing bowl stood on the table atop a piece of white silk on which the word *Buddha* had been written in blood. Zihen's bloodied finger was wrapped in a piece of cloth. Her sister, Ziyun, shouted tearfully:

"Little Brother, look at our sister . . ."

Orphaned nearly at birth, Li Naizhi had never laid eyes on his father or mother; as a small child, whenever he looked up, it was his elder sister's face he saw. That face—happy, angry, sad, joyful—was everything to him. But now, except for a mass of blisters and tears, there was nothing to see. The sound of sobbing brought the rest of the clan, men and women, young and old, running. When they saw the burns on Zihen's face and the bloody *Buddha,* they could not at first take in what had happened. They could not imagine that this woman would subject herself to such self-imposed cruelty, would render herself unmarriageable so as to assume responsibility for her own family. They could not imagine that this woman, who had never spent a single day in school, would sacrifice herself to give her brother and sister a chance to better themselves through formal schooling. All this she had done for the sake of her family, yet not one of the family's memorial arches commemorated the will and determination of this single unlettered woman.

Half a century later, guides in fashionable coifs and attire retold with gusto the legend of Silver City and the Li clan for the Chinese and foreign tourists who had traveled far to get there. The tourists scooped up the stories as if they were precious gems and flawless jade, but there was not one word for Li Zihen.

CHAPTER TWO

1

The first clan elder listed by name in the genealogy was Li Yi, who boasted that he was a twelfth-generation descendant of Li Er, famed philosopher of the Spring and Autumn period, also known as Laozi. In 25 A.D., the first year of the Jianwu reign of the Eastern Han dynasty, Li Yi was richly rewarded for helping the Guangwu emperor Liu Xiu overthrow the usurper Wang Mang. Over the next two thousand years, the Li clan flourished, outlasting dynasties and surviving one war after the other, moving from place to place, finally settling down to build a city and open a salt mine. According to the renowned British historian Joseph Needham, it was the first "percussion-drilled extra-deep mine" in the history of man and therefore among the most important scientific discoveries in China. The mine was a thousand meters deep, and it belonged to the Li clan. In front of the clan's ancestral home stood the two most imposing, most intricately carved stone archways in the city. They were called the Twin Arches, and etched into the stone was an imperial prescript: "Civil Officials Alight from Carriages, Military Officials Dismount from Steeds." The arches had been erected in tribute to a father and son—famous in the annals of the Li clan—both of whom had passed the imperial examination and were appointed by the emperor to exalted positions. Between the archways and the compound gate stood a five-hundred-year-old locust tree densely covered with leaves. "Ancient Locust and Twin Arches" were the most fabulous of Silver City's scenic wonders and became, over time, the symbols of the city.

But in January 1928, the care-laden clan patriarch, Li Naijing, stood in defiant opposition to his kin, and his actions would become the stuff of legends.

In January 1928, on the sixth day of the first lunar month, when Li Zihen scarred her face with joss sticks, Li Naijing stayed only a moment in his cousin's room before turning and walking silently out the door. Dejection so filled his heart that his chest throbbed painfully. For centuries the Nine Ideals Hall Twin Arches branch of the Li clan had enjoyed the status accorded Silver City's wealthiest families, having produced more officials than anyone could count. From one era to the next, the clan had subsidized the education of more impoverished citizens than anyone could calculate. Now, however, the clan's own children could attend school only through the charity of a woman willing to disfigure her face and live the austere life of an unmarried woman. This brought great shame to the clan's ancestors, an unspeakable loss of prestige. Who could have predicted that a family of such scholarly distinction, among whose members ceremony and propriety reigned, would one day owe its continuation to a disfigured spinster? None could deny Zihen the respect her strength of will deserved, but the truth was that the Nine Ideals Hall branch of the Li clan had reached its historical nadir.

On the sixth day of the first lunar month, 1928, as Li Naijing, laden with cares, followed a narrow winding path alongside

Willow Reflecting Pond past eight potted plants, then mounted the stone steps leading to the spot called Fragrant Hills, he was startled to hear boisterous laughter coming from the scattered peach trees. A cough announced his presence to two maidservants who immediately stopped laughing and emerged, flustered, from the stand of trees; holding freshly cut peach twigs in their hands, they stood, heads bowed, beside the columns of an arbor. Wordlessly and without pausing in his walk, Li Naijing gave the girls a stern look, noticing as he did so the black wooden placards with gold writing that hung from the columns:

A FLUTE IN THE COURTYARD GREETS THE MOON AT NIGHT

PEACHES AND PLUMS INTOXICATE THE GARDEN SKY WITH PERFUME.

The gardens belonging to this branch of the Li clan were filled with carvings, placards, and pillars hung with scrolls inscribed with ancient couplets; Naijing disliked this particular couplet more than the others, for it praised too lavishly the clan's ability to retain its wealth. Yet every member of Nine Ideals Hall, including some of the older servants, knew that this couplet was the favorite of Naijing's great-grandfather when he was patriarch. Back then, as the Silver City area was suffering the second year of a drought that created legions of starving refugees, the old patriarch had rescued an abandoned child lying at the Silver Creek ferry landing and brought him home, where he revived him with a thin rice gruel. The boy did not know his own name or where he came from, saying only that everyone called him Autumn's Child and that, not long after he and his parents had fled the famine, they had died of starvation. The old patriarch made the child his foster son and renamed him Floating Life. Sent to the clan's school, the boy surprised everyone by excelling in his studies. After ten years of diligent work, he began the long rounds of academic examinations, gaining laurels at the local, township, general, and, finally, imperial levels, bringing honor to his family by achieving the rank of "accomplished scholar." Two years later he was appointed a district magistrate. Floating Life's gratitude toward the clan patriarch knew no bounds, surpassing a child's love for his parents or a penitent's devotion to the Living Buddha. On the patriarch's birthdays, Floating Life sent lavish gifts to express his deep, boundless respect. Later on, when the patriarch expanded the clan's land holdings, he constructed Willow Reflecting Pond, Fragrant Hills, and this particular arbor. Floating Life, from the far-off district where he served as magistrate, sent a workman to measure the arbor columns and commissioned two wood hangings with a couplet in gold, then sent an emissary to the dedication ceremony. Floating Life's story, with its fairy-tale trappings, was a favorite of Silver City residents, and while the old patriarch lived, he never tired of repeating it, always with a broad smile. But to Li Naijing, this rags-to-riches district magistrate remained a beggar at heart, a worshiper at the altar of wealth and avarice; only someone like that could dream up a self-congratulatory, presumptuous phrase like "intoxicate the garden sky." If the sons of the Li clan had not lain under this "intoxicating garden sky" in the pursuit of debauchery, the clan would not have fallen to the depths it had now.

Among all the countless monarchs, ministers, generals, renowned scholars, and Confucianists throughout the nation's history, the current clan patriarch, Li Naijing, revered only Zeng Guofan, the Qing minister known as Lord Wenzheng, who quashed the Taiping Rebellion in the mid-1800s. A copy of *Lord Zeng Wenzheng's Collected Works* was never absent from the desk in Li Naijing's study, opened to such sections as "Letters," "Diary," "Poetry and Essays," "Memorials," and the like. And on the wall facing the door hung an eight-character couplet praising Lord Wenzheng in Li Naijing's own hand:

WHAT THE SAINTLY DECLARES

THE GENTLEMAN ACTS UPON.

He even commissioned a copy of Zeng Guofan's portrait, which he hung alongside his desk. With the removal of the emperor in the Republican Revolution of 1911, the landscape was littered with a kaleidoscopic array of contending "commanders in chief" and "presidents," which only deepened Li Naijing's reverence for Lord Wenzheng. He firmly believed that China was in dire need of a pillar like Zeng, one of those rare figures in a nation's history. The insurrection of December 1927 intensified his anxieties over the hardships of his age: a nation whose power was waning, a society in turmoil, a vast territory without an inch of "pure land" suited to someone interested in moral cultivation. Meanwhile, among the other descendants of the clan, once the words *spendthrift* and *hedonist* were eliminated, there was nothing to recommend them, since none showed any concern over the family's vanishing wealth. It was left to the three children of Third Uncle Li Sangong, bereft of doting parents and lacking a fortune to spend freely, to show what they were made of. Sixth Sister Zihen had taken the lead by cruelly sacrificing her beauty so that her sister, Ziyun, and brother, Naizhi, could gain an education without having to chip away at the meager inheritance left by their father. For once he had recovered from the initial shock of Zihen's action, Li Naijing purged his memory of any past disobediences toward him and vowed to ease her burden by helping with Ziyun's and Naizhi's tuition, thus honoring an obligation incurred sixteen years earlier. He also anticipated the possibility that in years to come he might need to rely upon Ninth Cousin Naizhi's education in his quest to see Nine Ideals Hall prosper anew.

On the sixth day of the first lunar month in 1928, Li Naijing, patriarch of the Li clan, a man who revered Zeng Guofan as a model of virtue, a paragon for all generations, could not predict that his cares and his wish to see the family prosper once more would come to naught through his own will and that ultimately it would be responsible for staining a stone wall with bright splashes of reds and grays. So, on the morning of the sixth day of the first lunar month, 1928, after he retreated from Zihen's room utterly dejected, he let his steps take him past Willow Reflecting Pond and into Fragrant Hills, where he coughed sternly and gazed angrily. Then, as was his custom, he headed for his beloved Emerald Sky Study, the only spot in the compound, with all its luxurious rooms and halls, where he could reflect quietly.

Emerald Sky Study had not always been blessed with such an elegant name; it had been just another vulgar, ornate room. Now, however, the walls were whitewashed, the beams and rafters were stripped of paint, and though the workmanship was of the highest quality, a delicate simplicity reigned. The view from the desk was of green banana trees so tall and lush that they blocked out the sky and sun. For Li Naijing, Emerald Sky Study was the perfect name. In the center of the whitewashed western wall hung a scroll directly in Naijing's line of vision. It had been presented to his grandfather by Fan Yunpeng, the esteemed minister of the imperial board of rites. Composed in *lishu,* the official script, the antique scroll grandly proclaimed:

SUN AND MOON IN ENDLESS CYCLE,
THE EYES OF HEAVEN AND EARTH
POETRY AND CALLIGRAPHY IN COUNTLESS VOLUMES,
THE SOUL OF SAINTS AND MEN OF WORTH.

Among the countless scrolls belonging to the Nine Ideals Hall branch of the Li clan, this was Naijing's favorite: two lines of verse that were one with heaven, a treasure to last for a thousand generations. Yet one day they, too, would sail into the stone wall fronting the old military parade ground, along with the top of his skull.

On the morning of the sixth day of the first lunar month, 1928, when Li Naijing, the clan patriarch, lifted the green satin curtain at the door to his beloved Emerald Sky Study, he was greeted by a breath of warm air. Wisps of gray smoke curled upward from the embers in a brass brazier on the floor in front of his desk. The brisk scent of aromatic sandalwood wafted from a Mount Bo cloud-etched heating kettle on an ebony slat bench. Naijing touched the porcelain teapot on the tea table—it was still warm, so he took a sip. Ever since Silver City's renowned physician Lin Jinmo had told him he was susceptible to stomach chills and urged him to treat them with black tea, Li Naijing had drunk nothing but the best Yunnan black tea. As he replaced the teapot and tried to focus his thoughts, he heard a voice at the door:

"Menglin."

It was the voice of Zhao Pu'an, his elderly adviser. Zhao was one of the last successful civil-service candidates at the metropolitan level before the whole system was scrapped; in 1905, the thirtieth year of the Guangxu emperor, when the examination system was replaced by so-called new learning, his widely acclaimed ability to quote the classics became irrelevant and he was forced to accept an invitation from Li Naijing's father to serve as adviser to the Li clan's Nine Ideals Hall. Zhao, who never did anything halfway or without considerable thought, repaid this kindness with unalloyed devotion to Nine Ideals Hall. After the death of his father, Li Naijing could not just put aside old affections and loyalties, so he kept Zhao Pu'an on as administrative adviser, treating him with the respect due any elder. Zhao became even more conscientious, negligent in nothing. Throughout Nine Ideals Hall, he was the only person who did not call the patriarch Old Master; as dictated by his own status, he used Naijing's courtesy name, Menglin.

Hearing a response from inside, Zhao entered Emerald Sky Study carrying a silver water pipe and announced to Naijing:

"Menglin, Commander Yang has sent someone with a birthday gift."

"*Commander* Yang?"

"Yang Chuxiong. His card gives his title as division commander."

"A title he came by rather easily. Why, he bled Nine Ideals Hall for forty thousand yuan in silver for military provisions alone! What did he send me in return?"

"Menglin, that's what I came to tell you. Commander Yang has sent eight gilded birthday scrolls."

"This isn't my eightieth birthday and there's only one person sending the gifts, so why eight birthday scrolls?"

"Now, Menglin, don't get angry, but I've seen those scrolls before. They were a gift from the eight Silver City salt merchants to Master Gao of Gao Mountain Farm on his fiftieth birthday, ten years ago. Commander Yang just changed the celebrant's name and the signature seal."

"That son of a bitch!"

"Menglin, when a scholar encounters a soldier, only the fool tries to be the bolder. We mustn't get worked up."

"How can Yang Chuxiong have the audacity to send me a birthday gift stolen from someone else?"

"Menglin, I think I should tell you what has long been on my mind. Nine Ideals Hall originally owed its status to the royal court. With imperial decrees carved into the twin arches, who would refuse to buy our salt? But the world has changed. As we learn from the Warring Kingdoms epic, the best-armed is king of the hill. Might makes right. Can you not have noticed? With no weapons to prop it up, Nine Ideals Hall is doomed to fall."

In point of fact, how could Li Naijing not have understood what Zhao Pu'an was telling him? Since assuming control of the clan's affairs, he had plunged into a chaotic world, and the prospect of difficult times ahead gave him no peace. Aggravation was a natural outcome, yet each time he felt the anger rising in him, he forced himself to push it down. Given the apparent deterioration of public morality, forbearance was his only option. Zhao Pu'an spoke in soothing terms about other matters until he saw that Naijing had regained his composure, then he raised another troubling issue:

"Menglin, you must make a decision on the Transocean mine. Commerce is no place for loyalty. We have been mining it for twelve years without seeing a drop of briny water or a hint of subterranean gas. It has already drained our coffers of over a hundred thousand. Bai Ruide's Prosperity Company is flourishing, and I think we should sell him 60 percent of our holdings. What difference does it make that he is in bed with foreign concerns or that he struts around like he was a foreigner himself? Nine Ideals Hall must borrow to pay its debts, and if we don't manage to rectify the situation, we are headed for bankruptcy."

This was another matter Naijing found difficult to discuss. Since he'd taken over the reins of Nine Ideals Hall, not a day had passed when he wasn't trying to lead the family back to prosperity. Drilling the Transocean mine had been his idea and he had urged all branches of the family to invest in the project. Who could have predicted such total failure? A bottomless pit, or near enough, and his investors, kin one and all, were clamoring for him to do something, threatening to withdraw what money was left and bring the drilling to a halt. If he couldn't come up with a solution, not only was Nine Ideals Hall in danger of collapse but the entire clan, having held together for more generations than anyone could count, could easily crumble and scatter to the four winds.

And so, on the sixth day of the first lunar month, 1928, the clan patriarch, a care-laden Li Naijing, having run out of options, was forced to accept, at the urging of his adviser Zhao Pu'an, the eight gilded longevity scrolls stolen by Commander Yang Chuxiong; he would also sell to Bai Ruide's Prosperity Company 60 percent of the Transocean mine, in which he had invested twenty years of blood and sweat.

As Zhao Pu'an lifted the curtain on his way out, Li Naijing, still troubled, stopped him:

"Old Uncle Zhao, when you accept those eight longevity scrolls, put them away and don't let them see the light of day again until we can return them to Gao Mountain Farm without letting on to Yang Chuxiong."

Zhao Pu'an nodded, a wry smile on his lips. "All right, Menglin, don't worry. I'll take care of everything."

Li Naijing's fiftieth birthday would fall two weeks after the sixth day of the first lunar month, 1928. But on this day nothing, neither family nor nation, would bring him a sense of well-being.

2

On the sixth day of the first lunar month, 1928, Li Zihen slipped quietly out of bed during the fifth watch. After folding her bedding by the dim candlelight, she held her breath and cocked her head to listen for any stirring. Reassured that her younger sister, Ziyun, was sound asleep in the adjoining room, she walked noiselessly to the brass basin resting on an ebony stand and splashed cool water on her face. She shivered slightly. Staying her hand, she looked into the mirror above the basin and saw beads of water on her pale, blurry face. The muffled sound of the night watchman's bamboo clappers spread through the predawn darkness; the rest of Silver City had switched to clocks and watches, but Nine Ideals Hall clung to the age-old tradition of night watchmen. Li Zihen bent over the placid basin again and splashed more cool water on her face. All was in readiness: the basin had been filled the night before; she had found the etched silver hair clip bequeathed her by her mother yet left undisturbed for years; the never-worn satin trousers and cheongsam, the woolen stockings, and embroidered shoes had been laid out beside the pillow before she went to bed. The floral hems of her satin trousers, the peonies on her cheongsam, and the lotus flowers on the shoes were all decorations she had personally embroidered years earlier. Back then she had vague notions that someday this trousseau might serve some significant purpose, but never had she imagined that this would be it.

Sixteen years earlier, on a cold, dark winter morning just like this, Li Zihen, who slept under the quilt at the far end of her father's bed to warm his feet, was awakened just before dawn by the sound of violent coughing. Her father's leg twitched on her back; terrified, Zihen got up to light a candle and spotted a pool of fresh blood in the bedside cuspidor. Only eight at the time, she burst into tears, but Father told her to stop crying and go wake up her younger sister and brother, for he had something to say to them. As Zihen stood at the head of the bed, her three-year-old sister beside her, her year-old brother in her arms, he said:

"Zihen, you're now eight, the eldest child, so what I'm going to say is for you: Schooling is all that matters in this world. When your brother is old enough, promise me you'll put him in school so he can make something of himself. Except for this one thing, I can die in peace."

Li Zihen nodded and promised to do as he said. Then it occurred to her what her father was saying. With a loud, tearful wail, she pleaded:

"Papa, you can't die . . . Mama's gone, you can't die . . ."

But he did, and after he was gone, Zihen had to shoulder the responsibility of protecting her siblings. At the age of eight she stopped being a little girl and became a woman. The men in the family would not fully appreciate that for another sixteen years.

On the sixth day of the first lunar month, 1928, in the cold, dark hours of predawn, as Li Zihen splashed her face with cool water from a brass basin, she recalled the vow she had made to her father on his deathbed and how his spindly legs had twitched as they lay atop her. It had taken sixteen years, but now she fully understood the meaning of her vow. After washing her face with clean water, she sat before the dressing-table mirror. She dipped her fine-toothed ox-horn comb in the water and combed her hair back so not a strand was out of place. Securing it with the silver hair clip, she dressed in her trousers and cheongsam, then put on the woolen stockings and embroidered shoes. Last, she opened her sister's compact and carefully dabbed scented powder on her cheeks with the tiny powder puff. Her toilette complete, she studied the new woman whose face looked back at her in the dim candlelight. Over the past sixteen years she had cast hurried glances at this same person every day, but this morning, for the first time, she was aware that the face looking out at her from the mirror belonged to a woman. Two rivulets of tears shone on the woman's cheeks. . . .

Zihen sat without moving, staring at the woman in the mirror; the predawn darkness and chill air froze them into an icy still life; a long, mournful sigh emerged. Now composed, Zihen coolly wiped away her tears, coolly removed the silver hair clip, and coolly stepped out of her embroidered cheongsam and shoes. Then she coolly dressed in her everyday gray trousers and jacket, meticulously fitting each cloth loop over its corresponding button. Once that was done, she picked up two joss sticks the thickness of chopsticks and tied them together with thread, then coolly held them over the candle flame and watched the tips blacken, begin to smolder, and, amid the green-tinged smoke, turn red as they caught fire. Before the embers could die out, Zihen clenched her teeth and jabbed the glowing tips into her cheeks. The predawn darkness and cold air were quickly suffused with the sickening smell of charred flesh.

On the sixth day of the first lunar month, 1928, Li Zihen was a young woman in her twenty-fourth year. After making a vow to her father on his deathbed, then watching over her younger sister and brother for sixteen hard years, she decided to bring matters to their logical conclusion. So on that morning, with a single action, she took the step that decided her fate. After disfiguring her face with the burning joss sticks, then pricking her finger and writing the word *Buddha* in her own blood, and before anyone discovered what she had done, Li Zihen quietly made her way down the shadowy corridors of her home, still dark at that predawn hour, to the family memorial hall, where the lantern that shone morning, noon, and night was aglow with a fresh quantity of oil placed there by the night watchman. As she entered, she could make out the twenty-four filial acts depicted on the ceiling; on the wall opposite the entrance hung three large black banners inscribed with gold letters. The one in the middle proclaimed: "Attend to funerals, perform ancestral rites." To its left was written: "Only trees have roots," and to its right: "Only water springs from wells." The carved idols in the center of the hall had the same sweeping curves as the building's outer eaves, and the ancestral tablets nestled among relief paintings of clouds and dragons identified themselves in neat printed script as Spirit Tablets of Generations of Ancestors of the Nine Ideals Hall Branch of the Li Clan. Their presence was mysterious, unnerving in the flickering light. Zihen walked past rows of ancestral tablets until she found those for her parents. She fell to her knees and bowed deeply, her face wet with tears. She whispered hoarsely:

"Father, Mother, now you can rest easy. . . ."

3

It would take Li Naizhi many years to shake the terror he felt at the execution of Zhao Boru, and throughout that winter he was visited nightly by a horrible dream: first his cousin Li Naijing approaches him menacingly, arms raised, then his teacher's head thuds to the ground and rolls toward him like a wheel, fresh red blood spurting skyward. "Just wait," Zhao Boru says. "Red flags will fly over the world of the future!" That was always when Li Naizhi woke up, drenched in cold sweat, his heart pounding as if to explode. By the time he was fully awake, he was alone with the freezing winter night.

Hidden in Li Naizhi's heart was a secret he had shared with only Zhao Boru. Outside the school gate one day, he had encountered Zhao, whom he hadn't seen for a while and who was obviously in a hurry. At the time, peasants from counties around Silver City were rising up in revolt, and sensational rumors about Mongrel Chen were spreading. Silver City was heavily fortified, its four gates sealed; it was an island surrounded by floodwaters, an anthill over which the gentry folk scurried in panic. Impulsively, Naizhi had blurted out:

"Teacher Zhao, I want to join the red detachment and help make revolution."

Taken aback, the teacher looked into the eyes of his student, then rested his hand on the young man's shoulder and said, "Naizhi, take my advice and stay clear of it."

"Why can't I join?"

"There is little chance they will win, and you are so young . . ."

At the time the insurrection was raging all around Silver City and hardly anyone thought the peasants' red detachments could lose; outside the school gate that day, Li Naizhi had no idea that he was in the presence of the insurrection's supreme commander. Now, in the winter, as he looked at the pallid, withered decapitated head of his teacher, it occurred to him that even at that chance encounter, his teacher had known exactly what fate awaited him yet had fought on fearlessly. Throughout the winter, Li Naizhi poured into his diary all the terror, depression, doubts, and despair that filled his heart:

JANUARY 5, 1928

Dreamed of Teacher Zhao again last night, and like every other time, it's the same terror and misery. My screams woke Second Sister. She ran in and asked me what I'd dreamed about. How could I tell her something so dreadful? How could the world tolerate a death so cruel? Oh, to be born into such a world is an unspeakable tragedy!

Since I've been denied the chance to die alongside my teacher or avenge his death, why live on? Everything he taught us was so inspiring. And now, in the snap of a finger, everything is drowned in a pool of blood, the world has turned dark and barbaric . . . Do I have the strength to leave it all behind?

JANUARY 10, 1928

Today I went to the city's east gate to gaze at my teacher's face. It's been nearly a month since the insurrection was crushed, and his features are now indistinguishable. I feel such sorrow! My teacher! I leaned against the wall and wept. I couldn't help myself.

More tragic still is people's apathy. The crowds passing through the gate are mostly peasants or city folk doing their Spring Festival shopping, and not one of them glances up at the wall. Have the victims been forgotten already? You selfish citizens, don't you care that the man up there gave his life for you? What chance is there for change in such an unfeeling world? Oh, sorrow! My teacher! Wherever you are your heart must be breaking.

JANUARY 13, 1928

I've never been so depressed or so dispirited. I tried rereading stories from Lu Xun's *Outcry,* but that only made things worse. Are people really nothing but cannibals, as he wrote in "Diary of a Madman"? I lost my appetite over a nagging sensation that Teacher Zhao's flesh was right there on my plate. Am I any different from those selfish, unfeeling citizens? . . . Second Sister sent for a doctor who checked my pulse and prescribed some medicine. She prepared it herself. I wonder if she guesses that I'm just tired of living.

JANUARY 17, 1928

I've been depressed so long I can't tell what I feel anymore. I saw Teacher Zhao again last night. The same horrible scene . . . Teacher, can't you somehow show me the way?

JANUARY 19, 1928

Third Sister returned from the provincial capital for the winter break. Just seeing her gave me a lift. She told me what was happening there and elsewhere in the world. It made me feel even more strongly that China is in desperate straits. She sneaked me a copy of a slim volume by Chen Qixiu that is all about the situation in Russia. The people there get along beautifully and society is at peace, like heaven on earth. It makes me want to go see for myself. I'd jump at the opportunity. If the Russian people can join in a common effort, why can't we Chinese?

JANUARY 25, 1928

The past few days have been one unending round of boring, stupid social obligations: paying respects to the ancestors, paying respects to our elders, paying respects to each other. The stony looks of a few days ago have been replaced by phony smiles. Everyone smiling at everyone else. Hypocrites! The power of money is evil and nefarious. If you've got it, strangers flock to you; if you haven't, your own flesh and blood shun you like a winter chill. My sisters share my feelings. But family ties are so strong that we must keep up the pretense, acting like we do because everyone else does. Debasing my life by appeasing other people, destroying myself by catering to the hypocrisy of others has made me just like them. I hate this smothering, crippling family! I hate the hypocrisy around me! One day I'll stand on my own two feet, and when that day comes I will break out of the Nine Ideals Hall cocoon!

JANUARY 26, 1928

I am constantly reminded that going with Third Sister to the provincial capital and entering school is my only way out of here. She says that students from poor families who must support themselves are the best students, that they are models of independence. If others can do it, why can't I? All that's holding me back is Second Sister. For more than a decade she has slaved for us, turning down marriage proposals in order to keep the family intact. Third Sister and I know only too well what she has done for us. The thought of her being alone if I leave is too much to bear. I, after all, have responsibility for our family. Each time I try to broach the subject, the words stick in my throat. So I tell Third Sister, and we both start crying. I don't know what to do. Life is filled with so many worries, so many trials, so many sorrows.

JANUARY 27, 1928

Today my schoolmate Qiuyun came to see Third Sister. She said that since the Silver City school had closed, her father was sending her to the provincial capital to prepare for college exams at the girls' school there. She arranged to travel with Third Sister after the winter break. When their conversation ended, Qiuyun came to my room, and she wept when she saw the memorial tablet I'd set up on my desk for Teacher Zhao. Qiuyun is the only person besides me who feels that way.

While we were talking about the provincial capital, Qiuyun asked me why I didn't come along and try to get into school there, since the Silver City school had closed. What could I say? She could not know that my heart was breaking over this very matter. She bragged about me to Second Sister, telling her how I always came out on top in exams. I guess it's best to hold off my decision and just avoid saying anything for now.

JANUARY 28, 1928

Today my heart has truly broken, my tears wet the pages my pen touches. Never in my life could I have imagined that Second Sister would disfigure her own face and take vows of abstinence so that I could continue my schooling in the provincial capital. If heaven has eyes, how can it bear to look upon such horrors? How much more pain and suffering can this loathsome world heap upon us? My beloved Second Sister has sacrificed everything for us. . . . Like me, she is only human, and like me, she has her own life to lead. Getting away from here is one thing, but not if the cost is my own sister's destruction. What can Father and Mother be feeling now, wherever they are? How in this life will I ever repay Second Sister? Tonight, without letting my sisters know, I burned a mark in my chest with a joss stick as an eternal reminder of the bitterness I feel. The pain was like a knife gouging out my heart. How could a frail young woman like Second Sister withstand such cruel torture, how could she ravage herself like that? Now we have both tasted the exquisite pain of branding. . . . Oh, such grief! My heart is rent. . . . I am adrift all alone in this world . . .

CHAPTER THREE

1

In 1913, when Bai Ruide, who was studying at the University of Wisconsin, received a telegram reporting the sad news of his father's passing and the resultant loss of his tuition, the fact that one day he would be the owner of the beautiful and elegant White Garden was the farthest thing from his mind. Eight years earlier, at the age of fifteen, he had ranked twentieth among the more than eighteen hundred students who took the school placement exam, and was matriculated in the School of Commerce, Mining, and Industry run by the office of the governor-general; his father, a farmer whose annual income was a mere thirty hectoliters of coarse grain, somehow managed to scrape up the annual tuition of a hundred taels of silver. Three years later Bai Ruide passed the governor-general's exam and continued his schooling in Japan on a government scholarship. Unfortunately, he had to study agriculture. While his father was delighted not to have to pay his tuition any longer, Bai Ruide, after years of studying mining, was less happy. But his world opened up when he arrived in Tokyo, and after only a year, at the age of nineteen, he decided to give up his government scholarship and quit the Japanese private college; he took and passed an entrance examination for the department of geology at the University of Wisconsin. A month later, he was on the deck of the *Kobe Maru* as it eased up to a pier in San Francisco; he went ashore and spent several exciting days in the city by the bay before boarding a transcontinental train to the shores of Lake Michigan, half a world away from where he had begun. Only then did he sit down and write to his family to inform them of what he had done. His aging father could only tighten his belt once more and recommence the flow of silver, this time across the Pacific Ocean to a place even the devil himself would not recognize.

There is a saying that fortunes can change from morning to night. Just as Bai Ruide, undergraduate degree in geology in hand, enrolled in graduate school to continue his studies, the telegram informing him of his father's death arrived. As the only son, he was obligated to return home to make funeral arrangements.

Before he boarded the train for San Francisco, his academic adviser invited him to dinner and promised him a full scholarship if he would come back to the university and complete his studies. But deep down, Bai Ruide knew there was more to this trip than his father's funeral, for his father had arranged a marriage for him with a girl back home. Foreigners could never understand how, for the past two thousand years, so many Chinese lives had been entangled in the business of marriages and funerals. Discouraging as it was to admit, there was no guarantee he would ever return to the University of Wisconsin. In San Francisco, he boarded a merchant ship, the SS *California,* and said farewell to North America. As he gazed out over the vast sea he could not shake the feeling expressed in the classics that "these wonderful times and places will soon be but a memory." How could he possibly know that a smiling god of fortune was waiting for him in the cocktail lounge of the SS *California*?

The monotony of the sea voyage either drove the passengers up on deck or forced them into the lounge below deck. Bai Ruide, who was traveling alone, had already read the only book he had brought along—Theodore Dreiser's new novel *The Financier*—three times and could not bear the thought of starting it again. On this particular day, he accepted a casual invitation to be a fourth at bridge after one of the original players got seasick. During the first hand, Bai learned that his partner, a Mr. Goss, not only had a Chinese name—Gao Hanqing—but spoke a little heavily accented Chinese. During the second hand, Mr. Goss was delighted to learn that his partner was a fellow alumnus of the University of Wisconsin and that they were both heading for the same Chinese province. Bai Ruide realized that he was in the presence of one of the targets of Dreiser's contempt yet someone whom he himself respected: a businessman—in this case, a resident manager for the Mobil Oil Company. Armed with this information, Bai played the most aggressive game he could manage, and a few hands later, he and his partner left the table big winners. Mr. Goss was so impressed that he used a Chinese saying to praise his partner: "Young shoulders, old head! Young shoulders, old head!"

So it was that Bai Ruide and Mr. Goss, on a crossing from the western to the eastern shores of the Pacific, went from being bridge partners to fellow alumni and from fellow alumni to friends; by the time the ship docked on the Whampoo River there were few secrets between them. As they disembarked from the SS *California,* Mr. Goss warmly invited Bai Ruide to travel inland with him on one of Mobil Oil's leased tankers, up the Yangtze all the way to their destination. Once aboard the tanker, Mr. Goss told Bai Ruide that Mobil was involved in heated competition all along the Yangtze with the British Asia Corporation and another American company, Texaco. Mobil had long entertained the idea of creating markets in the upper reaches, around Silver City, but so far had failed to find a distributor; British Asia and Texaco were on the verge of gaining a toehold. Pointing to the crates filling the hold, Mr. Goss said:

"See those? Filled with silver. Each jerry can of kerosene holds five gallons, and there are two jerry cans per crate. The price for each can is nine yuan ninety, the sales commission is forty cents for the two cans. We currently sell six thousand cans a month, so the commission amounts to twelve hundred yuan. By our estimates, the market for Silver City and its environs should be nearly a hundred thousand cans a month. Figuring conservatively, say sixty thousand a month, that still means a net profit of twelve thousand yuan. And that doesn't include a twice-monthly vending fee, which, at current rates, is a hefty sum. Now if we add British Asia and Texaco into the mix, with all three getting an equal share, the annual income is anywhere from thirty to forty thousand yuan. Not only that, Mobil's home office in America fully insures against losses due to fire, flood, or other 'acts of God.' But there's an even more important guarantee than that. Mobil products will be distributed in China free of the threat of extortion by civil authorities and warlords."

After finishing his lengthy speech on business practices, Mr. Goss made Bai Ruide an offer: "Mr. Bai, if you are willing to invest ten thousand yuan, we can sign an agreement here and now. Apply one-third of the cleverness you showed at the bridge table, and your success is guaranteed. I have always placed my trust in Wisconsin alumni!"

In the autumn of 1913, Bai Ruide, who had cut short his studies at the University of Wisconsin in order to return to China, carried out his filial responsibilities at the foot of his father's grave, then sold off the farm for twelve thousand yuan, despite his family's opposition. He added the five-thousand-yuan dowry of his new bride, a daughter of the Yang family six years his senior, and went to fetch her. Then, with steely determination, he tied his fate to the Chinese branch of Mobil Oil Company.

In Silver City, one lantern after another, now filled with Mobil kerosene instead of tallow, burned bright, and Bai Ruide's

Prosperity Company did indeed prosper. Bai Ruide took advantage of the boycott of British goods that followed the February 1926 Nanjing uprising to squeeze out the British Asia Corporation, and in a single stroke he repaid the debt to his astonished fellow alumnus by establishing a monopoly for Mobil Oil in Silver City. Before long, an ostentatious Gothic building, with verandas and peaked turrets, rose amid the rows of stone houses and stately homes of Silver City. The three-story mansion was constructed of imported carved and polished white stone; the courtyard was transformed into a flower garden complete with lotus pond, fountain, and arched bridge. White columns peeked out through lush green foliage. Bai Ruide called the place Bai Yuan, or White Garden, incorporating both his name and the pristine scenery.

As he pondered all the strange things that had happened over the past decade, good and bad, he proudly chose a name for the main room of the house, with all its varied windows: Riches and Ruins Abode. Then to make it easy to get around, he imported a four-cylinder Ford sedan and hired a chauffeur-bodyguard at a wage of a hundred yuan a month. Company VIPs arriving in Silver City were met by Bai Ruide, dressed in Western clothes, speaking clipped English, and riding in a chauffeured automobile. He even hired a Western chef to prepare their favorite meals. With the passage of time, Bai and his White Garden provided a spectactular peep show for Silver City residents. Next to the old-line salt merchants, he and his Prosperity Company were like long-necked cranes among a flock of chickens.

Bai Ruide knew that he could never enter the ranks of Silver City society unless he played a major role in the salt industry, that the established salt merchants would always treat him as an interloper, no matter how rich he became. So to insinuate himself into their company, he mounted a campaign against outdated mining methods and equipment. First, he advocated replacing woven bamboo cables for the overhead derricks with steel ones. The trend quickly caught on in the salt mines, just as Mobil lanterns had swept across Silver City; Bai, who made the cables, turned a tidy profit. By the time competitors entered the steel-cable market, he had moved on to replacing pumps run by draft animals or humans with steam-driven ones. His German engineers worked out all the technical details, and he now watched the brine come roaring up from a depth of two or three hundred meters ten times faster. The merchants flocked to Bai, virtually begging him for new pumps. In a place caught up in the rush to modernize, money flowed in with each new venture, and Bai was as content as a fish in its watery element.

Within fifteen years, Bai Ruide brought to Silver City lamps that burned Mobil kerosene, steel cables, and steam-driven pumps; but he kept the extent of his ambitions hidden from the citizens of Silver City. There was no point beating the grass to stir up the snakes until he had accumulated enough wealth, and the opportunity presented itself, to sink or own his own salt mine. For fifteen years, he quietly recorded the depth, location, production rates, rock formations, and history of each Silver City salt mine, nearly a thousand in all. Drawing on the technical knowledge he had acquired at the University of Wisconsin, he made a map showing the exact location of all of them; on nights when he was too agitated to sleep, which was often, he sat in his White Garden study dreaming of the day when, like J. D. Rockefeller or J. P. Morgan, he too would control a vast financial empire. Maybe, he allowed himself to dream, he would buy up Silver City, lock, stock, and barrel.

As the Spring Festival of 1928 approached, the moment for which Bai Ruide had waited fifteen years arrived: the local salt merchants had suffered considerable losses as a result of the recent insurrection and the salt market had stagnated. The target of his first assault would be the Nine Ideals Hall branch of the Li clan, whose salt holdings were plummeting in value; he took special aim at the Transocean mine, the one most deeply in debt, as the chink in the opposition's armor.

2

Bai Ruide's only child, fourteen-year-old Bai Qiuyun, was a pearl in her father's palm, but there seemed to be no hope that Lady Yang would ever present him with a son. For years she had urged him to take a concubine. Her reasoning was simple: A fortune such as ours requires an heir. Whether foreigners give a damn about such things doesn't concern me, but a Chinese family needs a son. Lady Yang had invested five thousand yuan in her husband's business, and she set great store by the family's holdings. But Bai Ruide had never taken his wife's suggestion seriously, always countering her arguments with equally simple reasoning: I can't be out there taking potshots from strangers all day long, then come home and take more of the same from the women in my family. If not for those twenty or thirty women, Nine Ideals Hall wouldn't have declined so rapidly, he pointed out. Their daughter also opposed the idea, for an even simpler reason: Do you plan to bring a second mother into the family while my real mother is still alive? And so the failure to produce an heir, the "great unfilial deed," simmered beneath the surface at the Bai home until one day Lady Yang brought home her cousin Liu Qiongju, a young woman of twenty-two who had recently graduated from the provincial girls' school. Qiongju had been passing the time at home, since teaching did not appeal to her. She was to find no peace there, owing to the demands of her parents, who had betrothed her to the son of another family when both children were still in the womb. She jumped at the opportunity to gain sanctuary at White Garden. At twenty-two, she could paint passably well, had some modest talent at the piano, and was something of an authority on the swains of romantic novels. But the greatest difference between her and Lady Yang was that she had acquired the airs of a modern city woman; the moment she laid eyes on Lady Yang's husband, she blurted out:

"Cousin, I'm called Qiongju—'living in poverty'—but I'm tired of the life of a poor country girl and ready to throw in my lot with my wealthy family in the city. Don't kick me out just because you're rich and I'm poor!"

Bai Ruide laughed. "Don't talk like that," he said. "With the two of you living here at White Garden, won't I have the good fortune of being shaded by both *yang* and *liu*—poplar and willow?"

Liu Qiongju quickly grew bored with life in the Bai household, so she took her cousin up on a suggestion to help Bai Ruide with some clerical work. She seemed born to the task. "Since teaching doesn't appeal to you," Lady Yang commented after a few days, "why not work for my husband at the Prosperity Company full-time?" The deal was struck, and from that day forward, Bai Ruide had a real secretary working for him. Twice he took her to social gatherings, where she acquitted herself well, chatting with ease and completely unintimidated by the guests. Now there was a new attraction in the Silver City peep show. The Prosperity Company had no need for a venerable adviser, since it had a real secretary—a female secretary!

On the seventh of February 1928, midway through the first lunar month, Bai Qiuyun was sunning herself on a swing in the yard, absorbed in the mournful sentimentality of "plump greens and wispy reds" in the book she was reading, *Pale Fragrance Lyrics,* when someone gave her a push from behind. "Hey!" she yelped. "You almost made me fall!"

Bai Ruide held the swing steady. He was smiling. "That's enough reading," he said. "Why so studious the day before a trip?"

"Papa, I'm going to ask Li Ziyun to ride in the car with us tomorrow."

"Fine with me. Your mother's going along, and that's all I care about. Take anyone you like, as long as there's room."

"Naizhi's coming too."

"Qiuyun, how come you're so close to the Nine Ideals Hall people?"

"Didn't you just say it was fine with you? If it bothers you, we can hire a sedan chair—and you can keep your old car!"

"Have I ever said no to you?"

Smiling again, he gave the swing a hard push, sending his daughter squealing into the sky.

While Bai Ruide was teasing his daughter in the yard, his wife was inside setting her tender trap. Gripping her cousin's hand, she instructed her with great earnestness:

"Qiongju, I'll be away for ten days, and I expect you to take good care of the man of the house."

Qiongju, guileless as always, blurted out, "I'll fatten him up, don't worry."

"Normally I turn the difficult chores over to Amah Liu and the other servants, so I can take care of the more personal tasks myself."

"Dear cousin, you may take care of his personal needs, but I certainly can't."

"Now, don't be like that. I wouldn't ask you to do this if you weren't family. Before he goes to bed at night, that horrid man demands a cup of coffee and a snifter of brandy to ensure a good night's sleep."

With that, Lady Yang fetched an alcohol burner and a coffee pot, then showed her cousin how to light the burner, how to add water, and how much coffee to put in.

"Every night," she said, "I prepare the coffee and pour the brandy before seeing him off to bed. I've suffered through this for nearly twenty years, like an indentured servant, but I've always felt awkward entrusting the chore to someone else."

Qiongju laughed. "I'll make his coffee for him, but I won't be seeing him off to bed," she said. "No mixing of the sexes, that I can tell you. He'll just have to come into the kitchen for his late-night grazing."

Bai Ruide walked in on them. Glib as always, Qiongju spun around and said, "Cousin, Sister here has put me in charge of you while she's away for ten days. I'm afraid you'll have to put up with me during that time."

Bai Ruide smiled and lit a cigar. But after Qiongju had gone upstairs, he asked his wife, "What are you up to?"

She looked at him knowingly. "I've done my part," she said. "The rest is up to you."

"Are you sure you know what you're doing?"

"This family must have an heir."

"You won't be sorry?"

The weight of this last comment was not lost on Lady Yang, who asked in reply, "Won't you be sorry if you have no heir?"

Bai Ruide left her question unanswered as he looked around the large, empty room and heaved a sigh. He sensed that domestic harmony would soon be a thing of the past.

The next day, Bai Qiuyun, dressed in her traveling clothes, climbed into the family Ford with her mother. Before they reached Nine Ideals Hall she saw Li Ziyun waiting for them beneath Twin Arches.

"Where's Ninth Brother, Ziyun?" she asked anxiously.

"Forget him," she replied angrily. "Let's go."

"Why?"

"He left right after breakfast. Said he felt like walking. Something about a social survey. I have his suitcase. He said Mr. Zhao had taken him and his friends on one of those surveys before."

Bai Qiuyun was close to tears. "Why didn't he tell me earlier? What fun is taking the car without him?"

Lady Yang looked at her daughter with astonishment. Since when had Li Naizhi become so important to her? she wondered. "Don't be upset," she urged her daughter. "We'll catch up with him in no time."

But the automobile never did catch up with Li Naizhi, who had left the main road and was walking through fields along earthen dikes and irrigation ditches. He wanted to see for himself how peasants who had once set off a prairie fire of revolution had turned into a pool of stagnant water.

When, fifty miles later, the automobile reached the town of Cockcrow, Bai Qiuyun complained of car sickness, and since neither a headache powder nor a damp washrag on her forehead helped, she insisted on stopping in town until she felt better. Lady Yang, no match for her daughter, reluctantly had the chauffeur drive them to the local inn. After dinner, Bai Qiuyun asked Li Ziyun to take a stroll with her. The two of them walked to the edge of town, where they looked out at farmland bathed in the rust-colored rays of the setting sun and at the red surface of the road that ran through it. Wretched little villages dotted the area. Off in the distance they saw someone in a school uniform and backpack heading toward them and knew who it was right away. Red-eyed, Bai Qiuyun asked her companion, "Ziyun, why didn't he want to come with us?"

Li Ziyun said nothing as she hugged the girl. She had discovered Qiuyun's secret, and it made her angry.

"Because he's an idiot! Your good thoughts are wasted on the likes of him!"

3

Li Naijing's fiftieth-birthday celebration could not have been more austere. His adviser, Zhao Pu'an, had made the arrangements for the big day, a major event in the life of most Chinese, and had handed the list of plans to Naijing, who shook his head and said no to the entertainment, no to the longevity pears and birthday cakes from the Gathering of Worthies Teahouse, and no to a sumptuous banquet that included fifty dishes with names like Golden Turtle Enters the Sea and Dragons and Phoenixes Bring Good Fortune. Except for a modest spread demanded by the occasion, to express gratitude to the people bearing gifts—a meal of birthday noodles, a couple of simple dishes, and tea instead of wine—he would celebrate his birthday with his family. Li Naijing wanted members of Nine Ideals Hall to understand that austerity was the path to success, and he was prepared to set an example. Zhao Pu'an accepted the list of rejected options with visible distress. "Menglin," he said, "I'm just not very good at arranging things, which only makes it that much harder on you."

"Old Uncle Zhao, please don't talk like that. The times dictate the way we live, and these are chaotic times. What worries me is that the family may fall apart, and then all the austerity in the world will be too late."

The smiles they exchanged could not mask the looks of worry on their faces. Beneath the window of Emerald Sky Study two plum trees sent the weak fragrance of their remaining blossoms up to those worried faces. Li Naijing knew that Zhao Pu'an would never mention the matter of the Transocean mine at a time like this, so it was up to him:

"Has Bai Ruide agreed to talk with us at Gathering of Worthies Teahouse?"

"Yes."

"On the twenty-ninth of this month?"

"Yes."

"Good. So long as he doesn't try to throw his weight around, I'll talk with him."

"Menglin, since you plan to sell him a 60 percent interest, maybe we should halt mining operations at Transocean for the time being. Otherwise, we're just lining his pockets with money."

"No. The family may sell its business interests, but not its integrity."

"All right. I'll send word to Bai Ruide confirming that the talks will take place on the twenty-ninth at Gathering of Worthies. If we agree on terms, we'll sign the papers. If not, we can try again later."

Li Naijing suddenly felt tears welling up in his eyes, and he turned to look out the window. "Old Uncle Zhao, who would have thought that these aging plum trees could smell so sweet?"

Caught off guard, Zhao could only echo the comment: "So sweet, they smell so sweet."

Neither man could say more.

When the silence grew oppressive, Zhao Pu'an considered saying something to lighten the mood, but he no sooner opened his mouth than Li Naijing stopped him with his hand. "Old Uncle Zhao," he said, "now that it's come to this, there's nothing more to be said."

Choosing Gathering of Worthies Teahouse as the location and the twenty-ninth as the date was part of Li Naijing's plan. Gathering of Worthies, the largest and grandest teahouse in Silver City, served pastries that attracted customers from far and wide. It was the city's news hub, a place where secrets passed from ear to ear. Nine Ideals Hall and Gathering of Worthies Teahouse shared a long history: there had been much intermarriage between the two families over the years and the proprietor of Gathering of Worthies, Mr. Chen, was the sole outside investor in the holdings of Nine Ideals Hall. Gathering of Worthies prospered because of that relationship, and Nine Ideals Hall's leadership in Silver City salt mining during those years relied in large measure on talk that emerged from Gathering of Worthies Teahouse, truth and rumor alike. In fact, virtually every major business deal had been settled inside Gathering of Worthies Teahouse. As for the date, the twenty-ninth of the month, it was commonly known in Silver City that all significant matters involving Nine Ideals Hall were decided on days ending in nine, days of talismanic importance for this branch of the clan.

Li Naijing awoke at dawn on the twenty-ninth day of the first lunar month, 1928, and asked his wife to attend to him personally as he washed up. Then he dressed in new clothes from head to toe: a white foxskin Chinese gown under a short buttoned jacket, felt shoes with thick white soles, and a purple marten cap; a jade pendant, shiny as a mirror, hung at his waist. This gem, more precious than any in Silver City, had an uncommon history. During the Taiping uprising of the mid-1800s, when government troops passed through the region on their way to annihilate Shi Dakai, pretender to the throne, they were welcomed by Nine Ideals Hall to the tune of a hundred thousand taels of silver. Later, on their victorious return, the clan chief was rewarded by the Tongzhi emperor with the rank of second-tier official and given this exquisite jade ornament. Normally kept in a fine crystal box in Li Naijing's bedroom, the pendant was taken out only on very special occasions. Such as today.

Li Naijing picked up a brass hand warmer and walked alone through the main hall, past the various private rooms, and out into the cold air; entering the clan's ancestral hall, he somberly offered up three lit joss sticks, then removed his cap, knelt before the tablets of his ancestors, and performed the rites of three kowtows and nine obeisances. His determination now properly reinforced, he emerged from the ancestral hall into the morning chill, solemn and stern.

Li climbed into the eight-man sedan chair with its green wool canopy and lowered the curtain just as Zhao Pu'an ran up with the manager of the Transocean mine in tow.

"Menglin, the manager of Transocean wants to know if he should stop drilling today."

One word, notable for its determined ring, emerged from behind the sedan-chair curtain:

"No."

Then two more words:

"Let's go."

Eight muscular bearers picked up the sedan chair, once the pride of Silver City and now the last remaining vehicle of its kind, and carried it with a steady rhythm through the main gate of the Li compound and past the two stone memorial arches, the city's tallest and most imposing. Following in the wake of the sedan chair were the clan's adviser and business manager, the bookkeeper, eight bodyguards, and two lantern bearers carrying tallow-burning lanterns made of bamboo strips, which had been brought on the orders of Li Naijing, who said he did not plan to return until after dark. In fact, the lamps were for the benefit of Bai Ruide. Li Naijing was saying: With or without Mobil Oil lamps, Nine Ideals Hall is still Nine Ideals Hall. But he had not anticipated that on the twenty-ninth day of the first lunar month in 1928, as he sat in his sedan chair like a true mandarin, somber and composed, he was walking straight into Bai's clutches.

Li Naijing sensed that something was wrong even before the sedan chair came to a halt. He climbed down past the curtain held open for him by a sedan bearer and was straightening his jacket when Zhao Pu'an rushed up, excited and nervous.

"Menglin, see what that damned Bai Ruide has done."

Glancing up in the direction of the outstretched hand, which shook from the old man's anger, Li Naijing saw to his astonishment that the gold-lettered signboard of Gathering of Worthies Teahouse had been replaced by another that proclaimed: Prosperity Teahouse. Parked beneath the new sign was Bai Ruide's Ford sedan, waxed to a high sheen. A pained look spread across Li Naijing's face. The battle had not even been joined and he had already fallen victim to an ambush. Bai Ruide, decked out in a Western-style suit, strode through the gate, beaming as he welcomed his guest:

"Ah, Master Menglin, forgive me for not coming out to the road to meet you!"

Bai Ruide was clearly gratified to see that his opponent had lost the psychological advantage. Mr. Goss had been right to say that Bai Ruide would succeed if he used even a third of the talent he had shown at bridge. Mr. Chen, whose teahouse was now under new ownership, appeared behind Bai Ruide. He, too, was smiling, but the smile could not hide his embarrassment.

"Menglin," Zhao Pu'an whispered to Li Naijing, "since he has abandoned decency, we are freed of our obligation to honor the agreement. Let's call off the negotiations."

Ignoring the advice, Li Naijing walked up to his host, smiling broadly, hands clasped in a show of reverence. "Elder Brother Ruide, you needn't have gone to such lengths to receive me properly that you bought the teahouse."

Then he turned to Mr. Chen, his eyes shining.

"Mr. Chen, for how much silver did you sell the good name of Gathering of Worthies?"

The caustic comment had the desired effect on Mr. Chen, whose smile faltered as he replied, "You flatter me, Master Menglin. This is just an insignificant little teahouse. You know how it is—the mountain stays put, so the water must detour. I have my livelihood to think of."

Li Naijing turned to his troops and said with mounting dignity:

"Can't you see that Elder Brother Ruide and Mr. Chen have come out to greet us? What are you standing around for?"

The twenty-ninth day of the first lunar month, 1928, may well have been the longest day in the life of Li Naijing, for it was then that he first experienced the rage and impotence of imminent defeat. Yet, for the sake of Nine Ideals Hall's business holdings, he had no choice but to fight to the finish, his back to the water.

In accordance with the agreed-on agenda, Li Naijing and Bai Ruide first spelled out the general conditions of the transaction, then Naijing left his adviser, bookkeeper, and business manager to hammer out the details with Bai Ruide while he repaired to Soul Nurturing Chamber, a second-floor room in Gathering of Worthies Teahouse that had long been his private sanctuary. Over the years, Mr. Chen had made sure that Soul Nurturing

Chamber maintained the elegance appropriate to its special guest. A curtain of amber beads hanging motionlessly behind a gold-lacquered folding screen parted to reveal a roomful of classical Ming furniture: a bench, a tea table, and armchairs, each piece crafted with simple grace. A century-old five-needle miniature pine rested atop a hardwood flower stand near the window. Years earlier, Mr. Chen had bragged to Silver City residents that he would sooner sell Gathering of Worthies Teahouse than part with that five-needle pine. But on the twenty-ninth day of the first lunar month in 1928, when Li Naijing revisited this place of respite, what greeted him was something entirely different: overstuffed sofas against the walls, glass-topped coffee tables covered with off-white tablecloths and a line of crystal ashtrays. The flower stand on which the five-needle pine had stood now supported a crank-handled phonograph, its arm at a rakish angle. Recalling Mr. Chen's boast of earlier years, Naijing could only grin ruefully. Everything is for sale these days. The grin was still on his face when an elderly waiter came up to greet him, still with the appropriate reverence:

"Master Li, Mr. Chen sent me to ask what sort of tea you would like. The usual, Yunnan black?"

"Thank Mr. Chen for me and tell him I'll take my tea downstairs in the Prosperity Tearoom. And I'll pay for it myself."

"Master Li," the embarrassed waiter replied, "we attendants rely on the owner for our livelihood. There is nothing I can do. We know how unhappy this makes you, and the fact that you still honor us with your presence, well . . ."

Sensing he had spoken too harshly and sympathizing with the elderly attendant who had served him for so many years, Li Naijing handed the man two silver coins.

"It's all right," he said, "Yunnan black will do just fine. But bring it to me in the tearoom downstairs."

Thanking his guest profusely, the old waiter slipped out the door. Li Naijing did not have to be told that the public room would be crowded with Silver City residents anticipating the unfolding drama, eager to see Li Naijing sell his family's business interests to Bai Ruide. A tall building coming down is a sight to behold, but a great house about to topple is a spectacle for the ages. The citizens of Silver City would not miss it for anything. For his part, Li Naijing was determined to show them that he, the pillar of Nine Ideals Hall, remained standing and to remind them that Nine Ideals Hall was still Nine Ideals Hall. With that bolstering thought, he smoothed his clothes and adjusted his cap, then lifted up the jade pendant at his waist for yet one more look before walking steadily down the stairway.

A hush fell over the tearoom, quickly broken by a series of greetings and best wishes. Li Naijing laughed.

"Welcome to all of you who are here to see what will befall Nine Ideals Hall."

The silence returned, this time with palpable embarrassment. Li Naijing continued:

"I'll watch along with you."

Some of the people in the tearoom laughed awkwardly. Li Naijing pulled up a chair and sat down. "I might as well get a good seat for the show," he said. Then, in an easy, confident manner, he called out, "Waiter, I'll take my Yunnan black now."

One of the customers offered some hollow commiseration:

"Master Menglin, the Prosperity people have gone too far this time."

"Oh? This is business, after all, which requires both a willing seller and a willing buyer. At Nine Ideals Hall we have had a change in fortunes, that's all, and Elder Brother Ruide has come to our aid."

"You're being generous, Master Menglin."

"Permit me a comment that may offend some of you. I'm sure that many of you here sold your salt mines to Nine Ideals Hall way back when. Well, mountains stand tall and waters run deep. Who's to say that things won't turn around again and that Nine

Ideals Hall won't be in a position to buy out the Prosperity Company? Nine Ideals Hall may be in difficult straits at the moment, but it will always be Nine Ideals Hall."

This time he laughed heartily, his laugh nervously echoed by the tearoom customers. Carefully noting the easy, confident manner of the Li clan patriarch, they found themselves truly curious as to just how the drama would play itself out. Li Naijing, on the other hand, knew only too well that when today's negotiations ended, Nine Ideals Hall would be left with only 40 percent of the Transocean mine.

Li Naijing could not have anticipated that while he was putting on a show of bravado for the sake of Nine Ideals Hall a horse was racing toward Gathering of Worthies Teahouse from Transocean mine, carrying a sweat-soaked messenger who jumped out of the saddle the minute his mount came to a halt outside the teahouse, rushed inside, and fell to his knees before Li Naijing.

"Master, Manager Wang sends news that they've struck briny water at the mine and that it's risen hundreds of feet. When I left it was already starting to pour out of the mouth of the mine. And a geyser of burning gas is shooting into the sky. Manager Wang is celebrating with fireworks."

Gasps of astonishment swept through the tearoom. Who could have predicted such a spectacular turn of events?

Amid a chorus of congratulations, Li Naijing's face suddenly went ghostly white. Then, after a fleeting moment, he said to the messenger:

"Run upstairs and inform Zhao Pu'an that shares in the Transocean mine are not for sale!"

Finally he turned back to the customers seated around him and announced, "Today's tea is on Nine Ideals Hall."

On the twenty-ninth day of the first lunar month, 1928, Li Naijing, his back to the water, could not have anticipated snatching victory from certain defeat. Had the breakthrough at Transocean occurred but moments later, Nine Ideals Hall would, in fact, no longer have been the Nine Ideals Hall of old. On the way home, as the swaying sedan chair hurried toward Transocean mine, yet another messenger came running up.

"Master," he said, blocking the road, "Mistress has sent me to report that Third Concubine has given birth to a young master!"

Li Naijing was dumbstruck. After so many years without an heir, even with the cooperation of three concubines, the day he had longed for had finally arrived. The timing could not have been more exquisite. How could such blessings have come to him all at once? He nodded absentmindedly as he mumbled "Fine" a time or two. Then, dropping the curtain in front of him, he fell back in his seat and let the tears flow down his face.

"Revered ancestors," he said in a tearful voice, "your unworthy descendant, Li Naijing, bows before you . . ."

CHAPTER FOUR

1

Word that the Nine Ideals Hall patriarch, Li Naijing, had been doubly blessed just when all had seemed lost quickly made the rounds of Silver City. If not for the moral courage he displayed by refusing to stop drilling, people said, that branch of the clan might now exist in name only, the controlling interest in the salt mine that ensured the family's wealth would now be in the hands of the Prosperity Company. Bai Ruide, for all his skill and talent, could only watch as the biggest fish broke free of his net. Once again, as in legends that had formed over the years, Nine Ideals Hall looked proudly down upon Silver City from high atop the two stone arches. Silver City residents both feared and hated Nine Ideals Hall, yet it was the support upon which they all leaned. Already there were people whose eyes were focused on Transocean mine, hoping that some of its briny wealth would come their way, and the quickest among them had already slipped into the Nine Ideals Hall compound bearing gifts.

In the midst of congratulations from the well-wishers who surrounded Li Naijing as stars encircle the moon, his adviser, Zhao Pu'an, came to Emerald Sky Study in deep anguish to announce that he was leaving. After reading his letter of resignation, Li handed it back.

"Old Uncle Zhao, what is this all about? Have I offended you somehow?"

"Menglin, what happened at the Transocean mine is cause for joyful celebration. But when I think of what might have happened, I see that my advice could have cost you everything. By urging you to sell shares all these years, I repaid the generosity of your late father in the most ignominious fashion. It would be a disgrace for me to continue in the service of Nine Ideals Hall. I've gotten old and useless."

Zhao Pu'an broke down and sobbed after he had spoken his piece, moving Li Naijing to tears as well.

"Old Uncle Zhao, you and I have been like family for many years now. We have relied upon each other. Of all the members of Nine Ideals Hall, old and young, you are the only one I can talk to. Do you really have the heart to simply walk off and leave me on my own? If I had listened to you years ago when you told me to sell off Transocean mine, we wouldn't have teetered on the brink of disaster in the first place. When my father was alive, the word *risk* was taboo. This time I took a risk by continuing the drilling and courted disaster in the process. But I wouldn't have stood a chance if not for the protection of my ancestors. Once we have moved past this critical stage, there will be many things to do. How can you think of leaving just when your services are needed the most?"

Then, ignoring their differences in station, Li Naijing helped Zhao Pu'an over to a chair and continued, "Old Uncle Zhao, as it turns out, there is something quite important I've been meaning to discuss with you for several days. For years now, Nine Ideals Hall has witnessed a steady decline in wealth and influence, with a corresponding impoverishment of spirit. This recent success at Transocean mine offers a wonderful opportunity, and I would like to hear from you how we can tame the wild steeds in the herd. There is also the matter of our outstanding debts to the moneylenders, Daheng and Datong. How can we get an extension?"

Zhao Pu'an sighed. "Since this is how things are, Menglin, I will pull these old bones together and stay with you a few more years. You are not the only one who has thought of these matters. The debts should be easy to manage. The Transocean mine is bringing in more than enough silver with all the brine and gas it's producing now. If we even utter the word *extension* the moneylenders will be displeased. But they will welcome us with open arms if we go to them to borrow more. With Transocean as collateral, a high return on their investment is assured. Dealing with members of your own family is a thornier issue, and I worry that you won't have the stomach to do what is necessary."

"Whatever you are thinking, old uncle, just say it."

"I can sum it up in two words: Be merciless."

"Merciless? How?"

"For years they were all clamoring to share in the anticipated profits of Transocean, then they clamored for their money back. Now that the mine has finally begun producing, I guarantee that they are eager to share in the good fortune. You should call a clan meeting at which the only item on the agenda is the return of their initial investment, with no talk of sharing in anything. Those who shouted the loudest about getting their money back will fall all over themselves apologizing. That's when you must keep a firm hand and insist on giving back some of their money. Naturally, they will be frightened and hurt, as if you were cutting off their very limbs, but it is crucial that you not yield, especially to the ones who made the most noise. Nairen, from Second Elder's home, has been sulking ever since he lost his bid to take over Nine Ideals Hall. He made the biggest fuss of all.

Last month he forced his shares on our steward, saying he needed money for the new year, and he walked off with half their value in silver . . ."

Catching himself in midsentence, Zhao Pu'an stopped and looked straight at Li Naijing.

"It doesn't bother you that I'm driving a wedge between members of your own family, Menglin?"

"Not in the least. Go on."

"I retrieved the certificates from the steward in your name." He reached into his sleeve and pulled out the documents. "With these in your possession, you can demand that he take the other half of his money and go, and there won't be a thing he can do about it. Then, if he wants his shares back, you can agree to sell them to him—at the original low market rate. Your display of magnanimity and fair play will silence all your critics. You can be sure that once you've made Nairen take his money back, no one else in the family will dare oppose you. But I warn you that resolving family squabbles can try even the wisest and most upright mediator. Are you up to the task?"

With a loud belly laugh Li Naijing said, "Old Uncle Zhao, there is no rust on your sword! Stay here today and share a bottle with me. This is the first time in years I've felt so happy."

So on the fifth day of the second lunar month, 1928, the heads of the Nine Ideals Hall branch of the Li clan were summoned to meet with the patriarch, Li Naijing, the following morning in the steward's office. Right after breakfast they rushed to the meeting as if vying to be first, and in no time the steward's office filled with smoke and the din of conversation. The talk was of Li Naijing's brilliant coup and how the Transocean mine had come through just when all seemed lost; yet behind the smiling faces there was a sense of foreboding. As part of his strategy, Li Naijing kept his relatives waiting; with each passing minute, and no sign of Li Naijing, the atmosphere grew more oppressive as the men began to speculate on the purpose of the meeting. Li Naijing, accompanied by his adviser and the steward, finally strode into the room at midmorning, looking very stern. With the arrival of Nine Ideals Hall's savior, all the men rose and welcomed him with wishes for his good health, long life, and the like, then bombarded him with congratulations. Naijing took his seat at the front of the room without saying a word, his stern expression frozen in place. When quiet returned, he announced to the assemblage:

"Gentlemen, drilling at the Transocean mine has proceeded uninterrupted for twelve years, but recently many of you have come to me clamoring for your money back. Some of you have even taken out your impatience on the family steward. I have asked you here today to arrange the return of your investment."

Shocked silence, followed by nervous laughter. Then came apologies and veiled protests such as "A worthy superior overlooks the mistakes of those beneath him." Two of the most prominent family members actually stood up, folded their hands respectfully in front of them, and apologized to their worthy nephew Li Naijing on behalf of all those present. Then, with a magnanimous nod, Naijing played his trump card:

"Well then, since everyone appears to want to drop the matter of getting their money back, we'll move on. But I do have Nairen's certificates, for which he has already received half the money."

Li Nairen blushed bright red. What could he say?

Li Naijing turned to his steward. "Did Second Master receive half the silver he had invested?"

"Yes."

"When Second Master took the silver, did he hand you these and say I could use them to wipe my ass?"

". . . Yes."

"Did you bring the remaining half with you today?"

"Yes, I did."

"Clear the books."

Beads of perspiration formed on the tip of Li Nairen's nose. Not even the twitter of a bird broke the silence in the room; instead it was broken by Li Naijing's stony voice:

"Nairen, do you accept this silver?"

With every eye in the room on him, Li Nairen walked up to the steward and took the weighty parcel of silver that had been prepared for the occasion. In the same stony voice, Li Naijing continued:

"Nairen, based on current production figures, these certificates of yours would have paid you a dividend of three thousand yuan in silver. You left half your silver unclaimed, which is fifteen hundred yuan, pretty costly toilet paper. If you think perhaps you made a mistake, you may buy back your shares at their original price."

Like a man mercifully reprieved, Nairen laid down the bundle of silver. "You are too generous, Elder Brother," he said. "I was foolish, I shouldn't have . . ."

At last the tension in the room dissipated; everyone agreed loudly that Nairen had been foolish and that Naijing had handled the matter with the generosity of a kindly father. But Naijing remained stern as he said:

"The drilling of Transocean mine has imposed heavy financial burdens on Nine Ideals Hall, and there is one more item I want to place before you today. Rather than divvying up the profits from Transocean's good first year, I propose to use that money to invest in new drilling equipment, make repairs to the saltwater pipeline, and pay off some debts that are singeing our eyebrows. Dividends on investments will be paid out in the second year. This is no time for Nine Ideals Hall to let down its guard. The cooperation of everyone in this room will be necessary if we are to get past this critical juncture and once again stand firmly on our own two feet."

Who would have entertained the idea of saying no? Instead, words of harmony and conciliation broke out around the table.

Finally, a genuine smile appeared on Li Naijing's face. "I will buy the shares returned by Nairen with my own money for Ninth Brother, Naizhi, and Eighth Sister, Ziyun. It is expensive to study at the provincial school, too costly for a fragile young woman like Zihen, burdened now with responsibility for them, to bear alone."

That, too, was met with approval all around, to which the assembled clan added praise for Naijing's selfless concern for their orphaned kin. Li Naijing and Zhao Pu'an, enjoying their success, exchanged glances. Then Li Naijing announced:

"Our meeting is over, but don't leave. The success at Trans-ocean calls for a celebration, so you are all my guests for lunch in Zhenghong Hall."

The crowd was delighted. Li Naijing's banquets were spectacular events, matched by no one, the pride of Silver City. Mere mention of them had a listener salivating.

Zhenghong Hall, located at the foot of the mountain, beside the lake near the Nine Ideals Hall woods, was where diners went for a relaxed, happy atmosphere. Each of five large rooms was divided in half by bamboo and gauze screens. A row of twelve-paned windows looked out over Willow Reflecting Pond, whose surface was covered with lotus leaves. The ring of linked verandas was set off by manicured bamboo groves. A finger of land called Embracing Autumn boasted a stand of weeping willows; in the distance Silver Creek snaked its way through mountain passes; the Jade Spring mountains themselves were outlined in evergreens. Sounds of rippling water merged with the gurgling of the springs that fed Willow Reflecting Pond, creating beautiful music the day long. The pillars at the entrance to Zhenghong Hall were draped with scrolls that proclaimed:

PEACE OF MIND AND A PURE HEART THE YEAR ROUND

SPARKLING WATERS AND BRIGHT MOUNTAINS FILL THE HOME.

So on the sixth day of the second lunar month, 1928, the heads of all the households in Nine Ideals Hall filled one of the rooms in Zhenghong Hall. Toasts were made, good wine was drunk, and heaven and earth were in perfect accord. The stormy scene they had all just weathered now seemed like nothing more than a temporary squall that left in its wake clear skies and a cleansed earth. Li Naijing raised his glass:

"Today the wine has cheered old Uncle Zhao, who has offered to sing a verse to enliven the atmosphere."

Zhao Pu'an, his face red as a beet, struggled to his feet and said, "I'll just make a fool of myself." He turned meditative for a moment, then began a rhythmic beating of his palm with his chopsticks; in an operatic tone of voice, he began to sing:

Pay no heed to those sounds,
piercing the woods, hitting leaves —
why should it stop me from whistling or chanting
and walking slowly along?
With my bamboo cane and sandals of straw
I move more freely than on horse.
Who's afraid?
Let my life be spent with a raincoat
in the misty rain.

A biting chill in the spring breeze
blows me sober from wine.
A bit cold,
but the sunshine that sinks on the hilltop
comes back to welcome me.
Turn your head to where you just were,
where the winds were howling,
go back —
on the one hand, it's not a storm;
on the other, not clear skies.

As the strains of "Calming the Waves" filled the room, Li Naijing could not help but feel that this meal would purge him of the residue of misfortune that had tormented him for years.

2

At the first knock, Bai Ruide placed his cigar in the ashtray, casually straightened his crimson silk pajamas, and went to the door. There stood Liu Qiongju, holding a serving tray with a cup of hot, fragrant coffee and his amber-colored brandy snifter. But what he really noticed was the shy, almost panicky look in her eyes, which she tried to conceal with a slight frown.

"This smells awful!" she complained. "How can you stand something so bitter before bed?"

Bai Ruide pointed to the bedside table. "Put it over there," he said.

As Qiongju slipped past him, a sweet fragrance filled his nostrils. She was wearing a tight purple cheongsam with a cream-colored shawl, and when she bent over to put down the tray, the dress highlighted her lovely figure: her waist curved softly as a violin, her breasts like peaches on the arched branch of a tree. "Will this body really bear me a son, an heir?" Bai thought. He walked over to Liu Qiongju, picked up the brandy snifter, and raised it to her lips.

"The first drink tonight is my gift of gratitude."

Liu Qiongju hesitated a moment before drinking the brandy. A pink flush rose to her pale cheeks almost immediately. She set down the snifter and had turned to leave when she was caught up in Bai's embrace; she felt herself falling into a void of blinding heat; at that moment she discovered the truth of all those romantic novels she was so fond of reading. With the biting stink of cigar in her nostrils, she blurted out her only thought, "What if your wife comes in?"—unaware that she was doing exactly what Lady Yang intended.

In the waning days of February 1928, over a period of ten balmy spring nights, Liu Qiongju wiped all concerns from her mind. She lived only to lose herself in the ardent embraces of her cousin's husband, now her lover, until her soul left her body. When she allowed herself to contemplate the terrifying prospect of her cousin's return, she saw herself condemned to the role of adulteress, and she yearned for a night that would never end. She was forever listening for the blare of a horn, dreading the moment when the Ford sedan would drive into the compound, its arrival heralding her banishment from White Garden.

After ten nights of soul-stirring passion, Bai Ruide finally knew what it meant to be with a woman, finally comprehended the depths of pleasure a man was capable of experiencing. Until then Prosperity Company had been his life, and women were kept at a respectful distance; he was content to honor the marriage vows to which his parents had committed him. Then once his daughter was born, he gave his affection to her, drifting farther and farther apart from Lady Yang, who was six years his senior, until the conjugal bed grew cold and cheerless. But from the moment that Lady Yang brought Liu Qiongju into White Garden, the implications of which were immediately obvious, Bai Ruide's feelings had been stirred in spite of himself. He found Qiongju, with her bright eyes and sparkling teeth, her endless prattle and ready smile, so desirable that the only way to control his feelings was to play the role of reserved elder cousin when he was around her. Now, after ten nights, each time he reached out hungrily to disrobe her, to bare her perfect body as if he were peeling a succulent lichee nut, he knew with absolute clarity that he would not part with this woman, even if it meant that his family would never enjoy another peaceful day.

It did not occur to Liu Qiongju that her cousin might return to White Garden silently on a sedan chair, might leave the Ford outside the walls of Silver City to return in the dark of night to the mist-enshrouded beauty and elegance of White Garden. After stepping down from the sedan chair, Lady Yang went directly to her cousin's room and pushed open the unlocked door; seeing the empty bed, she smiled knowingly. From there she proceeded to her husband's room and walked in with stealthy confidence. A lantern, fueled by Mobil Oil kerosene and covered by a milky gauze shade, cast a dim light, just enough for her to see that her place in the large brass bed was taken by her fair-skinned cousin; the naked lovers slept peacefully in each other's arms. Lady Yang felt as if the blood flowing through her veins had suddenly turned to ice water. She had thought of everything but the possibility that she would be the true victim of her own trap. Ten days earlier, her husband had asked, "You won't be sorry?" Now her careful orchestrations seemed utterly inept; she was dizzy with spite. In her confusion she picked up her husband's half-smoked cigar and lit it. She puffed mouthful after mouthful of burning, acrid smoke without tasting it—those cigars, whose biting smoke proved too much even for some men, would become a permanent habit. The man and woman lying side by side in the brass bed, spent from their night of passion, slept on, oblivious to all but their own erotic dreams. As Lady Yang looked down at the naked couple, two cold tears of despair trickled through the cloud of smoke; Lady Yang wondered how she would ever drive a wedge between this wanton pair of pleasure seekers, wondered how she would get even with this woman who had stolen her husband from her, wondered how her life would ever return to normal. She put down her husband's cigar, straightened up with renewed determination, and began to undress, calmly and unhurriedly. When she was as naked as the woman lying in bed she calmly and unhurriedly turned up the wick of the Mobil Oil lantern as far as it would go.

"Since shamelessness seems to be the order of the day," she muttered, "we might as well all participate."

Her comment woke the couple in bed, who opened their eyes on a woman as naked as they were. With a shriek, Liu Qiongju quickly covered herself with the comforter, but Bai Ruide bellowed:

"Are you out of your mind?"

And so, in the waning days of February 1928, in the pleasant warmth of early spring, Bai Ruide, who wanted only a son who would become his heir, found himself entangled in the very predicament he had tried so hard to avoid. And Liu Qiongju, who had only moved to the city to get away from her rustic surroundings, now had no choice, having been caught in such a compromising position, but to become Bai's concubine. From that moment on, the beautiful and elegant White Garden was notable for being the home of a poplar and a willow, a *yang* and a *liu,* a place where the climate was soured by female enmity and loathing.

3

After sending her brother and sister off to school, Li Zihen spent two and a half months cooped up in her room, painstakingly embroidering a nine-foot length of red satin with a life-sized image of the bodhisattva Guanyin, the goddess of mercy. The statuesque Guanyin stood atop her lotus plant, boundless mercy filling eyes that gazed at Li Zihen, who was moved to the depths of her soul. Sometimes this emotion drove her, inexplicably, to walk to the door, where she would look out into the distance. She could see the lofty blocks of derricks on both banks of Silver

Creek, the bamboo pipes coiled like a giant python, and the tight masts of salt barges tied up at the piers; and she could hear the salt miners as they sang the bleak refrains of a dirge. A hundred men strapped to salt cars like draft horses would bend low at the waist and creep forward to the rhythm of the dirge, dragging carload after carload of salt up hundreds of feet from the bowels of the mines. Seated atop the cars were girls from Hibiscus House and the Peach Palace hired especially to lead the singing. During the hot seasons, these "salt-car sitters" bared their shapely upper arms and hoisted their skirts up above silky white thighs. Often, to ease the labors of the human horses in their harnesses, the girls would raise their shrill voices in popular songs from operas like *Red Phoenix Jacket* and *The Jade Dragonfly.* They sang of things they would never do, would never in their lives be able to do:

After today we will not meet again,
In the halls of jade, I will remove my paint and whore no more.
I will marry a farmer with joy in my heart,
And be my own mistress, not the plaything of others.

Their songs ended, they returned to Hibiscus House and the Peach Palace to await the arrival of any human horse who could scrape together three hundred coppers from the sale of half a peck of rice for a night of pleasure. The next day the girls were back on the cars to urge the human horses on with their shrill voices. Sometimes when Li Zihen heard these songs, she wept.

Only one person connected to Nine Ideals Hall came every day to watch Li Zihen painstakingly embroider her merciful bodhisattva; only he knew that she filled her days and nights with this single-minded enterprise in preparation for the eighth day of the fourth lunar month, the Buddha's birthday, when she would donate her embroidered bodhisattva to the White Cloud Monastery on White Cloud Mountain. That was Winterset, the water boy. In Silver City, people who made their living delivering water were called clearwater guests. But there was a marked difference between Winterset and the other clearwater guests: his family had carried water for Nine Ideals Hall for generations. By now he had lost count of how much water he himself had toted; all he could remember was that, when his grandfather died, it was Nine Ideals Hall that had paid out ten ounces of silver for a coffin and a proper burial. And when his father died, Nine Ideals Hall paid out another ten ounces of silver. So Winterset took over from his father and carried water for Nine Ideals Hall. He was paid by the load, not by the month; each day he carried fifty or sixty loads from the well by the honey locust tree, a task that kept him busy from early morning to late at night. He delivered water to the kitchen, to the servants' quarters, to the guest rooms, and to the rooms of the various women in the family. Each delivery was accompanied by the respectful announcement of "Water delivery," at which point the cloth or beaded curtain was lifted from inside and Winterset would enter to pour the water into a vat, keeping his head lowered the whole time. As he left, he was handed a bamboo tally, which he turned in to the cashier for payment, one copper for each tally. The well by the honey locust tree was encircled by a red rock platform on which some words had been carved. Winterset was told that they commemorated the day long ago when someone from Nine Ideals Hall had dug this particular well: during the ninth lunar month of the ninth year in the Kaiyuan reign of the Tang dynasty. The well ropes had worn shiny grooves in the red rock, and as he looked down at the grooves and pondered the engraved date, Winterset was overcome with reverence for the venerable and serene Nine Ideals Hall branch of the Li clan.

Winterset never went anywhere without his pewter flask, and whenever one of the women of the family gave him a little something extra, he went straight to Three Harmonies public house at the nearby intersection to fill his flask up with wine and buy a packet of fried dough crisps; every now and then he splurged on a pig's knuckle salted a deep red. The sight of Winterset gnawing on a pig's knuckle generally drew comments about how he had traded his future wife for the chunks of pork now stuck between his teeth. Winterset would blush and grin apologetically. He knew how disgraceful it was to shun marriage. And in fact, thoughts of women often spurred him into sitting alone in a spot beneath the derricks, where he listened to the dirges of the girls on the salt cars. And as time passed, he fell under the spell of Little Eleven, a girl from the Peach Palace whose high-pitched voice betrayed hidden bitterness and held for him the same appeal as the wine in his flask. By forgoing many pig's knuckles, he managed to scrape together three hundred coppers to spend on Little Eleven. For the first time in his life, he followed the appeal of a woman to its logical conclusion with the tender body of Little Eleven. And from that day on, Winterset listened only to Little Eleven. Pewter flask in hand, he would rest quietly on his haunches, his eyes fixed on Little Eleven's shapely upper arms and silky white thighs; her high-pitched singing and the flask of wine together warmed his heart. Once her shift was over, he followed her at a distance, mesmerized by the sway of her body as she walked back to the Peach Palace. "I wonder which lucky man will sleep beside her tonight," he thought. Then one day she brought Winterset into the Peach Palace and paid the three hundred coppers for him. After closing the door behind him, she said that not all men could taste the delights of a woman's charms here just by handing over the money; it depended on whether the girl was willing. She told him that her body was his to enjoy on this night. As his face turned scarlet, he felt undeserving of Little Eleven's favors; and when he walked out of her room the following morning, some of the other Peach Palace girls teased him:

"Aren't you lucky, clearwater guest, enjoying our little sister and making her spend her hard-earned money for it."

Winterset hung his head in embarrassment.

Little Eleven came to the door. "Winterset," she said, "don't throw your money away around here anymore. Save it up to get a wife and live a good, peaceful life."

Mumbling a promise, he ran out the door in a panic; he never set foot in the Peach Palace again and went back to eating pig's knuckles.

Winterset often rejoiced over his good luck in inheriting an occupation from his father, and his grandfather before that. Earning a livelihood hauling water meant that he didn't have to strap on a harness and work like a human horse under the derricks and that he would never feel the sting of the overseer's lash on his back or his buttocks. He was free to fill his flask at Three Harmonies public house whenever he felt like it, and he was spared the painful redness and swelling of the feet and legs that tormented the human horses who worked on the salt cars.

In 1907, the thirty-third year of the Guangxu reign and the year he turned seven, he had witnessed an uprising by these laborers, the so-called red hooves. One afternoon he saw a mob of ragged red hooves surge into Silver City, hobbling along as they cursed and shouted slogans, complaining that their wages weren't enough to keep them fed. They broke down a restaurant door, swarmed inside, and ate and drank everything in sight. Then they broke into a fabric store, where they tore off enough cloth to wrap around their foreheads or tie around their waists. In the midst of the chaos, someone shouted that the soldiers were on their way. The red hooves scattered, but some were so crippled they lagged behind, and before long, as feared, a squad of quick-marching soldiers came into view. The dozen or so stragglers were caught almost immediately. They had alcohol on their breath and cloth bands around their foreheads. "We've caught the thieves outright," the commander shouted. "Off with their heads!" And so, the captured red hooves, who had barely wet their lips with alcoholic booty, were dragged to the riverbank by their queues and forced to kneel in a row. The commander drew his glistening sword, struck the pose of a cavalry warrior, and *swish,* a head rolled down the bank and into Silver Creek. Seven-year-old Winterset, running to catch up with the crowd, thought that the grown-ups were performing some thrilling play, and when he saw the head tumble down the riverbank, he was reminded of a rolling pumpkin. Another *swish,* then another, each sending a pumpkin tumbling into the river to turn the water bloody red. Winterset counted the pumpkins on his hands, but by the time all ten fingers were curled into his palms, he still hadn't counted them all. He looked down at his feet and wiggled all ten toes. When he looked up again, the haughty commander was leading his troops back to their barracks. A spectacular sunset served as background for the colorful banners snapping above the magnificent troops of soldiers, while on the riverbank sprawled a mound of corpses that would never again take a drink or utter a curse.

During the nights that followed, Winterset's sleep was interrupted by a bizarre dream: He was swimming in Silver Creek when all of a sudden a dozen or more human heads sprouted from his shoulders; not wanting to be bothered, he shrugged his shoulders, and the heads tumbled into the river, his own included. He dove in after it. "Come back!" he shouted. "Come back!" He would wake up crying, safe in his grandfather's arms. "The red hooves scared you, boy." That was when he knew he did not want to grow up to be one of them.

Following Winterset's amorous little adventure twenty years later, whenever any of the amahs or young maidservants handed him an extra coin given them by a family member, they couldn't resist poking a little fun: "Run this over to Little Eleven, Winterset." His head drooped lower than ever from the laughter that followed him; he hated the idea that people had discovered his vulnerability. The only person in Nine Ideals Hall who did not tease him was Sixth Sister, Zihen; she did not concern herself with his weakness, so he put extra effort into carrying water to her room. And there was more: knowing how hard her life was, he also did odd jobs for which he would not accept payment. Veneration for the young woman who had disfigured herself and taken Buddhist vows of abstinence for the sake of her family filled his heart. At times he even thought about how he, too, might have had a chance to study difficult works like the *Three-Character Classic* and the *Book of a Hundred Names* had he enjoyed the protection of an older sister like Zihen.

On the day Sixth Sister finished embroidering her bodhisattva, Winterset put down the water he had brought so he could take a long, careful look at the tapestry; he was captivated by its beauty but could not find the words to express his feelings. Finally, the praise tumbled out of his mouth: "Sixth Sister, this is beautiful. She looks like the white serpent goddess I've seen on the stage."

Li Zihen's face clouded. "Don't utter such blasphemies! The bodhisattva is the bodhisattva. All this talk of a white goddess. Aren't you afraid the heavenly devas will demand retribution?"

Beads of perspiration dotted Winterset's forehead as he fell to his knees and kowtowed, banging his head loudly on the floor three times to seek forgiveness. Once his expiation was completed, Sixth Sister told him she needed his help. The eighth day of the fourth lunar month, she said, was the Buddha's birthday, on which she planned to donate her embroidered bodhisattva to the White Cloud Monastery on White Cloud Mountain; she would prepare a vegetarian meal as a further offering and wanted Winterset to carry the two large food baskets for her. Still painfully aware of his offending remark, he could not agree fast enough.

But Li Zihen had failed to anticipate that the waters of nature would flow on the night of the seventh: rivers of blood flowed from between her legs. An unclean woman was not permitted entry into the temple, for she would defile it. With deepening misery, she gazed at the two large baskets of meatless food she had so painstakingly prepared; she felt oddly agitated. When Winterset showed up at the appointed time, she had no choice but to tell him they would not be going that day. "Why not?" he asked impetuously. "Not because of my blasphemy against the bodhisattva, is it, Sixth Sister?"

"Keep your silly guesses to yourself," she said resentfully as she let the curtain of the door fall. "I'm not feeling well."

With a sense of panic, Winterset stood alone in front of the curtain and cursed himself. He could never understand the people in this family, but this time he was sure the fault was his. Then the curtain parted again and Li Zihen said to him, "Winterset, get back to work. We'll go a few days later than we'd planned." She handed him one of the food baskets. "You can have this. I'll make a fresh batch before we leave."

Winterset gratefully accepted the fragrant gift of food, knowing that all was well.

White Cloud Monastery was the grandest and most famous Buddhist temple in the Silver City area. A path followed a narrow gully twenty li down to the quiet, secluded base of White Cloud Mountain, then veered left past the Silver City walls and out onto the broad plains. In the lush woods at the base of the mountain, where the path curved, stood an arch made of pure white stone, like a powdery cloud, on which two lines of tranquil verse were carved:

WHERE IS THE ROAD FROM HERE TO THERE?
NO GATE BETWEEN LIFE AND DEATH.

Looking upward from this white stone arch, Winterset was treated to the sight of White Cloud Monastery, its golden-tiled rooftops blazing through the lush green foliage. He stood in front of the stone arch with food baskets over his shoulder and a sweaty mist on his brow. Laying down his carrying pole, he looked back at Sixth Sister, who lagged far behind. The eighth day of the fourth lunar month had come and gone; now, ten days later, precious few pilgrims made the trek through the quiet, secluded valley under a hot late-spring sun. Li Zihen's pale face shimmered in the sun's rays, and Winterset felt sorry for her. Forty li on a day like this—her feet must be killing her. I wonder why she's doing this, he thought.

At the monastery gate, Li Zihen turned to Winterset. "Wait for me here," she said, picking up the food baskets and carrying them inside. Winterset sat down on the steps and quickly fell asleep. Some time later he was startled awake. The mountain and the monastery compound were bathed in silence and slanting rays of sunlight. Apprehensive, he scrambled to his feet to look for Zihen. He searched building after building and courtyard after courtyard, until he reached the third row of monastery buildings. There he spotted the trembling figure of Li Zihen kneeling on a rush mat in the doorway of a prayer hall. The embroidered bodhisattva hung before a gigantic painted sculpture of Guanyin. Three joss sticks in an incense burner had been reduced to ashes; gloom filled the darkened sanctuary. Clearly, Li Zihen was sobbing, and after a moment of indecision, Winterset turned away; he could not make up his mind to go to her and did not know what he would say if he did. So he returned to the steps at the front gate, where he sat back down with his apprehension.

When they finally left White Cloud Monastery and passed the white stone arch on the way home, Li Zihen broke the silence:

"When I die, bury me on this mountain ridge, as close to White Cloud Monastery as possible."

The sound of her voice was much like the slanting rays of sunlight: tranquil and dispassionate. All of a sudden the sight of the woman's back filled Winterset with foreboding.

CHAPTER FIVE

1

After her mother returned to Silver City, Bai Qiuyun asked Li Ziyun to move into Bamboo Garden at 6 Cathedral Street. Bamboo Garden was a Western-style cottage that Bai Ruide had bought from a French missionary several years earlier, a place where he could stay when he came to the provincial capital. Not long after arriving in China, the missionary had fallen under the spell of Chinese refinements: he would rather go without meat at the table than forgo the pleasures of living amid bamboo. So he planted bamboo all around his cottage: hirsute bamboo, dowager bamboo, phoenix-tail bamboo, speckled bamboo, purple bamboo, it was all there, forming a natural wind screen. He named the cottage Bamboo Garden. When he bought the cottage, Bai Ruide had to laugh at the missionary's ignorance of the art of bamboo planting; after cutting down the greater part of the bamboo wall, leaving some open spaces and creating little paths, he erected a small arbor and placed a boulder or rock formation here and there. His modifications lent the bamboo the serenity and restrained grace that the name merited. The Holy

Mother church belonging to the French overseas mission stood not far from Bamboo Garden. At mass, when the people inside sang their hymns, the lilting strains of music rained down from the steeple onto Bamboo Garden to merge with the rustling bamboo swaying gently in the wind; Bai Qiuyun preferred Bamboo Garden over White Garden.

Li Ziyun, who had grown tired of dormitory life, was overjoyed at the invitation to move into Bamboo Garden. She was not, however, unaware of the hidden reason for the invitation, and in that regard, she was secretly happy for her brother. The two lovely maidens spent their days together and were soon as close as sisters. Rarely was one seen without the other, entering or leaving Bamboo Garden at 6 Cathedral Street, and as time passed, the *yun*—the two clouds—of Bamboo Garden, Bai Qiuyun and Li Ziyun, became well-known around the provincial capital.

With Li Ziyun's help, Bai Qiuyun easily passed the entrance exam for the preparatory section of the girls' high school. Staged melodramas were all the rage at the provincial schools then, and the playwrights Tian Han, Xiong Foxi, Hong Shen, and Ding Xilin were particularly popular. The high school even had a student drama club, which both Li Ziyun and Bai Qiuyun joined. They invested much of their free time, their youthful passion, and their fantasies in such popular short plays as *A Maiden's Fan, Mei Luoxiang the Actress, Oppression, The Awakened Dream, The Young Wanderer,* and a Chinese rendering of Ibsen's *A Doll's House.* Since there were no boys in the school, all the parts were played by girls. Li Ziyun and Bai Qiuyun signed up for parts in Ding Xilin's *The Hornet,* which was one of the students' favorites. When Ziyun, in the role of Mr. Yu, took Miss Yu, played by Qiuyun, warmly in "his" arms, the student audience erupted in prolonged loud applause, until their hands stung and their faces burned. Such outbursts provided the girls with a means of releasing the emotions that swelled their hearts; they were each waiting for their own Mr. Yu, and they knew the stirring closing dialogue by heart. At night, after the lights were out and the girls were safely behind their mosquito netting in the dormitory, it was not uncommon to hear one of them utter in the plaintive voice of the love-struck Mr. Yu, "I need proof." Without missing a beat, another would reply, "What kind of proof do you need?" "Let me hold you," came the response. The mosquito netting vibrated with laughter.

But despite the release offered by all those tragedies and comedies, something still bothered Bai Qiuyun. One day as she and Ziyun were cooling off in the bamboo arbor, the conversation turned to the drama club. Bai Qiuyun said with a sigh:

"It's a shame all the parts are played by girls. It's not realistic."

"Let's go see Tian Han's *A Night for Catching Tigers*," Li Ziyun suggested. "Naizhi and the others are performing it on Sunday. We'll see what kind of job he does."

A Night for Catching Tigers was the last of the one-act plays on the program. At the end of the play, when Li Naizhi, as the doomed youth, was carried in, wounded and bloody, he spoke his lines with all the dramatic flair of a student; then, in a final desperate act, he drew his knife and plunged it into his breast. As they heard him utter the play's final line—"I can't bear it any longer. Miss Lian, it's time for me to leave. I'll wait for you"—and watched his tragic suicide, some girls in the audience broke down in sobs. Bai Qiuyun cried on Li Ziyun's shoulder. But her friend pushed her away:

"Why are you crying like that, sister Yun? Naizhi is just fine. Let's go backstage and find him."

When Li Ziyun walked up to her little brother with Bai Qiuyun, still teary-eyed, in tow, she rebuked him, "See what you've done to sister Yun, Ninth Brother."

The three of them laughed at that, though their laughter was tinged with awkwardness. They and several others talked about the performance until Bai Qiuyun thought it was time to leave.

"Let's get something to eat at Twin Wonders Garden. We can try their new dish, pearl-held prawns."

Once they were seated around a table in one of the elegant private rooms upstairs at Twin Wonders Garden, Li Naizhi insisted that they share the cost. "If I'd known you wanted to pay your own way," Bai Qiuyun protested, "I wouldn't have come." Her eyes were turning red and the mood was spoiled. "I'm the older sister," Li Ziyun said, breaking the silence, "so I'll be the hostess. We started out so happy, let's not ruin it." She glared at her brother to underscore her words. Hoping to patch things up, he said, "All right, it's my sister's turn to play host. Qiuyun can be the hostess next time, and then I'll host the time after that."

After everyone had sampled the new prawn dish, Li Naizhi walked the two girls home. They passed the church and had nearly reached the Bamboo Garden gate when Li Naizhi said good-bye, explaining that he wanted to see what was available at the used-book stalls. Li Ziyun glared at him. "What sort of mischief are you up to now?" she demanded. "You think all the books will be gone if you get there a few minutes later?"

Bai Qiuyun took Li Ziyun's hand. "Let's go, sister Yun. We can't force him to stay. I'm afraid our Bamboo Garden is too insignificant for one of Huaguang High School's top students."

His face reddening, Li Naizhi stood awkwardly in front of the two girls, not sure if he should leave or stay; they walked right past him, hand in hand. Li Ziyun looked back to make a parting comment:

"Idiot!"

The sun's rays on that early-summer day in 1928 slanted down through the clouds. The occasional pedestrians or rickshaw passengers on quiet, secluded Cathedral Street were, for the most part, ladies and gentlemen dressed in their finery. The little cottage set deep in the bamboo garden was visible through gaps in the emerald bamboo; atop the nearby church the bell pealed solemnly, its soothing chimes settling like leaves in a gentle breeze.

Actually, Li Naizhi had just been making excuses when he said he wanted to peruse the used-book stalls. He had often pored over the meager offerings, and among his discoveries were a dog-eared copy of the *Communist Manifesto* and an old edition of Qu Qiubai's *Travels in New Russia*. Strictly banned by the Nationalist government, these two books were his treasures, and he leafed through them like a starving man turning to food. He had lent his copies to a couple of fellow students, swearing them to secrecy, and these friends told him that the Chinese literature teacher, a Mr. Chen, had some similar books. So they went to swap books with Mr. Chen once, then several times, until these exchanges turned into a secret study group. Mr. Chen, a quiet man, smiled and told his students that a Ming scholar by the name of Li Zhi was credited with saying, "There is no greater pleasure than staying home on a snowy night and curling up with a banned book." Li Naizhi was caught up in the heated prose and the heroic, stirring deeds he read about, which often brought to mind his old teacher, Zhao Boru, and the student book club he had organized. On this particular afternoon he and some of his classmates were to go see Mr. Chen, who had warned them not to say a word to anyone, not even their parents. As soon as Li Naizhi saw his sister and Bai Qiuyun safely inside Bamboo Garden, he rushed off to the secret gathering.

His classmates were waiting for him when he walked into the dark, squat bamboo cottage at 5 Rush Alley. Mr. Chen's nearly blind old mother sat in her usual rattan chair next to the table, her kindly face raised slightly. Beneath the table, up against the old lady's leg, a pair of twins chattered away noisily and happily. One of the boys, Danan, had drawn eyeglasses and a moustache on the face of his brother, Ernan, with the red pen his papa used to correct student papers. "You're Commander Liu, who loses all the battles," he shouted gleefully. The second boy wrenched the pen out of his brother's hand. "I'm not Commander Liu! When I grow up I'm going to be a teacher, just like Papa, so I can smack your hand with a ruler!" That brought a laugh from the adults in the room, and the old lady wiped a tear from the corner of her eye; she stopped laughing long enough to say, "Even babies know that a certain Commander Liu's reputation stinks."

A heated discussion ensued, lasting all afternoon, with no one winning any of the others over to his side; then just as the guests' stomachs started growling, Mr. Chen's mother insisted that they all stay for dinner. Pointing to the pot of rice on the stove, she said with a smile, "We have a special treat for you tonight." They told her how tempting the aroma of the barbecued meat was, how they loved the smell of it with sweet rice, and how Mrs. Chen made the best pickled vegetables they'd ever tasted. That said, the students spread out the snacks and special delicacies they'd brought with them. Knowing Mr. Chen's situation all too well, they wanted to give Danan and Ernan a chance to enjoy themselves; with obvious embarrassment, Mr. Chen chided them for spending so much of their hard-earned money and warned them he wouldn't be able to invite them for dinner anymore if they kept this up. In the midst of all this polite wrangling, Li Naizhi was ashamed at the thought of the pearl-held prawns he had eaten at Twin Wonders Garden. It was common for him to be deeply moved by insignificant events at Mr. Chen's home, and sometimes he could not be sure if his unswerving belief in the *Communist Manifesto* was sustained by its heated prose or his teacher's blind old mother.

2

General Yang Chuxiong's success in routing the red detachments of peasants throughout the five counties earned him a considerable reputation among the province's warlord factions. As the commander of a new military division, he was able to expand his power base and increase his territorial jurisdiction. His peers looked to him with increased respect. But when Yang revealed the true extent of his ambition by enlisting even more soldiers and buying up even more horses, warlords in the upper Yangtze region issued stern warnings in communiqués they sent to the newspapers:

"A certain individual is setting up a separatist regime, oppressing the local populace, creating chaos, and forcing a military confrontation," read one. "We have no choice but to launch an attack to halt this usurpation of power. Our primary goal is to unite the nation and bring peace to the provinces. To that end we stand together in opposition of the aggressor."

The counterattack was not long in coming. A communiqué issued by the forces aligned behind Commander in Chief Liu, the leader with whom Yang Chuxiong, too, had seen fit to throw in his lot, proclaimed his "intention to relinquish power, thereby showing his desire for peace."

> But others have responded by seeking alliances with outside forces and hurling unfounded allegations. While they are willing to sacrifice our homeland and shatter the peace, burning the bean stalks to cook the beans, as the saying goes, our strategies are formed in the service of the people, conceived in response to military necessities. If we do not set up our defenses, we will be powerless against the enemy. Taking unity as our primary goal, we have urged Commander Liu to assume command over the united forces. With an army numbering a hundred thousand, we are certain to annihiliate the enemy.

Peaceful measures were quickly exhausted and force became necessary. When all efforts at conciliation failed, there was no alternative but a clash of weapons, and the smell of gunpowder filled the provincial skies. One savage battle followed another, until Commander Liu, having suffered a series of setbacks, sent off an elegantly phrased communiqué announcing that he was indeed relinquishing power:

"Gathering wood in the mountains and fishing in the river is the life I seek. I long for a glimpse of home, and the joy of strolling through the fields . . ."

And so, in the early summer of 1928, Silver City, which had only just regained stability after the chaos of the red peasants' uprising, found itself once again engulfed in the fires of war. The warlords of the upper Yangtze region, forming a united front, surrounded the forces of Yang Chuxiong on three sides with two divisions of soldiers and gave the city fathers an ultimatum that demanded Yang Chuxiong's surrender or retreat within three days. To inflame the soldiers' fighting spirit, the Yangtze commander proclaimed that whoever entered Silver City first would be appointed garrison commander. His two division commanders quickly made preparations to occupy the city. As they spoke of the battle ahead, they no longer bothered with the high-flown phrases of the communiqués; nor did they concern themselves with such troublesome matters as tactics. They simply said:

"Yang Chuxiong has gotten fat living off the riches of Silver City!"

Yang Chuxiong knew very well that he was faced with a serious challenge, that this was no red detachment of peasants armed only with knives and spears. He realized that this time he was confronting an army double the size of his own, in men and in weapons. But if he fled without a fight, his lofty ambitions and grand plans would simply evaporate. Once Silver City was lost to the enemy, he would never again have a base of operations; the best he could hope for then would be the life of a dishonored soldier and overthrown bandit chief. Worse yet was the thought of surrendering his entire army to the enemy without firing a shot, then fleeing for his life. He would forever after be known as a coward, a good-for-nothing, a disgrace to his profession. Having pondered the avenues open to him, he finally let his determination win the day: rather than live on ignominiously, far better to stand firm now and gain honor for his name.

Once Yang Chuxiong had decided to stand and fight, he moved quickly into action. First he and his chief of staff sized up the strengths and weaknesses of his adversaries, Huang Wanyu and Tang Zongfang, and devised a meticulous battle strategy of their own. Then Yang Chuxiong sent written invitations to the city fathers to discuss the plan of action. Finally, he ordered the four city gates barricaded, fortified the city walls with sandbags, and carefully deployed his troops. Fear and anxiety settled over the city. Time seemed to stop as every man, woman, and child trembled at the thought of the firepower that would soon rain down on their heads. With their very survival at stake, who among the city fathers would dare ignore Yang Chuxiong's invitation to discuss the plan of action?

Yang had early on claimed the imposing God of War Temple in the center of town as his headquarters; now, with the battle looming, the temple was ringed by heavily armed guards, the gate opposite the two crouching lions fortified with sandbags. After the terrified members of the gentry had filed into the temple's main hall, talking nervously among themselves, Yang Chuxiong, resplendent in full military uniform, made his entrance, clasping his hands in front and bowing to his guests:

"Fear not, gentlemen, every officer and man under my command is committed to sharing the fate of Silver City!"

His promise elicited cries of distress from the salt merchants in attendance. No one, they insisted, wanted war, and no one wanted to share the fate of the soldiers. Some of the miners were already fleeing for their lives. If fighting actually broke out, no one dared contemplate how many mines would be destroyed. Whatever the cost, the merchants wanted desperately to avoid this catastrophe. Yang Chuxiong noted the anguished looks on the faces around him but ignored them as he continued:

"Gentlemen, you need not be concerned, for I, Yang Chuxiong, have devised a means of defeating the enemy before Silver City is subjected to the fires of war. That is why I have asked you here today."

Responding to this revelation with silence, the gentry folk waited for the other shoe to drop. They did not wait long. Yang blurted out:

"Gather the sum of two hundred thousand in silver, and Silver City will be left in peace."

Seeing the salt merchants' eyes widen, Yang Chuxiong added icily: "Without that money, the man standing before you will have his back to the water and will be forced to fight to the finish."

Before a single shot was fired, Yang Chuxiong outlined his treacherous strategy to the members of Silver City's moneyed elite. The salt merchants, seeing the resolute expressions on the faces of the armed guards all around them and aware of the fact that they had less than three days to choose a course of action, knew they had no choice but to accede to Yang Chuxiong's demand. And so, after a brief consultation, they chose Li Naijing, patriarch of Nine Ideals Hall, to be in charge of collecting the money. And Li Naijing, seeing no alternative, accepted the assignment. After a moment's somber reflection, he said, weighing his words carefully:

"Commander Yang, during last year's uprising in the five counties, all the salt mines and warehouses spent heavily to supply the troops with provisions. No one has recouped that outlay, and that's just a fact. Yet we are duty-bound to spare Silver City a massacre, so the salt merchants and mine owners will contribute a hundred thousand, but they ask that you tap other sources for the remaining half." Without waiting for a response from Yang Chuxiong, Li Naijing quickly took another tack: "Not long ago, the Prosperity Company was prepared to spend a great deal of money to purchase a majority interest in the

Transocean mine. I am not at liberty to divulge the exact figure, but you can rest assured that it was much more than a hundred thousand."

Having spoken his piece, Li Naijing turned his uncompromising gaze upon Bai Ruide. To a man, the salt merchants marveled at this development, fully aware that Li Naijing had found a way of settling the score over what had occurred at Gathering of Worthies Teahouse; secretly rejoicing at the prospect of saving half the blackmail money, they were also deeply impressed by the astute maneuvering of the patriarch of Nine Ideals Hall, and they wasted no time in voicing their agreement. As for Bai Ruide, who was seated directly across from Yang Chuxiong, this sudden development caused his face to turn scarlet. With all eyes on him, it was too late to stall or take evasive action; every avenue of escape was sealed off. Allowing himself time to regain his composure and natural color, Bai Ruide announced boldly:

"Fine, we'll do as my friend Menglin says. You can count on me for a hundred thousand!"

With a hearty laugh, Yang Chuxiong proclaimed: "Given this tripartite cooperation, I, Yang Chuxiong, give you gentlemen my word that I will not let you down!"

And so, in the early summer of 1928, having with little effort obtained the vast sum of two hundred thousand in silver, a supremely confident Yang Chuxiong began putting his plan into action. All that night he sat up composing a letter, which he sent, along with a hundred thousand in silver, to Division Commander Huang, reaching him before dawn. In the letter Yang Chuxiong admitted candidly: "There is a vast disparity in troop strength between our two armies, and I am sure to be defeated in battle. However, I am not prepared to see Silver City turned to ashes for the sake of my own bravado. I have heard of your military prowess and know you are an implacable foe. On behalf of the city fathers, I invite Commander Huang to be the first to enter the city and preserve it from harm. This hundred thousand in silver for provisions is an expression of good faith. I urge Commander Huang to move his forward position ten li closer to town to make it easier to enter Silver City two days hence. To allay Commander Tang's suspicions, my troops will feign an attack on your position, then drop back ten li. After Commander Huang enters the city, I, Yang Chuxiong, will step down and hand over my military authority."

As promised, Yang Chuxiong's troops fired shots into the air the next day before retreating ten li. Richer by a hundred thousand in silver, Commander Huang advanced. When news of the advance reached Commander Tang, he frantically sent his chief of staff to find out why Commander Huang had taken unilateral action. "What was I supposed to do with Yang Chuxiong attacking?" came the answer.

The next day, the first stage of his scheme completed, Yang Chuxiong borrowed Bai Ruide's Ford sedan and drove to the White Cloud Mountain headquarters of Division Commander Tang to surrender in person, accompanied only by his capable and experienced aide-de-camp and bearing the second hundred thousand in silver. Having heard of Division Commander Tang's military prowess and implacability, he said, he was inviting Commander Tang on behalf of the city fathers to be the first to enter the city and preserve it from harm. The hundred thousand in silver for provisions was an expression of good faith, and he offered himself as a hostage, promising to ride into town alongside his captor. Commander Tang asked about the previous day's skirmish, to which Yang Chuxiong replied that his troops retreated when they saw they could no longer defend their position. With one hundred thousand in silver and Yang Chuxiong as hostage, Commander Tang happily climbed into the Ford sedan.

"Elder Brother Chuxiong," he said, "I don't mind admitting that this car is one foreign treat I've never sampled before."

And so, followed by the two commanders, clasping each other's hands and chatting cheerfully, Commander Tang's mighty army marched down White Cloud Mountain toward Silver City. When gunfire broke the silence, the car carrying the two commanders turned and sped away. Knowing that their own leader was in the car, Commander Tang's guards dared not open fire and could only scream and shout and look on helplessly as Yang Chuxiong drove off in the "foreign treat" with their division commander. Confused, they were utterly routed in the ambush that followed.

Thus, in the early summer of 1928, every newspaper in the province announced Yang Chuxiong's venture into the lion's den; they extolled his prowess in kidnapping Tang Zongfang and marveled over how he had miraculously defeated both Tang's army and the demoralized forces of Huang Zongfang. According to the reports, the Tang forces lost more than three thousand soldiers, and the hollows on White Cloud Mountain were filled with mass graves. Before long, Yang Chuxiong sent the newspapers a communiqué announcing his willingness to take orders from the newly appointed provincial governor and the commander in chief of provincial forces. He had chosen Silver City for his personal domicile, he said, and had absolutely no hegemonic ambitions. "This most recent armed response was unavoidable, and though I remain in Silver City to keep it safe, I will not claim all the salt taxes for the defense of the city. I am prepared to enter into negotiations with the authorities and other interested parties. I want also to assure everyone that my esteemed adversary Tang Zongfang is safe and sound under house arrest. He and I enjoy a game of chess and converse amiably every day. Very soon brother Tang and I will make a pilgrimage to the White Cloud Monastery, after which he will return to the provincial capital. I, Chuxiong, pledge the sum of fifty thousand in silver to the families of soldiers who gave their lives in defense of the city." And so on and so forth.

The brilliant tactics used by Yang Chuxiong in the defense of Silver City during that early summer of 1928 are not recorded in any military textbook. But by calling on his resourcefulness, cunning, ferocity, and courage, plus the ability to assess his position realistically and to act accordingly, Yang Chuxiong not only protected his own interests but won a battle when everyone said his situation was hopeless. From that moment on, Yang Chuxiong's exploits were hailed from one end of the province to the other, and his standing in Silver City was assured. In the early summer of 1928, after Yang Chuxiong had saved the city from certain disaster, he hosted a banquet at his headquarters in the God of War Temple to thank the city fathers for their support. During the toasting and feasting, the host, a career soldier, felt the joy of a fish in water, the happiness of a bird in the woods.

One year later, Yang Chuxiong increased his troop strength and raised a new flag, as commander of the entire provincial army. Not surprisingly, all the warlords in the province bestowed their recognition on this outstanding member of their martial society.

3

At four o'clock in the morning, Bai Ruide was awakened by the caresses of Lady Yang; his alarm increased as her caresses grew more fervent, her breath on his ear hotter and faster. Bai Ruide knew that his wife was trying another scheme from *Secrets of the Boudoir* to conceive a son. He knew, too, that she was holding fourteen red beans in the palm of her left hand and that in a moment, when her caresses had him so aroused that amorous activity was inevitable, she would put the beans in her mouth to await the exact second of eruption, when she would swallow them as if they were magic pellets. After that she would experience mild fear and trepidation for several days, then would be on pins and needles for several more, until finally her hopes for conception would be washed away in a tide of dark menstrual blood. This arcane remedy was something they had tried many times years earlier. After the birth of their daughter, followed by several barren years, Lady Yang had gone home to her mother to get this "secret." An uncle of Lady Yang's was a renowned obstetrician who had apparently helped more desperate women bear sons and daughters than anyone could count. Inexplicably, this remedy, which had been passed down from the legendary Pengzu and incorporated into the bedroom arts of Sunü, the goddess linked with the mythical Yellow Emperor, failed miserably for his own niece. At first she and Bai Ruide had followed the procedure exactly as prescribed—she had insisted on it—including the "seven taboos" and "sperm conservation," even making sure that the moon was full or the sun was directly overhead each time. But no matter how strictly they followed the procedures, no matter how devoutly they believed, nothing came of it, and with the passage of time, there was no more talk of any arcane techniques.

But since Liu Qiongju's entry into the family as Bai Ruide's concubine, in the wake of the night when the three of them had faced one another in their nakedness, Lady Yang had resuscitated this particular technique, applying it more rigorously than ever. She secured Bai Ruide's agreement to a three-point program: He was to reserve the day of the full moon for her, and for the seven days leading up to the full moon he was to sleep next to her, for the sake of sperm conservation. Finally, he was to drink a special potion mixed with wine and consisting of scrapings from young antlers, the polygala herb, and snake extract. Lady Yang's increasing fervor in all this was matched by Bai Ruide's growing disgust. Every bedroom episode was sheer torture; it was clear to him that this forty-four-year-old woman was risking everything in one last act of desperation, clinging to the fantasy that she would bear a son and to the even more fanciful notion that somehow she would win out over the rival she had invited into her life. Just as clearly, however, she noted how age had robbed her of both her looks and her skills, and by the time she managed, anxious and breathing heavily, to arouse her husband, Bai Ruide looked on the naked body beside him as a long-haired, red-tongued demoness intent on dragging him to hell.

Lady Yang realized that her husband was lying next to her as cold and inert as a wooden log. With feelings of deep humiliation she rose and asked him:

"Why aren't you moving?"

"I don't feel like it."

"What *do* you feel like? Who are you thinking about? That vile temptress, I'll bet!"

"It was you who brought that vile temptress to me."

His damning comment stunned Lady Yang for a moment as she lay there in defeat. Then she began screaming: "That shameless witch—I wanted her to give you a son, not to take you away. You've had your fun night after night, isn't that enough? All I ask are a few days, can't you even give me that much? What more do you want to take from me? Do ten years of marriage mean nothing to you? You shouldn't treat me like this, if only for the sake of Qiuyun . . . Don't keep pushing me, or is my death the only thing that will satisfy you two . . . ?"

In the early summer of 1928, as the full moon was setting in the west and the bright sun was rising in the east, at that moment of dawning when yin and yang meet, a woman's despairing wails floated through the air above the lovely, elegant White Garden, a terrifying sound that jolted every member of the household awake. The servants knew that peace and quiet had left White Garden the day the concubine was installed. Liu Qiongju, asleep in her room, was also woken by the wailing and she knew, with a clear and terrifying certainty, that sooner or later the woman making those chilling sounds would turn on her. And yet, ever since Bai Ruide had revealed to her the details of Lady Yang's trap, the fear and self-loathing she once felt were swept away and replaced by the determination to fight. In the struggle between these two women, the twenty-two-year-old Liu Qiongju, given the inherent advantages of youth, had only to bear a son to claim victory.

After Lady Yang had applied the special son-bearing technique from *Secrets of the Boudoir* several times, the first sign of pregnancy appeared: she missed her menstrual period. Tears of joy streaked her face at the good news, and she went immediately with her servant, Amah Liu, to the Temple of the Immortal Matron to burn incense and draw divination slips for guidance. After placing a hundred yuan in the temple donation box, she made a secret vow to the Immortal Matron of Sons and Grandsons: If the blessed matron favored her with a son this time, she would personally donate enough money to restore the temple to its original state. Returning home, she patiently waited another month to confirm once and for all that her missed period was no fluke. She then went alone to the home of Lin Jinmo, one of Silver City's most renowned physicians, who took the four essential diagnostic steps: he observed, he listened, he asked, and he felt her pulse. Lifting his hand from her wrist, Dr. Lin announced:

"Madame is not ill and is not pregnant. Madame has entered menopause."

Lady Yang sat frozen in her chair, her face pale as a sheet of paper. She heard none of the remainder of Dr. Lin's diagnosis: how her kidneys were weakened by heat, how her vital energy and her blood flow were out of synchronization, and the like. Nor did she take note of the remedy he proposed: crystal sugar mixed with silver fungus to restore her energy. On her way out the door, she turned abruptly and said:

"Dr. Lin, tell no one that I came to see you today, no one at all."

She took a gold ingot from her inner pocket, to which poor Dr. Lin reacted with shock.

"I cannot take that," he said, refusing the gift. "I truly cannot! I swear I will tell no one. Now, Madame, please put that away."

But Lady Yang, refusing to take no for an answer, laid the gold ingot on the table, turned, and walked out. In all his years as a physician, Dr. Lin had never dreamed that the most lavish fee he would ever receive would come from a patient in perfect health.

Just as Lady Yang's hopes of producing a son were dashed forever, Liu Qiongju became pregnant, and over the months that followed, her expanding belly stood out like a victory banner thrust proudly before the eyes of Lady Yang each and every day. As her pregnancy advanced, Liu Qiongju took to dragging her bloated, clumsy body out into the flower garden to stroll lazily, or rest on the stone edge of the fishpond and watch goldfish swim by, or perch on the swing beneath the banana tree for some light reading. At such times, Lady Yang would often stand at her upstairs window without so much as moving and glare down at her young cousin like a wild beast stalking her prey. But Liu Qiongju, now that she was carrying a child, frequently felt herself submerged in tenderness so abundant it even dissolved the enmity and loathing she felt toward her cousin. When these tender feelings rose up inside her, she was full of yearning that her goodwill could somehow flow into the bodies of everyone else in the household. She often sent Bai Ruide off to her cousin's bedroom, and she sometimes had Amah Liu take snacks and pastries she had prepared to her cousin. One time when Bai Ruide was not home, she walked into Lady Yang's bedroom, threw her arms around her cousin, and cried, openly pleading for them to reconcile and live as one big, happy family, with no more arguments and no more petty grievances. Naturally, none of this had any effect on Lady Yang. When her young cousin had stopped crying, she gave her a cold, hard look and said:

"All right, Qiongju, since you seem so sincere, let's do things the old way from now on. First thing every morning you must come pay your respects to me."

Qiongju saw what looked like two icy holes in her cousin's face. From those icy holes came a dreadful chill, a dark and gloomy menace that Qiongju, much as she tried, could not shake all through the long, hot summer of 1928.

But from that day on, Liu Qiongju did in fact walk upstairs each morning after her toilette to pay her respects to Madame, and even the servants talked about how the younger wife's pregnancy had turned her into a new woman. But this daily pageant tried Bai Ruide's patience:

"Why are you paying respects to that cadaverous witch? She's out to punish you, that's all!"

Liu Qiongju did not want to tell her husband of her fear, feeling that such a man could never understand what was in a woman's heart, could never comprehend that she was doing this to protect the child who would soon come into this world. Liu Qiongju was even hoping for a girl, since that might lessen her cousin's hostility and then she wouldn't have to worry so much.

Now that the two wives of White Garden seemed to be getting along again, Lin Jinmo dropped by often, at the request of the elder wife, to check on the condition of her pregnant cousin. He wrote out a few prescriptions to invigorate the mother and protect the fetus and he gave some advice on nutrition; on his way out, Lady Yang would see him off with a seemingly casual question: "As a doctor, what do you think my cousin is carrying, a boy or a girl?" Dr. Lin's response never varied: It was too early to tell, he wouldn't be able to predict until the eighth month. After seeing the doctor out, Lady Yang would return to oversee the preparation of the prescribed medicine, then instruct Amah Liu to take the concoction to the expectant mother. That had the servants saying that the elder wife had become a new woman, too, and that peace had returned to the family. What they did not know was that Liu Qiongju secretly poured every last drop of the medicine into the commode.

At the end of the ninth month, Liu Qiongju delivered a son, as Dr. Lin had finally predicted she would. An air of gaiety enveloped White Garden. At the end of the baby's first month, Lady Yang personally arranged an extravagant banquet, at which the guests congratulated Bai Ruide for having been blessed with an heir, a boy who would someday take over the Prosperity Company. And Lady Yang was praised for her willingness to put the family's well-being ahead of personal interests, lauded for being a kind and virtuous woman. At the banquet she draped a gold longevity necklace around the tender skin of the infant's neck and bestowed a "milk name" on him: she called him Hope Child. At that moment tears of joy filled the eyes of Liu Qiongju, and her vigilance and suspicions began to waver. Maybe, she thought, she had misjudged the woman, and what, after all, was so bad about being a concubine? Her heart brimming with contentment, she watched as her cousin proudly carried the child from one guest to the next.

But ten days after the first-month celebration, the child mysteriously spiked a fever, sending the inexperienced Liu Qiongju into a panic of confusion. Lady Yang promptly decided to take the baby by car to see Dr. Lin. The two women rushed downstairs, where Lady Yang flared up angrily at Amah Liu for bundling the baby too lightly; she insisted on wrapping it in a quilt, which the frantic Liu Qiongju ran upstairs to fetch. When they reached the home of Dr. Lin and peeled back the quilt, the baby was not breathing. Liu Qiongju fainted right in front of the doctor; by the time Bai Ruide came rushing in anxiously, he was greeted by the sight of his dead son and an unconscious Liu Qiongju.

Residents of White Garden were concerned that this turn of events might drive the younger woman mad with anger, and as a precaution, Bai Ruide personally spent every minute of the day with her for an entire month, after which the residents of White Garden realized that, instead of losing her sanity, Liu Qiongju had assumed an air of silent menace, frequently getting up in the middle of the night to wander the dark halls like a solitary specter. Finally, one day, Bai Ruide's Ford sedan sped Dr. Lin to the compound, and he was rushed into Lady Yang's bedroom. Hurriedly examining her, he forced her to vomit, then wiped his sweaty face and sighed:

"That was close! A few minutes later, and I don't think I could have saved her."

Dr. Lin, suspicion in his eyes, looked down at Lady Yang, who had been brought back from death.

"Madame, it appears you were poisoned. Can you tell me what you ate?"

Instead of answering, Lady Yang, her face ashen, merely looked unflinchingly at Lin Jinmo and said:

"Do not concern yourself, Dr. Lin. This is Bai family business."

Lin Jinmo's thoughts traveled back several months to that gold ingot.

The following morning, as soon as she had completed her toilette, Liu Qiongju went upstairs to pay her respects to her cousin as always. The two women understood each other perfectly; they stood there, neither willing to break the deathly silence. Finally, Liu Qiongju announced with fierce determination:

"Elder Cousin, I shall keep trying. A life for a life."

"Younger Cousin, I shall be ready."

CHAPTER SIX

1

Summers in Silver City are sweltering and seemingly endless. The year 1935 was no exception. One summer morning in 1935, the crisp, practiced sounds of someone reading aloud emerged from Emerald Sky Study, and the servants at Nine Ideals Hall all knew that Shuangxi, the beloved seven-year-old son of the elder master was reciting his lessons. Shuangxi's school name was Shenxiu—Cultivation of Body; the "milk name" Shuangxi—Double Happiness—commemorated his being born on the same day the Transocean mine broke through and Nine Ideals Hall was blessed with two joyful events. From the age of four or five, Shuangxi had studied under the strict supervision of his father; now, at the age of seven, he could recite the *Three-Character Classic* and *Book of a Hundred Names* flawlessly from memory, knew a hundred or more Tang dynasty poems and Song dynasty lyrics by heart, and was passably proficient with the writing brush. Everyone in Nine Ideals Hall sang his praises as a smart little boy and commended his father's skills as a teacher. But Li Naijing, not given to praising his son lightly, was a strict taskmaster, adding more and more essential works to the curriculum. He had decided against hiring a tutor, preferring to be the one who set his son on the road to knowledge. He hid his fervent hopes for his son's future behind a stern countenance; and so the refined interior of Emerald Sky Study now boasted two dedicated seekers of knowledge, one old, the other young. To such canonical texts as *Jade Garden of Children's Studies,* Li Naijing frequently added works of his own choosing. At this moment, Shuangxi was reciting a selection chosen by his father from *Letters from Autumn Waters Studio,* rocking back and forth as he intoned:

Our thoughts link us though we are far apart,
Words fail us when again we meet.
Each time you pass the golden platform,
My feelings and expressions are at their peak.
The fullness of my joy lingers on,
Our partings come too soon.
. . .
The day long I tarry from my lessons,
Placing my brush in the service of desire.
Scattered reds and random greens,
What good to recall them now?

Shuangxi had no idea what these dizzying lines of poetry meant, but he committed them to memory anyway, fearing his father's bamboo switch. Beyond the green window screen, cicadas in the shade of a banana tree sang joyously, lotus flowers floating atop Willow Reflecting Pond bloomed bright red; but Shuangxi knew he must memorize these lines, then fill ten pages with neatly written characters before he could go out to play. Just the day before he had caught a pair of crickets under the honey locust tree by the well out back; the servant called Winterset had fashioned two tiny paper cages, which they left on the windowsill, and those two crickets had filled the night with their pretty songs. He planned to go back out there today because Winterset said both their crickets were males, and he needed a male and a female for a couple, just like the people in Nine Ideals Hall, just like the elder master needs a wife. Now that his father was out of the room, Shuangxi quickly finished his ten sheets of practice characters, then wrote a note, as his father had taught him:

> The boy Shuangxi, kneels at his esteemed father's feet in gratitude for a thousand blessings:
>
> I have completed the studies my esteemed father assigned for today, which I invite you to peruse.
>
> In reverence, your son

Leaving the note where his father would be sure to see it, Shuangxi excitedly scooped up the paper cricket cages and ran to the honey locust tree, where he caught two more crickets after turning over only two rocks. But that didn't satisfy him. I need two more, he thought, for concubines. So he turned over another rock, and out jumped a huge cricket, right up onto the edge of the well. Shuangxi chased it excitedly, darting this way and that until suddenly he tumbled down into the well itself. Winterset, who was carrying a load of water past the well, heard terrified shouts from below, threw down his carrying pole and water buckets, and, without a thought for his own safety, grabbed the well rope and slid down into the water. Holding onto the rope, he clutched Shuangxi by the arms and held him until the two of them, master and servant, were hauled up to safety, dripping wet, while around them it seemed that all of Nine Ideals Hall was shouting and screaming. Someone picked up the young master and ran with him into the bedroom of Third Concubine, just as Shuangxi regained consciousness, which he announced with loud wailing. He told them he had fallen into the well looking for a "concubine." Li Naijing mopped his own wet brow and collapsed into an armchair.

Everyone tried to squeeze into Third Concubine's bedroom, except for Winterset, who hunkered down beneath the eaves, soaked to the skin and scared to death as he listened to the uproar inside. Someone came out to tell him that Elder Master wanted to see him. Fearfully he followed the messenger inside, falling to his knees the minute he passed through the door and apologizing for what he had done:

"Elder Master, it's all my fault. I shouldn't have told Young Master to go looking for crickets."

Li Naijing gently helped the clearwater guest to his feet. "Winterset," he said, "if you hadn't acted so quickly, my line might very well have ended today." He turned and gestured to Zhao Pu'an, who was standing next to him. "You will no longer be a clearwater guest, Winterset," he said. "I'm giving you five *mou* of paddy land and a house. Get married, start a family. Now go along with the family adviser—he'll take care of everything."

Jealousy in their eyes, the servants in the room gaped at Winterset, whom they urged to thank the elder master for his kindness. Poor flustered Winterset couldn't say anything for a long moment. Then he fell to his knees again.

"Elder Master," he said, "I only know how to carry water, I'm no farmer."

"You don't think it's too little, do you, Winterset?"

"Elder Master, I don't know if I should speak my mind."

"Go ahead. We'll see."

"Elder Master, I really don't want any paddy land or a house. What I want is to buy Little Eleven out of the Peach Palace."

Everyone in the room was amazed that this simple, honest clearwater guest, a coarse, tight-lipped man, carried such deep feelings inside him. With a sigh, Li Naijing said:

"Winterset, good, good Winterset, so honest and upright, you are a credit to Nine Ideals Hall. In the space of one day you have saved not one but two lives! I, Li Naijing, will buy Little

Eleven for you. Adviser Zhao, go to the Peach Palace and make the necessary inquiries. Tell them Winterset is buying Little Eleven's freedom, whatever the price."

With fear and trepidation, Winterset followed the adviser to the Peach Palace. But when he came face to face with the dark-skinned madam, she laid down her water pipe and said:

"The poor little thing never had a chance. Last winter she died of consumption."

She picked up her water pipe and continued: "Here at the Peach Palace girls come and go like the tides. Like oxen turning a wheel, a different one every year. Little Eleven died just after she had scraped together enough money to get out. I never heard her mention she had such a kind-hearted benefactor, but it simply wasn't to be. Fate said no."

The madam looked Winterset up and down as she spoke, sapping him of courage. He could not forget that he was in Little Eleven's debt for three hundred coppers but didn't know if the madam was aware of that, and all he could do was follow Adviser Zhao out of the Peach Palace. As they left, Winterset saw many new girls, many new faces, and all he could think was that he had stayed away from this place for probably seven or eight years. That thought was followed by another, that he had probably eaten too many pig's knuckles, which had kept him from seeing Little Eleven as much as he would have liked. As he passed through the gate in front of the Peach Palace, he saw the towering derricks on both banks of Silver Creek and he heard the strains of dirges; mixed with the bass intonations of men were the gossamer threads of women's voices, their delicate tones pinched and shrill:

After today we will not meet again,
In the halls of jade, I will remove my paint and whore no more.
I will marry a farmer with joy in my heart,
And be my own mistress, not the plaything of others.

None of them sing like Little Eleven did, Winterset thought, and he doubted if any of them had a body as soft and as comforting as hers. Regret washed over him—regret that he hadn't acted like a man, regret that he hadn't returned to Little Eleven's room. He took one last sentimental look at the Peach Palace; in a flash he thought back to those days seven or eight years earlier, and he could not recall how many times he had followed Little Eleven up to this very spot or how many times he had enjoyed the sight of her lovely figure swaying back and forth as she walked into the building. Zhao Pu'an, who was walking beside him, laughed kindly:

"Winterset, you poor infatuated boy, with your face red and wetting your sleeve . . ."

Frantically wiping his face, Winterset sputtered: "Venerable adviser, the wind made my eyes water . . ."

From that day on, Winterset grew even more taciturn, carrying his water like an automaton, the creaking of his carrying pole the only sound of his passage in and out of Nine Ideals Hall. With Little Eleven dead, he refused both the paddy land and the house, asking only that Elder Master permit him to go on serving as a water carrier. With a sigh over Winterset's devotion and honesty, Li Naijing instructed the bookkeeper to double the rate of exchange for the tallies Winterset turned in. He also told Winterset that, if he ever found the right woman and had thoughts of starting a family, Nine Ideals Hall would gladly pay all the wedding expenses. But Winterset, who silently trudged back and forth delivering water, appeared to have no thoughts for women at all. The pewter flask he kept inside his shirt was usually full, and he often treated himself to one of those tasty pickled pig's knuckles.

One day, around noon, when everyone was taking a nap, the

young master Shuangxi slipped out of the house and began dashing around the compound, winding up out back, where he heard someone singing under the honey locust tree by the bubbling well. To his surprise, Shuangxi saw that it was Winterset, who hardly ever said a word anymore. The song seemed long and drawn out, and so very slow:

After today we will not meet again,
In the halls of jade, I will remove my paint and whore no more.

With a loud "Hey!" Shuangxi ran up to Winterset, giving him such a start that he sat bolt upright.

"Hey, Little Ancestor, you know you're not supposed to come here."

Shuangxi grabbed hold of Winterset's arm. "Tell me what you're singing about."

"Young Master," Winterset blushed. "Just a crude song. Don't you dare try singing it, or the old master will spank you."

A loud chirping of crickets under the tree interrupted the conversation between master and servant.

That summer often found Winterset sitting alone under one of the two honey locust trees.

To Winterset, that summer seemed especially long.

2

In the summer of 1935, Lady Wang, wife of Li Naijing, patriarch of Nine Ideals Hall, fell seriously ill. She was bedridden for six long months and tried over a hundred nostrums and remedies prescribed by Silver City's renowned doctor, Lin Jinmo, but to no avail. Lady Wang knew that her days on earth were numbered, yet she seemed unconcerned. She often lay in bed, her head propped up by pillows, and brought her grief-stricken husband to tears by speaking about the arrangements to be made following her death. Her greatest concern was Third Concubine. She urged him not to delay but to elevate Third Concubine to the status of formal wife as soon as possible after the seven-week mourning period so as to keep the family intact. Reminding him of the great difference in age between him and Third Concubine, she explained that his young wife would rely on him for many things. But he shouldn't coddle her just because she had borne him a son or get carried away in bed just because she was so young and vibrant, for that would sap his vitality. Li Naijing frequently interrupted her: "You must take your medication and stop worrying about wives and concubines." She replied that she took her medication only out of love for him, that she drank the bitter liquids only because it made him feel better. "I wish I could share the rest of your life with you. I don't want to leave you, but fate will have its way, and in the days to come, I want you to rest and take good care of yourself." Tears slipping down his cheeks, Li Naijing said, "Why do you insist on saying things I can't bear to hear? Who said you're not going to get better?" With a smile and a few tears of her own, Lady Wang replied, "You must be getting old. Otherwise, where did all those tears come from? I'm just prattling away because I'm upset, and here you go taking it to heart."

In point of fact, Li Naijing's formal wife, Lady Wang, knew very well what would happen after her death, that, under any circumstances, sooner or later her position as wife would be taken by this woman who had produced a son. In point of fact, Lady Wang had personally managed the acquisition of all three of Li Naijing's concubines: she had consulted the fortune-teller and the zodiac, had even chosen the dates for their crossing the threshold and for the celebrations. While Li Naijing took charge of public affairs, Lady Wang always supervised the behind-the-scenes activities, and she was known throughout Silver City for her virtues, her wisdom, and her exceptional resourcefulness. Thus, before Third Concubine was chosen, Lady Wang had asked to meet her. The fifteen-year-old virgin had been carried through the visitor's side gate into the Nine Ideals Hall compound in a sedan chair and had no sooner stepped down than Lady Wang noted her moist, limpid eyes. This girl will bear a son, Lady Wang mused. For several nights before the virgin came to stay in the compound Li Naijing slept beside Lady Wang, at her insistence, to conserve his vitality. Then on the morning after Third Concubine was deflowered, Lady Wang slyly asked her husband to describe the event. Li Naijing laughed. The girl shook and shuddered like a jackrabbit, he said. You can rest easy now, his wife told him. Third Concubine will bear you a son. And as for Third Concubine, who bounced around the bed like a jackrabbit, she was transformed overnight from a fifteen-year-old girl into a woman. One year later, after she had borne a son, she became a true concubine, skilled in the ways of the world; her moist, limpid eyes had drunk in all there was to know about the people of Nine Ideals Hall, from top to bottom.

At New Year's and other holidays or when the family gathered around the banquet table to wish Elder Master good health and a long life, Third Concubine took her legitimate place beside him, cradling their son in her arms. She was fully aware that she was holding a ladder to the stars, the rock on which she could always lean, and a look of contentment floated comfortably in her moist, limpid eyes. Other than Elder Master, whose word was law to her, the only person Third Concubine treated with meticulous deference was Lady Wang, the formal wife. Owing to the considerable difference in their ages, Third Concubine acted like an obedient child around Lady Wang, piously respectful of her elder.

With the birth of Shuangxi, the patriarch of Nine Ideals Hall finally had the heir he had sought so long, a solitary rice sprout in a vast dry field, and the child was treated like royalty, so spoiled that he was still suckling at his mother's breast at the age of four. Shuangxi often went off to play and stayed away until he was thirsty. Then he would run straight to his mother, whether she was alone or not, lift up her blouse, wrap his lips around a nipple, and start sucking. So Third Concubine's full, jiggly breasts, a rolling expanse of soft white skin, were often exposed in all their glory. Eventually, inevitably, the other two concubines reacted to this display with vehement displeasure, but Third Concubine refused to be goaded into a dispute; instead, she waited for the right opportunity to deal with them, at least indirectly, and by and by the moment arrived. One day in Lady Wang's room, Third Concubine teased her son: "Shuangxi, Elder Mama's milk is sweeter than mine." Shuangxi rushed up to Lady Wang and demanded to be fed. Lady Wang had no choice but to let him have his way, and he sucked on her nipple until it itched. "Shuangxi," she said with an embarrassed laugh, "you're not going to get any milk out of these withered sacks." From that day on, no one in Nine Ideals Hall ever again had anything to say on the topic of breast feeding—especially not the other concubines, who had never produced an heir to suckle.

On the seventh day of the seventh month, Lady Wang's health suddenly took a turn for the better and she was in remarkably high spirits, so high, in fact, that she proposed a family outing to Cloud Shadow Arbor on Embrace Autumn Promontory to celebrate the annual meeting of the Cowherd—Altair—and the Weaving Maid—Vega—in the Milky Way. Li Naijing, overjoyed at his wife's buoyant recovery, ordered the arbor tended and instructed the kitchen help to prepare all the proper delicacies.

The sky that night seemed newly washed, the starry canopy sparkling like a glittery brocade. The Cowherd and the Weaving

Maid gazed at each other across the cold, distant River of Heaven. An altar had been set up in front of the bright, well-tended arbor, and the fragrant smoke from three sticks of incense curled upward into the glittering sky. Spread out over the altar was an array of deep-fried pumpkin twists, loquats, honeyed peaches, watermelon, and other seasonal fruits and melons. A cloisonné bowl, filled to the brim with water, sat on a bench in front of the altar, next to bean sprouts and pumpkin plant tips to be used during the divination ceremony. At the stroke of midnight, a girl would pick one of the two items and lay it on the surface of the water. If the reflection at the bottom of the bowl was shaped like a writing brush, she would someday give birth to a boy; if it resembled a flower, she would give birth to a girl. After reverently lighting candles on the altar and bowing before the two stars, Lady Wang was escorted by Third Concubine to a rattan chair brought out for her use alone. She smiled and instructed the women of the family to try their luck.

"Try it, all of you. See if you'll have sons or daughters."

Third Concubine, quick of eye and deft of hand, was first in line, as always. She picked up a pumpkin tip. "This one is for our mistress."

"An old lady like me," Lady Wang said, waving her hands in front of her, "what kind of child could I hope to have?"

"Then I'll ask for a good sign for our mistress."

Third Concubine laid the pumpkin tip on the surface of the water, and a gently quivering reflection at the bottom of the bowl came into view in the clear moonlight and candlelight. Third Concubine shouted happily:

"Mistress, Mistress, it's a writing brush! It looks exactly like a writing brush! Who knows, maybe our mistress will have a son someday!"

The other two concubines and the serving girls all crowded around to look; to the concubines the reflection looked neither like a writing brush nor, for that matter, like much of anything at all. They exchanged knowing smiles before adding their congratulations:

"Third Concubine did very well—it does sort of look like a writing brush. We couldn't have done nearly as well. Who knows what we might have come up with?"

Third Concubine stepped to one side and looked at Mistress as if she were being teased. But Lady Wang waved them away and said:

"Let's all see how we do, just for fun. No more talk of who has good luck and who doesn't."

From his vantage point Li Naijing watched the women carry on and was not altogether pleased with what he saw. But he kept quiet so as not to spoil the occasion for his wife. No one had to tell him that, when his wife passed on, these three women would be at each other's throats constantly; it was a distressing thought. What a headache. He was reminded of the proverb "Women and little children are hard to raise." With a look at Third Concubine, who was thirty-five years his junior and whose eyes were fetchingly moist, Li Naijing sighed. Why did it have to be this woman who gave me a son?

Lady Wang, starting to tire, asked to be helped to her feet. She walked slowly over to the stone ledge of Cloud Shadow Arbor and looked out at the lotus flowers covering the nearby pond and at the sky full of stars. Leaning against the railing, she asked her husband:

"Do you know how many times we came here hoping for a son?"

Li Naijing shook his head.

"Neither do I. Now there's no longer any need . . ."

She smiled, as if recalling something. Then she laughed. A shooting star streaked across the sky and fell from the glittering canopy; the sight startled both husband and wife. Li Naijing hurried to put the best possible face on this sign:

"The heavens were too crowded for that one, so it decided to come to earth to rest."

Lacking a reply, Lady Wang stood in quiet dejection for a moment, then said weakly, "I'm tired."

In the summer of 1935, three days after the "child seeking" on the night of the seventh, Lady Wang, wife of Li Naijing, patriarch of Nine Ideals Hall, gave up her husband and her family responsibilities and took leave of this world. Li Naijing personally took charge of his wife's funeral arrangements; the solemn and elaborate ceremony, on which he spared no expense, was an expression of the grief in his heart. One hundred and eight monks from the White Cloud Monastery were summoned to intone the scriptures and invoke the name of Buddha to escort her soul on its journey. Also invited were ninety-nine Taoist priests, who set up an altar and performed their rites to release the departed from grievances and clear the mortal slate. A music and drama troupe staged operas for three straight days, fireworks experts from three neighboring counties arrived to put on a display for three continuous nights, wine for the dead was set out for three days, and everyone who came to light incense or kowtow respectfully was given a turban of sackcloth and invited to the funeral banquet, which drew guests from miles around, all eager to sit at the tables of Nine Ideals Hall. All this splendor bore testimony to the truth in the saying "When one family's dinner gong sounds, ovens for miles around stay cold." On the day of the funeral, gentry folk from many surrounding counties and townships converged on Nine Ideals Hall, where the funerary dragon lanterns and lion dancers were too numerous to count. By the time the coffin carrying the body of Lady Wang had traveled ten li beyond the Twin Arches at the Nine Ideals Hall gate, there were still people in the compound waiting to set out on the procession. During the seven weeks of mourning, Nine Ideals Hall received countless funeral scrolls and funerary objects, as well as thirty-five thousand in silver currency, while the family bookkeeper paid out eighty thousand in expenses. Over a decade later, the funeral, unprecedented in its lavishness, was still being talked about in Silver City, and it was a rare individual who did not envy the woman whose service brought her such posthumous glory.

Not long after the rites were completed, a new item of interest swept through Silver City: Li Naijing, patriarch of Nine Ideals Hall, elevated Third Concubine, the mother of his son, to the position of formal wife.

3

Lady Yang, who six years earlier had barely survived an attempt by her cousin to poison her, sensed that she had gradually settled into an advantageous position, as over those six years Liu Qiongju had given birth to only a daughter, no sons. Qiongju, who six years earlier had suffered the loss of her baby son, still waited patiently for a chance to avenge that death; six years of nursing deep hatred had not aged her, had in fact bestowed on her the elegant beauty of a fairy princess. So when, in the summer of 1935, Bai Qiuyun returned from the provincial capital in high spirits to pass the summer at White Garden, she could not anticipate that she was about to land in the middle of a life-and-death struggle between two women whose hatred of each other knew no bounds.

Bai Qiuyun had turned into a lovely, poised young woman, and naturally a great many more girlish secrets filled her heart than ever before. She was now a first-year literature major at the provincial college, a path she had chosen not to satisfy some lofty aspiration but because Li Naizhi was a student at the same school. Her secret love sometimes invested her with the beauty of a fresh flower and at other times made her as melancholic as a stalk of bamboo. In the summer of 1935, Bai Qiuyun, beautiful as a fresh flower and melancholic as a stalk of bamboo, had no inkling of the net her mother was weaving for her homecoming. After putting down her bags and freshening up, she went upstairs to her mother's room, where she was surprised to see a pale, frail young man standing next to the open window. Her mother pointed to him.

"This is your cousin Wenda. Wenda, this is my daughter, Qiuyun."

Bai Qiuyun nodded to the young man, who returned the nod shyly. Lady Yang said:

"Wenda has taken a job at your father's office, so he'll be staying here with us. That way you youngsters can become good friends and he can do things for you."

With a little laugh, Bai Qiuyun said, "The only *things* I have are some unfinished assignments from this past semester, I'm afraid. Can Cousin do them for me?"

The young man's timid face turned positively red with embarrassment.

"Qiuyun!" her mother scolded. "Don't make fun. Your cousin may not have gone to college, but he graduated from a perfectly respectable high school, so you're no better than him."

When Lady Yang had brought her nephew to White Garden some time earlier, she had not minced words: "Wenda, I've done all I can—now the rest is up to you. If you can get Qiuyun to like you, dealing with her father will be a lot easier. Once you two are married, at least half of these vast holdings will go to the two of you. And if that demon doesn't produce another son, there will be a lot more than half."

The determination in his aunt's voice frightened the frail Wenda, who fretted over the possibility that he would not prove equal to the task. His very first day at White Garden, as he and Lady Yang were crossing the stone bridge over the pond, he bumped into the demon his aunt had spoken of. She was white from head to toe, including a dazzling pearl necklace around her neck. Pearly teeth glistened between the demon's captivating red lips as she smiled and said:

"Who might this charming lad be?"

Wenda, who was standing behind his aunt, blushed. To him, this demon was beautiful beyond description, so beautiful he had to look away, and he was thankful for the protection of his indomitable aunt, who replied evenly:

"This is Wenda, my nephew."

The demon smiled again. "Wenda, ah, such a nice-sounding name. Wenda, you may call me Auntie or you may call me by my name, Liu Qiongju, it's up to you. We don't stand on ceremony in this family."

Wenda responded clumsily, then brushed past the demon as he fell in behind his aunt again; the fragrance that filled his nostrils made his heart race and his nerves melt. Back in his aunt's room, he said:

"That woman is a demon for sure."

With a grim smile, Lady Yang said, "You be careful of her, for there's nothing she won't do."

Wenda's ears had been bombarded with his aunt's warnings about Liu Qiongju's evil nature, which included an implication that at one time she had even attempted murder. Now that he had seen her with his own eyes, Wenda called on his imagination to fill in the portrait his aunt had painted: a figure all in white, except for captivating red lips around dazzling pearly teeth, drifting among the shadows of trees and bamboo in White Garden late at night under a full moon, a ghostly, glistening dagger in her hand. But for some reason, not only did this image fail to frighten him, he was actually reminded of the sensual writings of the Tang poet Li Shangyin.

To get into his uncle's good graces, Wenda was careful to do everything just right at the Prosperity Company and to be scrupulous about every assignment he was given. Bai Ruide saw in him a young man who had a great deal of promise; he was quite unaware that this promising young man was burdened with a far more arduous mission. Liu Qiongju, on the other hand, knew at first glance exactly what Lady Yang was up to and found the aging woman's ineptness quite laughable—to think that she had chosen a fledgling, a boy who blushed every time he opened his mouth, as a match for her; too bad, since he had such a pretty face. Deciding she'd have some fun with Lady Yang, Qiongju assumed the airs of a young aunt, ordering the charming young man around all day long, sending him upstairs to fetch her handbag one minute, having him bring her a cup of tea the next. Young Auntie's commands were not to be disobeyed. But the stern look on his older aunt's face made Wenda squirm awkwardly as he blushed with embarrassment. One day as they all sat in the garden Liu Qiongju brought Lady Yang's scheme out into the open:

"Ruide, do you really think that someone with Wenda's looks and abilities is the right person for our Qiuyun?"

With a wave of his hands, Bai Ruide said, "What gave you that idea? Qiuyun hasn't even laid eyes on him, so why bring it up? I don't want either of you getting involved in Qiuyun's marriage plans."

Liu Qiongju, feeling very pleased with herself, looked knowingly at the enraged Lady Yang and her mortified nephew, as if to say: Don't think this will be easy! Wenda, feeling humiliated to begin with, was sufficiently enraged by Qiongju's barbed comments that he uncharacteristically raised his eyes to glare daggers straight at her. He had not anticipated having his glare engulfed by the tender allure of her moist gaze. With studied nonchalance, Liu Qiongju sized up the young man and said:

"Wenda, you don't think your auntie talks too much, do you?"

Opening his mouth to reply, Wenda quickly swallowed his words as, to his surprise, the image of a woman all in white, a dagger held threateningly in her hand, flashed before his eyes.

On the eve of Bai Qiuyun's return to White Garden for the

summer holiday, the preliminary skirmishes of the battle between the two women, whose antagonism sometimes broke into open strife and at other times simmered beneath the surface, had been concluded. Now all that was needed for the decisive phase to begin was the return of the central figure. But Bai Qiuyun was too preoccupied by the secrets in her heart to take much notice of what was going on around her. Granted, over the years she had witnessed the enmity between Mother and Auntie many times, yet just now she could think only about Li Naizhi, who was still back at college in the provincial capital, and about whether she should reveal to him the secret she had for so long kept hidden in her heart. The book she carried with her wherever she went, an annotated edition of *Pale Fragrance Lyrics,* seemed full of messages meant just for her. The melancholy of "plump greens and wispy reds," the coyness of "slipping a smile to her suitor," and the self-pity experienced by "a girl more fragile than a chrysanthemum"—these phrases often made her toss and turn through sleepless nights.

Lady Yang, increasingly eager to make a match between the two youngsters, regularly dreamed up chores they could do together. On this particular day, she had sent them to buy some satin for summer dresses she intended to make for her daughter and herself. When the family's Ford sedan pulled up in front of the Heavensent Silk Emporium, the beaming proprietor was standing there to greet them before they even stepped out. Once inside, Bai Qiuyun pointed to this fabric and that, and when the proprietor asked how much she wanted, she nonchalantly ordered a bolt of each. All but falling over himself out of sheer joy, the proprietor ordered his clerk to carry the fabric out to the car, and as his customers were leaving the emporium, he beamed once again and said, "Next time anyone in the family wants something, just send a servant and we'll bring it over so you and your mother can make selections in the comfort of your home. There's no need for you to make this unnecessary journey." Bai

Qiuyun turned to her cousin and complained, "I told you Mother is just dreaming up things for us to do." Wenda agreed, then suddenly remembered the request made of him as they were leaving White Garden.

"Oh, Auntie asked me to buy some silk for a cheongsam she wanted to make."

With a wry smile, Bai Qiuyun warned him, "I'd avoid getting caught between those two if I were you. Believe me, there's more trouble there than you can handle."

She was correct. As soon as the silk was brought into the main hall, Liu Qiongju, hearing the noise, came downstairs, opened the bolt of fabric intended for her, and rubbed her hand over it to test its quality; then she praised Wenda for being so clever and asked him to carry it upstairs for her. From where she stood nearby, Lady Yang frowned and noisily snapped her sandalwood fan shut.

"Wenda," she said, "since when have you been so willing to degrade yourself? Have you become her slave, eager to do her bidding?"

Wenda, stung by the reprimand, put down the bolt of fabric. Smiling, Liu Qiongju approached him, gently patted his shoulder, and said:

"Wenda, I owe you an apology. It's all my fault, I should have been more attentive. You're not my slave, but by treating you like one I've made you suffer."

As he felt his shoulder being rubbed so gently, so softly and smelled that intoxicating fragrance, Wenda turned bright red, hung his head, and said nothing. Liu Qiongju summoned Amah Liu to take the bolt of fabric upstairs, then fell in behind Lady Yang's trusted servant. "Amah Liu," she said, "since you are a slave, by rights you are the one who should do my bidding."

Finding such barnyard squabbles unbearable, Bai Qiuyun stormed off to her room, leaving the hall to an angered Lady Yang and her nephew.

"Wenda," she rebuked him, "don't you understand? I told you that demon was capable of anything, so why do you listen to her?"

"Auntie, she told me to buy it. I couldn't just ignore her."

"What do you mean, 'couldn't'? You gave her plenty of face today. Just wait and see if she does the same for you any time soon. You ignore the people you should be paying attention to but can't wait to be with the ones you would do well to ignore."

"I won't have anything to do with her anymore, Auntie."

For several days after this incident, Wenda was the picture of dejection, going to the office during the day, then moping around the house at night, either staying in his room or walking alone in the garden in the dark, a lonely, melancholic young man surrounding himself with the faint aroma of damp grass. He sighed over his ineptness, wondering what he had to do to win the heart of his cousin, wondering whether he would prove equal to the task. He often leaned up against a tree to gaze vacantly at the light shining from his cousin's window and to indulge his fanciful musings and hopes, unaware that another pair of eyes was watching him all the while.

On this particular night, Wenda was walking in the garden, as usual, when he saw Liu Qiongju, all in white, step out from behind a banana tree and stand still before him. Transfixed by fear and elation, he stared at her motionless body as if she had appeared in his imagination. Liu Qiongju's red lips curved into a smile.

"Wenda," she asked, "what makes you sad all the time?"

"Auntie . . . I'm not supposed to talk to you . . ."

Liu Qiongju laughed out loud. "I know you're scared to talk to me and worried because you can't get in the good graces of the one you want to talk to, am I right?"

"Auntie . . ."

"Wenda, I've come here tonight to tell you that you shouldn't concern yourself with good graces."

No response.

"Read this letter. Then you'll know I'm here to help you."

She handed him a letter and turned on a flashlight she had

with her. Recognizing Bai Qiuyun's graceful handwriting, Wenda tore open the envelope and started to read, but after the first line he dropped his arms in dejection.

> Dear Naizhi,
> I love you.
> I've held back for seven years, but today I have finally found the courage to tell you. . . .

Pleased with the results of her efforts, Liu Qiongju took pains to explain: "Amah Liu may be your aunt's slave, but the driver is mine. Qiuyun instructed him to take this letter into town tomorrow. I can't bear to see you mope around for no reason, and that's why I've let you read it." She drew up next to him and ran her cold hand through his hair.

"I feel sorry for you, Wenda."

First there was the cold hand, then Wenda felt himself enfolded in that strange intoxicating fragrance—an unexpected, sudden, shocking turn of events. Raising his head in the midst of his dejection and embarrassment, Wenda found himself looking into a lovely, soul-stirring, yet coldly haughty face framed in bright, clear moonlight. Unable to stop himself, he fell to his knees, wrapped his arms around Liu Qiongju's waist, and buried his face in her fragrance.

"Auntie . . ." A moan, a cry for help.

Without moving a muscle, Liu Qiongju laughed. "Even now you call me Auntie?"

Without waiting for a reply, she pulled his arms from around her waist.

"Wenda, the door to Qiuyun's room is closed to you, but mine is open. Your uncle is out of town for a few days."

The invitation given, Liu Qiongju turned and disappeared into the bamboo shadows, leaving the badly shaken young man all alone.

The loss of hope is misery, but longing is agony. Following

this wondrous nighttime encounter, the frail, delicate Wenda was in an agony of longing, and for days on end he could neither eat nor sleep; the sound of Liu Qiongju's invitation still rang in his ears. Time and again he leapt out of bed, ran to the door, and grabbed the doorknob; but at the very last moment, his nerve deserted him and he went back to bed. He lacked the courage to flirt with taboo; at the mere thought of his uncle's rage he broke out in a cold sweat. He knew that if it were ever discovered that he had dared step into that upstairs bedroom, he would be banished from White Garden for all time, condemned to live out his life disdained and loathed by all. And so he went back out into the garden late at night, wandering like a specter among the trees and bamboo. No longer interested in Qiuyun's window, he now gazed longingly at the light streaming from Liu Qiongju's room and at the demon's shadow as it moved about; he waited to see the demon open or close the curtain, then watched with despair as the night gave way to total, hopeless darkness. Impatiently, he yearned for another of those wondrous encounters, yearned to see her, all in white, step out from behind the banana tree, even if she held a dagger in her hand and even if that cold dagger was plunged deep into his chest. But Liu Qiongju did not return to the garden; one night she lifted her curtain and saw the despondent figure in the shadow of a tree, but all she did then was extinguish her lamp, and the harsh darkness that streamed toward Wenda set him trembling with despair.

For three nights in a row Liu Qiongju slept with her door unbarred, calmly waiting for Wenda to slip into the room. But on each of those nights he held back from taking that fateful first step. In the light of day, either in the main hall or on the stairs, when the two of them met, Liu Qiongju took note of Wenda's increasingly pale, gaunt face and his dark eyes, made bright by longing. She greeted him with a silent smile, to which he reacted with the uncontrollable panic of a wild animal being stalked. On this particular day, Liu Qiongju smiled, then brushed past the wild animal and reminded him:

"Wenda, your uncle returns tomorrow, and he wants you to have this month's accounts ready."

The stalked prey stopped cold and turned toward Liu Qiongju.

"Did you hear what I said?" she asked.

Wenda nodded, suddenly sensing that he was teetering on a high precipice above a dizzying, beckoning abyss, at the bottom of which birds dipped and circled and cold winds waited to stroke his face. . . .

This final deadline turned the young man's timidity into boldness. At two o'clock in the morning, Wenda, trembling uncontrollably, pushed on the upstairs door that had become his obsession. It was not locked, and the lamp inside was still lit; Liu Qiongju, in her nightclothes, was sitting up in bed.

"Wenda," she said, "did your aunt ever tell you that I tried to kill someone?"

Puzzled by the question, he smiled. "I can't begin to tell you all the terrible things she's said about you."

"But in this case she wasn't making it up. I did try to kill someone, and that someone was your aunt. Because she killed my son."

"Why are you telling me this?"

"Aren't you afraid I'll kill you too? Anyone can buy arsenic."

But Wenda was fortified by his desire. He blurted out:

"Qiongju, if you poisoned me, I would die without regret."

As she looked at this pale, delicate young man who had just opened his heart to her, his love greater even than death, Liu Qiongju was deeply, if fleetingly, moved, and she felt slight stirrings of remorse for having set a trap from which he could never escape. But it was too late. For at that moment, Bai Ruide pushed open the door to her room. A vicious slap sent blood gushing from Wenda's nose.

"You bastard!" Bai Ruide thundered. "I refused to believe what your aunt told me about you, but I see what an utterly shameless bastard you really are!"

Bai Ruide's thundering rage shook the whole house and awakened its inhabitants; Wenda fled to his room, pursued by the astonished looks of everyone in the household. He knew that no one would want to hear his side of the story, nor would they believe it if they did. He began packing his things, but he had barely opened his suitcase when he shut it again, an incomparably tragic smile spreading across his blood-streaked face.

The following morning, when a panicky Lady Yang ordered a servant to break down Wenda's door, they saw his cold, stiff body stretched out on the bed. It was clear he had not died easily, for the bedding was all twisted and torn, and dried blood showed at the corners of his mouth, in his nostrils, and in his ears. A note on the table had but a single line:

Qiongju, unfortunately I killed myself.

With a shriek, Lady Yang threw herself onto her nephew's body, mourning both his fate and her own disastrous defeat. She cursed Liu Qiongju with every fiber of her being. Now that things had reached this point, Bai Ruide was forced to take action: blaming Lady Yang for having brought Wenda into the household, he offered her a grim choice. She could either accept divorce papers and return to the home of her parents or she could retain her wifely status but move to Bamboo Garden in the provincial capital; in either case, she must never show her face in Silver City again. These cataclysmic events made it impossible for Bai Qiuyun to stay at White Garden any longer, so she decided to accompany her mother to town. On the eve of her departure, she went to find Liu Qiongju.

"Auntie, why did you have to destroy Wenda?"

To Bai Qiuyun's astonishment, Liu Qiongju broke down in tears:

"Qiuyun, that's exactly what I did, destroy him. But he didn't have to die. He was so cowardly, I never thought he had the courage . . . To think that he had such strength of character after all. Now there'll be peace . . . White Garden will be at peace again. First my son and now Wenda. It's enough. Those who shouldn't have died, died anyway, and now those who remain, the living dead, will have peace . . . Qiuyun, on that day six years ago when your mother killed my son, I stopped living . . ."

As she watched her cold, haughty aunt weep in front of her, Bai Qiuyun was unable to prevent the hot tears from streaming down her own cheeks. What she could not understand was how, amid the beauty and elegance of White Garden, her mother and her aunt had become such bitter enemies.

In the summer of 1935, as Bai Qiuyun, her face tear-streaked, left White Garden in the company of her mother, she saw her beautiful, elegant home in a new light: a place of sorrow and revenge, and of battles unto the death. . . .

CHAPTER SEVEN

1

Li Naizhi received Bai Qiuyun's soulful love letter as he sat in his room, distraught, after a sleepless night. Not sleeping had been only part of it; he had vomited twice and washed his hands with soap and water at least ten times, but he still could not wash away the horrible sensation in his palms and on his fingers. The terrible spasms of the man's struggles as he died traveled from Naizhi's hands to the rest of his body like the searing heat from a branding iron. What was he feeling? Terror? Excitement? Compassion? Relief? Torment? Or perhaps just cold, dispassionate righteousness? Li Naizhi was not sure.

That summer of 1935, the provincial newspapers had reported startling news. According to the Provincial Garrison Command, a sizable group of Communists had recently "come out of the shadows," thanks to a succession of traitors, making it possible to catch the entire Communist underground in a dragnet. The local Communist Party secretary, Wen Tianlei; the organization department head, Chen Shijie; and the propaganda chief, Ma Qianli, had all been arrested, and, according to the reports, "just sentences for the foolhardy individuals" would be carried out at the East City parade ground over the coming days. "We will press on," insisted the Provincial Garrison Command, "until the last remnants of the Communist underground have been wiped out. Party leaders are urged to turn themselves in while they still have a chance. Leniency will be shown to all who freely admit the error of their ways, and past mistakes will be forgiven."

Throughout the summer of 1935 terror reigned in the provincial capital, where wanted posters went up overnight and arrests and public executions became common occurrences. But the Garrison Command underestimated its enemy's tenacity; the local Communist leadership issued an order to the faithful to fall back and regroup, at the same time resolving to purge the party of traitors. On the eve of the summer holiday, Li Naizhi received instructions to remain in the provincial capital, using a work-study program as his cover while he awaited a special assignment. About two weeks later, in a noisy, dingy teashop, a man with the code name Lao Ma—Old Nag—gave him his assignment: the traitor he was to kill was none other than Chen Shengshen, the literature teacher. Naizhi was shocked, unable to believe what he was hearing, unable to comprehend how that simple, impoverished man could be linked to the unspeakably evil concept of traitor. But for all Li Naizhi's emotional resistance, there was no way to deny the cold, hard reality. Lao Ma, himself icily composed, told him that the party, now considering Li Naizhi's application to join, had decided to use the campaign against traitors to test his loyalty. And so, on a moonless night, Li Naizhi, Lao Ma, and a man whom Li Naizhi never got a good look at hid in a gateway across from 5 Rush Alley, which Li Naizhi had visited so many times. According to their intelligence, Chen Shengshen returned home to his mother and children every night at two or three A.M.; he carried a drawn Mauser with him at all times, so the only chance to get at him was when he put the gun down to open the gate. Standing in the pitch darkness, Li Naizhi could see nothing but could hear the other two men's breathing and the sound of his own racing heart. As they waited endlessly, he could not help recalling the old woman's kindly, slightly upraised face, the enticing aroma of barbecued meat, and Danan and Ernan as they drew moustaches on each other under the table; the children would find it impossible to imagine him lying in wait to murder their father. Li Naizhi forced himself not to contemplate the scene inside the little cottage the next morning when they had opened the gate and found the body lying in the dirt.

Each man had his assigned task. After pouncing like panthers on their victim, Lao Ma grabbed Chen's wrist to prevent his seizing the pistol, while the second man slipped a cord around his neck and pulled it tight from behind and Li Naizhi held his legs to keep him from kicking. Clean, neat, no noise except for the occasional thuds of bodies thrashing in the darkness. Mr. Chen struggled briefly, then went limp and lost control of his bodily functions, releasing a cloud of vile odors into the air. Just to be safe, they knotted the cord tightly around his neck as if tying up a sack, then pinned a slip of paper to his chest with the words: Death to traitors! Their mission accomplished, the three men ran to the end of Rush Alley, then scattered in different directions.

For the next hour, Li Naizhi threaded his way through countless alleys and intersections, making sure he wasn't being followed, then headed back to the dormitory at the university; he threw up as soon as he entered his room, and a short time later his stomach betrayed him again. So as not to attract attention, he hurriedly cleaned up his mess, changed clothes, and washed his hands with soap over and over. But no matter how many times he plunged his hands into the warm water, he could not wash away the dirty, crawling sensation that stuck to them.

So when Li Naizhi tore open Bai Qiuyun's clean white envelope and read the opening sentence, what filled his heart was neither excitement nor joy but a sense of the absurd. Why, he thought, did it have to happen like this—murder and love, extreme and irreconcilable, entering his life at the same moment? With a bitter laugh, he returned to the letter:

> Dear Naizhi,
>
> I love you.
>
> I've held back for seven years, but today I have finally found the courage to tell you. Do you recall that time seven years ago when you played the tragic young man in *A Night for Catching Tigers*? When I saw you end your life with one thrust of the knife, tormented by love lost, I cried my eyes out. But it wasn't until later that I realized that my tears were shed not for the character on stage, but . . .

Li Naizhi finished reading Bai Qiuyun's letter and felt empty, as if all his memories had been swept away. Would Bai Qiuyun have written it, he wondered, if she knew that he'd just murdered Mr. Chen? He was sure of only one thing: after last night, he could never return to the way he once was.

As the summer of 1935 drew to a close, Li Naizhi, with Lao Ma as his sponsor, was formally inducted into the Chinese Communist Party and became a member of the underground, a person at risk of being killed anywhere, anytime. The ceremony was a hurried affair held in a room of a small hotel; to avoid undue attention, the new member whispered his oath before a miniature Communist flag: I swear that I will be loyal to the Communist cause; that I will safeguard party secrets; that I will not betray the organization or my comrades, even at the cost of my life; and that I will struggle to further the Communist cause for as long as

I live. The ceremony completed, the two men left separately and disappeared into the crowds in the street.

As the summer of 1935 drew to a close, Li Naizhi, newly admitted member of the Communist Party, thought often about Danan and Ernan and their nearly blind old grandmother. Finally, after much struggle with himself, he went to 5 Rush Alley, where he handed the old lady twenty yuan. She thanked him over and over again, and gripping his hands tightly, insisted that he stay for some barbecued meat. He was just as insistent on leaving, unable to bear the thought of staying in that house and of looking the old lady in the eye. He was fearful that her failing eyes would see the secret in his. Danan and Ernan were nowhere about. They had dropped out of school, the old lady said, and were working as rickshaw boys, the taller brother pulling from the front and the smaller one pushing from behind. She praised Ernan for his determination, proud that he was eager to grow up so he and his twin brother could each have a rickshaw and put more food on the table. The old lady actually managed a smile at that. Li Naizhi stood up to go. He could not stay in that house another minute.

Naizhi was severely reprimanded by the party over the incident; Lao Ma told him that this sort of behavior was tantamount to playing with the lives of his comrades and putting the entire organization in jeopardy. It was petit bourgeois behavior, totally at odds with what was expected of a member of the Communist Party. On behalf of the party, Lao Ma coldly announced that Li Naizhi was to be excluded from party activities and suspended until further notice as punishment for his unauthorized visit. A record of the punishment would remain in his political dossier for the rest of his life. As the meeting came to an end, Lao Ma patted Li Naizhi on the shoulder and said, "Go to the East City parade ground and take a long look. The heads of Comrades Wen Tianlei and Ma Qianli are still hanging from the city wall. This sort of butchery leaves us no choice. Revolution is nasty business! Our revolution must eradicate the reactionary camp!"

The cessation of Li Naizhi's party activities was almost more than he could bear. He felt like a beached fish gasping for air within sight of the waves lapping at the shore; being cast off by his comrades was unbearable, even though his expulsion was only temporary. And so, as the summer of 1935 gave way to autumn, Li Naizhi, tormented by remorse and self-recrimination, had no interest in anything, including the love of Bai Qiuyun.

2

There was no reason in the world Li Ziyun could have expected to be offered a job as a principal right out of college—and at the renowned Silver City High School at that. The idea of being called "principal" was so tempting she didn't feel disquieted when her elder sister asked, "Do you really think there are no strings attached to the man's offer?" Eagerly, Li Ziyun decided to accept the offer and asked her cousin Naijing to inform Commander Yang. Li Naijing could not praise her enough: "Eighth Sister, I knew you had ambition, and you are wise to recognize the commander's kind offer for what it is."

And so in the summer of 1935, a rickshaw regularly traveled between Twin Arches and Silver City High School, and whenever the bell heralded its passage down one of the city's streets or lanes, people commented: "Look, there's Eighth Sister of Nine Ideals Hall, just out of college and already a high school principal!"

Silver City High School had been closed since the peasants' uprising in 1928. In response to appeals from all quarters, Yang

Chuxiong, leader of Silver City's civil and military government, reopened the school in the summer of 1935. He placed great importance on the school, taking twenty thousand in silver out of that year's salt tax as seed money to repair the buildings, buy teaching materials, and hire teachers. Silver City residents applauded his civic-mindedness, and when he recommended hiring the young mistress of Nine Ideals Hall as principal, he encountered no opposition; after all, Li Ziyun was Silver City's first-ever female graduate of the provincial college. But all the same, the citizens of Silver City were still a little surprised at this unprecedented step of hiring someone who barely had her degree in hand.

Not so the patriarch of Nine Ideals Hall, Li Naijing, who had earlier been apprised of Yang Chuxiong's intentions. Indeed, the matter had been decided before the school refurbishing had even begun. After one of the early planning sessions, Yang had asked Li Naijing to stay behind; he said he had found the perfect person to serve as principal. Li Naijing asked who that might be. "Who do you think?" Yang said with a laugh. "The talented Eighth Sister of Nine Ideals Hall is about to graduate from college, isn't she?" Li Naijing protested that Li Ziyun was too young and could hardly live up to people's expectations. But Yang assured him, "I was younger than Eighth Sister when I became a battalion commander. I'm only worried that she has her eye on better opportunities in the city and might consider this beneath her." Li Naijing, too, laughed, as he began to suspect Yang's true intention. But he was cagey: "Chuxiong, my friend, it's up to Eighth Sister. She's not one to be forced into doing something she doesn't want to do." Commander Yang pressed his hands together in a reverent gesture. "You're like a father to Eighth Sister, she'll listen to you." With another laugh, Li Naijing hedged a little more: "Times are changing. Young people these days are more interested in freedom than in anything else."

Again Commander Yang clasped his hands. "Menglin, my friend, I'll be forever in your debt. Eighth Sister is a rare talent!"

This time Li Naijing agreed to give it a try. He wasn't worried that Eighth Sister would not want the job, but she might not agree to whatever else Yang Chuxiong had in mind. He was aware that she was currently tied up with someone else, a schoolmate a class ahead of her by the name of Lu Fengwu. Apparently he was a journalist, his shirt pocket always sporting a brass badge with his newspaper's name on it. The previous summer he had spent a few days in Silver City. Li Naijing had met him on the veranda beside Willow Reflecting Pond, where he was chatting with Li Naizhi and Li Ziyun. When Eighth Sister introduced him, Lu Fengwu bowed and paid his respects, but although little was said, Naijing detected a haughty look in the young man's eyes.

Bai Qiuyun was the first—and, for a long time, the only—person to know that Li Ziyun had been offered the position as principal. The final term had not yet ended, so both young women were still at Bamboo Garden on Cathedral Street. Li Naijing's letter thrilled and excited Ziyun, who told Qiuyun she'd love to accept.

"What are you afraid of, Elder Sister Yun?" asked Bai Qiuyun, who could not have been happier for her friend. "You be the principal, and as soon as I graduate, I'll join your staff!"

"Don't tease me, Little Sister Yun. I'm so confused I don't know what to do."

"Confused about what?"

"You-know-who will be fit to be tied. His greatest fear is that I won't stay in the city."

"If he really loves you, he'll still want you even if you go to the ends of the earth. Do you think he's all talk? Do you think he wrote *Spring Waters Flow East* just for fun?"

Spring Waters Flow East was a romantic novel Lu Fengwu had written for serialization in his paper, the *Jinjiang News*. With every installment, his reputation grew, especially among high school girls, for whom he was quite a celebrity. They did not know, of course, that their favorite author already had someone special in his life and that, when he wasn't spicing up the romantic lives of characters in his novel, he was sending love letters to Bamboo Garden, filled with professions of devotion that made Li Ziyun blush and set her heart pounding. Once in a while she would take out his letters and read passages to Bai Qiuyun, who would sigh and say:

"Elder Sister Yun, you are so lucky."

"Don't worry, Little Sister," Li Ziyun would say comfortingly. "Someday you'll get letters just like that."

"If anyone ever wrote things like that to me, I'd follow him to the ends of the earth."

Then the two girls would sink dreamily into their private romantic fantasies.

In the days following the commencement ceremonies, Li Ziyun and Lu Fengwu discussed their future several times. When the time for departure came, she and Bai Qiuyun rode back to Silver City together in the Bai family's Ford sedan. There was no need, therefore, for the traditional farewells that wished a traveler well as he journeyed "six miles down the road," proceeding from "large oases to small." Her eyes red, Ziyun said simply, "I'm leaving now, Fengwu." And he replied, "I'll come see you in Silver City, I promise." With that, the American car gave a couple of automotive snorts and sped off, leaving behind the serene Bamboo Garden. As the car pulled away, Li Ziyun sobbed and dried her eyes with a wadded-up handkerchief; the sight affected Bai Qiuyun, who cried along with her. After she had cried enough, Ziyun handed Qiuyun a paper fan: "Look what he wrote. . . ." In an elegant flowing script Lu Fengwu had penned a line of plaintive verse by Liu Yong, a poet who had lived—and suffered—nine hundred years earlier:

Though there be a thousand sentiments
To whom can I speak them?

The words and the thought behind them reduced Ziyun once again to tears, but though she lay sobbing on the backseat, the Ford sedan never slowed as it brought her back to Silver City, delivering her into her new world of official duties and social obligations.

With Li Naijing's and Yang Chuxiong's tacit backing and Li Ziyun's industriousness, Silver City High School quickly regained its former renown; but that was not enough for Li Ziyun, who wanted to try something new, something unprecedented. She had her heart set on organizing Silver City's very first athletic meet, a competition with the area's other two private high schools. She wanted the people of Silver City to see what modern education was all about and also wanted them to take note of her boldness and initiative. But athletic meets cost money, so she went to her cousin, Li Naijing, for advice; urging her to consult Commander Yang, he wrote and sent a letter on her behalf. The next day one of Yang Chuxiong's staff officers came to the school to invite her to meet with the commander at his headquarters. Li Ziyun was secretly delighted. Yang Chuxiong had granted all her requests so far, and she had a measure of respect for this rash and somewhat crude military man's enlightened views and enthusiastic promotion of mass education. Li Ziyun accompanied the officer to the city's heavily guarded God of War Temple; entering through the front gate and skirting the main hall, they negotiated a maze of passageways until they came out into an elegant little courtyard. Facing the entrance was a large Lake Tai stone serving as a screen, and behind it a flagstone path lined with phoenix-tail bamboo. The fragrance of chrysanthemums hung in the air. The officer led Li Ziyun into a guest room and offered her a seat. "I must ask that you wait here a moment while I tell the commander you are here," he said with a salute. As she sat there alone, Li Ziyun took in her surroundings, noting the bare white walls free of decoration, except for a single large scroll opposite the door; on it, in the bold calligraphic style of Liu

Gongzhuan, was a quotation from *The Art of War:* "A soldier who gains victory without a fight is boldest of the bold." Li Ziyun's thoughts went back to the military incident of seven years before, when all the local newspapers lauded Yang Chuxiong as a brilliant and courageous figure of near-legendary proportions. Her thoughts were interrupted by the arrival of Yang Chuxiong himself, looking quite dashing in his uniform.

"Eighth Sister, my apologies for keeping you waiting."

The affectionate form of address made Li Ziyun blush, but Yang appeared not to notice.

"Eighth Sister, you needn't be so modest. Have I ever said no where money was concerned? I asked you here today to show you something. Come with me. I want to see if it pleases you!"

Relaxed and at ease, Yang Chuxiong walked over and helped Li Ziyun up by her hand. Once again she blushed over someone's taking such liberties with her. This time Yang noticed and he apologized with a rousing laugh. "I'm a coarse man, please don't take offense. When you see what I have for you, I'm sure you'll be pleased."

She was. When Li Ziyun walked into the courtyard and saw the resplendent military band assembled there, she could scarcely contain her joy. With a wave of his hand, Yang Chuxiong commanded, "Men, a song for Principal Li!" Then, with the triumphant martial music swirling around them, Yang Chuxiong turned to Li Ziyun. "With this band putting on a show, Eighth Sister, you needn't worry about how your athletic meet will go over with the people, will you?"

Li Ziyun sparkled, she was so happy. "Commander Yang, you've thought of everything."

"This is nothing, Eighth Sister." Yang Chuxiong laughed heartily. Then, suddenly earnest, he continued, "Eighth Sister, today is the ninth day of the ninth lunar month, a holiday to enjoy the beginning of autumn. Stay for dinner and try one of my famous crab feasts!"

And so on the evening of Double Ninth, 1935, Li Ziyun followed Yang Chuxiong through a series of gates to another courtyard ringed by verandas. The first thing she saw was a vast panorama of lush chrysanthemums, their subtle aroma thick in the air. A stone table and four stone benches stood beneath a wisteria trellis in the center of the courtyard. A wonderful spread had been laid out on the table. Yang Chuxiong smiled and gestured to a bench.

"Double Ninth is a perfect day for this humble abode to be blessed by the presence of graceful Eighth Sister. Please enjoy our chrysanthemums and crab feast. What's the point of keeping all this for the likes of me?"

Yang Chuxiong then turned his attention to the food on the table, describing each dish to Li Ziyun: crab roe and sea cucumbers, crab and roasted anchovies, steamed whole crab, sliced crab and chrysanthemum-petal hot pot, crab roe pastries . . . and, of course, old-cellar white wine. They feasted on crab until the moon rising in the east created shadows amid the bamboo. When Li Ziyun said that she must be going, that she couldn't take up any more of Commander Yang's time, he summoned his personal guard to escort her home. At the front gate, as Li Ziyun was leaving, Yang Chuxiong clasped his hands in front of him and said:

"Eighth Sister, from now on, anything you desire, so long as it's within my power to get it for you, just say the word."

Li Ziyun, slightly tipsy, thanked him profusely, and as she turned away, she was reminded of her sister's caution: "Do you really think there are no strings attached to the man's offer?" The rickshaw's bell rang out, the guards' cadenced footsteps sounded behind her, and Li Ziyun could not help laughing at her sister's suspicious mind. On the night of Double Ninth, 1935, a slightly tipsy Li Ziyun sat in the rickshaw in the deep darkness of an autumn night and smelled the heady fragrance of chrysanthemums.

3

In the summer of 1935, while the patriarch of Nine Ideals Hall was overseeing the spectacular funeral of Lady Wang, Bai Ruide, the general manager of Prosperity Company, spent several days in the provincial capital. Before long, rumors reached Li Naijing that two old-style financial brokerages, Da Heng and Da Tong, were merging to form a modern bank. Intuitively Li Naijing perceived that this was no insignificant development, since Nine Ideals Hall owed the two institutions six hundred thousand in silver, a loan negotiated decades earlier. The two lenders virtually held the future of Nine Ideals Hall in their hands. Fortunately, both Nine Ideals Hall and the two lenders were venerable institutions that had done business for generations, and relations between them had always been cordial; but while there was no history of legal wrangling, this new development was troubling. Yet with the funeral rites under way and a steady stream of callers at his door, Li Naijing had no time to spend on anything else. So he sent the old family adviser, Zhao Pu'an, to look into the matter.

It took Zhao five days, traveling by day and resting at night, to arrive in the provincial capital by sedan chair; as custom dictated, he stayed at the lenders' guest house. First thing the next morning he went to call on the heads of the two firms, to whom he delivered handwritten letters from Li Naijing plus some Korean ginseng and a pair of young deer antlers for medicinal use. The lenders extended their condolences over the death of the mistress and insisted that there was no need for Zhao Pu'an to have traveled all this way for such a trivial matter, that a messenger would have been sufficient, since generations of amicable dealings with Nine Ideals Hall ensured that no changes could affect their good-faith relationship; Menglin had no cause for concern. The heads of the two firms then urged the adviser to stay for a few days, to enjoy good food and watch some opera, before setting out on the arduous return trip. Satisfied with the responses he had received, Zhao Pu'an took them up on their offer. He was impressed by the warm reception and the lavish entertainment, in particular by the unanticipated company of Fifth Mistress Xiao from Cinnamon Garden. He was in high spirits as he set out in his sedan chair to return to Silver City, where he reported to Li Naijing that all was well.

What Zhao did not know was that while he was on the road a news item appeared in the provincial newspaper reporting that Da Heng and Da Tong, two venerable financial institutions on the verge of bankruptcy, had merged with Silver City's Prosperity Company to form the Tri-Summit Bank. Inasmuch as Prosperity Company had supplied 60 percent of the capital, Bai Ruide would assume the duties of Tri-Summit's general manager. To consolidate the bank's business dealings, he was sending a team of lawyers and accountants to Silver City to recoup outstanding loans from the owners of the salt mines and the salt merchants. Its assets strengthened, the bank would be in a position to expand—and so on and so forth.

This audacious move by Bai Ruide created quite a stir in the financial circles of the provincial capital. Everyone knew that only on the surface was this a joint operation by all three firms, that in reality Prosperity Company had annexed the two badly managed lending institutions, and that by merging their rights as creditors Tri-Summit would now exercise considerable control over Silver City's salt industry. People in the know, without exception, felt secret admiration for this bold financial coup.

And so, in the summer of 1935, not long after the spectacular funeral rites for Lady Wang had been completed, Bai Ruide's lawyers came knocking at the door of Nine Ideals Hall. When they stated the purpose of their visit, Li Naijing and Zhao Pu'an broke out in a cold sweat. This time, there would be no miracles. After the lawyers left, Zhao Pu'an beat his chest and stomped his foot in anger:

"Menglin, Menglin, I let myself be hoodwinked by that turtle spawn, and now I have brought Nine Ideals Hall to the brink of ruin . . ."

Li Naijing stared blankly at the venerable adviser for a long moment. Then, as if to himself, he said, "I suppose he really does want to crush us . . ."

And so, after seeing Bai Ruide's lawyers, Zhao Pu'an went home and sat in his study, sighing mournfully. His wife and children tried to comfort him, but he shooed them out. A fearful silence settled on the house as night fell. Finally, Zhao's wife summoned up the courage to go see why there were no sounds coming from the study. She had barely opened the door when she drew back with a moan. Her sons and daughters, following her, burst into the room but were stopped by the sight of their father's body hanging from the rafters. Their shrieks and wails brought the neighbors running. On the desk lay two letters, one for his family, instructing them to keep his funeral simple and austere to ease the burden on friends and relatives and especially to spare the members of Nine Ideals Hall any inconvenience; no condolence gifts were to be accepted. The second letter was addressed to the patriarch of Nine Ideals Hall, Li Naijing:

> Worthy nephew Menglin:
> Thanks to the benevolence of your late father, I have served Nine Ideals Hall for three decades. For two generations of your family, while I have done little that deserves praise, I have poured my heart into every endeavor. On my latest trip to the provincial capital, however, I failed to carry out an important mission, which led to disaster. I have no one but my miserable self to blame.

> Since the very first day I served your late father, I wanted nothing else in life except to share the fate of Nine Ideals Hall. I am heartbroken that, in a single day, I brought down a family that has thrived for hundreds of years, but there is nothing I can do to repair the damage, for which I am agonizingly remorseful. Ending this wretched life, letting my death acknowledge your family's benevolence, is the only way I can pay for what I have done. From now on, we shall travel two different roads, one in this world and one in the next. I can no longer accompany my master in life. Still, my ghost will always be with you. I write this letter through tears of sorrow and regret. I pray that my worthy nephew will restrain his grief and not be distraught by this turn of events. Someday your fortunes will rise again, and may that happy knowledge be conveyed to this resident of the Yellow Springs.

News of his esteemed adviser's death hit Li Naijing hard; hot tears ran down his face as he read the letter. All members of the family were told to don mourning attire and follow him out the gate past Twin Arches, where their cries of sorrow and haggard appearance shocked bystanders. Once again Silver City was rocked to its foundations. The actions of Tri-Summit had caused a man's death, and everyone was grumbling about the new bank as they grieved over the death of the loyal adviser Zhao Pu'an. The Nine Ideals Hall patriarch, Li Naijing, did not respect his esteemed adviser's last wishes; he saw to it that Silver City witnessed yet another spectacular funeral. This one, though, had an added purpose: it was a show of force directed at Bai Ruide—an army burning with indignation cannot lose. The moral condemnation provoked by the adviser's death would surely snuff out Bai Ruide's arrogance. So during the course of the rites, Li Naijing, dressed in mourning, went looking for Bai Ruide at White Garden.

"A man dies but once, and any man unafraid of death cannot be intimidated," he said menacingly. "I wonder if our Mr. Bai is afraid of death."

In the summer of 1935, after careful deliberations and a series of secret moves, Bai Ruide had felt assured that Nine Ideals Hall itself would soon be his. But he had not anticipated the suicide of Zhao Pu'an, which created a completely unexpected obstacle. Everyone in Silver City's salt industry was incensed over what had happened; knowing how unwise it would be to provoke mass outrage, Bai Ruide once again drew in his claws, temporarily abandoning his original plan and authorizing an extension of the outstanding loan. Nine Ideals Hall put up the profitable Trans-ocean mine and the Open Road pipeline as collateral and agreed to pay 120,000 in silver annually for six years, until the loan was paid off, interest included. In the event of default, the two mortgaged properties would be forfeited to the bank. But in the end, no matter how angry the old salt merchants might have been, Bai Ruide had still managed to consolidate his position in Silver City.

The old adviser could not have predicted that his worn-out life would rescue Nine Ideals Hall and block Bai Ruide's plan to take it over. After the conflict over the outstanding debt was resolved with the help of local officials, the courts, and the salt merchants and mine owners, Li Naijing led the entire family to his adviser's funeral chamber, where they knelt before the coffin and wept openly. As he thought of Zhao Pu'an's loyalty, of the double loss of his loving wife and his closest friend, and of the long days ahead, empty and contentious, Li Naijing wailed piteously. No one, not the old adviser's wife and children nor the members of his own family, was spared the shock of witnessing the patriarch cry. Who could have imagined that Li Naijing, known for his cold exterior and fierce demeanor, would expose his innermost feelings with no regard for who witnessed the scene?

Once the mourning period had ended, Li Naijing settled his

old adviser's two sons into his own home and had his bookkeeper give the bereaved widow ten thousand in silver.

In the summer of 1935, virtually everyone in Silver City reflected on the trials and tribulations Nine Ideals Hall had withstood within a few short months, and no one was unmoved by the loyalty and devotion between employer and employee; they sighed over the cruelties of life and the fickle nature of fate.

CHAPTER EIGHT

1

On the last day of 1935, Li Naizhi, who was only one semester shy of receiving his diploma, was expelled from the provincial college. The expulsion notice, signed by the principal himself, was posted on a wall facing the main gate, under the watchful gaze of a sentry, one of a number of armed guards stationed around the campus. Ten days earlier, a massive protest had been broken up by bayonet-wielding soldiers, but Li Naizhi had once again proved to the party's underground organization his loyalty to the revolution, demonstrating exceptional organizational skills and unyielding courage in the anti-Japanese student movement sweeping the nation. Naizhi, who was already chairman of the provincial college students' association, was elected chairman of the united students' association of institutes of higher learning in the provincial capital. As chairman, he led the student-organized protest demonstration, gave street-corner speeches, passed out handbills, and called on all people to resist Japanese encroachments into northern China. Even now, years later, Li Naizhi's emotionally charged communiqués remain as proof of his ability to inspire awe in the name of justice: "We must pull together in this national crisis," began one public communiqué to the Central Agency in Nanjing, warning that eastern Hebei had declared autonomy and that Tianjin and Beijing, now known as Beiping, were threatened.

> China's very existence is at a crossroads. Students from all of Beiping's schools must heed this call to rise up for our nation's salvation. Anyone who harbors malicious designs on our territory or sovereignty, under whatever name, must be opposed. Our passion and our zeal can win over even the dead, the righteousness of our cause will spread throughout the land and bring justice to all our people. Our best defense is our determination: we will stir up the consciousness of all the people, until every one of our countrymen answers the call and pulls together in the name of survival. We must sacrifice to defend the motherland. I call upon the students from all of Beiping's schools to swear their support.

"Protect the patriotic movement!" he urged in another communiqué, this one addressed to the chairman of the Nationalist government in Nanjing.

> The nation is beset by difficulties, and the situation has grown desperate. Eastern Hebei has been betrayed; now the traitors have their eyes on Beiping and Tianjin. Heaven and earth will not tolerate their vicious deeds, though our ridiculous bureaucracies are corrupt from top to bottom. The students of Beiping must seek nothing less than national salvation. If justice and righteousness lead only to arrest, what legacy will we leave? We entreat the Beiping municipal authorities to release any students

they have detained and publicly support all legal patriotic activities, in the name of principle and order, and as a means of safeguarding national interests.

But the author of these emotionally charged manifestos had no sooner been summoned to the police station for interrogation than he spotted the announcement signed by the principal of the college and posted at the main gate. He sneered to show his contempt, then glared defiantly at the sentries—the enemy. Calmly and confidently, he went back to his dormitory room and packed his belongings. The indignant young student of seven years earlier had now become a veteran revolutionary. Following a recent clandestine meeting with Lao Ma, where he had learned that leaders of the provincial party underground were pleased with his activities in the struggle, he had been told that, because of the untenable local situation, he would be sent away from the provincial capital, first to undergo two months of training in underground operations, then to return to Silver City. There, under the protection of Nine Ideals Hall, he was to spread anti-Japanese propaganda, organize the salt workers, reconstitute the local underground, and serve as its secretary. Lao Ma had also informed him that the party had considered his report on Bai Qiuyun and had decided on a slow approach, insisting on further observation so as better to understand this daughter of a family known for class exploitation. Lao Ma reminded him that he was being tested, since unconditional obedience to the party is the first principle for a revolutionary.

On the last day of 1935, as Li Naizhi calmly and confidently forfeited his college diploma and returned to his dormitory room to pack his belongings, his heart was filled with revolutionary fervor and with contempt for a society cowed by the points of bayonets. He was convinced that the revolutionary enterprise for which he and his comrades were prepared to sacrifice their lives would eradicate China's moribund society and bring new hope and a bright future to his country. In the service of this grand ideal, he resolved to offer up not only his life but his love as well. After agonizing over his predicament, he had finally made up his mind to break off his association with Bai Qiuyun. In truth, he could not bear the thought of dragging her into danger, and he worried that she could not survive the hardships that were sure to follow.

And so, on the eve of his departure from the provincial capital, Li Naizhi invited Bai Qiuyun to lunch at Twin Wonders Garden, making a point of ordering the specialty called pearl-held prawns. He waited and waited, wondering why she hadn't shown up; finally, when the lunch hour was nearly over, Bai Qiuyun burst in, talking excitedly as she sat down.

"Naizhi, I got fifty students to sign a petition protesting your expulsion from school. I just came from handing it to the director. He nearly blew up, calling us lawless and threatening to expel all fifty of us. That's why I'm late, I was arguing with him."

This news made Li Naizhi, who was already feeling guilty enough, wonder how he would find the will to say what he needed to say. He held his tongue through lunch, then through tea, and still hadn't said anything by the time he walked Bai Qiuyun all the way home to Bamboo Garden on Cathedral Street.

"Qiuyun," he finally said, "I never gave you an answer to the letter you sent over the summer holiday."

Hard though it was, Li Naizhi looked straight into Bai Qiuyun's anxious eyes and forced himself to continue: "Qiuyun, I've given this a lot of thought, and I cannot accept your affection. Our relationship must end here."

Naizhi expected Qiuyun to burst into tears, to scream, to curse, but she surprised him by staring at him silently, as if she were looking at a stranger. The word "You . . ." was all she said before her face collapsed and her body slumped. On the last day of 1935, as Li Naizhi clumsily held Bai Qiuyun in his arms, one of the Bamboo Garden servants came running out to the gate, just steps ahead of Lady Yang, who grabbed Li Naizhi by the shirt and demanded:

"What have you done to Qiuyun? What did you say to her just now?"

Knowing he could never explain himself to such a woman, Li Naizhi stood there and let her scream at him, never taking his eyes off Bai Qiuyun. At that moment he felt that he had made a terrible mistake.

The ugly scene continued a while longer, until the servant slammed the cold, heavy iron gate shut; the thunderous metallic noise shook Li Naizhi from his stupor, and he looked up at the barrier that now separated him from Bai Qiuyun. At that moment he understood with exceptional clarity and intensity the differences between them: the two sides of that iron gate represented separate worlds, just as the two sides of Twin Arches represented separate worlds, one of which Li Naizhi had left for the other. Thoughts of the responsibility he carried made him ashamed of his momentary lapse of will. His resolve restored, he turned and walked away from the heavy iron gate, determined to put as much distance as possible between himself and the quiet elegance of Bamboo Garden.

2

Lu Fengwu was preparing to leave when the editor in chief of the newspaper came by to lecture him. "Fengwu, my friend, why is she the only girl you're willing to marry? Do you mean to tell me there isn't a single girl around who can compare to the Eighth Daughter of Nine Ideals Hall? The love stories of Liu Lanzhi and Zhu Yingtai are fairy tales, opera, not real life. The author of *Spring Waters Flow East* should know that better than anyone. Well, I suppose I can't stop you. The sooner you leave, the sooner you'll be back. Don't forget, we need your sequel for the literary supplement next week."

Lu Fengwu ignored his editor's advice, convinced that debating with a vulgarian was beneath him; his only response was a sardonic grin. Confident by nature, Lu Fengwu never once doubted himself or his affections. The idea that he might have fallen in love with the wrong person simply did not cross his mind; nor did it occur to him that she might not agree to marry him. He believed that all their temporary separations merely added to his storehouse of fond romantic memories. So when he'd copied Liu Yong's mournful sentiments onto the folding fan, what filled his heart was elation, not melancholy.

Lu Fengwu had no idea that several months earlier his editor had received a hand-delivered letter from Li Naijing, patriarch of Nine Ideals Hall, informing him that a matchmaker had brought Lu Fengwu's proposal of marriage to Eighth Sister and asking to be kept informed of Lu Fengwu's situation and activities. Consequently, Nine Ideals Hall was aware of Lu Fengwu's trip even before he set out, and a reception for the young suitor was already taking shape. Lu Fengwu, certain of his talents, never felt unworthy just because he came from humble origins, and he refused to entertain the idea that he was in any way inferior to the people of Nine Ideals Hall. He believed that the adage "In books there are castles of gold, in books there are jadelike countenances"—the credo of learned men since ancient times—would be further substantiated by his own experience. And so in December 1935, when he set out for Silver City, alone and very cocky, in addition to his brass press badge, a gold-plated fountain pen was clipped to the breast pocket of his tunic, a Parker pen for his beloved, purchased with the earnings from his writing. In December 1935, Lu Fengwu, bearing his gift, was carried into the cold wind on a sedan chair, invigorated by the brisk chill of the winter air as he rushed toward Silver City like spring waters. At a rest stop in Cockcrow Township, Li Naijing's envoy was waiting for him, and he was only too happy to switch to a warm and comfortable palanquin.

When Li Ziyun strolled into the God of War Temple with her cousin, Li Naijing, she knew only that Commander Yang had asked them there to discuss a very important matter. But after they had dispensed with the tea and finished their meal, Yang Chuxiong had still not brought up the important matter. Li Ziyun, whose thoughts were on Lu Fengwu and his imminent arrival, was beginning to fidget. She addressed Li Naijing.

"I thought Commander Yang had something important to say to us," she said.

Yang Chuxiong stood up, looking very uncomfortable. "Eighth Sister, in this crucial matter, everything depends on you."

"What kind of problem could a powerful military commander have in which everything depends on me?"

Li Naijing also stood up. "Eighth Sister, believe me, in this matter, everything does depend on you."

All of a sudden Li Ziyun felt cold, as if the chill air on that December day were wrapping itself tightly around her. When she finally learned what the two men had in mind for her, she cried out:

"You're asking me to give up Fengwu to be a concubine? You think it's appropriate to ask a high school principal to become somebody's concubine? What have you done to Fengwu? I demand to see him."

"Eighth Sister," Li Naijing said soothingly, "don't get so upset. I've already sent someone to Cockcrow Township to bring Fengwu here. You have my word that nothing will happen to him. Eighth Sister, if you really care for him, then you should try to understand that I'm going to all this trouble for you."

Li Ziyun would have none of that, and the silence of the room was broken only by the sound of her crying. After a while, once she had cried herself out, Yang Chuxiong said with an angry edge to his voice:

"Eighth Sister, in a lifetime of soldiering, I've killed at least a thousand men, so one more, in the person of Lu Fengwu, would make little difference. The only reason I've stayed my hand is you. If you agree to marry me, I will give you anything you desire. If being a concubine is what bothers you, then you can be my formal wife. I'll send those other two crones back to their families. I find it hard to believe that a military commander is less impressive than some poor pen-wielding pedant. I think I deserve a little respect. This is the first time in my life I've ever asked anyone for anything."

That night a smallish sedan chair carried Third Concubine, who had only recently been elevated to the position of Li Naijing's formal wife, from Nine Ideals Hall to Commander Yang's headquarters. Third Concubine and Li Ziyun stayed in the same suite; Third Concubine sat up with Li Ziyun shedding a woman's tears, lamenting her own cruel fate, having suffered through all those years in the role of concubine. She envied Ziyun with all her heart. "Eighth Sister, you will come into the household as formal wife," she said, "and you will never have to suffer the others' dirty looks. Who could have imagined Commander Yang losing his heart like this? If this marriage takes place," she continued, "you will have rescued Nine Ideals Hall, an entire household of people. You will be a woman who has rendered outstanding service. From now on, Bai Ruide's Prosperity Company will be no match for us, no matter how mighty it grows. Eighth Sister," she said, "you must accept this match in order to rescue the family, and you will, I know, for you are not the type to sit idly by and watch others fall to ruin." Third Concubine's monologue ended in a torrent of tears, and Ziyun could not be sure which of them felt greater melancholy.

Early the next morning, Lu Fengwu, eager to see Li Ziyun, was ferried across Silver Creek and went straight to Twin Arches, where he was ushered in to meet with Li Naijing. The pleasantries were quickly dispensed with, and talk turned to the issue at hand. When Lu Fengwu asked why Li Ziyun was not there to greet him, Li Naijing asked Lu Fengwu to hear him out, since that was, after all, the reason he had sent an envoy to Cockcrow Township. Lu Fengwu demanded to know where Ziyun was. Li Naijing told him he'd know everything in a few minutes if he would just be patient, but Lu Fengwu said he couldn't wait a few minutes. Someone was coming right over, Li Naijing explained, and then he'd know everything. The words were barely out when a servant entered and informed them that Adjutant Chen had arrived with Commander Yang's betrothal gifts. A moment later, Adjutant Chen, flanked by soldiers in dress uniform, stood in the guest hall. Ordering his men to open the elaborately wrapped boxes and jeweled crates, Adjutant Chen unfurled a red scroll, the list of gifts, which he read aloud. As Li Naijing surveyed the roomful of treasures—the jewels, brocades, silks, and satins—he asked Adjutant Chen if Eighth Sister had asked to see anyone. No, replied the adjutant, at the moment she was celebrating with Commander Yang at his headquarters. Li Naijing turned to the confident suitor Fengwu. "Didn't Eighth Sister tell you of her intentions?" he asked. Lu Fengwu was overcome by rage and humiliation. Regaining his composure with great effort, he managed a weak smile and asked Li Naijing to deliver his congratulations to Eighth Sister on her forthcoming nuptials and his wishes for a lifetime of wealth and happiness. With that he turned and walked away, trailed by Li Naijing's courteous protests: "You needn't rush off like that, Fengwu. Since you've come this far, why not let me put you up a few days, then lend you my warm sedan chair for the trip home? If you leave like this, Eighth Sister will be upset with me for not treating you better." Lu Fengwu did not, could not, turn his head, for at that moment, hot tears were streaming down his cheeks; having lost everything else, he could not then turn around and lose face as well.

Lu Fengwu emerged onto the street, as if dazed. Suddenly he

heard someone call out to him: Do you need that engraved, sir? He stopped and noticed an engraver's pushcart. The craftsman was pointing at the gift Fengwu had planned to give his beloved. Smiling sadly, Fengwu removed the gold-plated fountain pen from his breast pocket. Then he slowly recited a famous line of poetry to the craftsman, who carefully engraved it on the barrel of the pen:

> *The east wind is cruel, happiness is ephemeral. A bosom of tangled silk, many years of separation. Wrong. Wrong. Wrong.*

As the artisan engraved the characters, he congratulated Lu Fengwu on his good taste, and Fengwu could only smile as he recalled the inscription he had written on the folding fan when he and Li Ziyun had said farewell. When, he wondered, had the true somehow become false, an unchangeable reality, cold and ruthless? The lofty tower of the God of War Temple stood nearby in plain view, and from it emerged the joyful strains of pipes and drums and raised voices at the celebratory party. Lu Fengwu felt his heart breaking. All alone, far from home, at this moment of sorrow and lost hope, he was comforted only by the lines of a poet who had lived nearly eight hundred years ago. Pen in hand, Lu Fengwu retraced his steps to Twin Arches and sought out Sixth Sister, Li Zihen. Handing her the pen, he said it belonged to Eighth Sister and asked her to return it for him. Then he walked to the bank of Silver Creek, where a ferry boat was tied up at the nearly deserted, silent pier, the ferryman the only person in sight. On that winter day, the water in Silver Creek was the soft green of fine jade, and after Lu Fengwu had been poled out midway, his heart felt as empty as the deserted river valley and as cold as the water flowing silently under his feet, and he was reminded of another line of poetry: "Hoist my skirt and slip off my silk stockings / Stand up and walk to the clear pond." A lovely, sorrowful girl filled his thoughts. The bleak strains of a dirge drifted over from the base of a nearby derrick. Lu Fengwu stared blankly at the lovely, sorrowful girl in the soft green water and, without a sound or trace of emotion, walked toward her. . . .

The moment the panic-stricken ferryman noticed that his passenger was gone, he shouted for help, but Lu Fengwu had long since stopped breathing by the time he was brought to the surface. None of the curious onlookers knew who this water-soaked, ice-cold man was, nor had they any idea how he could have been so heedless as to fall into the river. The ferryman, fearful of being held accountable for the death, loudly protested his innocence to all who would listen: Don't blame me, I was ferrying the gentleman across when he just disappeared, some water sprite must have dragged him off the boat. . . .

When Li Naijing came running up to the God of War Temple to report the news, Yang Chuxiong bellowed ecstatically:

"Who can be sure it wasn't ordained by heaven? What can Eighth Sister say now? Let's go tell her!"

"Chuxiong, we mustn't be hasty. We don't want Eighth Sister to think we meant for this to happen. That would ruin everything."

"What should we do, then?"

"She must feel the pain of the curing needle. Let her go look at the corpse and listen to the ferryman plead his case. We'll ruin it if we say a word."

Li Ziyun wept as if she might die; never could she have imagined that in the course of a single night she would both save her beloved and lose him. The ferryman was so badly shaken he fell to his knees and begged Eighth Sister not to blame him, but she was too caught up in lamenting Fengwu and blaming herself for his death to notice. Li Naijing told his people to pull her away and take her home, then sent someone to buy a coffin, in which the body of Lu Fengwu was placed and returned to the provincial capital. A week later, where the latest episode of *Spring Wa-*

ters Flow East should have appeared, the *Jinjiang News* ran the following announcement from the editor in chief:

> On behalf of the employees of this newspaper I am saddened to report that Mr. Lu Fengwu, author of *Spring Waters Flow East,* drowned in Silver City while on a visit to a friend, leaving his novel unfinished. We have lost a respected colleague, and you readers have lost a good friend. Our heartfelt sentiments . . .

3

When Li Zihen accepted the gold-plated pen on her sister's behalf, she sensed that something was very much amiss. Sure enough, within a few hours, she learned that Lu Fengwu had fallen into the river and drowned, news that threw her heart into turmoil. When Winterset came in with a load of water, he found Li Zihen in her room, a tear-soaked handkerchief in her hand. He asked what was wrong.

"Mr. Lu has just drowned in the river," she said.

"Which Mr. Lu?"

"The one who came looking for Eighth Sister."

Winterset shook his head. "How could that be? I saw him walking out the gate when I was fetching water."

But Li Zihen, no longer interested in conversation, left the house. Flustered, Winterset laid down his water buckets and quickly followed her. When they elbowed their way through the crowd of curiosity seekers, they saw Lu Fengwu's water-soaked body lying on the cold stone steps of the pier, his hair matted, his ashen face streaked with mud, his black lips slightly parted to reveal blindingly white teeth. Just like that, a living, breathing man lay dead on the stone steps. Overcome by sadness, Li Zihen knelt and wiped the mud from the young man's face with her handkerchief, while Winterset, standing behind her, mumbled over and over, "I watched him walk out the gate just a while ago, so how could he be drowned." The crowd of curiosity seekers swelled as people learned that the dead man had come to visit Nine Ideals Hall. The ferryman went on repeating his defense to all who would listen: "Don't blame me . . . I don't know which water sprite dragged him into the water." Li Zihen, unable to bear the sight of poor Lu Fengwu exposed to the circle of greedy eyes, covered his face with her handkerchief, and as she did, her glance lit upon the pair of mandarin ducks she had embroidered on the handkerchief, two ducks paddling toward a lotus flower floating on a rippled surface.

"How could you two have been so foolish . . ." she wailed.

On that December day, Silver Creek flowed with cold indifference below the stone steps, feeling no remorse for having drowned a heartbreaking story or for having swallowed up a youthful, confident soul.

Not until Lu Fengwu's body had been taken away did Li Zihen return home and hand the gold-plated fountain pen to Li Ziyun, who handed it back with cold indifference.

"Elder Sister," she said, "I don't want ever to see this again and I don't want to talk about what has happened."

"Little Sister, this relationship between you and Commander Yang—what are you thinking?"

"Nothing, that's their business."

"You realize, don't you, that Commander Yang is twenty years older than you?"

"He could be fifty years older, for all I care. I'll marry him and that will take care of everything."

"Little Sister," Li Zihen sobbed, "I stayed home all these years so you could get an education, I did it all for you . . ."

Li Ziyun laughed. "You're such a fool. Is Commander Yang the most important man in Silver City or isn't he? By marrying him, don't I ensure that we three and Nine Ideals Hall will have all the backing we'll ever need? Yang Chuxiong will carry us to heights other people only dream of. What's wrong with that?"

"Don't be angry with me, Little Sister, I know how unhappy you are deep down."

"I'm not unhappy, I just don't feel like thinking or struggling anymore. I feel nothing. There's only this one life to get through, and death awaits us all at the end."

Li Zihen's wails grew louder. "Little Sister, Little Sister, I've lived a pure Buddhist life. And for what? So you can live a meaningless existence? Is that all this life of mine is worth?"

Moved by her sister's plea, Li Ziyun, too, began to sob. She took the gold-plated fountain pen to read the inscription, then sobbed some more. "Wrong, wrong, all wrong, the wrong incarnation, born to the wrong family, I shouldn't have come into the world at this time to meet him . . ."

Li Zihen took her younger sister in her arms. "Go ahead and cry, Little Sister, you'll feel better if you cry."

The sisters were startled by Winterset, who suddenly appeared at the door with his buckets of water. Instead of the coarse, simply dressed man they were used to seeing, he now stood there neatly dressed in a high-collared tunic and matching trousers.

"Winterset, where did you get those?" Li Zihen demanded.

"They belonged to Mr. Lu," he answered, guileless as always. "When they dressed him in burial clothes, no one wanted these wet things, so I took them. It would have been a shame to throw them away."

Crying and shouting at once, Li Zihen demanded, "Winterset, you cursed idiot, don't you know anything? What made you think you could wear Mr. Lu's clothes? You'll be the death of Eighth Sister! Take them off this minute!"

His face scarlet with shame, Winterset begged forgiveness.

"Please don't be angry, Eighth Sister, it's all my fault. I don't know anything, I didn't know I shouldn't wear Mr. Lu's clothes, I didn't know you'd be angry, I didn't want to see them thrown away, see how new they are. Everybody said it's unlucky to wear a dead person's clothes, but I said I wasn't frightened, and besides, Mr. Lu wasn't just anybody, he was a good man."

Winterset rambled on and on until he saw the tears running down Li Ziyun's cheeks. Then he fell silent. It was a bad thing he had done, and he didn't know how to put things right. Li Ziyun came to his rescue when she saw how terror-stricken he was.

"Winterset," she said consolingly, "don't be afraid, I don't blame you for anything. Just don't wear the clothes anymore and everything will be fine."

That afternoon, Li Zihen and Li Ziyun went with Winterset to the path leading up to the monastery at White Cloud Mountain, where they found a secluded corner and buried Lu Fengwu's clothes beneath a pine tree. Then they watched Winterset cover the spot with stones, making a tidy mound atop the buried clothing. In that brief moment, Li Ziyun sensed that her past and her future were buried in the cold earth under Winterset's mound of stones; she felt the cold stones pressing down on her and sighed deeply. Lifting her eyes to the heavens, she saw a cloud so filmy it was barely visible against the blue sky, so vast and so deep. She said to Li Zihen, as if talking to herself:

"Elder Sister, I didn't understand before and I didn't believe. But now I do."

Her sister's words expressed exactly the feeling in Li Zihen's heart. The sisters stood beside the new grave for a long while, saying nothing, the silence broken only by the cold wind whispering to the trees as it rushed past the two of them and the cold grave.

Li Ziyun fell gravely ill, but when she had been nursed back to health, she formally accepted Yang Chuxiong's proposal, with one condition: she wanted a bridge erected over the site where Lu Fengwu had drowned and a promise that she could cut the ribbon at the opening ceremony. Yang responded with a hearty laugh. "Eighth Sister, by not demanding that I fetch stars from the sky or hold up the moon, you have made me a very happy man!" A single command brought workmen from several counties converging on the spot to hammer and pound and hew and carve, day and night. Two months later, a bridge with stone pillars cleaved the creek into three streams downriver from Fish Listening Pond. Commander Yang then ordered the workers to erect ceremonial arches on each bridgehead and commissioned a five-foot-high engraved stone tablet at one end. The words etched into the tablet were in his own calligraphy: Ziyun Bridge. The dedication of the bridge was, of course, a major event in Silver City. Following a thunderous burst of fireworks, Li Ziyun, protected from the wind by a marten cape, gently cut the red satin ribbon, then, in full view of the onlookers, headed out to the middle of the bridge. The murmuring of the crowd grew louder as she walked to the railing, removed the fur cape from around her shoulders, and let it fall. Stretching out its wings, it floated gracefully to the tranquil green water below and sank serenely to the river bottom. To herself, Li Ziyun said softly:

"Don't hate me, dear Fengwu."

Three days after Li Ziyun dedicated the bridge, Yang Chuxiong threw a wedding of unprecedented lavishness; like the funeral for Lady Wang, wife of the patriarch of Nine Ideals Hall, it would be talked about in Silver City for years to come. As throngs of Silver City residents streamed across Ziyun Bridge, trampling underfoot the tragic tale of love and death, they were filled with awe and envy over the events that had led to this marriage between two great and envied families.

CHAPTER NINE

1

After the collapse of the 1927 Silver City insurrection, the provincial Communist Party organization was in shambles, its leaders slaughtered, its followers cowed; a reign of terror sent the revolution plummeting to its nadir," Silver City's party committee recorded in its official history of party activities. "But in February 1936, in accordance with directives from the provincial committee," it continued, "Comrade Li Naizhi returned to Silver City to assume the position of underground party secretary." Comrade Li Naizhi rebuilt the underground organization, set up a night school for salt miners, and formed an anti-Japanese patriotic choral troupe. Inasmuch as the miners had for centuries formed guilds among themselves, Comrade Li Naizhi saw fit to join the largest established guild, the Fire God Guild, rather than attempt to form a labor union on his own. By throwing in his lot with the workers—leaving behind forever his aristocratic origins—and looking after their interests, he gained their trust and was able to organize and launch the biggest salt miners' strike in Silver City's history. Although the strikers' enemies did everything possible to obstruct and intimidate them in their quest for better wages and shorter work hours, ultimately the strike was successful. Party funds were severely limited, but Comrade Li Naizhi organized the transportation and sale of his share of table salt and the distribution of tobacco, in accordance with provincial committee directives. These initiatives generated enough income not only to solve the party's financial problems but to enable the provincial committee to establish an underground printing operation and purchase weapons—all in all, a substantial contribution.

Particularly worthy of note is the fact that Comrade Li Naizhi, following provincial committee directives, joined Silver City's Elder Brothers Society. Elected one of the three chieftains of the patriotic Robed Brotherhood of Propriety and Virtue, he was thereby able not only to conceal his Communist activities but also to raise a good deal more money through his illustrious connections.

During this period, however, the reactionary Nationalist regime, the Guomindang, carried out extreme anti-Communist repression in which the Silver City underground organization suffered crippling losses. Using the cover of resistance to Japan and wielding the dictatorial fascist slogan of "One Party, One Doctrine, One Government, One Army," the reactionary Guomindang secretly implemented a policy to "oppose Communism, restrict Communism" and wantonly butchered Communist Party members in the course of two brutal "anti-Communist waves." First, they routed the Communist Eighth Route Army; then, in a move that shocked China and the rest of the world, they massacred the Communist New Fourth Army in the "southern Anhui incident." In 1939, troops of the Silver City garrison commander, Yang Chuxiong, surrounded salt miners who were celebrating the victorious conclusion of their strike and opened fire, killing fifteen workers and injuring forty-nine. Acting on information supplied by traitors, enemy forces arrested another fifteen members of the Communist Party, including the municipal secretary, Li Naizhi. Ultimately, on secret orders received from Chiang Kai-shek's headquarters, fourteen of the comrades were executed in Silver City's prison on the fifth of December. Li Naizhi, who was related by marriage to Yang Chuxiong, managed to escape with the help of his sister, Li Zihen (at the time, she, too, was a member of the Silver City underground), and, thanks to his eminence in the Robed Brotherhood of Propriety and Virtue, was spirited away. After his escape, Li Naizhi, with the sympathetic help of the brotherhood, managed to relocate some of his Communist comrades and so preserve the party's revolutionary force and leave behind some seeds of revolution in Silver City.

The fourteen comrades executed in the fifth of December massacre were: Chen Juesan, organization department director; Wu Nianci, head of propaganda; Luo Bin, secretary of the Workers Committee; Qiao Guoliang, secretary of the Western Henan branch; Yang Wenda, branch secretary of the Salt Bureau; Wu Dajiang, secretary of the Transocean mine branch; Lin Jianyi, secretary of the salt processors' branch; Deng San, secretary of the water workers' branch; and Yang Wenwu, Liu Yongtai, Huang Shuangfa, Zeng Yongdi, Wang Jinfu, and Li Dahan, all rank-and-file members of the party.

2

In the eyes of Yu Zhandong, leading chieftain of the Silver City Brotherhood of Propriety and Virtue, also known as Master Dragon Head, the years between 1936 and 1939 were the most gratifying and enjoyable period of his life. Until his dying day he believed that accepting Ninth Brother Li of Nine Ideals Hall into the brotherhood and choosing him to sit in the second chair as sage was a turning point in the history of the organization, his cleverest move ever. Even though he nearly lost his head because of Li Naizhi, whenever Naizhi's name was mentioned, Yu Zhandong gave a big thumbs-up. "Ninth Brother Li, what can you say except he's got guts?" That was always followed by a regretful sigh. "Too bad he became a Communist." But then he'd soften his tone. "In the end, what's the difference? Back around the turn of the century, when our robed brothers fought the Manchu overlords, there was a price on their heads for the same activities the Communists are accused of."

Silver City's Robed Brotherhood was divided into three halls: Benevolence, Righteousness, and Propriety. Benevolence Hall was called the Brotherhood of Obedience and Charity, Righteousness Hall was called the Brotherhood of Filial Devotion, and Propriety Hall was called the Brotherhood of Propriety and Virtue. In its earliest days, the brotherhood was a secret society dedicated to overthrowing the Manchu dynasty. In the wake of the Republican Revolution of 1911, which ended with the fall of the last Manchu emperor, the brotherhood emerged into the open. It quickly fragmented into a dizzying array of splinter groups, which in turn led to the formation of independent orders, each with its own motto. The Benevolence banner read, Gentry and Farmers; the Righteousness banner, Commerce and Trading; the Propriety banner, Rob and Plunder. Yu Zhandong's Brotherhood of Propriety and Virtue claimed fifty cells with a total membership of twenty thousand, but most of its members belonged to society's underclass: clearwater guests, porters, waiters, cooks, peddlers, and the like. And so the Propriety and Virtue Brotherhood was viewed with disdain by the Benevolence and Righteousness Halls as a motley conglomeration of domestics and common laborers, all beneath contempt. Every day, Yu Zhandong was surrounded by underlings who flattered him with Elder Brother this and Elder Brother that, yet the fires of resentment burned within him. What bothered him most were the factional struggles within his own brotherhood and the open defiance of several of his lieutenants, apparently coveting his place as leader. All this internal fighting had lowered Propriety Hall's status even further in the eyes of the other brotherhoods. Yu Zhandong had just about had enough when Ninth Brother Li of Nine Ideals Hall appeared on the scene.

On the third day of the third lunar month, 1936, Yu Zhandong called a special brotherhood meeting at Gathering of Worthies Teahouse (so it continued by many to be called) to welcome an honored guest. On the invitations he warned the members: "Our guest is from the brotherhood in the provincial capital, so we must be on our best behavior and follow the rules of decorum. We mustn't give our guest the impression that we are a bunch of nobodies who have no concept of dignity." What luminary were they coming to meet? the robed brothers wondered. Yu Zhandong kept them in suspense, saying only, "You'll know him when you see him."

On the morning of the special meeting, Yu Zhandong and his lieutenants filed into a second-floor private room in Gathering of Worthies Teahouse and sat in two rows facing each other as etiquette demanded. The moment the guest of honor made his appearance, everyone recognized him as Ninth Brother Li of Nine Ideals Hall, and while they knew that he was a student in the provincial capital, they were amazed to learn that he had joined the capital's robed brotherhood. Once all the members had saluted their guest, the protocol officer made the introductions in accordance with established procedure.

"In the seat of honor, Elder Brother Yu Zhandong, known in the brotherhood as Master Dragon Head."

Yu Zhandong clasped his hands together and announced, "I am unworthy to be placed at the head."

All the members chimed in with "Congratulations and great wealth."

"In the seat next to him, Elder Brother Wang Zhenfa, known in the brotherhood as Oceans of Gold and Grain."

But before Oceans of Gold and Grain had a chance to say, "I am unworthy to be placed in such an exalted position," Li Naizhi laughed. "Elder Brother Yu," he said, "we're all from around here and I see no need to go on." The others laughed along with Li Naizhi. Then he announced, "Benevolence Hall and Righteousness Hall both have private teahouses. Only the Brotherhood of Propriety and Virtue has no meeting place of its own. I have recently spoken with my elder cousin, who has agreed to lend us East Wind Pavilion for brotherhood meetings. Nine Ideals Hall can reclaim it when the brotherhood has a teahouse of its own. Please accept this as a first-meeting gift. I have been studying in the provincial capital for many years but have returned to the branch in Silver City to benefit from the advice and counsel of you gentlemen." Everyone warmed immediately to Li Naizhi, who seemed in all respects to be a frank, straightforward man of action.

Taking advantage of the general good spirits, Yu Zhandong announced:

"Ninth Brother Li of Nine Ideals Hall has honored us by joining the Brotherhood of Propriety and Virtue. Never in the history of the brotherhood has anyone of such standing, a student of the provincial college, honored us with his membership. I ask you all, what should his rank in the brotherhood be if we are not to disgrace him?"

The men responded unanimously: "Whatever you think is fitting."

"Ninth Brother," Yu Zhandong asked, "would you consider it beneath you to serve as sage in the Brotherhood of Propriety and Virtue?"

"I cannot accept such an honor," Li Naizhi protested with a wave of his hand, "I cannot."

"Don't turn us down, Ninth Brother," the others pleaded. "Don't deny us the prestige your acceptance will bring."

Hands clasped humbly in front of him, Li Naizhi acquiesced: "Then I shall accept the honor of second in command."

"Congratulations and great wealth!" roared the robed brothers, unaware that they were accepting a Communist into their ranks.

After Li Naizhi had taken his place as sage, someone lodged a private complaint with Yu Zhandong: "Elder Brother, how can we give Ninth Brother Li the position of second in command on the very same day that he enters the brotherhood?"

"What the hell do you know?" Yu Zhandong thundered. "If any of you can think of a better way to raise our stock than fraternizing with Nine Ideals Hall, I'll give you the title of Master Dragon Head."

Events proved the wisdom of Yu Zhandong's decision. For one thing, as soon as word was out that Ninth Brother Li had thrown in his lot with the Brotherhood of Propriety and Virtue, the ambitious lieutenants who had coveted Yu Zhandong's position backed off. For another, the Nine Ideals Hall workers, from salt roasters to treadmill operators and porters, who belonged to a Propriety cell of the Robed Brotherhood, all gladly followed Li Naizhi, who had always been good to them. Before long, Li Naizhi had a supply of salt from Nine Ideals Hall mines delivered to Yu Zhandong for open sale. But before the salt arrived, Yu Zhandong sent brotherhood representatives to establish good relations with all the dockworkers. The protection of these robed brothers guaranteed a flourishing business, and within six months the Brotherhood of Propriety and Virtue had accumulated enough money to build its own teahouse, which it called Propriety and Virtue Tower. The grand opening was a festive occasion with many guests.

Now that Yu Zhandong was secure in his position as Master Dragon Head and the brotherhood was prospering, someone came to ask him, "Elder Brother, aren't you worried that Ninth Brother Li won't be satisfied with being second in command?"

Yu Zhandong chuckled. "All you're good for is stuffing rice into! Can't you see that Ninth Brother Li is merely using our monastery to turn himself into a Buddha? Where is he going to find time to worry about anything so insignificant as the Master Dragon Head?"

By then Li Naizhi had set up a night school for workers at the Fire God Temple and founded his anti-Japanese patriotic choral troupe, both of which quickly became well-known organizations in Silver City. On one occasion Yu Zhandong told Li Naizhi:

"Ninth Brother, if you must keep at these kinds of activities, make sure you have an escape route."

Li Naizhi responded with a shrug, then turned the subject to how to make money from selling cigarettes.

On the seventh day of the tenth lunar month, 1939, Yu Zhandong witnessed the passage of Commander Yang's heavily armed troops through town and felt certain that Li Naizhi would be caught in the dragnet. As he feared, within a couple of hours men came running from the salt mines to tell him that there were several loads of Li Naizhi's salt on the pier that Ninth Brother had asked them to deliver. Yu Zhandong knew what they were telling him. "Has Ninth Brother been caught?" Yu Zhandong asked. The men nodded. Without another word, Yu Zhandong summoned one of his people to go with the messengers to the pier. Just before they set out, he told them, "After you deliver the salt, keep the money for your troubles." Surprise showed on the faces of the workers, but before they could thank Yu, he waved them away, saying, "That's enough. I'm not doing this for you. I wouldn't be doing this if it weren't for Ninth Brother."

Imagine Yu Zhandong's surprise when he himself was trundled, arms bound behind him in the classic "five-flower" position, into Yang Chuxiong's headquarters that very night. Commander Yang, who rarely received callers, was seated at the head of the main hall. Without giving Yang a chance to speak, Yu asked:

"Commander Yang, why have you arrested me and brought me here?"

"Because you are a Communist."

Yu Zhandong, unruffled, refuted the accusation: "Yu Zhandong is too principled a man to straddle two camps. As long as I am a robed brother, I cannot be a Communist!"

"Take this hoodlum outside," Yang Chuxiong exploded, "and give him twenty lashes! We'll see what that does to all his tough talk."

As he was being dragged out by Yang's soldiers, Yu Zhandong shouted, "Commander Yang, I know you are flushing out Communists to make a name for yourself, but you've got the wrong man. My Brotherhood of Propriety and Virtue has over twenty thousand members and I advise you not to tangle with us."

Yang Chuxiong's anger scorched the heavens: "Make that forty lashes!" he thundered.

Forty lashes later, a raspy-voiced Yu Zhandong was dragged back into the main hall, where he saw Li Naizhi standing in shackles.

"Ninth Brother, is he a Communist?" Yang Chuxiong asked.

"What is it you want me to say?" Li Naizhi asked with a grim laugh. "That he is or that he isn't?"

"Ninth Brother, don't be difficult. You must give me someone, so I can ask my superiors to spare you. Don't force me into a corner."

"If Elder Brother Yu is a Communist, then you should go out and round up the twenty thousand members of the Brotherhood of Propriety and Virtue as Communists as well."

"Commander Yang," Yu Zhandong spoke up, "did you hear that? Do you not even believe your own brother-in-law?"

Li Naizhi turned around. "Elder Brother Yu, I beg your forgiveness for getting you involved in something you had nothing to do with."

Hot tears slid down Yu Zhandong's cheeks. "Ninth Brother Li, please don't talk about forgiveness. We are sworn brothers, and I will always stand by you!"

His arrest and beating took a physical toll on Yu Zhandong, but it brought him a bit of added glory: he became known as a man of iron who had withstood forty lashes. But he knew that a simple nod of the head by Li Naizhi that day would have sent him, Yu Zhandong, to meet Yama, the king of hell. His admiration for Li Naizhi knew no bounds, and his pride at being the man's sworn brother was deep and abiding.

Yu Zhandong never forgot the calm look on Li Naizhi's face as the young man stood shackled in the middle of the hall. "If every Communist is like Li Naizhi," he said, "sooner or later the world will belong to them!"

Yet one thing puzzled Yu Zhandong. Why had Ninth Brother Li, the scion of Nine Ideals Hall, turned to Communism? Wasn't that biting the hand that feeds you? Did he think that Nine Ideals Hall had too much money? If someone was going to communize the world, shouldn't it be the poor members of the Brotherhood of Propriety and Virtue? They should be the ones to take from those dog-fucking rich people and spread it around for everyone to enjoy!

3

During that period, from 1936 to 1939, Li Zihen made one of the most dramatic decisions of her life, a decision that lent those three years of Silver City history a legendary quality. People from Silver City never recall those times without thinking of that amazing woman.

Li Zihen sensed that her brother was flirting with danger, and on a steamy summer night in 1936, her suspicions were confirmed. After her brother's return to Silver City from the provincial capital, Nine Ideals Hall was often visited by mysterious strangers who spent the night sitting around a mahjong table talking about things she could not comprehend. Living a chaste life of abstinence and Buddhist devotion, Li Zihen knew little beyond her needlework. She had no idea that her brother was the party secretary of Silver City's Communist underground and the author of all those inflammatory communiqués to the newspapers in the capital. That steamy night she woke up drenched in sweat and noticed a light coming from her brother's room. Tiptoeing to his door, she was shocked to see him leading a worker in swearing allegiance to a red flag. She recognized Wu Dajiang, a worker at the Transocean mine. Though they spoke in hushed voices she could hear what the two men were saying:

". . . will remain loyal to party causes, safeguard party secrets, and die before I betray the organization or my comrades. I will struggle for the Communist cause every day of my life . . ."

Having completed the oath ceremony, the two men turned and looked straight into the ashen face of the woman standing just beyond the raised curtain.

"Couldn't you sleep, Big Sister?" was all the startled Li Naizhi could say.

Li Zihen, cold fear gripping her heart, her face drained of blood, just nodded. "I saw everything."

Li Naizhi and Wu Dajiang exchanged glances, then Naizhi quickly saw his guest out. He rushed back to his room, where the kerosene lantern added to the stifling heat. In her terrible confusion, Li Zihen didn't know what to say. Scenes of Silver City's insurrection and the terrible carnage of 1927 played before her eyes.

"Little Brother, they chop off the heads of rebels."

"I know that."

"And you're still determined?"

"Yes."

"Little Brother, there's a world of opportunity waiting for you. I can't believe that I have more sense than a person with a real education."

"Big Sister, it was that education that spurred me to make revolution."

"I know nothing about revolution. Can't you find a cause that will leave your head intact? I burned my face for that education of yours. Was it all just so you could end as a forgotten martyr? What will I have to live for if your head is hanging from the city wall? Won't you have some pity for your own sister . . . ?"

Li Naizhi may have had a storehouse of arguments capable of convincing legions to stand with him beneath the red flag of revolution, but no logic in the world could convince this woman that his choice was the right one. The last thing the party secretary of the Silver City Communist underground expected, therefore, was that a decision that had taken shape over seven years of schooling, seven years of careful reflection, was one that his sister could make in a single night. But the next morning at the breakfast table, Li Zihen announced: "Little Brother, I am going to make revolution too. If that means dying, then we shall die together!"

Li Naizhi laid down his chopsticks. "Sister, you'll have to let me think about that."

"What's there to think about? Death doesn't frighten me."

"Sister—"

"Don't waste your breath, I've made up my mind to follow you." Li Zihen's face was washed by a flood of tears. "Ziyun has made her life with Commander Yang, you're out making revolution, what am I supposed to do here at home all alone? Ziyun was right, after all, when she said there's only this one life to get through, and death awaits us all at the end."

And so, on that sweltering summer day, Li Zihen made the one and only political decision of her life, transforming herself from an unworldly devotee of Buddhism to a fearless member of the Communist underground. From that day forward, she became the most trustworthy messenger for Silver City's party secretary. Over the years she passed on information, stored seditious documents, and, of course, did the laundry and cooking for Li Naizhi and his comrades. To protect his sister's cover, Li Naizhi permitted her to keep her religious vows, for which she was especially grateful, as this spared her the agony of having to choose between her faith and her brother. And so things remained until the day Li Naizhi was bound in the five-flower position and dragged off to the cells of the condemned.

In truth, the victory in the salt miners' strike played right into the hands of their enemies. As Li Naizhi's responsibilities in Silver City expanded, the provincial committee sent him a deputy. No sooner had this man learned the ins and outs of the operation than he ran to Commander Yang with the information. Astute and patient as always, Yang Chuxiong stayed his hand for the moment, telling the deputy secretary to carry on as before.

The moment for action arrived as Li Naizhi and his comrades met at Fire God Temple to celebrate their victory in the strike. As heavily armed troops surrounded them, the deputy secretary stepped forward and pointed out each and every party member to the soldiers. Yang Chuxiong had received orders from Chiang Kai-shek's headquarters to interrogate all suspects, then execute them summarily; thus, in the winter of 1939, the 1927 Silver City massacre was reenacted. Overnight, in one swift, violent rash of arrests, the underground operation Li Naizhi had labored to rebuild fell apart.

On that winter afternoon of 1939, as troops marched through the city, Li Zihen knew that the catastrophe she had dreaded for so long was about to occur. With horror she watched the cold glint of bayonets passing against the blood-red setting sun.

• • •

Bright red lanterns were raised high atop the flagpole outside Fire God Temple, where the salt miners were celebrating their greatest victory, oblivious to the impregnable wall of advancing bayonets. Without a second thought, Li Zihen fell in behind the troops, but she was stopped in her tracks by a military guard. There she stood and watched as two columns of soldiers moved toward her herding a line of individuals whose arms were bound in the five-flower position, and right in front she saw her own brother. A gawker just beyond the military cordon shouted:

"Look! Look there! Ninth Brother Li from Nine Ideals Hall has been arrested!"

Li Zihen tried but failed to push her way forward. Trapped in the middle of the crowd, she forgot that she, too, was at risk—only one thought filled her head: she must, at all costs, rescue her brother from the jaws of the lion. That thought enabled her to cast aside her terror and walk to Yang Chuxiong's heavily fortified, menacing headquarters. There she sought out the private quarters of Commander Yang's wife, where she said to her sister:

"Commander Yang cannot take my sister *and* kill my brother!"

"What do you expect me to do, sister?" Li Ziyun asked.

With studied composure, Li Zihen took her month-old nephew from her sister and said, "This boy is the lifeblood of the Yang family. Our brother is the lifeblood of the Li family." Li Ziyun understood her sister's threat.

Later that day, when Commander Yang Chuxiong returned home after mapping out his next moves, he was caught by surprise.

"What do you want from me?" he asked the two sisters. "I can't just let him go, or I'll wind up under lock and key myself."

"Do whatever you have to," Li Zihen said fiercely. "All we want is Ninth Brother returned alive."

Li Ziyun was equally determined: "If anything happens to my brother, I will not live another day!"

That night, Yang Chuxiong, who had crushed the Silver City party underground organization almost single-handedly, didn't sleep. He squeezed his brain dry to come up with a strategy, knowing he would have to release his wife's brother, even if the man was the party secretary of the Silver City Communist underground.

Li Naizhi, who spent the night in a cell for the condemned, didn't sleep either. As he lay on the cold stone floor, heavily shackled, he thought about his youth—he was only twenty-nine years old—and the nearness of death, and how life went by far too quickly and was over far too soon. Eleven years earlier he had experienced the dreadful crushing of the Silver City insurrection, and four years earlier he had witnessed the failure of the Communist underground in the provincial capital. Now, finally, it was he who would forfeit his life in the name of revolution, he who would offer his life as proof of his faith in Communism. He recalled the calm resignation on the face of Zhao Boru eleven years earlier and remembered the courage the principal had displayed in refusing to turn back, even when he knew that the insurrection was doomed to fail. Li Naizhi had no regrets at this moment, except for a deep sense of self-reproach for not having spotted the traitor in his ranks.

Freezing night winds swept in through the metal bars, and the tattered cotton quilt wrapped tightly around Li Naizhi did little to protect him. Darkness forced the dim light of a kerosene lantern to cower in a corner. For three days and nights the only people Li Naizhi saw were guards, their movements the only outside noise he heard. He paced the floor to keep warm, his clanking shackles filling the cell with icy cold sounds. Li Naizhi suddenly began to sing:

"Flowers bloom in the wilderness, petals cover the blood of martyrs . . ."

He sang as loudly as he could, hoping that his comrades would hear him. But there was no response in the inky darkness, not even the trace of an echo—nothing but the cold light of a lonely kerosene lantern illuminating his final moments. Life went by far too quickly, he reflected again, and was over far too soon. There is so much a person can do, providing he doesn't die at the age of twenty-nine.

After several interrogations had yielded nothing from him, Li Naizhi found himself waiting out the last afternoon of his life. The members of the underground were herded into the prison compound, and there he was finally able to come face to face with the comrades he had been aching to see since his arrest. The firing squad stood ready, their faces blank. Yang Chuxiong, in full dress uniform, waited beneath the veranda to witness the execution personally. Wu Dajiang burst out crying when he spotted Li Naizhi.

"Ninth Brother, I've got a seventy-year-old mother at home and four little children . . ."

Li Naizhi held Wu Dajiang's hands. "Don't cry, Dajiang. We mustn't lose face in front of the enemy."

But for Wu Dajiang it wasn't that easy, and tears continued to streak the scruffy growth on his cheeks. Yang Wenda, branch secretary of the Salt Bureau, was also crying and complaining loudly: "You people arrested everybody I know, so whom can I give up to save myself? Ninth Brother Li, you shouldn't have made me go along with you—look what it cost me." He walked off crying, leaving an unsightly trail on the rocky ground from the urine dripping down his pant leg. Li Naizhi straightened up proudly and exhorted his troops:

"Comrades, revolution demands sacrifice. Our revolution is bound to succeed one day, and the reactionaries will be beaten back. Someday we will be avenged!"

Soldiers in full uniform shoved fifteen members of the Communist underground up against a high stone wall. A few scattered snowflakes fluttered down through the hazy sky. The afternoon was exactly like any other, and when it was over, everything would be just as it was before. Not a single person beyond the wall was aware that an execution was taking place on the other side; not a single person knew that fifteen lives were about to be snuffed out. Li Naizhi raised his arms resolutely. "Long live the Chinese Commu—" Before he could finish, Yang Chuxiong gave the order, explosions from fifteen rifles rocked heaven and earth, and fifteen shackled men crumpled to the ground at the base of the cold wall. They would henceforth lie sprawled, drenched in their own blood, in the local party committee's official history of party activities.

What Li Naizhi, whose faith in Communism allowed him to stare death in the face, did not know was that, on secret orders from Commander Yang, the bullet intended for his heart merely shattered his collarbone. When he regained consciousness, he was lying on a salt barge, with Li Zihen and Yu Zhandong beside him. Behind Li Zihen stood a woman wearing a white scarf. Li Naizhi recognized her as Bai Ruide's daughter, Bai Qiuyun. He opened his mouth to speak but Yu Zhandong stopped him.

"Don't move, Ninth Brother, and don't ask any questions. Miss Bai will tell you everything after you're on the road. This is as far as I can take you, so you'll have to look after yourself from here on." Yu Zhandong opened a cloth bundle. "Ninth Brother, here are two thousand yuan and some ointment for the bullet wound. Let this count as your traveling expenses, from one brother to another. At the next stop you will be met by members of the Brotherhood of Propriety and Virtue."

Li Zihen grabbed Bai Qiuyun's hand and said tearfully, "Qiuyun, I'm putting Ninth Brother in your care. He is the lifeline of the family, the only son . . . I have lived my life for him and him alone."

On that black, bitter-cold December night in 1939, as the salt barge was swallowed up by the darkness, the sorrowful, almost musical sounds of a woman crying came from the bank of

Silver Creek. Li Zihen knew that this moment could very well be the last one she shared with her brother in this life. She knew that he would not waver, that he was fated to make revolution for as long as he lived.

The salt barge passed beneath Ziyun Bridge, headed downstream, as Bai Qiuyun grasped Li Naizhi's icy hand and said:

"The minute I heard you had been arrested, I went looking for Eighth Sister, who told me to wait here for you . . . Naizhi, don't say anything. I've thought it all out."

But Bai Qiuyun, who had thought it all out, could not have imagined that three days after she wrote a note to tell her mother she was leaving the tranquil and elegant Bamboo Garden on Cathedral Street, Lady Yang would loop a rope around her neck and hang herself.

Six months later, when Li Naizhi was sent to a remote area by the provincial party secretary to continue his life as a revolutionary, he would be accompanied only by his wife and the child in her womb.

INTERLUDE
1937–1946

1

As Li Naizhi's comrades were crumpling under the fatal blow, their opponents were on the verge of an era of wealth and prosperity.

Hostilities with the Japanese had broken out in July 1937, in the wake of an attack on Chinese civilians. Li Naijing, having foreseen such events, had quietly begun to buy up as much of Silver City's salt as he could lay his hands on. He had also instructed the Chongqing branch of the family to buy vast quantities of table salt, whatever the cost, but discreetly and behind the scenes. Tianjin fell to the Japanese, then Shanghai, Nanjing, Jinan, Guangzhou—virtually every coastal city. Hundreds of millions of Chinese were cut off from their source of ocean salt, and the value of Li Naijing's tons of table salt skyrocketed. By the time the Nationalists imposed a government monopoly on the sale of salt, he had already paid off his debt to the Tri-Summit Bank and had converted vast sums of French francs into silver dollars, further protecting himself from Bai Ruide's might.

Finally, after so many years, Li Naijing had extricated himself from the miseries of debt and economic vulnerability. Respect for Li Naijing increased tenfold when people in Silver City learned of his shrewd manipulations. To which he responded happily as he stroked his beard: "During the religious uprisings of the Xianfeng reign in the 1850s, the Taiping rebels ran rampant and cut off the source of ocean salt, but Nine Ideals Hall had planned ahead and so enjoyed an era of prosperity. All I am doing now is following the example of my forebears."

While Nine Ideals Hall was growing more prosperous by the day, Bai Ruide was not idle. Drawing on the strength of the Tri-Summit Bank and the cachet of his American education, he transformed himself into a powerful representative of the Silver City salt industry to the Nationalist government. Appointed director of the Silver City Salt Bureau for the War of Resistance against Japan, he was responsible for implementing the government's table salt monopoly, which involved huge business transactions. Silver City's salt merchants flocked to this power broker with the same enthusiasm they had displayed when pursuing him years before for his Mobil Oil lanterns and steel cables.

But while the fortunes of these two industrialists rose dramatically in Silver City, real power rested with Yang Chuxiong, who stepped up to assume the duties of Silver City's mayor. His first official act was to install Li Naijing and Bai Ruide as members of Silver City's Nationalist Council and appoint them as vice mayors. From that moment on, Silver City's three tycoons worked together to implement the proverb "When government works, the people are compliant and neglected matters are neglected no more."

2

Li Naizhi never imagined he could be so profoundly moved, so deeply shaken by a color: a murky yellow that covered heaven and earth, rising and falling as it crossed mountains and ravines. Eyes accustomed to seeing red soil, paddy fields, bamboo groves, and white-feathered egrets were now dazzled by the yellow earth of Yan'an, the sacred cradle of revolution, where Mao and his followers ended the Long March in 1935. Yan'an, praised in so many songs, revered in so many essays, talked about by so many comrades, and imagined in so many dreams, was transformed by that murky yellow into a land of unfathomable wildness and sanctity. Bai Qiuyun shook her husband in alarm as unexpected tears wetted his face.

"Naizhi, Naizhi, what's wrong?"

Li Naizhi dried his eyes. "I've thought about this place for so long."

In January 1946, on orders from Party Central, Li Naizhi had left his post as secretary of the provincial party underground and traveled thousands of li across yellow plateaus chilled by freezing winds until Pagoda Ridge came into view. Unlike the zealous young revolutionaries pouring into the newly liberated areas, Li had been ordered into Yan'an to submit to the party's investigation of his past in a general cadre review. Once settled into the cave assigned him by the central organization department, he discovered that his neighbor to the left was Zhou Juesan, party secretary of Qinghai Province, and to his right Zheng Yunong, party secretary of Gansu Province. All three had been working in the Nationalist-controlled "white" areas and all had been summoned for investigation.

Li Naizhi felt invigorated and inspired by everything he saw in Yan'an. The highly charged revolutionary spirit that pervaded every corner, the pulsing music that filled the air morning, noon, and night, the solidarity between soldiers and civilians, the children's corps with its red-tasseled spears, the troops marching by in all their might and grandeur. Even the faint tinkling of goat bells drifting over from the mountain ridges put him in touch with the vitality of the revolution. Since he was frequently summoned to listen to some report or other, it wasn't long before he saw Mao Zedong, Zhou Enlai, Zhu De, and Liu Shaoqi, the great leaders of the revolution; standing behind podiums in their coarse army greatcoats, they spoke stirringly, and sometimes even humorously, about China and the world. Li Naizhi felt himself gain a deeper understanding of the ideals in his heart now than he'd ever had looking down the barrel of a rifle; he could not find words to express the joy and inspiration that filled his days.

But soon after his arrival, Li faced a test as grim as the firing squad, one that demanded that he offer up not only his life but his soul as well. The comrade responsible for leading the investigation told him that questions remained about his behavior in the enemy prison in 1939: fourteen of his comrades had died before a firing squad, and he was the only man spared. Unable to determine if he had collaborated with the enemy, the party had decided to suspend his membership and demand a detailed report. The comrade sincerely hoped Li Naizhi would be able to pass the party's test.

How, Li Naizhi wondered, could he have been sent to the sacred cradle of revolution, only to be driven out? He reminded himself, however, that he had withstood any number of threats; he was no longer an inexperienced student living in a dormitory at the provincial college. Concealing his agitation, he replied to the comrade: "I am confident that the party will reach the correct conclusion in due time."

That afternoon, when Li Naizhi returned home full of dread, his distraught wife greeted him with the news that their neighbor, old Zhou, had committed suicide; the body had just been taken away. Bai Qiuyun took out a pocket watch.

"Old Zhou came over just before he killed himself, even played with the children a while. As he left, he handed them this watch. I told him he shouldn't do that, but he said to let them play with it, that he'd come get it tomorrow. And now look what happened. Naizhi, why would old Zhou choose to die like that? Was he really a spy?"

Although Li Naizhi could not bear to look at his wife, she saw how pale his face was amid the shadows in the cave.

But revolutions never run according to plan, and soon something much more important overshadowed the fuss about one particular individual. In March 1947, with General Hu Zongnan's Nationalist troops bearing down, the Communist Central Committee decided to abandon Yan'an. In the midst of preparations for the massive retreat, Bai Qiuyun went into labor with her third child. Li Naizhi, released from his duties when the word came, rushed home to help with the delivery. As he placed his newborn daughter in his wife's arms, he said:

"Let's name her Yan'an. When she grows up, she'll always remember the place where she was born."

That afternoon, Bai Qiuyun, dressed in a coarse cotton jacket and trousers, a towel wrapped around her head, took her three daughters in tow and fell in with the panicky mob of peasants fleeing into the hills. At day's end she and a dozen or so others crowded into a cave thick with weeds. There her older daughters, fear radiating from their eyes, huddled around her as the swaddled newborn cried with hunger. Bai Qiuyun patted Yan'an gently and said, both to her children and to herself:

"Don't be afraid, your father says we're going to win the war very soon."

In March 1947, General Hu Zongnan, at the head of a massive army, took Yan'an with overwhelming force. The mighty, valiant general standing at the base of Pagoda Ridge had no idea that three hours earlier his victory had put a pregnant woman into labor and had then driven her deep into the hills, into a primitive cave where her infant daughter would spend the first month of her life before her mother carried her out into the sunlight.

CHAPTER TEN

1

On May 17, 1951, the day he entered prison, Li Naijing was calm. The last day of his life, he felt sure, had finally arrived. An entire company of People's Liberation Army soldiers had surrounded Nine Ideals Hall and dragged dozens of Li clan men from their rooms. As they were paraded through Twin Arches, bound in the five-flower position, only the face of the clan patriarch showed no fear. His hands tied behind his back, the seventy-three-year-old Li Naijing, denied the use of his customary cane, walked proudly, his chest thrust out. Passing beneath the stone arches, he heard the sobs of people behind him, including those of his son, Shuangxi, who had turned twenty-three a few months before; he thought of his grandson, barely six months old, and the daughter-in-law who had died bringing the boy into the world. Holding his head high, he passed the gaping crowds of people and looked up at the red halo of the setting sun in the distant sky; Silver Creek was like a scar, its red-crested ripples seeming to roll out of the sun itself. His heart dry as an abandoned well, Li Naijing dully followed the armed guard; he had witnessed so many debacles in his seventy-three years, had seen so many soldiers, that nothing existed in his eyes and his heart but the soft red aura of transcendent calm.

In 1948, almost a year before the PLA attacked and occupied Silver City, Bai Ruide had paid a call on Li Naijing. Having sold off his holdings, Bai Ruide was leaving China. At this final meeting, the two lifelong antagonists put aside their differences and wiped out decades of ill feeling. When Bai Ruide asked Li Naijing about his plans for the future, Naijing responded with a shake of his head and the words "I'm an old man."

As Li Naijing witnessed the Communists seizing one town after another, beating back Chiang Kai-shek's Nationalist army, he knew that a change of dynasty was only a matter of time, and he prayed he would meet his death before the start of this cataclysmic change; so much pain could be avoided by the simple act of dying. And when the PLA soldiers entered Emerald Sky Study and, amid angry shouts, bound him with ropes, he understood that there would be no escape this time, that the change of dynasty in Silver City meant it was time for him to die, time, too, for Nine Ideals Hall to die. As he walked through Twin Arches, his ears assailed by the wails of his family, Li Naijing could hear the reverberations of buildings crashing down behind him and smell the strong, acrid odor of destruction.

Silver City's prison, which had swallowed up the followers of Sun Yatsen's Revolutionary Party of 1911, the peasant insurrectionists, the striking salt miners, the bandits and highwaymen, and the Communist underground, now, with spring turning to summer in 1951, shut its doors behind hundreds of "counterrevolutionaries" found guilty by the people's government. The sudden arrival of an adequate food supply sent the breeding rate of the prison's vermin skyrocketing; frenzied, the bedbugs and lice sucked the life out of their unwitting donors and mated frantically in a wild race to bring forth the next generation before these healthy humans were turned into walking corpses. While many of his fellow inmates wept at the misery of being eaten alive and the fear of impending death, Li Naijing was calm as an old tree that has shed its leaves. He spent each day sitting wordlessly on his cot; when the prisoners were let out for exercise, he stood alone for a moment in the entrance to his cell, then returned to his cot to sit, his eyes shut.

Shuangxi, in the adjoining cell, had been almost hysterical since the moment of his arrest, overwhelmed by fear, wanting desperately to go on living. Time and again he had asked the other prisoners, "What could I have done during the two days I served as district party secretary to deserve a death sentence? Just because Yang Chuxiong fought hard to defend the city, what does that have to do with me?" But no one answered him, and in the end his questions turned into incoherent mutterings. Shuangxi wanted desperately to talk to his father, to hear Li Naijing assure him he would not be executed. But they were let out for exercise at different times, so all he could do was stare out the barred window at his father standing in the doorway. One day, he could bear it no longer and thrust his arms between the bars, calling tearfully, "Papa, Papa, come over here . . ." His pleadings were immediately cut short by guards. Li Naijing turned to cast an indifferent look toward his son's cell. He saw the guards unshoulder their rifles, then watched as three or four rifle muzzles and the same number of uniformed backs converged on the cell door. He turned and walked back into his own cell.

The visit of Sixth Sister, Li Zihen, was totally unexpected. A guard summoned Li Naijing from his cell. "You have a visitor," he said, and as Naijing followed the rifle down the corridor, he wondered who it could be. Third Concubine, whom he had elevated to the status of formal wife, had died two years earlier, and his other two concubines, who had never stopped grumbling, would surely not risk showing their faces at the jail at a dangerous time like this, not if they could help it. Naijing was astonished when he saw Li Zihen seated on a bench in the visiting room.

"Sixth Sister?"

She stood up. "Elder Brother, I came here to tell you that I'll take care of Shuangxi's son."

That was when Naijing spotted the blue bundle on the bench behind her. His swaddled grandson lay there fast asleep. Li Naijing's dulled, heavy eyes began to smart; he had a sudden vision of that morning decades earlier when Sixth Sister disfigured her face with burning joss sticks. The room abruptly grew quiet and peaceful. A moment later, though, his cold detachment returned.

"Sixth Sister, why do you want to do this?"

"I want to see this child grow to adulthood."

"You are foolish, Sixth Sister. What difference does it make whether he grows to adulthood or not? He'll just have to endure shame and humiliation from now on—so why insist on making him suffer? A man who grows to adulthood amid shame and humiliation is no member of Nine Ideals Hall . . ."

"I want to raise this child. Elder Brother, I came here to beg you to give him a name, that's all I ask, and I ask it for him."

Tears rolled down Li Zihen's cheeks; a string of teardrops fell on her sleeve. The sight threw Li Naijing's parched heart, which had shriveled like a leafless, dead branch, into turmoil. In the end, he softened.

"Don't cry, Sixth Sister, don't cry. I'll do as you ask."

Naijing told Zihen that the child belonged to the "zhi" generation, so he should be called Zhisheng. She asked him to trace the two characters in her palm so she could commit them to memory. Once she had the name firmly in mind, she picked up the sleeping baby, holding his face so Li Naijing could see it. Then she got down on her knees before him and said to the baby:

"Come, Zhisheng, it's time to say good-bye to your grandfather . . ."

Li Naijing could hold back no longer; his tears flowing freely, he bent toward the baby, and as he did, his eyes clouded over.

"Sixth Sister, you shouldn't have brought him here."

He straightened up, turned, and walked away, leaving the woman and the infant alone in the visiting room.

From that moment on, Li Naijing ate nothing, drank nothing, and said nothing, no matter what anyone asked him. Unlike the other prisoners, he wanted only one thing: to die. But his wish was perceived as an act of resistance against the revolution. After severely reprimanding him several times, the guards finally pried Li Naijing's mouth open with a bayonet and forced one bowl of rice porridge after another down his throat. Li Naijing was a parasite on the body of China's working masses, the prison warden told him, a counterrevolutionary who, along with the reactionary clique, was responsible for the deaths of so many Communist Party members that he had no choice but to submit to trial by the people. Resistance on his part would only add to the severity of his crime. Li Naijing was forced to give up his hunger strike, abandon all hope that he could choose the means and time of his death, and await the people's judgment.

There was no calendar in the prison, so Li Naijing could not follow the passage of time; he knew only that on the day of his execution the weather had turned cold and rainy. So many people had crowded onto the parade ground that it took on the air of a temple festival. A particularly martial-looking soldier stood on a platform waving his arms and declaiming fervently. When the harangue was finished, Li Naijing felt someone push him hard from behind; he stumbled and fell forward into the mud but was quickly jerked upright. Turning his head, he spotted a PLA soldier with a bandolier across his chest whose face he thought he'd seen before. In fact, the whole scene seemed familiar somehow, as if he had witnessed one exactly like it somewhere at some other time, but just where and when he simply could not recall. After that, nothing. He did not hear the shot, nor did he see the powdery white and bright red splatters that stained the stone wall. And of course he could not have seen that, after him, the wall was stained the same way a hundred and seven times more. This time, the stain of victory forever obliterated the Silver City of old.

2

After the People's Liberation Army broke through Yang Chuxiong's lines of defense, Yang abandoned the remnants of his forces, gathered his family, and, following Chiang Kai-shek, fled in a panic to Taiwan. There he would die, not yet an old man. On one of the white silk funeral scrolls hanging high in the mourning hall, a tearful Commandant Chiang wrote four words: "Faithful Service Eternal Gratitude."

In Silver City, the Communist underground came out into the open, red flags flying, the heavens thundering with gongs and drums and slogans. It was a new world, and the people of Silver City went about adapting to a host of new realities. In this new world, the biggest surprise was Li Zihen. People were astounded to learn that the woman they had known as a devout Buddhist had actually been a member of the Communist underground, risking her life for the revolution, and that it was she who had rescued the party secretary, her own brother, the celebrated Ninth Brother of Nine Ideals Hall, who, it was said, was now a high-ranking official in Beijing. As this astonishing tale spread through Silver City, people were hard-pressed to understand how such mountain-crumbling, earth-splitting events behind Twin Arches had failed to bring the family utterly down.

Li Zihen could never have predicted that her brother's revolution, begun in this very city, the revolution that she had resolved to die for, would lead to the virtual extermination of their own clan. On May 17, 1951, from her vantage point behind a military escort, she stared wide-eyed as PLA soldiers herded dozens of Nine Ideals Hall men out the gate of the family compound and through Twin Arches; horrified, she began to understand exactly what her brother had brought about. After the glinting bayonets had passed, she could not shake the feeling that she had witnessed a similar scene once before. Terrified, she turned back to look at the city, with its rows of houses, and saw a boundless void and desolation threatening to engulf her. She thought of the child and rushed to Shuangxi's room, where, amid the clutter and mess, the wet nurse cried:

"What a cruel fate awaits this child, with his grandfather and father taken away and none of the concubines willing to care for him."

Li Zihen picked up the baby and said, "Don't worry, he's mine to raise."

As she carried the baby through the rooms and hallways of the house, the Nine Ideals Hall women watched her pass in shocked silence, like cicadas caught in a cold snap, wondering where this woman found such courage, wondering, too, why she was doing this, daring to raise the child of an "enemy of the people." Years before, they had wondered what had driven her to sear her face with joss sticks. Li Zihen ignored their looks of suspicion and fear as she strode to her room and laid the baby on her hand-carved sandalwood bed.

"Little one," she said, "call me Great Aunt."

The baby started bawling, so she picked him up to coax the tears away, but to no avail. She hesitated only a moment before lifting the hem of her upper garment and putting the baby's mouth to her nipple; at the first sensation of sucking, she began trembling like a stalk of bamboo standing before the wind, and the tranquility she had worked so hard to cultivate for most of her life abandoned her. When she had regained her composure, Li Zihen took the baby to see Ninth Brother's comrades. By then, they were ensconced in Yang Chuxiong's headquarters, caught up in the myriad tasks of setting up a new political regime. She said to all present that she wanted to visit Li Naijing in prison. Puzzled by the request, Ninth Brother's comrades said:

"Sixth Sister, why go see counterrevolutionaries?"

"Revolutionaries, counterrevolutionaries, what do I know?"

"Sixth Sister, if Ninth Brother found out, he'd say you lacked conviction. He'd be angry."

"I went to see *him* when he was in prison, so what's the difference? What's there to be angry about?"

"This is different—times have changed."

"Whatever the times, it's still one person's head propped up by a pair of shoulders."

Li Naizhi's comrades were momentarily speechless. But there was no denying her great contributions to the revolution, so how could they refuse her request? And so it happened that one afternoon Li Zihen walked down the long, dark prison corridor leading to the cells of the condemned, carrying a baby in her arms.

Later, having failed to talk sense into Li Zihen and get her to change her mind about raising the child of a counterrevolutionary, Ninth Brother's comrades handed her a letter from Li Naizhi. In the strongest possible language, he reminded her that, even though she was no longer active in the party, she was still a Communist and must never lose sight of class struggle and her position in it. Li Zihen sent a reply to her younger brother through an intermediary: When our parents died, you were about as old as this baby is now. I have decided not to come to Beijing to be with you, and my "position" is to remain here at home in Silver City to bring up this child who also has no parents. She went on to remind him that the child was his fraternal grandnephew and, in line with generational practice, Ninth

Brother would henceforth be called Ninth Elder; the boy's name was Li Zhisheng.

The matter settled, Li Zihen hunted up a cradle, which she placed alongside her embroidery rack, so she could rock the baby for hours each day as she busied herself with her sewing. Sometimes she sang to the baby: "Rock, rock, to and fro, to Grandma's bridge we shall go, at Grandma's house a gala fair, and all your cousins will be there." She rocked as she sang, her thoughts drifting back to the distant past, when a seven-year-old girl sang this same song to her baby brother. The boy in the cradle beside her was like a tender sapling; in the void and desolation around her, Li Zihen was tending its soft green leaves. Day in and day out, whatever the time, she never took her eyes off this baby who had been born to someone else; in the void and desolation, she felt a force tugging at her that was fine as gossamer yet sturdy and profound. Sometimes tired of embroidering, she would revert to her old habit of standing in the doorway and staring into the distance, at the meandering Silver Creek, the towering derricks, and a forest of ships' masts. The earth-shaking events that had occurred all around her had done little to change her; they were hardly worth mentioning, it seemed. Li Zihen gave in to the fine yet profound force tugging at her.

All of Silver City turned out at the old parade ground on the day the mass executions were carried out. Li Zihen was not among the crowd; she stayed home to rock and soothe the baby as a silent autumn drizzle fell, casting its gloom over row upon row of empty houses, over the whole city, heightening her solitude and foreboding. The clamor of the crowd, the shouts and slogans, echoed through the drizzle, and Li Zihen was wracked with cold shivers. Then came the soul-pounding explosions of gunfire. Li Zihen abruptly stopped shivering; she dropped her prayer beads, her legs fell open inelegantly, and she tumbled backward in a dead faint alongside the cradle. Startled by the gunfire, the baby began to shriek . . . Li Zihen came to in bed,

Winterset standing over her looking worried. When he saw she was awake, he said:

"I didn't go, Sixth Sister, I was too frightened to watch the killing."

Li Zihen quickly sat up to look in the cradle, where the baby lay sound asleep.

3

Following the execution of thirty-two men from Nine Ideals Hall, Li Naizhi's comrades confiscated all the Li clan's wealth, including the vast compound behind Twin Arches, and announced that the buildings lining Archway Street now belonged to the people, the new masters of Silver City. Those days were remembered for the songs that rang through the city:

Three yellow oxen. Hooray! A single horse,
This old driver can't stop laughing,
Hurrah, ha ha, see me laugh.
In years past, this wagon here
Could never belong to a poor man like me,
But now, hurrah,
Big-wheel wagon, turn, turn,
Big-wheel wagon, turn, turn,
Turn, turn, turn, hooray!
Ta-dah,
Turn right into my yard!

The song had the same effect on Silver City as a spring thunderstorm, cheerfully swirling in the air and driving the big-wheel wagons day and night.

After the last dregs of the feudal classes were removed from the vast family compound, a committee member came looking for Winterset.

"Don't be scared," he said, "we're not going to eliminate you."

Winterset felt as if a big-wheel wagon were turning in his heart.

"Until now you served the exploiting classes. From now on you will deliver water to Sixth Sister. Delivering water to her is revolutionary work, for which there is no bickering over wages. Do you want the job?"

"Yes, yes, I want it."

Like a man finding salvation, Winterset understood the man's meaning and nodded vigorously in the midst of his terror.

Winterset had carried water in this compound all his life. Until now it had been his livelihood and he had never given a moment's thought to whether he was working for the exploiting classes or for the revolution. For decades humble Winterset had carried water for the family, and now, shedding none of his humility, he carried water for the revolution, on orders of the party, in a city that was rewriting history. It was a different world, but he was the same old Winterset. Before, his work was finished only after he was drenched with sweat; now his work was finished after a single delivery of water. Each morning, he stood in front of Li Zihen's door with two wooden buckets and called out with customary diffidence: "Sixth Sister, your water's here." When the door curtain parted, Winterset would look into the pale, scarred face of Li Zihen, and he could see the boundless void and desolation in her eyes.

Over time, his morning delivery of water became a ritual that enabled Winterset to bridge his past and his present. For decades, his exchange with the family seldom went beyond a few simple words, respectfully uttered: "Your water's here." Confronted by those towering stone arches, the mysterious calligraphy and hanging scrolls, the endless courtyards, meandering paths, ancient trees with their cloudlike canopies, and the glorious stands of emerald bamboo, Winterset had held fast to his humility as he prowled the grounds over the long months and years with his creaky bamboo pole, drawing water from the well beneath the honey locust tree to irrigate the vast compound and slake the thirst of the flourishing family that lived there. In all that time—so many years that it made his head swim—he had never imagined that the day would come when this mighty family in this vast compound would be reduced to a single woman and a baby.

Before long, a flood of new tenants inundated the ancient compound, bringing their pots and bowls and spatulas and basins, their wives and children and elders, and the turbulent currents of their lives. Tattered diapers and ragged clothes hung from carved ridgepoles in the corridors, imposing piles of excrement dotted twisting paths and out-of-the-way corners, and noisy children overran the man-made hills and bamboo groves all day long, while late at night green lamps illuminated the private rooms, from which emerged masculine roars and feminine moans of pleasure. . . . A vague gloom descended on Twin Arches. The parasol trees shaken by an autumn drizzle, the purple swallows calling in the waning evening light, the slanting shadows cast by bamboo swaying under a bright moon had all faded; in the turbulent currents of those lives, they had grown shabby and pale.

The new tenants, forever in awe of the Li clan of Nine Ideals Hall, were endlessly curious about the previous occupants and the old compound. They would stop Winterset in the yard to ask all sorts of questions:

"Winterset, what do shark's fin and bird's nest soup taste like?"

"Winterset, did all the women and girls know how to read and write?"

"Winterset, were you there the day Sixth Sister seared her face?"

"Winterset, what sort of sleeping arrangements were there with the wives? A different one every night or all together?"

"Winterset, how come they all had three or four wives but you stayed a naked rod all those years?"

Winterset's response to these questions never varied: a humble smile and the simple comment that a clearwater guest is a servant and whatever the masters and mistresses do he neither sees nor hears. But his discreetness only served to pique their curiosity further, and the new tenants could not refrain from probing the personal affairs of the Li clan, especially those aspects that bore on their own uncertain lives.

"Winterset, what is Ninth Brother's official position? Why doesn't Sixth Sister go see him in Beijing? Why is Sixth Sister raising that boy? Winterset, we know we're not your equals and that if Ninth Brother comes back some day we'll all have to move out of here. We can't afford to cool our heels in other people's houses. A stump with no roots cannot stand firm."

Still no response from Winterset, who stood before the new tenants, fearful, humble, and blushing with embarrassment. He did not know why Sixth Sister didn't go to Beijing to see Ninth Brother, nor did he know why she was raising the orphaned child or what it was that kept her in the vast compound, just as he had not known why she had scarred her face and taken vows of abstinence years ago or why she had later joined the Communist underground. Deep down, all he really hoped was that Sixth Sister would stay put, so he would never have to leave the only home he'd ever known. So long as he could serve her at Nine Ideals Hall, he could remain at home, secure, and yet—as they'd told him—work for the revolution. It never occurred to him that rumors would spread about him and the woman who was all that was left of the once-mighty clan. Winterset held Li Zihen in awe; every time he saw her, his thoughts drifted to the white ceramic goddess of mercy that sat on her square table. Just as his profound humility made him forget that he was a man, so his respect for Li Zihen made him forget that she was a woman.

Thus things went on until one sweltering summer. Summer, when the world turns green and lush, is the season when stories are born.

It all began when the baby reached out and pulled open Li Zihen's blouse. She was lifting the screaming boy, who was deathly afraid of water, out of the bath, and as Winterset bent down to move the unwieldy basin out of the way, he saw the hungry baby pull open Li Zihen's blouse to reach for her nipple; two soft white breasts spilled out—white moons that shone upon his soul. He caught his breath, as if struck by lightning, frozen in place by the vision before him. As Li Zihen turned her back to him in embarrassment, a thought occurred to Winterset:

Sixth Sister is a woman.

That thought was followed by another: Sixth Sister is an unmarried woman.

And then Winterset was done in by fear and humility, so unnerved by these improper thoughts that his soul took flight and his courage crumbled; the basin crashed to the floor, spilling his terror and humility at the feet of the bodhisattva whose back was to him. . . .

On that lush, green summer day, Li Zihen turned around with extraordinary calm and said to Winterset:

"We're both well along in years, so why are you so flustered?"

"Sixth Sister, I deserve to die . . ."

"If you did, who would bring me water?"

"Sixth Sister, I'll bring you water as long as I live . . . unless Sixth Sister doesn't want me anymore?"

"Winterset, I want to ask you something."

Winterset looked up into Li Zihen's eyes. He could feel the summer story racing breathlessly toward him.

"Winterset, would you be willing to raise this child with me?"

Knowing full well what lay behind her question, Winterset saw the extraordinary calmness of her eyes, the look of a woman's steely determination.

Sixth Sister is a woman, he thought.

And then again: Sixth Sister is an unmarried woman.

His head sagged under the weight of his great humility.

"Does my unsightly face bother you, Winterset?"

"Sixth Sister, you are beautiful, you are beautiful all over . . . Sixth Sister, I've been a naked rod for years and years, but I never ever dared to imagine . . ."

"Winterset, go fetch some water. I'll wash up and let you see for yourself."

Winterset understood, and his blood turned as hot as the searing summer.

After fetching a bucket of clear water from the old well beneath the honey locust tree, Winterset placed the basin inside the mosquito net for Li Zihen, heated the water, then filled the basin with the hot water and added just the right amount of cold. Pointing to a chair next to the square table, Li Zihen said:

"You sit there quietly. The baby just fell asleep."

Winterset sat without making a sound, and soon heard splashing sounds from behind the netting. Suddenly he felt hot all over and his mouth was parched. He walked over to the water jug and scooped out half a ladleful to cool off and to quench his thirst, then went back to his seat, where splashing sounds reached him again. "It's Sixth Sister sitting in the basin," he thought. And that kindled even greater heat in his chest and thirst in his mouth. Finally the splashing sounds came to a stop. Then his ears filled with the chirping of cicadas. Winterset got up and walked toward the mosquito net. Lifting up a corner, he saw a body as pure as jade and as clean as ice, snowy white like the white ceramic goddess of mercy on the square table. With a heart full of terror and humility, Winterset said:

"Here I am, Sixth Sister."

After that, the only sound to be heard on that lush, green summer day was the soulful chirping of cicadas.

When Winterset sat up, drenched in sweat, the baby sleeping at the head of the bed started to bawl, rolled onto the snowy white softness Winterset had just moved away from, and began to suck. Winterset looked on amazed as blood seeped from the body of the woman lying before him and tears rolled down her cheeks. Raising himself on the carved sandalwood bed, Winterset knelt before Li Zihen.

"Sixth Sister, I will stay with you always, in the next life too, even if I come back as an ox or a horse . . ."

On that sultry day when all that existed was the soulful chirping of cicadas, a woman whose body was oozing tears and blood liberated two men, one to become a son, the other a husband.

CHAPTER ELEVEN

1

When Li Zihen took the baby Zhisheng home with her, she never dreamed that the thundering big-wheel wagon would one day bring the Cultural Revolution, which would crush her world underfoot, reduce everything she had struggled to accomplish to a simple six-word wooden sign:

ANCIENT LOCUST TWIN ARCHES OLD SITE

In 1964, the boy Li Zhisheng gained a measure of notoriety in Silver City. Having scored first in the municipal exams, he had been admitted to the city's best school, the Boru Middle School, which had been closed after the aborted insurrection in December 1927. In the flower bed beside the school's main gate stood the bust of the man for whom the school was renamed, the revolutionary martyr Zhao Boru, the former principal who had been beheaded when the insurrection failed. The former principal now stood for all eternity in the school's flower bed, his eyes fixed on the city that had slaughtered him.

To reward Zhisheng for doing so well at his studies, Li Zihen opened her trunk on the first day of school and dug out the Parker pen that had lain there for decades. The words engraved on the barrel turned her thoughts to her younger sister and her brother and to the young man who had drowned in the icy waters of Silver Creek. Seeing the tears in Li Zihen's eyes, Zhisheng asked:

"Why are you crying, Great Aunt?"

"So many people are no longer with us . . ."

"Which people do you mean?"

Li Zihen answered the boy solemnly:

"Someday I'll tell you, Zhisheng. For now, just make yourself worthy of this pen by studying hard."

Zhisheng happily clipped the pen—and its sad, noble history—to his breast pocket as he raced across Ziyun Bridge and all the way up to the revolutionary martyr. He did not know that it was his own grandfather's friends who had made the school principal a martyr or that it was the statue's comrades who had made him an orphan. He stood with innocent curiosity in the school gateway feeling both reverence and fear, but then quickly moved out of the line of the martyr's fixed gaze. Zhisheng lowered his head, removed the gold-plated pen from his pocket in front of the statue, and read the engraving on the barrel, pausing after each word:

"The . . . east . . . wind . . . is . . . cruel . . . happiness . . . is . . . ephemeral . . . a . . . bosom . . . of . . . tangled . . . silk . . . many . . . years . . . of . . . separation . . . wrong . . . wrong . . . wrong."

Zhisheng wasn't sure what the words meant, nor did he know that the gloomy lines of poetry had been written seven hundred and fifty years ago by the poet Lu You. He felt that the pen should have been engraved with a saying by Chairman Mao, something like: "Study well, and make progress every day" or "Learn from Comrade Lei Feng." He could not know how much trouble those words would cause him. Two summers later, he was again transfixed before the martyr's statue, but this time he was on his knees, forced by his schoolmates to declaim these lines of poetry as proof of his crimes. All the while, his schoolmates would beat him with the buckle ends of their belts and the dummy wooden rifles they used for military drills, until blood dripped from his nose, past his chin, and onto the ground.

"Don't hit me," Zhisheng cried out, "don't hit me, you're hurting me . . ."

His schoolmates shouted, "Admit it, admit you hate our new society. Why did you curse the east wind, the socialist camp, as cruel, knowing full well that it has prevailed over the west wind of the capitalists?"

"Yes," Zhisheng wailed, "I hate the new society, and I cursed the east wind."

"Say it," his schoolmates demanded, "say 'I am a Nine Ideals Hall dog whelp.' "

Zhisheng repeated, "I am a Nine Ideals Hall dog whelp."

Then his schoolmates beat him again. Belt buckles and wooden rifles thudded mercilessly against Zhisheng's body, knocking him to the ground. The boys jerked him back up and kept beating him. He fell to the ground again; they jerked him back up.

"Confess your crimes to the revolutionary martyr, you dog whelp!" they demanded.

Zhisheng, bruised and bloodied, wailed to the revolutionary martyr:

"I'm guilty, guilty, a dog whelp . . . O martyr, I didn't know it was my grandfather who killed you. It's my fault! Please forgive me . . ."

The summer of 1966 seemed so long to the residents of Silver City that all they could remember of that year was sweltering summer days; they were baked by the sun until the blood in their veins seemed to boil. In that summer of 1966, the sun baked the streaks of blood on Zhisheng's face into black scars. After washing the boy's face with cool water, Li Zihen held him in her arms and cried piteously:

"Zhisheng, Zhisheng, if only I had listened to your grandfather instead of letting you grow up to suffer in a world like this. Little one, your great aunt's heart is breaking, she has been unworthy . . ."

"Great Aunt, they all say it was my grandfather who killed the martyr. Is it true?"

"Little one, for decades this city has seen nothing but killing."

"Great Aunt, they all say I was born the son of a counterrevolutionary . . ."

"Zhisheng, all the babies in the world are born to their mothers, and they enter the world innocent of any crimes."

"But they beat me and cursed me and said that the engraving on my pen is a reactionary slogan. I'm scared, Great Aunt. Why can't we go away? We can go to Ninth Elder in Beijing. Please, let's leave. I hate this place!"

"Don't be afraid, little one, I'll protect you with this old life of mine!"

Two days later, Zhisheng's schoolmates dragged him to Ziyun Bridge to "reeducate" him. By then, the stone marker at the head of the bridge had been knocked over and smashed to bits, and someone had written three words on the stone piling under the railing in dark red paint: "Red Guard Bridge." All of Silver City's landlords and counterrevolutionaries—the "ox demons and snake spirits," as Chairman Mao called them—were being dragged up to the bridge and thrown into the water to be "reeducated." Day in and day out, the banks were crowded with revolutionary masses loudly roaring their approval. Neither tearful retractions, nor pleas for mercy, nor fearful shrieks saved the terrified Zhisheng from being dragged up to the bridge and hurled into the river. But at the very moment he hit the water, some of the onlookers saw a gray-haired man dive into Silver Creek and swim desperately toward the thrashing boy.

"Zhisheng," Winterset shouted as he swam, "Zhisheng, stay where you are! I'm coming!"

After dragging Zhisheng onto the bank, Winterset fell to his knees in front of the mob and declared tearfully, "Masters, mistresses, uncles, aunts, comrades, the boy has been afraid of the water since he was a baby—please don't throw him in again, or he might drown. Spare him, he's just fifteen. If you must throw somebody in, throw me. If you must beat somebody, beat me."

Someone in the mob recognized Winterset. "This man once rescued the son of the patriarch of Nine Ideals Hall," he shouted, "and today he's come to rescue the old man's grandson. Once a loyal slave, always a loyal slave. A beating is what he deserves!"

Within moments, Winterset lay bloody and almost unconscious beneath a hailstorm of flying fists. Then someone shouted:

"Drag both of them over and reeducate them!"

That was all the brawling, shouting mob needed to carry the old man and the boy back to Red Guard Bridge. But after the water sent up two columns of spray, nothing rose to the surface. By the time Li Zihen heard the rumors and raced to Silver Creek, the banks were deserted and the water flowed silently beneath the bridgehead; the fiery rays of the setting sun turned the bony frames of old abandoned derricks on both banks black and brittle, like so many towering skeletons. Li Zihen sat limply on the bridge steps, the cold from the icy stones spreading through her body. So much had happened to her on the banks of this silent, unfeeling stream, so many things she could not bear to recall, yet she had endured them all. But on this afternoon, as she sat on the stone steps above Silver Creek gazing at the skeletons blazing in the sunset, she knew that her endurance had withered. Years earlier, as she sat at her embroidery rack and gazed out the door with tired eyes, she had heard the strains of songs wafting from the derricks, songs that often moved her to tears. Now there was nothing left in her eyes, nothing but those black, brittle skeletons, nothing but inexpressible despair and grief. For once, self-recrimination tormented the wretched, friendless Zihen; she reproached herself for being obstinate, for insisting on raising the boy herself, and for dragging the trusting and innocent Winterset down with her. She had never dreamed that the humble, timid Winterset could possess such courage that in front of a crazed mob he would dive into the water to rescue the boy.

Li Zihen sat in the dying rays of the sun on that summer evening without stirring, like an aged, time-worn stone, staring at the water slowly flowing east, wanting to cry but empty of tears, wanting to speak but not knowing where to begin.

2

Before diving headlong into Silver Creek, Winterset had waited in dread for the calamity he sensed was coming. During that summer, the ancient city that had been home to generations of his family was transformed into a place where nothing was familiar. Walls were painted red, Chairman Mao's quotations appeared everywhere, every surface was plastered with posters and slogans. Ziyun Bridge was now Red Guard Bridge; at Fish Listening Pond, Su Dongpo's calligraphic engraving had been chiseled away and replaced, in red, by the four words "Torrents Rush Boldly Forward." Archway Street had been renamed Workers and Peasants Street, and Three Harmonies public house, where he had gone to drink all his adult life, was now called Workers and Peasants Diner. Even then the people were not satisfied. Men drove up in two large trucks to pull down Twin Arches, cut down the five-hundred-year-old locust tree, then hack at the fallen objects with sledgehammers and axes until they were completely destroyed. On the day they brought down the arches, Winterset hunkered on the steps at the main gate, watching from a distance as the stone pillars and the locust tree came crashing to the ground amid a chorus of shouts, leaving a huge void; he was deeply saddened, and deeply afraid. With dread, he took the measure of the city, unable to comprehend what had happened to this place he'd lived in all his life. Looking out beyond the empty vista, he saw dark gray brick walls and a giant chimney belching black smoke above the brickyard on the other side of Silver Creek. It was all so unnatural and so unsightly. He thought of the flasks of wine he had drunk while leaning up against the old locust tree, the dirges he had listened to, and how, mixed in with all those coarse men's voices, he had been able to pick out the high voice of Little Eleven. . . . But now the blinding rays of an unfamiliar sun shone down on a wasteland. Quietly, he reached inside his shirt for his pewter flask, from which he took a long drink. The warm wine brought him courage, and he hurled curses at the razed tract of land: "You turtle spawn, you evil monsters!" Unsatisfied by this first outburst, he took a quick look around and fired off another volley in the direction of the crumbled stone and splintered wood: "Bandits! Fiendish villains! Defilers of heaven and pillagers of earth!" This time his curses ended in tears. What good did it do? He felt ashamed. You're just wasting your time, you old ghost! he reproached himself. Except for that carrying pole, what in this city ever belonged to you? Even Sixth Sister and Zhisheng you only stumbled on by accident. When he had finished reproaching himself, he poured some more wine down his throat as tears fanned out over his wrinkled face. The world is changing so fast, he muttered, it won't let people go on living in it. Suddenly his sobs were interrupted by a voice:

"Winterset, why are you sitting out here crying like that?"

Quickly wiping his wet face, he lied, "I'm not crying, Sixth Sister. It's the sun, it's hurting my eyes . . ."

"Winterset," Li Zihen said, "you were crying."

Ashamed, he nodded. "I've gotten old, Sixth Sister, too old to be of any use, too old to go on living . . ."

Li Zihen bent toward him, her gray-streaked head drawing close to his. A moment later, they spotted Zhisheng, his face bloodied, coming toward them through the scattered stones and splintered wood. The words "dog whelp" had been written on his ripped shirt in black ink. The old couple gasped in horror. Under the blazing sun of that 1966 summer day, Zhisheng ran crying toward the two people who loved him, and as the three of them stood holding one another, Winterset could only think: This really is the end for me, I've lived as long as I want to live.

Once they were back home, Winterset raced to the well to get water to clean up Zhisheng, but he was so flustered he let the bucket slip off the winch hook. He watched it thud to the bottom of the well. He was so angry he wept, and once again he reproached himself: Too old to be of use, too old to go on living. Many years earlier, when Shuangxi fell down the well, Winterset had shinnied down the rope without a second thought. He had been sitting in the shade of the honey locust tree singing snatches from an opera, lines he had learned from Little Eleven, her favorite lines from *Red Phoenix Jacket:*

After today we will not meet again,
In the halls of jade, I will remove my paint and whore no more.
I will marry a farmer with joy in my heart,
And be my own mistress, not the plaything of others.

But in the end, Little Eleven had died in the Peach Palace. He'd gone with the esteemed adviser to buy her way out, but they had made the trip in vain. No matter how rich you are, no matter how pure your heart, it is never enough to redeem someone from Yama, the king of hell. In that moment, Winterset had truly understood that death is eternally closed to the living, a place where the living are forever shut out. Now such thoughts led to more self-recriminations: Someone whose addled brain thinks about death and the dead has no right to go on living. Having lost one of his buckets, Winterset was forced to put down his bamboo pole and carry the remaining bucket back in his arms. It was very hard going, and he had to stop and rest several times on the trip home. The sight of Li Zihen weeping as she cleaned Zhisheng's face reminded Winterset of that summer day more than ten years earlier, a day that had baked under a searing sun much like today's, another occasion when he had fetched water to bathe the boy. First came Zhisheng and then Sixth Sister, as he sat beside the white goddess of mercy on the square table, separated from them by a mosquito net, hot all over and terribly parched, listening to the splashing water as it ran down the woman's body and feeling the blood in his veins flow hot and fast. Then he heard the soulful chirping of crickets from the trees outside the window. And after lifting up the corner of the mosquito net, he gazed on Sixth Sister's body, which was as white as the ceramic goddess of mercy on the square table; he fell to his knees and said, Sixth Sister, I will stay with you always, in the next life too, even if I come back as an ox or a horse. . . . More than ten years had passed since that day, but it seemed like only yesterday. Now, though, the wooden basin could no longer hold the boy who was so afraid of the water. The sight of Zhisheng's battered face, tense with fear, cut into Winterset's heart like a knife.

"Zhisheng," he said, trying to comfort the boy, "don't be scared. You'll take a couple of days off from school and just stay home. Great Aunt and I will stay with you."

"I can't," Zhisheng sobbed, shaking his head. "They'll come get me."

"If those turtle spawn so much as try," Winterset nearly shouted, "they'll answer to me. I'll die if I have to! I've lived too long as it is!"

At that very moment, with Winterset's reckless shout hanging in the air, a propaganda truck rumbled by, its half dozen speakers blaring a song that the whole nation was singing that summer of 1966:

We are Chairman Mao's Red Guards,
Forging our red hearts in the stormy waves,
Armed with Mao Zedong's thought
To sweep away the enemy leeches.
We dare to criticize, we dare to struggle,
Revolution and rebellion will never cease,
We dare to criticize, we dare to struggle,
Revolution and rebellion will never cease,
Destroying forever the old world,
Revolutionary power, red for ten thousand generations!

The song reverberated through the skies over Silver City, shaking the universe with the power of thunderbolts. So the next day, when Zhisheng's schoolmates swarmed into the house to seize the dog whelp, chanting slogans and singing the song, Winterset's resistance hardly registered; it took only a few boys to deposit the gray-haired old man in a corner while the others, shouting loudly, dragged off their "spoils of victory." Winterset, humble Winterset, found his resolve at that moment. "Sixth Sister," he said, "you stay here. I'm going to the school to see what's happening." Li Zihen, noting a look of determination she had never seen in his eyes before, cautioned him tearfully:

"Please be careful, Winterset. It would kill me to lose either of you."

Winterset ran to the school and from there to Ziyun Bridge. The bridgehead was sealed off by a mob, so Winterset had to elbow his way down to the edge of the water, whose surface, reflecting the sun's blistering rays, nearly blinded him. Though he couldn't see a thing, he shouted, "Zhisheng! Zhisheng! I'm here, don't be afraid!"

His shouts were met by Zhisheng's shrieks: "Don't throw me in, don't throw me in . . ." Then Winterset saw Zhisheng fall from the sky, arms and legs flailing, and hit the surface of Silver Creek. As the mob stared wide-eyed, Winterset dove into the water and swam toward the thrashing arms that kept dipping beneath the surface.

"Zhisheng," he shouted as he swam, "Zhisheng, stay where you are! I'm coming!"

The old man and the boy no sooner dragged themselves out of the water than the irate mob closed around them. Finding such open defiance of the revolution intolerable, they beat Winterset to the ground, ignoring his pleas, but they had not counted on the strength of the old man, who struggled to his feet out of a pool of his own blood and shook the earth with his thundering voice: "I'll die here if I have to! I've lived too long as it is!" He threw himself into the mob like a crazed bull, knocking people to the ground and pouncing on them. The mob's fury was multiplied a hundred times by the crazed Winterset; a dozen men seized Winterset and Zhisheng, hoisted them high in the air, and carried them, face up, to the bridge. Shrill screams, sputtered curses, flying fists merged to form a boiling stream of humanity. Winterset felt the blistering heat of the sun in his blood-filled eyes turn everything to a red haze. It took hardly any time for the mob to swarm up onto the bridgehead and from there to the center of the bridge. Suddenly, Winterset felt himself flying through the air, and he shouted:

"Zhisheng, Zhisheng, don't be afraid . . ."

Two columns of water rose into the air, then the stream was still. The chorus of shouts on the bridge and along the bank stopped abruptly as people stared wide-eyed at the deep, dark green water below, expecting to see something come bobbing to the surface. But nothing did, nothing at all, and the deep, dark green stream flowed gently, like a wandering poet, moving slowly and silently up to the stone wall rising out of the water at Fish Listening Pond to stop for a fleeting moment before continuing on its leisurely course under the bridge and beyond. The ancient, time-worn Silver Creek flowed as if oblivious to the bold torrent of the new age.

3

Silver City residents saw Li Zihen's hair turn completely white over that endless summer; in the blistering rays of sunlight her snowy white head seemed conspicuously out of harmony with the lush greenery as she made her way through the streets of Silver City. On the day Winterset and Zhisheng were flung into the waters of Silver Creek, she was seen sitting at the water's edge late into the night. The next morning someone observed her walking down the dirt road by the riverbank to a dam twenty li downstream to wait for the bodies to surface. She hired an oxcart and bought a pair of coffins for her loved ones, whom she had carried up to White Cloud Mountain. As the cart negotiated the bend at the foot of the mountain path, she saw the cloudlike stone arch of White Cloud Monastery rising above the lush green foliage. Telling the driver to stop, she pointed to a small clearing and said, "Right there," then sat wordlessly on a rock and watched the peasants climb down off the cart and begin to dig; when the holes were deep enough, she watched them lower the coffins and fill in the two new graves. Two mounds of fresh red earth rose at the edge of a grove of emerald-green bamboo—too red, it seemed to Li Zihen, as if drops of blood were seeping from them. The tired, sweaty peasants sat off to the side smoking, keeping their eyes on this strange old woman, waiting for her to offer up something, to burn spirit money, then to wail for the dead. Her silence frightened them. All they saw her do was light three joss sticks beside the graves and stand with her hands clasped together, as silent and motionless as a gloomy stone arch.

After a long while, she turned, handed the men some money, and said, "You can go on back now." They urged her to return with them, reminding her that the mountain monastery had been sealed up long ago and the monks sent back to their homes to work the fields. What the peasants did not know was that many years earlier the white-haired woman had come to this very spot with the man they had just buried, pointed to the clearing, and said, "When I die, bury me on this mountain ridge, as close to White Cloud Monastery as possible." Who could have predicted that decades later it would be she who came here to bury him? Li Zihen gazed up at the stone arch as beams of sunlight slanted down the tranquil mountainside, covering the two mounds of red earth with the gentle shards of bygone years. Many times she had walked past that stone arch, which she now recalled was engraved with two lines of verse she had never quite understood but knew had something to do with the passage of time and the essential sameness of life and death. Now, however, life and death stared each other in the face, and only sorrow was left to the living, left to a lonely old woman with no one to lean on.

Li Zihen was haunted by a vague feeling that two ghostly white faces hovered above the blood-red mounds of earth. After dragging them out of the water, one old man and one boy, and laying them side by side atop the dam, she had gazed at their ghostly white faces in the bright sunlight, their eyes tightly shut, and could not believe they were dead. She sat between them to smooth their hair, then began talking to them softly. First she called out Winterset's name, then Zhisheng's. "Don't frighten me like this," she said. "You're not going to abandon an old woman, are you? If you don't say something," she went on, "I won't leave. I'll sit here until you get up." Some people approached her then, helped her to her feet, and said, "Let's put them in the coffins and nail down the lids, old woman. It's not a good idea to leave them out here like this." After that, a flurry of hands lifted the old man and the boy into the grim white boxes, then nailed the lids shut. The thuds of hammer on nail made the people's hearts pound with dread but convinced Li Zihen that Winterset and Zhisheng were dead, drowned the day before when they were thrown off Ziyun Bridge. Li Zihen had brought money along to pay for the burial, for she had already made up her mind that her two loved ones would lie at the foot of White Cloud Mountain and that when she died she, too, would be buried there, so that in death the family would be together, as close to White Cloud Monastery as possible. She loved the tranquility of White Cloud Mountain, loved the emerald-green bamboo that grew on its slopes, loved the slanting rays of sunlight that fell upon its lushness. She had chosen it as her burial site back when she was a young woman and had done so with Winterset at her side. Maybe there was something to the lines of verse engraved on the stone arch after all:

WHERE IS THE ROAD FROM HERE TO THERE

NO GATE BETWEEN LIFE AND DEATH.

Since everyone died sooner or later, what purpose was served by making life a struggle? But these vague thoughts brought her no comfort, for as she stood before the two new graves, all she could feel was that her two loved ones had taken her life with them, leaving behind only the black void of death.

The peasant laborers she had hired could not bring themselves to leave her. "Please get back on the cart, old woman," they urged. "We don't dare leave you here alone. We'd have the devil to pay if something happened to you."

So Li Zihen climbed onto the oxcart, and when they made the turn on their way down the mountain and she could no longer see White Cloud Monastery or her loved ones, wails of grief burst from her throat. The carters sighed with relief. "Go ahead, old woman," they said, "go ahead and cry. You'll feel better afterward . . . You scared us half to death back there."

Not long after that, Silver City residents saw that Li Zihen's hair had turned completely white; in the blistering rays of sunlight her snowy white head seemed conspicuously out of harmony with the lush greenery as she made her way through the streets of Silver City. Sixth Great Aunt probably won't be with us much longer, people were thinking. But there was so much to think about that blood-boiling summer. The great leader Chairman Mao's "supreme directives" came down one after the other and the Chinese people raised one revolutionary tide after the next; in such glorious times, the people had neither the time nor the energy to take much note of one old woman. Every once in a while someone saw her on her way to market. Or noticed her straining to carry a wooden bucket only half filled with water, hobbling and wobbling all the way from the well to her room. Or observed her sitting under the eaves of her house, the embroidery rack she had used for decades propped up in front of her but bare, unused. Sometimes a fine piece of silk or satin appeared on the rack, adorned with indescribably beautiful and lifelike flowers or birds or fish or insects, or maybe floating clouds and wild cranes; but these pieces had been fashioned many years before. Some of her more observant neighbors guessed that Sixth Great Aunt wasn't about to die after all, since Ninth Elder sent money from Beijing every month and she was surely waiting for him to return. When they thought about the many strange and wondrous things that had happened in her life, this assumption seemed plausible. Gradually, the old woman was seen less and less frequently and, as time went by, people's interest in her waned. And so, following a very short winter and a spring, it was summer again, and suddenly people realized they hadn't seen Sixth Great Aunt for several months. Someone went up and knocked at her door, but there was no answer. Someone went for a pry bar. When they got the door open, it was like entering a hive; the walls were black with crawling flies, as were the table and chairs. There was a resounding buzz, and as thousands of flies swarmed to the door, nearly knocking people over, the walls, table, chairs, and hand-carved sandalwood bed erupted into view. A sickening smell of rotting flesh churned the stomachs of everyone in the room, sending them scurrying out the door. When a few hardy souls returned, they found Sixth Great Aunt's corpse. To their astonishment, the old woman's body was clad in resplendent wedding clothes: silk and satin from head to toe, all beautifully embroidered by her own hand. They held their breath as they stood above the silk-draped cadaver, looking at what was once Silver City's most amazing woman. They did not know when she had died, or whether it had been in agony or joy, or why she had dressed her death in such beauty.

The people gazed at the beautiful cadaver, not daring to get any closer and not wanting to stay in the terrifying room any longer. They puzzled over what to do with the corpse until someone recommended taking down the door and carrying the body outside on the bed to burn it in the courtyard. Somehow the crowd found itself standing outside watching a blazing fire turn Silver City's remarkable woman into a pile of cinders.

CHAPTER TWELVE

1

Li Naizhi never imagined that the reverberations of the mass execution at Silver City's prison in December 1939 would sound all the way to his death in 1970.

When the Cultural Revolution had raged for more than two years, the great leader Chairman Mao signaled a "May Seventh" campaign of reeducation through manual labor for the ranking urban cadres. So in 1968 Li Naizhi was lifted by a surging tide of humanity and carried all the way from Beijing to a May Seventh Cadre School in Jiangxi Province, where he and several other vice-ministers were locked up in a row of buildings encircled by high walls.

Li Naizhi gazed out the window as he was driven from the train station in Nanchang, and when he saw the rust-colored fields and rolling hills, he was suddenly gripped by unbearable homesickness. The place was remarkably similar to Silver City: earth so red it seemed to ooze blood, red dirt roads that churned up mud, a little river that hugged the highway in all its twists and turns, distant villages that cowered in the dank, cold air, dark waves of hilltop pines. The landscape seemed so familiar to Li Naizhi that he was reminded of a day many years before, when he was strolling through a similar vista, a schoolbag over his sun-warmed back, and saw the two people dearest to him, two girls at the far end of a deserted road, raising their hands in greeting, one holding a handkerchief that fluttered in the rays of the setting sun like an egret in hesitant flight. On impulse, he lifted his eyes heavenward, searching for the sun, but he couldn't find it. The hazy sky pressed down while all around there was only cold murky light.

The stone-faced chief of the special investigative team, wrapped snugly in an army greatcoat, sat pressed up against him as he stared at the bumper of the car in front. Up ahead of the caravan of cars, rows of uniform brick buildings rose out of the wasteland. "We're here," someone said. The cars came to a rocking stop when they reached a clearing. The chilled May Seventh warriors stomped their feet and rubbed their hands together as they were herded with their bags into a courtyard to await room assignments.

The May Seventh Cadre School was a former labor-reform farm from which the prisoners had been moved, leaving behind the rows of encircled buildings, a small herd of cattle, and a few peasants hired to look after things. Li Naizhi was assigned to first company, second platoon, third squad, which was reserved for those of vice-minister rank and higher who had been targeted for "purification"; they were "the big fish" caught in the campaign to purge class ranks and unearth traitors. The big fish, all of them old men, particularly sensitive to the cold, sat huddled on top of their luggage. Li Naizhi took out a small bottle, unscrewed the cap, and took a drink. The fragrant aroma of strong Lüzhou wine slowly spread across the courtyard; his son had secretly handed him the flask just before he boarded the train. The chief of the special investigative team scowled at the smell.

"Li Naizhi, this is a May Seventh Cadre School, not one of your dens of vice!"

All eyes turned to look at a face that showed only apathy and fatigue. This sort of tongue-lashing had little effect on Li Naizhi, accustomed as he was to it after being shut up for nearly two years in a "cowshed," the makeshift quarters where landlords, rightists, and other bad elements were locked away. The chief of the special investigative team walked up to him, snatched the bottle from his hand, and flung it against the nearest wall; glass splintered and the courtyard was quickly flooded with the aroma of wine. Li Naizhi looked impassively at the irate team chief, then turned and gazed sadly at the shattered bottle. One of the big fish behind him said softly, "Let it go, Old Li." But after moving into his assigned quarters, Li Naizhi waited until the monitor was called out to attend a meeting before reaching into his coat and drawing out another wine flask, like a magician. He unscrewed the cap and took two deep drinks, then passed the flask to the man who had cautioned him earlier. "Have some, Old Chen." Old Chen smiled. "What are we going to do with you?"

And so, from the very first day in the May Seventh Cadre School, the Traitorous Li Naizhi Special Investigative Team and the military representative in charge had no choice but to initiate a succession of struggles against Naizhi over the wine issue. They explicitly prohibited him from drinking or buying wine, searched his belongings on a regular basis, and even convoked a special criticism session for him alone. But they could not keep him from his liquor; he found ways to buy wine and opportunities to violate the prohibition against drinking. It became a game for him, his sole pleasure. In the midst of the Great Proletarian Cultural Revolution, an ideological campaign unprecedented in human history, Li Naizhi stubbornly insisted on playing this game so incompatible with the seriousness of the times that its only outcome could be his death.

Li Naizhi was the most junior vice-minister among the big

fish that had been caught, having been promoted from bureau chief in 1965, the year before the Cultural Revolution was launched. During that year, he had suffered from fatigue brought on by chronic hepatitis, eventually coughing up blood and collapsing at the office. After receiving emergency medical treatment, he spent six months regaining his health and pestering his superiors until they finally let him return to work. The promotion order came soon after, but the position granted him was largely symbolic, with few if any responsibilities.

The May Seventh Cadre School was no convalescent hospital, and owing to Li Naizhi's legendary intransigence, the military representative forbade any contact with other people, assigning him work as a cowherd and a toilet cleaner. To everyone's surprise, Li Naizhi loved tending the cattle, and by the end of winter he had the small herd in perfect shape, as well behaved and neatly turned out as a troop of soldiers. The herd leader, a sharp-horned animal that always held his head high, was his favorite; he called him Old Yellow and often fed him buns he bought in the dining hall. After each day's work, he patiently cleaned the mud off Old Yellow's hide, and over time, the shrewd animal came to know and appreciate his patient master. Li Naizhi had only to stand at the pen's open gate for Old Yellow to throw back his horns and amble over with a look of recognition in his big eyes. Li Naizhi saw trust in those eyes and was frequently moved by Old Yellow's behavior. He'd step up, pat the animal's neck, and say, "There's nothing to do, Old Yellow, I just wanted to say hello." Then he would busy himself putting feed in the trough or spreading fresh dirt over the ground inside the pen. If he had already performed these tasks, he would pick up his palm-leaf broom and brush down Old Yellow, who followed his movements with his head, to the ringing accompaniment of the cowbell around his neck. Then came the lowing, soft and slow and filled with longing. Li Naizhi would pat his neck: "Let it go, Old Yellow, you're too kind to me."

Gradually people at the May Seventh Cadre School discovered that, instead of carrying a whip when he tended the oxen, Li Naizhi went out with only a bamboo flute that he had made. He had now found an outlet for what he had learned years earlier in the anti-Japanese choral troupe. He played his flute as he led his charges up the mountain and was still playing it when he brought them home. Gradually the people discovered that he played "The East Is Red" on his way up the mountain and "The Helmsman Leads Us across the Seas" when he herded them back down. As soon as Old Yellow heard the flute, he led the other animals out of the pen, all of them falling in behind Li Naizhi. In the morning and at dusk, a straw hat hanging down across his back and a flute held up to his lips, Li Naizhi looked indeed to have become an old cowherd. One day, while he was tending Old Yellow, watching the stream flow gently past the mountain and listening to cowbells far off on the slope, he suddenly remembered the communiqué Commander Liu had written decades before, upon relinquishing power:

"Gathering wood in the mountains and fishing in the river is the life I seek. I long for a glimpse of home, and the joy of strolling through the fields . . ."

On that early evening in 1969, as the setting sun blazed blood-red, Li Naizhi sat on his mountain slope watching the ancient and time-worn dusk close in, soothing his aching heart. He turned his head slowly and asked:

"Had enough to eat, Old Yellow? Time to go home."

Then he began to play his flute, and with the first notes, Old Yellow raised his head from a clump of weeds and began plodding steadily down the mountain; at the base of the slope, he turned and bellowed majestically for the others to follow. Li Naizhi laughed, then began playing the tune everyone knew so well, "The Helmsman Leads Us across the Seas."

Old Yellow raised his horned head and bellowed loudly again.

As Li Naizhi prowled the grounds of the May Seventh Cadre

School with his herd of oxen, he frequently met up with a coarse, dark-faced peasant whom everyone called Hayseed. Hired by the former labor-reform farm to look after the empty buildings and the oxen, Haywood was kept on when the May Seventh Cadre School replaced it. At the end of each day, when Li Naizhi led his herd back to their pen, he turned them over to Hayseed, and together the two men threw feed into the trough. Then Li Naizhi watched as Hayseed closed the gate and secured it with a thick board. Hayseed never said a word, but Li Naizhi always heard the man's ragged, heavy breathing. On one occasion, as Li Naizhi was pulling a flat cart up to the pen, loaded with artemisia he had cut down to spread over the ground, the cart got stuck in the mud beside the road; he struggled to free the wheel, and was getting nowhere, when all of a sudden the cart lurched forward. Straightening up, he saw Hayseed quietly pushing with all his might. When they were back in the pen and had spread the artemisia, Hayseed abruptly broke the silence:

"Old Li, are you really a bad element?"

Caught by surprise, Li Naizhi looked at the dark-faced peasant, then corrected him: "They don't call me a bad element, they call me a traitor."

"Are you really a traitor?"

"Do I look like one?"

"No."

"Why not?"

"A bull wouldn't trust a bad person."

Li Naizhi laughed. "That view is not in accord with the concept of class struggle."

Li Naizhi's laughter embarrassed Hayseed, whose dark face flushed darker.

Following this brief exchange, Hayseed did not speak to Li Naizhi again, but Naizhi often returned to find that Hayseed had cleaned the pen and noticed that the man took all the heavy jobs on himself. Li Naizhi would wait for him in front of the pen.

"Hayseed, thank you," he would say when the man showed up. Hayseed wouldn't reply or even look up, but one evening as he walked off, he said, "I'm strong. It's easier for me." He added, "Old Li, don't drink so much. The doctor says wine is bad for the liver." Then, without waiting for a reply, he took a cautious look around and walked off. In the dying light, a surprised Li Naizhi watched the broad back move into the distance, then removed the board from the gate and went up to Old Yellow, patting him on the head.

"Old Yellow, Hayseed is a good man."

He reached inside his shirt and took out a bottle of wine. "But he doesn't understand wine," he said.

After two quick swigs of the strong white wine, he felt his heart catch fire, and that brought a familiar, comforting warmth as sweet munching sounds rose from flickering shadows in the pen.

2

Li Naizhi was puzzled as he opened the envelope, because instead of his wife's familiar handwriting, it was addressed in a child's crooked scrawl. A single line of writing appeared on a sheet of exercise paper torn out of a notebook:

> Papa, Mama died yesterday, Brother and Sisters aren't home, I'm scared Papa, hurry back Papa.
>
> Xiaoruo

The letter wasn't dated, so Li Naizhi looked at the postmark, the numbers fading where the ink was light . . . 11–16–1969. Li Naizhi's younger son, Xiaoruo, a second-grader when the Cultural Revolution began, was barely ten years old. Li Naizhi read the words again. His son's voice rang in his ears. I'm scared Papa, hurry back Papa.

On the eve of his departure from Beijing, the military representative and the revolutionary committee had released a circular urging all cadres to strike out on the May Seventh trail with firm resolve and steely purpose, and to that end, family members had been prohibited from seeing them off at the station. For "ox spirits" and "snake demons" like Li Naizhi, who were isolated for investigation and subject to the absolute will of the proletariat, the rules were stricter: all contact with outsiders was forbidden. But as Li Naizhi stood in the station waiting to board the train, his younger son, Xiaoruo, squeezed through the crowd and handed him a wool scarf, wrapped around a bottle of strong Lüzhou wine.

"Mama asked me to give you this, Papa," his son said. "She's over there." Li Naizhi looked in the direction his son was pointing and there, beyond the disorderly crowd, across the street, he spotted his wife. Bai Qiuyun, wearing a dark gray padded coat with a dark gray scarf looped around her neck, was standing before a gray wall in the winter sunlight, her pale face showing bright against the dull background. Li Naizhi looked down and ruffled his son's hair.

"You go on, now, Xiaoruo. Tell Mama not to worry."

The boy nimbly threaded his way through the crowd, and very quickly two pale faces showed against the dark gray wall, one high and one low. Bai Qiuyun had presented Li Naizhi with five children, four of whom had already left Beijing, either to join a labor team in the countryside or to take up work elsewhere, leaving only Xiaoruo at home with his mother; the large, boisterous family was now dispersed to the four corners. Xiaoruo waved to Li Naizhi, who forced a smile in reply, though he couldn't be sure they saw it. It seemed to him that his wife was crying, that her face had begun to glisten. The ranks began to stir just then, and the densely packed rows of heads blocked his view. . . . Li Naizhi never dreamed that this would be the last time he would see Bai Qiuyun. "Papa, Mama died yesterday," his son had scrawled the words, but ever since that night so many years ago when they drifted down Silver Creek on a barge, he had assumed they would grow old together, partners till death.

With his son's letter in hand, Li Naizhi went to ask the military representative for a furlough, but the man interrupted before he had a chance to finish.

"We got the news three days ago, and were just about to come talk to you. Bai Qiuyun died by her own hand; she committed suicide and so alienated herself from the people. Given who she was, the daughter of a bourgeois family, her action is unmistakable proof of her contempt toward the Cultural Revolution, the party, and the people. When you're home taking care of the funeral arrangements, we expect you to handle this politically charged issue with the seriousness it deserves. Do not choose the same path of alienating yourself from the party and the people."

As he listened wordlessly, watching the snowy chips of white enamel shining from between the military representative's bright red lips, Li Naizhi could not understand why they had held back the news of his wife's death. Suddenly he noticed that the three or four other people in the room were staring at him. Then he spoke: "I won't die by my own hand. I trust the party to clear my name. And until that happens, I will not die."

But even as he spoke, he could barely conceal his disgust. Who would have thought that the secret execution in December 1939 would dog him all these years, from Silver City to Yan'an and from Yan'an to Beijing? As long as he lived he would remember how he had shouted slogans while looking down the cold, menacing barrel of a gun; had he been sacrificed at that moment, he would have fallen a pure and noble defender of his ideals. But no, instead of dying, he had been saved by his sister. She could not have known that, while he would narrowly escape death that day, he would never be able to escape the dark legacy of his survival or the vengeance of those who had revolted against his clan. Except for him, there was not a single living person who could testify to his stainless history. How was it that the very ideals he had risked his life to pursue could now be used against him in an accusation he was helpless to disprove? "Papa, Mama died yesterday," his son had written, and in his agony, Li Naizhi felt his heart fill with such crushing disgust that for a second he forgot the sorrow of losing his wife, forgot his body-and-soul love for Xiaoruo.

The experimental farm near Beijing where he and Bai Qiuyun had lived while he was a vice-minister and where Bai Qiuyun had died dealt with her crime of "alienating herself from the people and from the party" by cremating her without delay and calling a special workers' meeting to subject her to one final round of criticism. By the time Li Naizhi arrived, Bai Qiuyun's ashes filled a white ceramic urn that the children, reunited, had placed on a makeshift altar, alongside a photograph of her taken many years before. He took down the photograph but quickly put it back. It was impossible to believe that the woman with whom he had shared his entire adult life, a life of mutual reliance and support, had vanished into thin air, leaving only a handful of ashes and a photograph—stiff, dead, and fraudulent. Li Naizhi picked up the snowy white urn, and as he held it in his hands, a terrible coldness traveled from his palms to his head. Once again he experienced a sense of hazy unreality: this cold ceramic urn, was this the sum total of his wife and everything she was? Straining to rise out of his haze, Li Naizhi said to the children:

"Let's put Mama in the bedroom. I'll stay with her for a few days . . ."

Before he could finish, the children, gathered around him, began to sob. Through his tears, Xiaoruo said, "Papa, I didn't know Mama took sleeping pills . . . When I woke up in the morning she hadn't made breakfast . . . I didn't know . . ."

Once again, Li Naizhi strained to rise out of his haze. "Xiaoruo, I don't blame you, it's not your fault. Mama died because of Papa . . . Leave me alone with Mama for a little while. Afterward, there's something I want to say to you children . . ."

He stopped in midsentence, overcome by the meaninglessness of it all; nothing in the world could make up for the death of his wife or fill the void that had opened in him. So many years, a lifetime of emotions, had in one brief moment been transformed into a handful of gray ashes in a cold ceramic urn. Li Naizhi felt himself inexorably drawn into an ancient and time-worn story; he was old, and his withered heart held the dreariness of the ages. Death had not just taken his wife from this room but taken him as well, taken that boy of so many years before who had chased his ideals, a schoolbag slung over his back. As that youngster walked down an old rust-colored path, there at the far end, in the halo of a red sunset, he saw two girls, one waving a white handkerchief at him, an egret floating in the air. . . .

Li Naizhi closed the bedroom door, the sound of the children's crying in his ears. With an old man's tears streaking his face on that cold November day in 1969, Li Naizhi looked at the white ceramic urn and said:

"Qiuyun, Qiuyun, I've come home . . ."

3

Li Naizhi was forced out of a hospital bed to be sent back under escort to the May Seventh Cadre School in Jiangxi. The pain of losing his wife had caused his chronic hepatitis to flare up, and he had had no choice but to enter the hospital for treatment. But immediately following a discussion between the physician in charge and the chief of the special investigative team, he received word that he was to be discharged. His children rushed to the train station to see their father off, all but his third daughter, Yan'an, who did not appear. Throughout the mourning period, Li Naizhi had waited for Yan'an, hoping with all his heart that the pain of losing her mother might bring her to his side; but his hopes were dashed. Not only did Yan'an, who had "resolutely made a clean break" with her traitor father, fail to return home, but she sent no word. Yan'an stood unwaveringly in the front line of Chairman Mao's revolutionary battle, her heart as hard and unyielding as iron; she had volunteered for service in northern Shaanxi, the cradle of revolution, driven by enmity and anger toward all traitors. Even as Li Naizhi languished in the cowshed, Yan'an had put up a poster in the corridor of her father's ministry in Beijing, announcing that she had "resolutely made a clean break with the big traitor, Li Naizhi." Then she had answered Chairman Mao's call to travel to the plateaus of northern Shaanxi to join the peasants. Not long after that, Yan'an wrote a letter to her mother from Shaanxi, informing her that in order to sink vital roots into the rural village and be forever integrated with the workers and peasants, she had married a local shepherd. Li Naizhi knew that his daughter's actions were all in response to him, all born of her enmity toward him. And as he looked down from the railroad car at his other children, their eyes red and swollen, and at the teeming masses of people pushing and shoving on the platform, he suddenly felt as if he were separated from his daughter by a thousand mountains and ten thousand rivers and by tens of thousands of years; he suddenly felt that he might never again in this life lay eyes on his daughter Yan'an.

On Li Naizhi's return to the May Seventh Cadre School, the first thing the special investigative team did was search his belongings; as expected, they found two bottles of strong wine. But after lights out that night, the heavy aroma of wine wafted above Naizhi's quilt, and during a second search the chief of the team discovered that the rubber water bottle that Li Naizhi used to warm his bed was actually filled with sixty-proof sorghum wine. The next day, the two bottles of wine and the hot-water bottle were brought along to Li Naizhi's criticism meeting, where the military representative and the assembled crowd loudly denounced him for his cunning opposition to the Cultural Revolution; the military representative pointed out that Li Naizhi's drinking habits were nothing less than a counterrevolutionary means of slow suicide. Li Naizhi had lost track of how many criticism meetings he had been subjected to, but this was the first one that attacked him for his drinking. Standing apathetically in the cold sunlight of that January day, he looked down at the crowd massed below the stage and spotted Hayseed squatting way in the back; when their eyes met, Hayseed lowered his in obvious discomfort, which brought a faint smile to Li Naizhi's lips. He noticed that the eyes of many of the people watching him were smiling at the fact that he had hidden wine in a water bottle and at the absurdity of the criticism meeting in the first place.

Getting his hands on wine now became a major problem for Li Naizhi. The military representative posted orders in the doorways of all the local shops prohibiting the sale of alcohol to Li Naizhi. Deprived of his wine, Li Naizhi still went out to work every day, tending Old Yellow and the rest of the herd as usual, though people commented that he suddenly seemed much older; some tried to comfort him: "Old Li, not drinking will actually improve your health." He nodded and smiled in agreement, but there was a dull quality to his smile. Li Naizhi tended his herd, walking dully up and down the mountain that January of 1970. When he sat in the grass on the mountain slope with the herd, thoughts of his wife often came to tear at his heart, and he felt how old he had grown, and how feeble. Tormented by a great thirst, he would long for a swig of wine, recalling with exquisite clarity the rush of burning pleasure that the first drink always brought. Turning to his companion, he would blurt out:

"Old Yellow, a day without wine is as long as three autumns."

At the sound of his voice, Old Yellow would turn his big, black, trusting eyes and gaze into Li Naizhi's face. Sometimes Li Naizhi would be so moved by his companion that he would recite lines from "Wine Immortal," a poem by Li Bai. In the cold sunlight of January 1970, a great many ancient and time-worn scenes were summoned by those lines:

A flower-dappled horse,
Furs worth a thousand in gold,
Tell the boy to exchange them for good wine,
And we'll drown the woes of ten thousand generations!

After reciting these ancient words, Li Naizhi often laughed at himself as he patted his companion's neck: "Let it go, Old Yellow, since you can't understand what the man said." But then an irrepressible ache would rise in his throat and he would turn in embarrassment to his companion to apologize: "Sorry, Old Yellow, but you're better off not understanding."

Li Naizhi never dreamed that Hayseed, who had once urged him to stop drinking, would be the one to come up with a brilliant solution to his wine problem. One day, as Li Naizhi was bringing his herd down the mountain slope, Hayseed rushed up and led Old Yellow away with the excuse that he needed him to turn a millstone. A short while later, Old Yellow returned alone, and Li Naizhi saw a pouch hanging from around his neck. Inside were a bottle of strong white wine and a bag of peanuts. When he looked up, he spotted Hayseed's broad back moving down the road off in the distance. Later that afternoon, when they met in front of the pen, Li Naizhi said with a laugh:

"Hayseed, won't that bottle of wine damage my liver?"

Hayseed looked serious. "Old Li, I'm like you. I lost my wife too." With his eyes fixed on Li Naizhi, he added, "Old Li, you can't call someone back from the dead, so don't let yourself get too sad. You're a leading cadre, you ought to know that better than me."

Silently they filled the trough with feed, shoveled up the animal droppings, and took them to the manure pile; after latching the gate with the board, Li Naizhi watched Hayseed gradually disappear down the road. I need a drink, he thought to himself, a drink to Hayseed. He took out the bottle, which was still half full—he had planned to save the rest for the next day—tipped back his head, and drank to the very last drop, flinging the empty bottle on the manure pile when he was finished. The burning sensation in his chest brought pleasure all the way to the marrow of his bones. Maybe, he thought, he wouldn't have to wait till his name was cleared, for there was no one left to prove his honor to. At that thought, the fire in his chest vanished and he was as tranquil and clear as a pond in autumn.

Death came quietly on a snowy New Year's Eve.

That day, the May Seventh Cadre School cadres had organized a New Year's dinner. The military representative, who had declared a five-day holiday, joined in to drink and celebrate. Ox demons and snake spirits were excluded, however, so Li Naizhi tended his herd as usual. As he led them up the mountain, he wondered whether Hayseed would come today. But he didn't. He had been sent to the kitchen to slaughter and prepare a pig, which had kept him busy all day. Li Naizhi still hadn't seen him by the time the herd was back in the pen and the gate latched. But when he laid out his quilt that night, a bottle of rice wine rolled out and he had to laugh, knowing this was Hayseed's doing. Quickly he opened the bottle and took a couple of swigs, then let the wine burn its way down; the fiery sensation turned his thoughts to his children, and he wondered how they were passing this New Year's Eve. He took two more deep drinks and felt the burning power of the wine seep into his heart. He was warm and sleepy; the lamp seemed bright and hot. He lay down and fell asleep almost at once. As he slept, snowflakes the size of goose feathers fell just beyond his door, huge snowflakes floating silently to the ground, coating the world in a gentle, silvery down.

Just before dawn, sharp pains startled Li Naizhi awake. Foul-smelling liquid surged up into his mouth. He knew it was blood; the same thing had happened once before. Flicking on his flashlight, he pulled the spittoon close to his face and spat out a puddle of red. Then he noticed the thick layer of glittering whiteness on the windowsill. It's snowing, he thought to himself.

By the time the others had woken from their dreams, Li Naizhi's spittoon was half full of bright red blood. The nearest hospital was twenty li away. "Are the roads slippery in weather like this?" the military representative asked. "Yes," the driver replied. "Well," the military representative said, "since it could be dangerous, let's wait till the sun's up." Li Naizhi lay in bed without saying a word; he knew he didn't need a hospital and didn't need the sun. Old Chen, with whom he shared his room, asked, "Old Li, is there anything you want your family to do?"

Li Naizhi thought for a moment before saying, "Tell my third daughter, Yan'an, to come wash my soiled quilt and clothes."

"Old Li," Old Chen persisted, "is there anything you want us to tell the party?" Li Naizhi knew exactly what Old Chen had in mind, and he shook his head. Then he turned and spat up another mouthful of dark red blood.

As they were placing his stretcher onto a truck, Li Naizhi felt something cold melting on his face. He opened his eyes and saw the snow-covered rooftops and the trees' white canopy and the ground covered with pure white snow. The sun wasn't up yet and the space between heaven and earth in that predawn hour was one of soft serenity. In the snowy peace, Li Naizhi felt the final speck of life depart into the deepest recesses of the blue-black heavenly void. He remembered that on that December day in the Silver City prison, on the day of the secret execution in 1939, it had also been snowing, in a high-walled courtyard just like this one.

That afternoon, the internal medicine department of the Meiling Hospital issued a death certificate:

> Bed number: Eighteen. Patient's name: Li Naizhi. Sex: Male. Age: Sixty. Time and Date of Admission: 9:30 A.M., February 15, 1970. Symptoms: Spitting blood, liver rigidity, ruptured varicose vein in stomach.
>
> Medical summary: At 4:00 A.M. patient spat up 2,000 milliliters of blood, at approximately 1:00 P.M. spat up another 1,200 milliliters. Emergency treatment futile. Patient died at 5:15 P.M., February 15, 1970.
>
> Cause of death: Excessive loss of blood, producing hemorrhagic shock.
>
> Physician: Liu Shuxiang
> 7:00 P.M., February 15, 1970

Looking through his effects that evening, the military representative found an issue of the *People's Daily* covered with handwriting. Li Naizhi had filled every inch of available space with a single word over and over: revolutionrevolutionrevolutionrevolutionrevolutionrevolutionrevolutionrevolutionrevolution . . . no lead-in, no follow-up, no punctuation, no space between the words, just a mass of cramped, tangled letters. No one understood what Li Naizhi meant by this or comprehended the frame of mind he was in when he filled the sheet of newspaper with his handwriting.

Members of the May Seventh Cadre School waited and waited for Li Naizhi's third daughter to come and wash her father's blood-soiled bedding and clothes.

But Yan'an never came.

CHAPTER THIRTEEN

1

After two years of reform through labor, Bai Qiuyun had become a model field-worker, equally adept at weeding crops, harvesting wheat, carrying water, winnowing grain, picking cotton, and spraying insecticide. She had even learned how to fertilize the cabbage patch—men's work. A wellsweep had been set up at the manure pits alongside a ditch, with a willow dipper at one end and an iron weight at the other. The dipper was lowered into the manure with a rope, then raised by means of the weight, and swung slowly out over the ditch, where its contents were tipped into the flow of water. The blackish yellow muck turned the clear ditch water into a murky substance that seeped into the fields. Bai Qiuyun soon became inured to the soaring stench of the stomach-churning night soil slopping over the sides of the dipper, to the squirming maggots, and to the foul objects, some expected and some not, that clung to the dipper; she even got used to eating her lunch beside the manure pit during the farm's busy seasons.

Zhang Cai, a burly farmworker, was in charge of the ox-demon and snake-spirit team. In his eyes, only people who worked with their hands were real laborers. Everyone else he divided into two categories: the men were called officials; the women, officials' wives. He was delighted to be designated labor-reform team leader, since he had the pleasure of wielding the whip over all those officials and officials' wives. Lumped together, they were all dog shit. Each morning he summoned the ox demons and snake spirits to the edge of the fields to study one of Chairman Mao's quotations before going to work; he, of course, chose the quotation for the day. Calling up one of the officials or officials' wives, he would hand the person his little red book and say:

"You read, the quotation at the bottom of page 16."

And the reading began: "The diehards may be stubborn, but they are not stubborn unto death, and in the end they change—into something contemptible, like dog shit."

At this point, Zhang Cai would wave his hand. "Stop! Hear that? Dog shit! You fucking officials and officials' wives are nothing but dog shit! Me, Zhang Cai, I'm a third-generation peasant. My grandfather was a coolie laborer in a coal mine at Mentougou, my father was a rickshaw boy at Tianqiao, and I'm a fucking farmer. Why the hell did we stink and sweat for three generations, hm? Why the hell should you people lie about doing nothing but drinking your fancy wine and still rake in all that fucking money? Does that make any fucking sense? No. And that's why Chairman Mao launched his Cultural Revolution. And why you people are such eyesores to Chairman Mao. You fucking dog shit! Now get to work, ladies and gentlemen, and see what it fucking means to be a real laborer!"

Of all the ox demons and snake spirits, Bai Qiuyun interested Zhang Cai the most, for a very simple reason: she was the most distinguished official's wife in the entire labor-reform brigade. In August 1967, her house having been searched and her possessions confiscated, she had been assigned to her first labor-reform work detail. Zhang Cai grinned as he pulled her out of the ranks that August day and told her to read the dog shit passage from Chairman Mao's quotations. When she finished, he took away her canvas work gloves and said with a laugh:

"We have a VIP with us today—a fucking minister's wife. Just look at how clean and white her gloves are. I hear that our minister's salary has been stopped and his savings book confiscated by the special investigative team, which puts us on an equal footing. I've worked my whole fucking life without splurging on a pair of gloves like our princess here has. Maybe you think you're some fragile jade leaf, but you're exactly like the rest of them: dog shit!"

His tirade over, Zhang Cai sent Bai Qiuyun to work at one of the two manure pits at the edge of the field. "Here's an easy job. Just move the muck from that pit to the other one today. You'll have to work through the noon hour. But don't worry, we'll bring you some food."

That day Bai Qiuyun learned how to operate the wellsweep. With the August sun beating down fiercely, the pit spewed a foul stench and powerful ammonia fumes that all but asphyxiated her; she was nearly smothered by the flies that swarmed over her, landing on her hands and eyes and nose and lips. Her stomach erupted, sending her breakfast out her mouth and onto the ground, a sticky white mess that baked under the sun, drawing hordes of happily buzzing flies that quickly turned it to a sticky black mess. Bai Qiuyun inadvertently bumped the wellsweep, which swayed slightly in the sunlight, like a useless marionette with its arms hanging limply at its side.

Zhang Cai was as good as his word, for he personally brought her lunch out to the field: a plate of fried kidney beans and two chunks of hard cornbread. He laid the food down on the cement ledge of the motorized well beside the manure pit and called Bai Qiuyun over to eat. As she came, he turned on the well motor and watched clear water gush from the spigot.

"Come on, Madame Minister, I'm at your service while you

wash up and eat. We don't want people to say we mistreat our prisoners, do we?"

Bai Qiuyun washed her hands, then buried her face in the refreshing water, like farmhands everywhere, gulping down mouthfuls of cool water. When she was finished, she dried her face with a handkerchief and said:

"No food for me, I'm not hungry."

Zhang Cai laughed. "Not hungry? OK. That way you won't waste good food. But I'm telling you, when you come out tomorrow, ask the other pieces of dog shit if not eating got any of them out of work. Don't think Madame can get sent some other fucking place just because she doesn't like it here!" Zhang Cai picked up the plate and started to walk off, before adding: "Not hungry? Madame on a diet? The way you gulped down that water, you looked no different from any other fucking farm animal. You'll see, we'll make a laborer out of you yet."

Bai Qiuyun sat blankly on the edge of the now-still well, blinded by the blazing rays of the August sun. The steamy fields were still as death, but the buzzing of flies nearby was loud and clear and the soaring stench kept pressing toward her.

Bai Qiuyun didn't feel like eating, not a bite.

The next day she did not eat lunch, nor the day after that.

Every day for a week, Bai Qiuyun was sent out to work at the wellsweep, where she stood between two manure pits, assaulted by buzzing flies and a soaring stench. Eventually, strenuous labor won out over a delicate digestive tract, and on the last day of the week she was so weak and so hungry that she finally picked up a piece of hard cornbread. Zhang Cai stood off to the side brimming with satisfaction, relishing the munching sounds of one more humiliated individual.

At long last, Bai Qiuyun reformed herself into a qualified farmhand. At long last, she grew accustomed to the bitter cold and cruel heat, to the filth and exhaustion. Often, when she looked over at the wellsweep, she thought back to "The Revolution of Heaven," which she had read at the provincial school.

With casual elegance, the Taoist philosopher Zhuangzi had written: "Have you not seen the workings of a wellsweep? When the rope is pulled, it bends down; and when it is let go, it rises up. It is pulled by a man, and does not pull the man; and so, whether it bends down or rises up, it commits no offense against the man." Remembering this casual elegance, Bai Qiuyun felt deeply ashamed. Since throwing in her lot with her husband and joining him on the road to revolution, she had been reminded constantly that she must reform herself, that she must make a clean break with her bourgeois, class-exploiting family. Now, after all her efforts, she looked down at her calloused palms and suddenly felt wearier than words could describe. A hopeless wellsweep, that's what she was, made to bend down time and time again, then made to rise up time and time again. Weary beyond words, she dimly recalled the lush green of White Garden and the peaceful seclusion of Cathedral Street, recalled the swing set and her young dreams, recalled her mother's banishment. If indeed there was life after death, she was determined to make it up to her mother, whatever it took. Thoughts of life after death, she knew, implied thoughts of death, and as the profound weariness spread through her body, death was precisely what she thirsted for. She thirsted for death to bring an end to this limitless, inescapable weariness, to free her from the guilt and sorrow that plagued her.

2

Bai Qiuyun finally completed her preparations: a bottle of sleeping pills, a glass of water, and a note for her son Xiaoruo. She laid these objects out with no expression on her face and a heart as calm as still water, and when she was done, she discovered how familiar the procedure seemed. Maybe she had thought about it too often or had waited for it too long, so that now that the moment had arrived it seemed ordinary, simple, and dull. The table was empty but for a bottle of pills, a glass of water, and a slip of paper. Calmly, she faced them. Lamplight touched her sober figure, still as a tree standing lonely in the snow, a single tree. Bai Qiuyun did not know the date or the time. She had no special reason for choosing this particular night, nor had she experienced any particularly strong provocation or suffered any particular harm; she simply didn't want to put it off any longer. She had spent the day teaching Xiaoruo how to prepare breakfast, lunch, and dinner, and even though he was only ten, he did a passable job of all three meals. After dinner, as mother and son cleared the table, Bai Qiuyun patted him on the head and said:

"Son, you've grown up."

Xiaoruo looked at his mother, unaware of the deep sorrow this observation caused her. She patted his head again.

"Son, you've grown up."

"Ma," Xiaoruo replied, "I'm only ten."

"But you've grown up," Bai Qiuyun said.

Bai Qiuyun had been teaching her son to do housework—laundry, sewing, cooking, lighting the furnace—taking him carefully and patiently through each step, knowing that each skill learned brought her closer to the day. Sometimes she watched him struggle along until he managed to accomplish the task she had set, and she would laugh, a soft, distant laugh that somehow unnerved Xiaoruo. He could not know that his mother was calmly contemplating her death, but he was concerned enough to call out, "Mama." Startled out of her reverie by the sound of her son's voice, Bai Qiuyun would focus on him again and her eyes would regain their warmth.

"Son, you've grown up," Bai Qiuyun said.

"Ma," Xiaoruo replied, "I'm only ten."

"But you've grown up," Bai Qiuyun said.

Once these words were spoken, Bai Qiuyun felt freed of all cares and worries, like a ship tossed about on the waves until its ropes finally snap and let it go. Now everything had become so simple; all she faced was a bottle of pills, a glass of water, and a slip of paper, illuminated by the bright lamplight above. Everything had become so simple, so very familiar. She had always associated death with unrelieved darkness, but now that she was about to enter its realm, what she saw was a vast stretch of cold and cheerless emptiness in brilliant light.

A cold winter night without wind or sound gripped the world outside her room. Many years before, on another black winter night, as she risked her life to drift along on a barge, to flee with her husband, she never dreamed that she would end that life alone in this cold and cheerless emptiness. When her father, who had driven to the provincial capital on business and was staying over at Bamboo Garden, told her that Li Naizhi had been arrested, she had made up her mind immediately. Telling her parents she was going to spend a few days with friends, she secretly made her way back to Silver City and straight to the headquarters of Commander Yang to see Eighth Sister Li Ziyun.

"Sister Yun," Li Ziyun said after learning of her decision, "I never knew your feelings for Ninth Brother were so strong that you would give up everything for him . . . Ninth Brother's life is in grave danger. His fate is in your hands." Li Naizhi came to as the barge headed toward Ziyun Bridge. The light from a hanging lantern framed his pale face and penetrated the unbroken darkness of the night around their boat; Bai Qiuyun was moved by the most profound happiness she had ever known. "Naizhi," she said, "don't say anything. I've thought it all out." The river was in no hurry, the solitary lantern was like a beacon, and Bai

Qiuyun rejoiced at the good fortune of finally being here with the man she had longed for, drifting on the boat of life.

Close to thirty long years passed, filled with revolutionary fervor and nation building. And then, almost overnight, Bai Qiuyun's husband was transformed into a "big traitor" and a spy, and a blizzard of posters and slogans nearly blotted out the house and the courtyard; someone had even painted the walkway from the garden to the front gate with a slogan that read, "Ferret out the big traitor and spy Li Naizhi," and it was over this slogan that they had dragged her husband, cursing and spitting on him. As they trampled her husband's name, they ordered her to break completely with the big traitor and spy, expose and denounce him, and report immediately to the experimental farm's ox-demon and snake-spirit team for reform through labor. "Otherwise," they warned her, "you, like Li Naizhi, will be filthy, contemptible dog shit."

Sitting in her ransacked house, Bai Qiuyun suddenly felt that her home, for all that its contents were spilled and scattered across the floor, was as bare as a dead tree that had lost its leaves. Suddenly she felt that the insults hurled at her, the "stinking daughter of a capitalist family," might have some validity, that on the black night so many years before, when she had risked her life to drift along on that barge, it had all been for the man she loved, not for the revolution to which he had dedicated his life. As he was dragged out the door, her husband had turned and said, "Qiuyun, trust the masses and trust the party. My name will be cleared sooner or later. My conscience is free." But his words were swallowed up by shouts of "Stubborn resistance is the road to death."

At that moment, Bai Qiuyun felt that none of the things she had struggled to believe in could alter the fact that her husband had been taken from her, and she had the sudden sense that he might never return; at that moment she recalled that her cousin Wenda had committed suicide by swallowing arsenic. In his death agonies, he had made a shambles of his bed—the pillow on the floor, the sheets twisted into a ball, and the blankets all in a heap. In an instant, her refined, immaculate cousin had become something ugly, a repulsive pile of filth. Bai Qiuyun did not want to die like that; she would choose a cleaner, neater way. Comforted by that thought, she looked around her at the books, letters, and photographs strewn across the floor, then bent and picked them up, one at a time. One particular yellowed photograph caught her eye. Someone had stepped on it, leaving a dirty footprint. The person in the photo seemed familiar somehow, then she realized that the girl sitting on the swing was her. She had been relaxing on the swing, taking advantage of the shade of a banana tree to read *Pale Fragrance Poems,* and enjoying her favorite line from Li Qingzhao: "Desolation, misery, and woe." Had it all been a dream? Was the carefree girl rocking in a swing under the banana tree the same Bai Qiuyun who was now sitting amid the shambles of her house? What had she done in the years between? What had she seen? What was it all for? Sorrow flooded her heart.

Bai Qiuyun had been sitting for some time when she heard a child's hurried footsteps. Xiaoruo, out of breath and covered with mud, came running into the yard. The air was thick with the stink of Chinese ink and paste baked by the blistering rays of the summer sun, and Xiaoruo stood terrified in the midst of all the posters and slogans denouncing his father. He was holding a pair of dragonflies between his fingers; somewhere along the way the dragonflies had been squeezed to death, and they fell from his fingers now to lie shimmering in all their red beauty in the blistering sunlight. When Xiaoruo looked down and saw that he was standing squarely on his father's name, he grew flustered and instinctively jumped off to cower alongside the path. He looked up to see Bai Qiuyun coming down the steps.

While his family's house was being turned upside down,

Xiaoruo was out by the windbreak, snaring dragonflies in the rice paddy. The dragonflies called red chili peppers were his favorites; perched atop the rice tassels, they turned a glorious ruby red in the bright sunlight. Xiaoruo couldn't believe his luck at being part of something as fun as the Cultural Revolution; day after day it kept him out of school, with no homework and the freedom to play to his heart's content, which meant going off to catch dragonflies with his playmates. As he reached out with the sticky end of his bamboo pole, absorbed in snaring one of the red chili peppers, someone knocked the pole out of his hands. He spun around angrily and was face to face with Zhang Dafu looking triumphant.

"Hey, go home and see the big traitor and spy!"

"You looking for a fight?"

"You think you're a big shot but you're just a fucking dog whelp. Tomorrow your mother's going to be part of the ox-demon and snake-spirit team, where she'll take orders from my dad!"

Xiaoruo handed the two dragonflies he was grasping between his fingers to his friend Xiaobao. "Hold these for me," he said before turning and punching Dafu squarely in the chest. "Any more wisecracks?" he said as he watched the other boy land on his backside in the rice paddy. Dafu was the worst student in his class, forever being made to stand in the corner by their teacher. The other boys all scorned him. But this time Dafu wasn't backing down. He picked himself up out of the mud and came at Xiaoruo with curses and flying fists, shoving him into the water.

"You fucking dog whelp, who do you think you're hitting? Wait'll my dad gets his hands on you. Hear the loudspeaker? Hear who they're talking about?"

That took the fight out of Xiaoruo. Sure enough, the high-pitched loudspeakers atop the experimental farm's water tower were blaring slogans, sending them his way, steaming in the blistering sunlight. Zhang Dafu wasn't lying: Xiaoruo heard his father's name loud and clear. He got back up, took the dragonflies from Xiaobao, and started running home. He knew all about dog whelps: they were the children of landlords and rich peasants, the sons and daughters of class enemies, as his older brother, Li Jingsheng, had told him. The previous summer, at the very beginning of the Cultural Revolution, the farm's elementary school had let out early for the day; out by the windbreak, Xiaoruo and Xiaobao came upon a yellow-winged woodpecker among the trees. They took after it with their slingshots, chasing it all the way to a village called Five-Li Fort, where they spotted a crowd gathered on the threshing ground, red flags fluttering overhead. Elbowing their way through the crowd, they came on a group of Red Guards engaged in a struggle session. Some people with placards reading "Landlord" and "Bad Peasant" around their necks were standing in a line, bent over so low you couldn't see their faces, just a line of large, heavy placards hanging beneath a row of heads. The Red Guards were beating them on their backs and heads with leather belts and shouting at the top of their lungs for the accused to hand over their "restoration accounts," records of usurious loans the landlords extended in anticipation of the revolution's failure. The placards swung back and forth as the belts, shrieking through the air, found their targets. As every last man and woman slumped to the ground, Xiaoruo saw a row of bloody faces. Then he watched as someone picked up a jug and poured scalding hot water over them. Heartrending screams and angry curses fused in the air. The people on the ground clambered to their feet, but they were knocked right down again. The smell of blood and blistered skin hovered in the sun-drenched air; hanks of burned-off hair fell to the ground and stuck to torn, bloody faces. Xiaoruo's heart was pounding so fast he could hardly breathe when Xiaobao began to wail loudly; Xiaoruo's body tensed, and a stream of hot liquid ran down his leg and onto the hard, dry ground. Suddenly, he heard a shout.

"Xiaoruo! Xiaobao! What are you doing? You two get home right this minute!"

Xiaoruo saw Li Jingsheng coming toward them wearing a red armband. "We're going," Xiaoruo told him, "but you have to come with us."

The hot summer sun beat down so fiercely it forced their eyes shut. When Li Jingsheng saw his brother's soaked pant leg, he scowled in disgust.

On the road home, Xiaoruo asked his brother, "What were you doing there?"

"The peasants from the village asked some of the Red Guards from school to attend their struggle session."

"Why were you beating those people?"

"Because they're class enemies who want to restore the old order, and Chairman Mao called upon us Red Guards to sweep away all ox demons and snake spirits!"

"What are restoration accounts?"

"That's enough questions. You wouldn't understand even if I told you. From now on, you kids stay away from places like this. All you do is cry and make a scene, not to mention wetting your pants!"

Xiaoruo hung his head in embarrassment; his wet pant leg stuck to his skin. Xiaobao sobbed in the blistering air. The sun's rays made their scalps itch painfully, and the glare from the mirrorlike patches of water in the rice paddies stung their eyes. It seemed to Xiaoruo that all of heaven and earth was burning with blistering sunlight; the prickly sensation on the skin of his forehead bored its way into him, as the heartrending screams from the threshing ground followed him on his way. Red flags fluttered in the bright sunlight like a shifting sea of blood.

That night, Xiaoruo had a frightful nightmare. Cows and horses lay in an empty field, all of them legless, for some strange reason—just a mass of bloated torsos lying in the mud. People were beating them with sticks, flailing at their flesh to get them up and running. But how could they, without any legs? The animals just writhed and squirmed under the savage assault. "Don't hit me," they pleaded, "don't hit me." But the people kept flailing away with their sticks. With loud thuds, they beat them on their heads, they beat them on their backs, never even pausing. "Get up! Get up!" But the cows and horses could only wail and weep, their bloodied torsos writhing as they sought out one another's bodies for protection. Xiaoruo ran into the field shouting, "Run away, hurry, get out of here, how can you be so stupid?" But the cows and horses just looked up at him, wide-eyed. Too panic-stricken even to speak, Xiaoruo stood beneath the blazing sun and bawled. Startled awake by his own wailing, Xiaoruo opened his eyes and saw his mother standing by his pillow shaking him. He wrapped his arms around her, still sobbing. "Mama," he said, "Mama, they were beating all the animals to death."

Xiaoruo had no way of knowing that one day he, too, would become a dog whelp or that he would hear the news from Dafu, the person he despised most in the world. Even before he reached the house, he saw the slogans and posters plastered all over the compound. He ran into the yard and was immediately surrounded by angry black writing, that and the stink of Chinese ink and paste baked by the sun's rays. He looked down at the red chili peppers in his hands, both having died somewhere along the way; they fell to the ground, glorious red in the sunlight, next to his feet, which were planted squarely on his father's name. Flustered, Xiaoruo jumped off to cower alongside the path, and that's when he noticed his mother coming down the steps.

Bai Qiuyun said to the boy, "Let's go inside, Xiaoruo. It's too hot out here."

"Mama," Xiaoruo said.

With staring eyes, Xiaoruo saw everything, and he knew that, from today on, he was nothing but a dog whelp.

"Mama," he said again, as he followed her into the house and saw her lean against the door jamb. She was crying.

3

Barely a month after marrying Waiwai, Yan'an received a letter from Xiaoruo, her little brother, and learned that her mother was dead. After reading it two or three times, she laid it on the table.

"What's it say?" Waiwai asked.

"See for yourself," Yan'an replied.

Waiwai laughed. "Hah, as if I knew how to read."

"My mother died."

Waiwai's face darkened. He studied his hands and began picking at the callouses on his palms with grubby fingernails. After a moment or two, he said, "Yan'an, I've brought you nothing but trouble. Joining your fate with that of a lowly shepherd has brought a peasant's miserable destiny on your mother too, and only a month after we were married. I'll go cut up some black cloth, so you and I can wear mourning bands for the old lady."

"Qin Wanbao," Yan'an replied, "I never thought you'd take the old feudal superstitions so seriously."

"Ah, Yan'an," Waiwai said, "here in our village, the two most important kinds of people are those who give birth to us and those we give birth to. If we don't mourn for our elders, we're no better than animals."

"No mourning bands for me," Yan'an said, "and none for you either. As a party member, I'll have nothing to do with old thinking, old culture, old customs, or old habits, and I can't allow any of it to stand in the way of our revolutionary work. Tending the fields is much more important than those rituals. Besides, when I joined the commune, I made a clean break with my family, and I'll never go back."

Waiwai gaped at Yan'an, shocked. What kind of a woman is she? he thought. But her response only increased his belief that he was unworthy of her, that he would never be able to shed his illiterate, ignorant ways.

No one in Five-Man Plot called him by his real name, Qin Wanbao. When he was a toddler in split-crotch pants playing in the mud, not once did he manage to pee in the mud itself; later on, after he had grown up, become a shepherd, and stopped wearing split-crotch pants, everyone in Five-Man Plot—men, women, and children—still called him Waiwai, Little Crooked.

Waiwai caught his first glimpse of Yan'an on a mountain path. The commune leaders had come to inform the people of Five-Man Plot that Chairman Mao had sent his Red Guards back to northern Shaanxi Province to learn from the peasants. Having never seen one of these alien urbanites, the villagers gaped at them in wonder. Waiwai, who was on the mountain with his flock when the city youngsters entered the village, could not attend the welcoming ceremony, so he rushed to their assigned caves as soon as he returned that evening; too shy to enter, he stood outside with his hands tucked into the sleeves of his coat as the city youngsters sat in the brightly lit caves talking and laughing excitedly. The cave to the left was occupied by boys, the one to the right by girls. The sound of their laughter was so infectious that Waiwai couldn't help joining in, and as he stood there laughing in the night, someone in the cave to the right opened the wooden door and flung out a basinful of dirty water, splashing Waiwai's feet and legs. A girl in a checkered shirt appeared in the light of the entrance. "Oh, I'm sorry!" she screeched.

Waiwai took a step backward. "Don't worry, it doesn't bother me," he said with a smile.

"Won't you come in?" the girl said with an easy manner.

"I have to go," Waiwai blurted. "I need to take the sheep out tomorrow morning."

As he walked away, Waiwai was troubled by thoughts of what he had just seen: Who washes up before going to bed? There was enough in that basin to water two sheep. Located high up on the plain, Five-Man Plot was an arid place, and water had to be hauled up from a distant gully, which meant a round trip of two or three hours—an entire morning's labor. Those baby-faced students had no idea how valuable plain water was. Waiwai could not imagine that back in Beijing the students always washed their faces and feet before going to bed at night. The next morning, up on the mountain, Waiwai met one of the girls carrying a load of water, hobbling crookedly as she held the carrying pole out in front in her soft, white hands; what she lacked in strength she made up for in dogged determination, straining to hold her body straight. Pained by the sight, Waiwai set down the buckets he was carrying and went to take the pole from her. As he did so, he noticed fresh blood stains on the shoulder of her white shirt.

"This is no job for a girl," he said as he picked up her water buckets. "The weight will crush you." Back at the cave, after he had emptied her buckets into the water jug and put down the pole, the girl said:

"Thank you."

Waiwai smiled. "Why thank me for a piddling job like that? It's what a man's supposed to do."

Without warning, the girl thrust out her hand and said, "My name is Li Yan'an. What's yours?"

"I'm called Waiwai. They all say I . . ."

Waiwai's face flushed bright red as he stopped in midsentence, knowing how vulgar the story would sound to her. The city students weren't coarse like the local women, and you couldn't just say anything in front of them. Waiwai stared red-faced at the lily-white outstretched hand. He knew what the gesture meant—the girl wanted to shake his hand. He had seen cadres at the commune cooperative market shake hands when he was there buying salt licks for his sheep. Waiwai had never seen a hand so white, so soft, and he just stared at it, like a man on whom a great and undeserved honor has been bestowed. Apologetically, he said:

"Look how polite you are . . . My hand's too dirty . . ."

Before he had a chance to finish, Yan'an had his hand in her grasp. "Chairman Mao tells us," she said, "that 'the workers and peasants are the cleanest of all, that even though their hands are black and their feet covered with cow dung, they are cleaner than the bourgeoisie or the intellectuals.' "

The delicate soft hand nestled in his calloused palm, and a lascivious thought rushed into his head. As he greedily held her soft, white fingers, Waiwai said, "Dirty is dirty and clean is clean, and nothing you say can change that. Let's compare hands if you don't believe me."

Waiwai held out his free hand, large and calloused, and as he looked into Yan'an's face, he realized he was squeezing her hand too tightly and holding it longer than he should. For the rest of the day, he kept raising his hand to his nose so he could smell the lingering fragrance. After getting into bed that night, he thrust the hand down into his crotch, unable to stop himself, even though he knew it was wrong to do so. He cursed himself:

"You're the warty toad who wants to feast on the tender flesh of a swan. Dream on!"

Waiwai was unaware that Yan'an was a "model" comrade or that after breaking with her vice-minister father she was the first person to sign up for resettlement in the northern Shaanxi labor brigade. He did not know that Yan'an was determined to stay away from Beijing for as long as she lived, to never return home, preferring to roll in the mud and grow callouses on her hands, to remold herself in the sacred place, the cradle of revolution, where she was born. Nor did Waiwai know that Yan'an would soon submit a pledge to the commune party committee to marry a peasant and raise her children in the sacred revolutionary province. Waiwai thrust his hand down into his crotch because he couldn't help himself, because he was a bachelor well past marrying age.

Yan'an's and Waiwai's lives fused on the mountain. One morning, Waiwai was heading down to the gully for water when, at a bend in the path, he saw that he was being followed. Taking no notice, he began singing a sad little tune as he kept walking down the mountain:

Who's that damned woman on the knoll over there?
Nobody but my second sister . . .

His song was interrupted by a voice calling, "Qin Wanbao."

Still taking no notice, Waiwai kept walking and singing. The voice behind him shouted louder, "Qin Wanbao!"

Then it occurred to Waiwai that someone was using his real name. Waiwai turned around, and there was Yan'an. He waved at her. "Call me Waiwai, it saves trouble. I almost forgot that Qin Wanbao is my real name."

"Qin Wanbao," Yan'an said, coming closer, "I want to ask you something."

"What?"

"I want to ask if you'll agree to marry me."

"What? Marry? Who?"

"Me."

The white winter sun hung high in the sky. An endless vista of rolling yellow hills stretched all the way to the edge of heaven. The winding mountain path beneath Waiwai's feet was frozen, dry and hard. He looked down at the tattered sandals he was wearing, then up at the white sun high in the sky. He wiped his nose with his sleeve and said:

"I don't feel like swapping nonsense with you in the middle of the day."

Flustered, Yan'an took out a copy of the pledge she had signed. "Look here, Qin Wanbao, I made this pledge to the commune party committee. I want to put down roots in northern Shaanxi and spend the rest of my life here. I want to marry a peasant and raise my children here to carry on the revolution from one generation to the next."

By the time Yan'an had spoken her piece, Waiwai had picked up his pole and walked off, the buckets creaking noisily. "If you won't do it," Yan'an shouted after him, "I'll find someone who will. One way or another I'm going to marry a peasant and stay here in Five-Man Plot!"

Yan'an's shout stopped Waiwai in his tracks. "You can't do that. It's first come, first served. I never said I wouldn't."

"Then I'll write your name on this pledge," Yan'an said.

Meat pies had dropped from heaven. Waiwai gazed off into the distance. The rolling yellow hills stretched all the way to the edge of heaven; he had taken his herd of sheep out onto these hills every day, more times than he could count.

"Yan'an, what is it about me you like?" Waiwai asked.

"You come from a true peasant family. Your grandfather came to northern Shaanxi with the Red Army and was the commander of the peasants' regiment. I want to be with a genuine member of the peasant class, a true peasant."

"Yan'an, I can't afford a betrothal gift," Waiwai said.

Yan'an waved her written pledge. "I don't want a penny. I want a revolutionary wedding. I want to smash the old and build the new."

Dizzy, Waiwai exclaimed, "Damn, something good has finally happened in my life."

As he watched Yan'an walk away in high spirits, Waiwai picked up his pole and headed down the mountain, his buckets creaking. Joy made his load light, and he sang loudly as he went:

The east is red, the sun has risen,
China has produced a Mao Zedong
To work for the good of the people.
Hey, hey, hey, ho,
He is the people's liberator.

As he finished the song, Waiwai turned to look at Yan'an's retreating back and was overcome by emotion. "Worthy ancestors, if not for Chairman Mao, how could I have ever found anything this good?"

Yan'an's pledge was sent by the commune to the county headquarters, from there to the prefecture, and from there to the provincial committee, which sent a reporter. After completing his interview, the reporter told Yan'an that the story of her proposal would appear in the newspaper within a week. But a month passed with no story. Each time the postman arrived on his weekly visit, Yan'an scanned the entire week's newspapers from beginning to end, until finally the postman delivered a letter from the reporter saying that the provincial authorities still considered her a model cadre and complimented her on her exemplary spirit. But given her family's political problems, they felt that her proposal should not be given undue publicity. Yan'an wept when she read the letter, wondering what she had to do to remake herself once and for all, to escape her father's shadow and convince people that she was a true revolutionary. Yan'an passed the news on to Waiwai, crying the whole time. Momentarily speechless at the sight of her tears, Waiwai finally said:

"Yan'an, since they won't publicize the news about us, are you having second thoughts? Because if you are, we can just forget it. I haven't given you a single betrothal gift, after all. I never really believed that meat pies drop from heaven."

Abruptly Yan'an stopped crying. "Qin Wanbao," she said, "I'm going to see this through to the end. Tomorrow we'll take out a marriage license at the commune. I'll show them what a real revolutionary looks like!"

Yan'an's determination threw a bit of a scare into Waiwai. What kind of a woman was she?

The next day they went to the commune to take out a marriage license, then bought a cooking pot and some bowls and a spatula and a basin. Yan'an also bought a new blue worker's outfit and a pair of cloth People's Liberation Army shoes. She handed the new clothes and ten yuan to Waiwai.

"Qin Wanbao," she said, "I'll take this other stuff back to the village while you go to the Red Flag Bathhouse in town and take a bath."

His face flushed with happiness, Waiwai said, "I've never had a real bath."

The Red Flag Bathhouse was closed by the time Waiwai had walked the fifty li from the commune to the county town, so he splurged half a yuan to spend the night at the wagoners' inn by the city gate. He returned the next morning, only to find that the bathhouse was still closed. Someone pointed to a wooden sign hanging on the door. "Can't you read? It's closed for repairs." That was that, so he walked the fifty li back to Five-Man Plot, weary and travel-worn, carefully keeping his new clothes tucked safely under his arm the whole way.

The wedding ceremony was just as Yan'an said it would be: revolutionary. In the presence of the other brigade members, the party branch secretary and the brigade commander led them in three bows before a likeness of Chairman Mao; then they read aloud two passages from Chairman Mao's quotations. When that was done, the branch secretary said, "Let's have a song from you two—try 'The East Is Red.' " So Yan'an and Waiwai sang it together, Yan'an with rhythm and style, Waiwai off-key from start to finish, which drew loud laughter from the guests. The singing and laughing had ended but no one left, so it was up to Yan'an to break the uncomfortable silence settling over the courtyard: "All right, I'll sing another song."

Be resolute, fear no sacrifice,
Let nothing prevent victory!
Be resolute, fear no sacrifice,
Let nothing prevent victory!

Yan'an sang with such passion that her normally pale face turned bright red. Her comrades were awed as they watched her sing, flushed with excitement; they all knew she was doing something they could never do. When Yan'an's song was finished, silence returned to the courtyard, and still the guests stayed put, as if waiting for something to happen; once again, there was an uncomfortable silence in the courtyard. The branch secretary clapped his hands impatiently and announced, "Enough bullshit, now it's off to the bridal chamber!" The guests watched as the bride and groom walked toward the red wedding couplets flanking the entrance to their cave. Yan'an had written them herself. "Take root in northern Shaanxi to serve the peasants," the first one read. "Remold yourself to make permanent revolution," read the second. No true parallel structure, no proper tonal patterns, just a couple of revolutionary slogans. Waiwai, dressed in brand-new clothes, followed Yan'an into their cave, then shut the wooden door, leaving behind the two gloriously red sheets of paper fastened to the pitted walls of yellow earth. Suddenly from the crowd came a shout:

"Waiwai, you piece of dog shit, what about thanking Chairman Mao? If not for Chairman Mao, where would you ever have found such a wife?"

Inside the cave Waiwai smiled. "Hear that, Yan'an? Those pieces of dog shit out there are jealous of me!"

After dinner, as they were making up the bed by lamplight, Waiwai could not keep from telling Yan'an he hadn't taken a bath in town.

"If you're worried about the dirt, I can boil some water and wash up," he said in an apologetic tone.

"I'll wait outside," Yan'an said.

It was dark outside and very cold. A half-moon hung coldly in the starless sky, its icy moonbeams highlighting the unrelenting bleakness of the plateau. Yan'an was thinking how she had been born on this very plateau, how Papa had asked to be relieved so he could rush to their cave and help with the delivery before rushing back to his work. Mama had picked her up and taken her and her sisters to hide in an even more remote, even bleaker cave. Now, at last, she had returned to her birthplace. As she stood bathed in the icy moonbeams, Yan'an heard splashing sounds on the other side of the door. Without warning, her tears fell like rain; she shed a torrent of hot, time-worn tears as she stood on that bleak yellow-earth plateau, the icy beams of a half-moon her only witness.

When the splashing sounds had stopped, Yan'an opened the cave's wooden door. Startled by the sound, Waiwai instinctively covered his nakedness with his hands. "Yan'an," he said.

Yan'an looked, then squeezed her eyes closed. She had not imagined that Waiwai could be so brawny or so dirty.

"Yan'an," Waiwai said, "half a basin of water isn't nearly enough . . ."

Yan'an walked to the brick bed and blew out the lamp, instantly turning the cave as dark as a sealed tomb. Waiwai heard the sounds of clothing being removed in the darkness as Yan'an slowly undressed.

The darkness emboldened Waiwai, who let his hands drop as he felt the blood sing in his veins.

"No regrets, Yan'an?" he said.

"No regrets."

But when his masculine odor and the stench of sheep came crushing down on her, Yan'an yelped as if she had been stuck with a knife; she shoved, she pounded, she screamed, she struggled. Waiwai pushed down on her with savage boldness, panting and crying out and pleading, until suddenly, like an avalanche, a gush of pleasure erupted between his legs, soaking the sheet beneath them. With a wail, a spent Waiwai rolled off to the side.

Yan'an grabbed the towel covering her pillow and frantically wiped down every inch of her body, until the soreness worked its way into her heart.

"What the hell are you doing?" Waiwai asked her. "Are you a woman or not?"

Just before dawn, Yan'an got up and lit the lamp, then turned to face Waiwai and said, "Qin Wanbao, I've thought of nothing else all night. I'm going to see this through to the end."

CHAPTER FOURTEEN

1

Twenty years after Sixth Great Aunt's death, the people of Silver City could no longer pinpoint its date. Her neighbors remembered breaking down her door and finding her body lying on the hand-carved sandalwood bed; they remembered how thousands upon thousands of flies nearly knocked them over. It must have been in the summer of 1967, they calculated. Prior to that, Zhisheng, the boy Sixth Great Aunt had brought home with her, and Winterset, her husband, had both drowned. So many people had died during the Cultural Revolution that no one paid much attention to who died when, but the death of Sixth Great Aunt and her family had spelled the end of Nine Ideals Hall. People would point to the vacant lot and talk about the two beautiful stone arches that once stood there, tall as a three-story building, the tallest stone arches in Silver City; they would remember the imperial edict carved into the stone—"Civil Officials Alight from Carriages, Military Officials Dismount from Steeds"—and the locust tree that had stood there for over five hundred years. Back then "Ancient Locust and Twin

Arches" was one of Silver City's eight scenic wonders, but it was razed to the ground during the Cultural Revolution. The people of Silver City told the story time and time again, to the party history office, to the editorial committee of the local archival gazetteer, and to officials in the tourist bureau. In the end only the tourist bureau showed any interest; on the vacant lot they erected a sign with a mere six words:

ANCIENT LOCUST TWIN ARCHES OLD SITE

When Li Jingsheng came to Silver City and stood before the sign, people did not immediately know whom he was asking about.

"That Li Zihen you're looking for, was she one of the Nine Ideals Hall Li clan?"

Li Jingsheng nodded.

"Then it's Sixth Great Aunt. We knew that Li was her surname, but we all just called her Sixth Great Aunt. Are you with the tourist bureau, comrade?"

Li Jingsheng shook his head.

"Writing party history? Or maybe a local journalist?"

"No, Li Zihen was my aunt."

The neighbors were suddenly wary. "Are you here to claim her house?"

Li Jingsheng shook his head again, unsure what to say. He stared at the vacant lot, where peddlers had staked out space to sell a colorful array of cheap clothes, toys, kitchen wares, and other odds and ends; they hawked their goods loudly, in accents that had a singsong lilt to Li Jingsheng's ears. His standard Beijing Mandarin sounded out of place; every time he opened his mouth, he attracted curious stares that immediately drew a curtain of difference around him. No one who heard him speak would have believed that he had grown up hearing Silver City's singsong lilt or that he was one of the Nine Ideals Hall Li clan. The moment he stepped off the train, he felt overwhelmed by feelings of estrangement. He walked through the streets, mingling with crowds of people speaking the dialect of his childhood. The bright sun shone down on a city sprawled across rolling hills, on the gentle little river spanned by two bridges—an old one made of stone and a new one made of steel. This was Silver City, a place he'd heard his parents talk about so many times, a place Eighth Aunt had written about in letters and spoken of over the telephone time and time again. If his father and mother and Eighth Aunt hadn't mentioned it so often, he would never have believed that this provincial city was tied to his family in so many ways or that this was the ancestral home whose memory reduced Eighth Aunt to tears as she spoke to him over the telephone. After forty years of silence, Li Ziyun, now living in Virginia, near her sons, had sought the help of the Office for Overseas Chinese in tracking down her younger brother's children. Through an exchange of letters, Eighth Aunt had learned that everyone of her generation had died; Li Jingsheng was the only family member to respond. A flurry of letters was followed by telephone calls in which she always made the same tearful plea:

"Son, go back to Silver City to see the family home and the Twin Arches of Nine Ideals Hall, and visit the grave of Sixth Aunt . . . Please go, and please send me some photographs."

Li Jingsheng wasn't sure he would ever have made this long trip into the interior if not for Eighth Aunt. He remembered his mother once showing him a yellowed photograph. "This is your Eighth Aunt," she had said. It hadn't made much of an impression on him at the time, but during the Cultural Revolution he'd often seen her name on the posters denouncing his father. He learned that she was called Li Ziyun and that her husband, Yang Chuxiong, had been a major general in the Guomindang army. All his father's crimes were linked in some way to these two people, and at the time Li Jingsheng felt only hatred for the aunt who had caused his family so much trouble from so far away. Back then, Li Jingsheng could not have imagined that an aunt about whom there had been no news for so long would someday manage to locate what remained of her family on the other side of the Pacific Ocean. In each of her first ten or twenty letters, Li Ziyun had enclosed yellowed photographs, on the backs of which were notes in a shaky hand: "The only picture from back then"; "A picture of your mother and me as students"; "Taken on my last day in Silver City before I left China. I planted the chrysanthemums you see behind me. I watered them that day for the last time"; "Me in front of the school in Taipei where I was principal"; "A little mountain path. I loved this old place, which reminded me of home"; "An air-raid drill outside the school"; "Your uncle's funeral. Even today I can't bear to look at it"; "At the airport when my son left for school in America"; "Going to America with my grandson"; "The old-age home where I live"; "My living room"; "My flowers are like those back home"; "My bedroom"; "My church, where I often pray to the Lord to allow me to see my family in China once more before I die." . . . One yellowed photograph after another, linking the vanishing threads of a woman's life to those of an ancient and time-worn story. As he looked at the photographs, Li Jingsheng knew that his aunt was sending home, to her birthplace, the years and months of her life, returning them to the bosom of her family. But the city rooted in her soul and wound into her dreams had long since changed beyond recognition.

Li Jingsheng wondered what Eighth Aunt would think if she could see this vacant lot and the wooden sign with its six words. The grand residence Li Ziyun had talked about was now a cluttered compound, with one family crowded in alongside the other, one bamboo lean-to kitchen jammed up against the next; amid the junk, the debris, the laundry hanging out to dry, here and there a vestige of the old days had survived—a scarred veranda column or the remnants of a carved window frame. The mounds of junk and debris seemed to follow the outline of a section of the old veranda, but Willow Reflecting Pond, which had once bordered it, had given way to a row of new brick buildings and a very large public outhouse from which an overpowering stench emerged. Li Jingsheng took a few photographs, then put away his camera; what, after all, was served by shattering Eighth Aunt's nostalgic dreams of home?

The neighbors who had been so eager to point things out to Li Jingsheng just moments before were suddenly on their guard when they saw him taking pictures in the courtyard. One of them walked up and grabbed him by the arm.

"Did the housing authority send you to take photographs, comrade?"

Somewhat puzzled, Li Jingsheng replied, "What housing authority?"

"Listen carefully, comrade. We're long-time residents here, we've lived on this spot for generations, and it won't be easy to get us to move away."

"Who's asking you to move?"

"Don't play dumb with me. See those new houses over there? The housing authority told us they had rights to the property and that houses would go to long-time residents. But when the turtle spawn finished building the houses, we didn't get a single one, even though we've been living like this for years. I tell you it won't be easy getting us to move. We'll get it in writing from the notary office. Then see who's going to move!"

Li Jingsheng tried to reassure the excited residents that he had merely returned to his parents' birthplace to look around and take a few pictures. He had no interest in the houses here and no intention of taking anything back. "You people can live here as long as you want—until these buildings collapse around you." Having finished his speech, Li Jingsheng turned and walked off, suddenly sick of the whole business.

He returned to the vacant lot, where a tour bus was parked alongside the wooden sign. A gaggle of blond, blue-eyed tourists was surrounded by a Chinese crowd whom the impatient tour guide, fashionably coiffed and attired, was trying to fend off with a bullhorn. No sooner had she driven off the people to the left than the vacuum was filled by others on the right, until she gave up in frustration. Her charming smile was on her face again by the time she turned back to her charges; raising the bullhorn to her lips, she began her prepared talk:

"Ladies and gentlemen, what you see here was one of Silver City's eight scenic wonders: an ancient locust and two splendid twin arches stood on this site. Silver City's most venerable family once lived in the grand estate beyond the arches, Nine Ideals Hall. The family was Silver City's oldest, its pioneers. The first clan elder listed by name in the genealogy was Li Yi, who boasted that he was a twelfth-generation descendant of Li Er, famed philosopher of the Spring and Autumn period, also known as Laozi. In 25 A.D., the first year of the Jianwu reign of the Eastern Han dynasty, Li Yi was richly rewarded for helping the Guangwu emperor Liu Xiu overthrow the usurper Wang Mang. Over the next two thousand years, the Li clan flourished, outlasting dynasties and surviving one war after the other, moving from place to place, finally settling down to build this city. The last member of the Li clan to live in the family compound was a woman named Li Zihen. The first woman from Silver City to join the Communist party, she died in 1967."

The tour guide went on talking about the city's antiquity and its various legends. But when Jingsheng heard Sixth Aunt's name along with his family's history, a profound sense of alienation filled his heart; here he was, listening to stories of his clan, his family, as if he were just one more tourist. Two thousand years of hardship, of accumulating power, generation after generation. Li Jingsheng, Beijing born and bred, speaking standard Mandarin, was overwhelmed by the enormity of it. His imagination paled. He turned for another look at the wooden sign, a mere six words:

ANCIENT LOCUST TWIN ARCHES OLD SITE

2

In point of fact, Li Jingsheng had another purpose in making this trip: the book on which he had been working for three years, *A History of China's Salt Industry,* was nearing completion and he had long planned to do some on-site research for the portions dealing with Silver City. On the eve of his departure, he had written to the editorial committee of the Silver City archival gazetteer to notify them of his visit and request an interview. But he never expected to hear back that no fewer than three local officials—Deputy Director Zheng of the party history office, Deputy Director Lin of the Office for Overseas Chinese, and Deputy Director Liu of the editorial committee—proposed to fete him at one of Silver City's restaurants. Li Jingsheng had little trouble finding the restaurant—it was Silver City's finest and everyone knew it—but again he was surprised by the warmth of his reception. Almost immediately, Deputy Director Zheng invited him to write a short biography of his father, Comrade Li Naizhi, Silver City's underground party secretary, for the *Silver City Party History Compendium.* The time for rehabilitation had long since arrived, and it was only appropriate that victim and victimizers alike should turn grief into strength. As the deputy director spoke, talking both of joy and of sorrow, Li Jingsheng felt in himself an ineffable sickness at heart, an unspeakable abhorrence of this vaunted dialectic of turning grief into strength.

Deputy Director Zheng went on to praise Li Jingsheng's maternal grandfather, Bai Ruide, Silver City's first successful industrialist, the person who had mechanized the city's salt mines and introduced chemical engineering to its salt industry. The city's leaders emphasized their hope that Comrade Li Jingsheng would want to contact his overseas relatives and, as a service to the people of Silver City, encourage them to return to their hometown to make investments and promote new industry. Naturally, they would be welcomed with open arms. Deputy Director Liu said that he had read portions of Li Jingsheng's *History of China's Salt Industry* in scholarly journals; he encouraged Li Jingsheng to maintain close ties to his hometown and even to submit articles to the local gazetteer. The three deputy directors told Li Jingsheng that they had arranged for him to spend the night in the White Garden Guest House, which had once been Bai Ruide's manor. Following several rounds of toasts, Deputy Director Liu, emboldened by the wine, told Li Jingsheng that, based on their generational standings, "I, Liu Guangdi, ought to call you uncle, since your father's elder cousin, Li Naijing, was my maternal uncle." Having thus reintroduced himself, Deputy Director Liu toasted his uncle on his first visit home. The sound of this man in his mid-fifties calling him uncle made Li Jingsheng very uncomfortable, and the poetic sentiments over returning home to his roots, which had germinated in Beijing and flowered on the long train ride, vanished; all he wanted now was to conclude his business as fast as possible and leave.

A full bottle of aged wine was consumed before Li Jingsheng finally freed himself from the chain-smoking trio of earnest deputy directors and stood alone at the entrance to White Garden. Back in Beijing the cold of autumn held sway, but here it looked and felt like midsummer. Through the lush green trees he could just glimpse an elegant, pristine white building. Li Jingsheng took a black-and-white photograph from his pocket, and even though it was old and fading he was able to imagine the lush greenery surrounding the young girl in a gauzy white dress sitting on the swing, gazing innocently out of the photograph at the summery beauty of that autumn day in 1937. He tried to locate the spot where the swing had once hung, but with no success, and his thoughts drifted back to a summer day twenty years before when, in the company of the people who had just ransacked his house, he had carried his father's belongings to a car. The driver, a man named Huang, used to bring Father back from Beijing in a Volga sedan nearly every weekend; Father always invited him to stay for dinner, and he had the children call him Uncle Huang. Now, after loading the car and stepping back to watch them bundle his father into the backseat, he happened to catch the eye of the driver; when their gazes met, for some strange reason he waved good-bye to the man, who turned away in embarrassment. There was an explosion of caustic laughter from the mouth of a woman in the car. Li Jingsheng blushed scarlet and dropped his arm as if it had been stung by a wasp, then glared at his sweaty hand, wishing he could chop it off then and there. Baked by the midday sun, he walked home and found his mother sitting in the ransacked house amid her strewn belongings, holding this very photograph in her hand and weeping bitterly. . . . After that day, he would see her only rarely. The Red Guards were needed elsewhere.

The green world beyond the borders of the photograph turned to a green haze, but once the haze had lifted, Li Jingsheng caught another glimpse of the elegant, pristine white building behind the green banana trees. Maybe he shouldn't have come back, he was thinking, maybe he shouldn't have returned to the heart of all those eternally irretrievable events of the past. None of this mattered at all to anyone else, and it was all far too alien to him. Not only would it never find its way into *A History of China's Salt Industry*, but no history book would ever record this unrecordable past.

Li Jingsheng could not have known that his mother thought of him as she lay dying, wishing desperately for one last glimpse of her oldest son. She could not have imagined as the breath left her body that the son whose presence was denied her would one day return to Silver City to stand before White Garden—in all its jadelike purity, tucked amid the banana trees and bamboo stalks, as elegant and as beautiful as ever—weeping openly not for history but for his mother.

3

By car, the trip to White Cloud Mountain took hardly any time. As they negotiated the curve at the base of the mountain, Deputy Director Liu said, "Here we are." The first thing Li Jingsheng saw as he stepped out of the car was the white stone arch standing amid the green foliage; then his attention was caught by the towering monastery halfway up the mountain. Deputy Director Liu pointed to a grove of green bamboo beside the road and said:

"See over there, Uncle, that's where Sixth Great Aunt is buried, by the side of the bamboo. When she died, they burned her, bed and all, in the courtyard. I was working at the security bureau at the time, and I witnessed the cremation. Her neighbors said she had buried Winterset and Zhisheng on White Mountain, so we buried her ashes alongside them. I witnessed that too. See there, Sixth Great Aunt is on the right, Winterset is in the middle, and there, a little to the left, is Zhisheng's grave. The Cultural Revolution was raging at the time, and we didn't dare leave a mound over Sixth Great Aunt's grave, so we just put a stone marker on the spot. The bamboo grove wasn't nearly as big then."

"Where's the stone marker?" Li Jingsheng asked.

Deputy Director Liu parted some tall weeds to reveal a piece of green marble about a foot high; no words, no evidence of any carving, a simple stone that could be found anywhere in the river valley. "I'd like to be alone for a moment, if you don't mind," Li Jingsheng said to Deputy Director Liu.

Li Jingsheng took a photograph, then sat on the ground before the marble stone, listening to the crisp staccato of a woodpecker attacking a tree somewhere deep in the shadowy valley. He knew nothing about this great aunt of his whom he had never met, except for what his mother had told him when he was very young: she said that after searing her face with joss sticks so his father could go to school, Sixth Aunt had taken vows of abstinence and become a Buddhist devotee. It wasn't until he traveled to Silver City that he learned about her role in the Communist underground. Eighth Aunt cried every time she mentioned Sixth Aunt during one of her transpacific phone calls, but even then, Li Jingsheng could not comprehend the depth of her emotion or the profusion of memories that provoked her mournful sobs. All that remained was a foot-high stone marker, a patch of dense weeds, and a lush wall of soft bamboo. The boundary between life and death had been reduced to a single sentence: The bamboo grove wasn't nearly as big then. . . . The bamboo grove wasn't nearly as big then. . . . All that was left were the peaceful rays of the setting sun and a luxuriant patch of grass, the surrounding stillness, deep and eternal, and the pock-pock of a woodpecker.

As he and Deputy Director Liu walked back past the stone arch, Li Jingsheng stopped to read the two lines of faded verse carved upon it:

WHERE IS THE ROAD FROM HERE TO THERE?
NO GATE BETWEEN LIFE AND DEATH.

Deputy Director Liu told him that Sixth Great Aunt had been an abstinent Buddhist devotee all her life, someone who had taken this path up White Cloud Mountain more times than anyone knew; she didn't stop coming to burn incense here until the Cultural Revolution, when the Red Guards smashed her porcelain bodhisattva and sealed the entrance to White Cloud Monastery.

Deputy Director Liu was worthy of his position as a cadre charged with compiling a local gazetteer, for he told a good story, relating one Silver City anecdote after another as they walked back to the car. "Uncle," Deputy Director Liu said, "don't underestimate the significance of White Cloud Mountain. Years ago, your aunt's husband, Commander Yang Chuxiong, ringed Silver City with soldiers and held off two enemy divisions. He set up an ambush right here in the White Cloud Mountain valley, then let himself be taken prisoner to draw the enemy troops into the valley, where they were routed. For more than five li in each direction, this gully was strewn with the bodies of dead soldiers. Uncle," Deputy Director Liu continued with a sigh, "don't be fooled by that fine poetry. All the poetry and joss sticks in the world couldn't release all those souls." Gazing about him, Li Jingsheng found it impossible to conjure up the thousands of bloody bodies strewn across the valley; he wasn't sure he even believed the story was true. Could Eighth Aunt's husband actually have slaughtered thousands of men in a single battle? How could a valley in which thousands had died violently now be so still and calm? "No one is recording the history of our Silver City," Deputy Director Liu continued excitedly. "If they did, it would take a dozen volumes—even more. Why don't you do it, Uncle? There's more material than you could ever use, take my word for it."

Li Jingsheng laughed. "Weren't you the one who just said all the poetry and joss sticks in the world couldn't release all those souls? So what good would a dozen volumes do?"

In the warm rays of the setting sun, in the surrounding stillness, deep and eternal, there was only the distant sound of a woodpecker knocking against a tree.

EPILOGUE

Li Jingsheng phoned his aunt as soon as he had his ticket in hand. He phoned her again from San Francisco and Washington. Then, after arranging a time to visit her, he ordered a taxi and set out, taking with him the many photographs she had sent with her letters. He was looking forward to hearing about his father and mother and Sixth Aunt, whom he had never met. Li Jingsheng approached the manicured lawn of the old-age home, a simple building tucked behind a grove of white birches. His aunt's photographs and letters had journeyed from this peaceful building all the way across the Pacific to Beijing. His aunt herself had drifted from a small town in the heart of China to Taiwan and then to this peaceful building in Virginia. Full of excitement and trepidation, Li Jingsheng stood quietly for a moment to compose himself before pushing open the glass entrance door. A foreign odor of perfume met him as soon as he stepped inside his aunt's room. Li Jingsheng saw her sitting in front of a clock; she had been counting the minutes, waiting for him to show up. As he drew near, he saw that she was much older than her photographs showed. Seated behind an aluminum walker, she stretched out her arms like a helpless child, but before she could utter a word, tears streamed down her cheeks.

"Your auntie never believed she'd see this day . . ."

Li Jingsheng waited for her to compose herself before handing her, one at a time, the gifts he had brought. She politely thanked him for each, but when he drew out the photographs, he quickly discovered that Li Ziyun was in her dotage. She had no recollection of the past; she could not even recall her father's name. Li Ziyun looked at the photographs with no sign of recognition. "I can't recall . . . Who are these people?" was her only comment. And before long, she was crying again. "Such a useless thing . . . Time for your auntie to die . . . All I can say is, sooner or later everything passes . . ."

Finally, Li Jingsheng abandoned his efforts, unable to bear his aunt's futile attempts to probe her memory. He stopped asking questions and just held her hand. Beyond the French windows, a birch tree was shedding its leaves. Ravens circled the treetop, flashing their wings as their caws sounded in the gentle sunlight. Li Jingsheng was struck by the familiarity of the scene, as if he had only to walk through the French windows to be in China, back in the quiet, secluded valley of White Cloud Mountain.

It was time to end the family reunion Li Jingsheng had been talking and thinking about for so many years.

One day, three months later, Li Jingsheng found two pieces of mail waiting in his mailbox. One was a letter he had written to his aunt two weeks earlier; the second was a postcard. No signature, just a pair of initials beneath an official-looking sentence:

This is to inform you that Madame Yang Li Ziyun passed away peacefully on January 11, 1988.

TIMELINE

1911	THE QING (MANCHU) DYNASTY IS TOPPLED BY SUN YATSEN AND HIS REPUBLICAN FORCES.
[1927	THE SILVER CITY PEASANT INSURRECTION IS PUT DOWN.]
1934–35	MAO ZEDONG'S COMMUNIST FORCES UNDERTAKE A LONG MARCH FROM JIANGXI PROVINCE IN THE SOUTH TO THE CAVES OF YAN'AN IN NORTH-CENTRAL SHAANXI PROVINCE.
1937	FIGHTING BREAKS OUT BETWEEN JAPANESE AND CHINESE TROOPS AT THE MARCO POLO BRIDGE NEAR BEIJING, RESULTING IN EIGHT YEARS OF HOSTILITIES.
[1939	A MASS EXECUTION OF COMMUNISTS IS CARRIED OUT IN SILVER CITY.]
1941	THE ANHUI (OR NEW FOURTH ARMY) INCIDENT, IN WHICH A NATIONALIST ARMY AMBUSH RESULTED IN THE DEATHS OF MORE THAN 3,000 COMMUNIST TROOPS, OCCURS.
1945	WORLD WAR II AND THE SINO–JAPANESE CONFLICT END.

1947	NATIONALIST GENERAL HU ZONGNAN ATTACKS AND OCCUPIES YAN'AN, DRIVING THE COMMUNIST FORCES NORTH INTO MANCHURIA.
1949	COMMUNIST FORCES DEFEAT THE ARMIES OF CHIANG KAI-SHEK, WHO FLEES TO THE ISLAND OF TAIWAN.
1950–51	A LAND REFORM CAMPAIGN IS LAUNCHED, DURING WHICH AS MANY AS A MILLION LANDLORDS ARE EXTERMINATED.
[1951	LI NAIJING, PATRIARCH OF NINE IDEALS HALL, IS EXECUTED ALONG WITH MANY MEMBERS OF HIS FAMILY AND HIS CLASS.]
1966–76	THE GREAT PROLETARIAN CULTURAL REVOLUTION ENGULFS CHINA.

DATES IN BRACKETS ARE FICTIONAL.

TRANSLATOR'S ACKNOWLEDGMENT

The translation of this novel was aided substantially by several people. I would like to thank in particular Shelley Wing Chan for checking the entire manuscript and the author, Li Rui, for supplying clarifications and additional material and for graciously acceding to suggestions from me, copy editor Roslyn Schloss, and our superb editors, Sara Bershtel and Riva Hocherman.